Praise for

TOGETHER WE CAUGHT FIRE

"A book that doesn't hold back. Even when the characters travel to their darkest places, there is an undeniable spark of light, of hope, at the center. . . . Gritty, bold."
—Rachel Lynn Solomon, author of *Today Tonight Tomorrow*

"Captivating . . . An addictive page-turner that begins with a forbidden romance but turns into so much more."
—*Kirkus Reviews*

"Fans of Kathleen Glasgow and Nina LaCour will appreciate this sometimes lyrical, sometimes brutal, always unflinching portrayal of a girl struggling with her past in order to find her future."
—*SLJ*

ALSO BY EVA V. GIBSON

Together We Caught Fire

WHERE SECRETS LIE

eva v. gibson

SIMON & SCHUSTER BFYR

NEW YORK   LONDON   TORONTO   SYDNEY   NEW DELHI

An imprint of Simon & Schuster Children's Publishing Division
1230 Avenue of the Americas, New York, New York 10020
Text © 2021 by Eva Gibson
Jacket photograph © 2021 by Stocksy
Jacket design by Laura Eckes © 2021 by Simon & Schuster, Inc.
SIMON & SCHUSTER BOOKS FOR YOUNG READERS
and related marks are trademarks of Simon & Schuster, Inc.
For information about special discounts for bulk purchases, please contact
Simon & Schuster Special Sales at 1-866-506-1949 or business@simonandschuster.com.
The Simon & Schuster Speakers Bureau can bring authors to your live event.
For more information or to book an event contact
the Simon & Schuster Speakers Bureau at 1-866-248-3049
or visit our website at www.simonspeakers.com.
Interior design by Hilary Zarycky
The text for this book was set in Adobe Garamond Pro.
Manufactured in the United States of America
2 4 6 8 10 9 7 5 3 1
First Edition
Library of Congress Cataloging-in-Publication Data
Names: Gibson, Eva V., author.
Title: Where secrets lie / by Eva V. Gibson.
Description: First Simon & Schuster BFYR Edition. | New York : Simon & Schuster BFYR,
2021. | Summary: Sixteen-year-old Amy, her cousin Ben, and Teddy, longtime friends until the
previous summer, must put aside their differences and confront truths that tie their families to
tragedy when Teddy's sister disappears in River Run, Kentucky.
Identifiers: LCCN 2020014558 |
ISBN 9781534451223 (hardcover) | ISBN 9781534451247 (ebook)
Subjects: CYAC: Friendship—Fiction. | Cousins—Fiction. | Artists—Fiction. |
Missing children—Fiction. | Family life—Kentucky—Fiction. | Kentucky—Fiction. | Mystery
and detective stories.
Classification: LCC PZ7.1.G523 Whe 2021 | DDC [Fic]—dc23
LC record available at https://lccn.loc.gov/2020014558

For Brandon and Henry,
who were there at the start

WHERE
SECRETS
LIE

The brain fills it in, lets us see what we know is real. Pieces together sky and clouds, scatters trees; draws the earth itself upward in familiar, jagged chunks. We take in the world the way we always have—from the surface up. We ignore the scuttle of crayfish, the soft swoosh of river rays over our toes; leap away from the insistent, ankle-snagging curl of grass and reeds. We close our eyes tight before ducking under.

So it was and always had been—Ben and Teddy and me, from childhood into eternity. Everything beginning and ending with one another.

Summer belonged to the three of us—belonged to the cove and the trees, the green pull of the Kentucky River, the rolling, swooping land of horse country. Our world was the outskirts of River Run, where the prefab houses gave way to mansions and trim, black fences butting up against a tangle of wild, dark woods. Summer was land-lines and cicadas, sunscreen and bug spray every day. It was a swimming hole without a bottom that we leaped into together, year after year, hand in hand.

World without end.

It was always going to fall to pieces once we opened our eyes.

They weren't there.

I let the storm door close at my back, shutting out the river-soaked fever of the afternoon. My eyes adjusted to the dim indoor light, taking in the frown of the grandfather clock in the corner and the spatter of color on its polished face—broken sunbeams twisting their way to rainbows through the cluster of antique prisms in the entryway window. The air was cool and dry, sweet with almond oil and the soft flora of my grandmother's perfume. Fat to bursting with the tension of unsaid words.

I hadn't made it past the foyer, and the summer was already ruined.

"They haven't been by?" I asked, hating the panicked twist of my own voice. Hating the glimmer of hope I'd let bloom into flame. "You're absolutely sure?"

"No, sweetheart, they haven't." Grandma's eyes slid from me to my mother and back to me again, her brow furrowed. "Teddy finished up early today and went on home. Didn't say a thing about coming around this evening. As for Benny, he's been a bit of a pill these past several months. Your aunt Madeleine called earlier, said he won't leave his room, and—well, she wouldn't repeat his exact words. You know how he gets."

"They must be down at the cove already. I'll go see if they're waiting for me."

"Amy. They're not." She sighed, distressed as always by unpleasant conversation. "I'm sorry, dear. Let's go out to the kitchen, have a talk. It'll be okay, I just know—"

I was already gone.

Mom's anger was narrow, a thin, fine needle piercing the back of my head as I fled up the curved staircase. Louder in its silence than my shoe soles on the polished oak, or the worried lilt of Grandma's voice trailing at my heels. I focused on my retreat to the heavy bedroom door and its solid lock—my mother's old room, a child's room, yellow and pink and tucked under an eave. They put me there every year, as if they hadn't noticed that the short, slight girl who'd once squeezed her tiny body into all the hidden recesses of this big Victorian fun house had spent the past few summers bumping her head on the stupid slanted ceiling of that room. Sixteen years old and looking down at the world.

I dropped my stuff on the frilly duvet and crossed to the window, stared out at the empty trailhead. Tamped down the tears crowding the back of my throat.

For the first time since I could remember, the boys weren't waiting for me.

There was no point in texting Ben. River Run was too goddamn backwoods for its own cell tower, the property too removed to access what little coverage managed to straggle over from the nearest one. Even if it did, he probably wouldn't answer—Ben with a grudge was Ben at peak asshole, eclipsed in magnitude only by Teddy and his injured pride. I should have known better than to hope they'd show.

It was simple math that screwed us, really: We were an odd number—a prime number, divisible only by itself. Impossible to split into two equal parts. This natural discrepancy was one we gladly overlooked when the distance between us was literal, remedied by a first-class plane ticket, the end of the school year, the start of my parents' clockwork season abroad. And once together, it never mattered anyway—it was easy as anything to ignore the subsurface shifts and tectonic pressure, bound to end in cracks.

A blur of memories clamored for space in my head, so many summers rushing back at once, and *this* was how they wanted things to end? Fuck the phone. Fuck them, too—if they wanted to play cold shoulder, they'd damn sure picked the wrong opponent. I'd dissolve into mist before I'd let them see me beg.

The doorknob's rattle shook me from my thoughts. The lock clicked and gave; she was in the room before I'd even turned around.

"The door was locked for a reason, Mother."

"As if I don't know the trick to this old door. Freshen up and change your blouse. Grandma's got dinner planned, and . . ." She paused, studied my wet, red eyes and quivering chin. Her mouth tucked itself into a delicate sneer. "You shouldn't cry. It's showing."

"I don't care. Tell them it's allergies."

"You look miserable, Amy. Hold still." She crossed to the bed, pulled my Chanel compact from my purse. My vision sharpened to a surreal collection of shapes as her face neared mine and I shut down, withdrawing into the pocket of my mind—the noiseless, empty safe space that let me endure the blotting and blending as she coaxed me back to unblotched perfection. "I'm sorry he disappointed you, but it's no big shock, is it? Typical River Run boys."

Her words were venom-tipped darts designed to sting. What little I'd said on the subject last fall had still been too much. It was all I deserved, trusting that she'd give a fuck about my emotions apart from the impact they had on my art. Her fingers tightened on my chin as I tried to turn away.

"I'm not discussing him with you, Mom."

"He's never *been* up for discussion. Your focus is your work and your future, not a dead-end summer fling—if you can't uncouple one from the other, he's better off at arm's length. I can only guess at the real reason you came home empty-handed last year."

"Seriously? I told you I lost my satchel, along with my sketchbook and everything else in it. And I made up the work, remember?"

"I remember that's what you *said* happened. Not that carelessness is an excuse. Don't forget these trips abroad are for your benefit as well—everything about my life, every extra moment beyond the bare minimum spent with your father—all of it is to ensure your success. All so you'll never be chained to this place, or anyone in it."

"Whatever. If you hate River Run so much, maybe you shouldn't drop me off here for months at a time."

"Watch your tone, young lady. Your grandparents love you, and I make allowances for that. What I won't do is nod and smile while you throw away the world." She brushed a final swipe of powder over my skin, turned me to face the vanity. "There. Much better."

She had indeed worked magic. My face was blank and lovely around smoke-lined, arctic blue eyes; the pale, tousled mess of my hair skimmed a perfectly blended jawline. My mother stood behind me in darker shades of everything, smile cold as the teeth of winter. I only had to look at her for one more day.

It would be easier once she was a literal world away. My parents would have a whole overseas flight to repress their marital issues, then they'd trek through the world behind a united front—through Johannesburg, Budapest, Jerusalem, wherever—my mother's eyes glued to the camera, every image another staggering paycheck when paired with my father's words. Jake and Eleanor Larsen, the husband-and-wife photojournalist powerhouse duo whose political and humanitarian projects overrode their forever-impending divorce. Those summers abroad kept me in the top private schools, hired the most prestigious art instructors to shape my future, kept my mother's closet overflowing with Kate Spade, and kept my father's Tesla Roadster in the garage of our enormous Great Falls home, for the few weeks a year he bothered showing up to park it there.

My father. A snow-washed glacier who'd much prefer to sink into the sea alone than endure even the idea of footprints. Mom's coldest cold shoulders were desert sands compared to his indifference. I'd learned *that* little trick from the best, to be sure—I'd never been a daddy's girl, but I was certainly his daughter, down to my frost-studded core.

It wasn't that he'd left us, gradually and without any sort of official verbal indicator—I of all people understood the undeniable urge to flee my mother at all costs. He was his own special brand of uninhabitable, who gifted his feelings to pages rather than people. Still, it was that he'd left *me,* young and defenseless, alone with her in a too-quiet house. A house where even a four-year-old was subject to her hovering hands and frantic voice, and rabid, relentless standards.

It hadn't taken her long at all to turn an exceptional preschool art project into a vicarious set of goals—to swap crayons for pastels, then pencils, then charcoals and ink, all before I'd learned to write

my name. My childhood bled into an endless blur of figure study and cramping fingers, color wheels and still lifes and thumbnail sketches, all framed by the edges of my mother's shadow. She monitored the progress of the hands I'd inherited from her as if she wasn't the inspiration behind my desire to redraw the world. As if my hands couldn't just be my own, no matter what their shape. Now, my talent had surpassed even her most far-fetched hopes, opened doors neither of us expected—doors that triggered my own personal countdown, once I realized I could walk through any one of them without her, then slam it in her face when she tried to follow.

Twelve years and hundreds of miles from the first spark, that flame still burned. It fed on the grind of pencil lines and brushstrokes; on my apprenticeship and private tutelage. On my acceptance into an elite high school for the arts, where I joined the cutthroat seethe of students, all aspiring to unmatched greatness. We worked side by side and neck and neck, rivalries bleeding into resentments, the nature of our shared ambitions superseding personal connections— and that was before adding in our parents and their vicarious hopes, their personal issues and social aspirations, that culminated in more private lessons and hours of practice, leaving no time for sleepovers or shopping trips or, until recently, boy-shaped distractions.

That last one—well, that was a situation best left on the Eastern Seaboard, folded down into a memory and tucked safely in the pocket of his fucking sweater-vest. None of it had meant a thing beyond the first resentful impulses.

It had made Mom happy, though. Holy shit, had it ever—that old-money, furnace-eyed prospect, with his sharp cheekbones, his own credit card, his actual pressed slacks. A musician, of all things—a

seventeen-year-old piano prodigy, who'd supported my goals, sympathized with the constant practice and constraints on my time, which very closely mirrored his own. He'd existed in smudges of skeletal branches and winter frost; in the twinkle of holiday lights on white DC marble. He'd whirled me through a season of gilt-edged, upscale recklessness and melted away in time for spring.

She'd taken that breakup harder than he had, my mother. Not that I gave a flying shit concerning her thoughts on the matter, but he'd made for a good cover story while it lasted. Much easier to hide behind her rules and expectations when his very presence canceled out her deepest fears. Easier to let the prodigy escort me through tree lightings and gallery openings, let him kiss me on New Year's Eve over glasses of vintage champagne he didn't have to pay for and, later, pretend he hadn't meant to feel that far up my skirt. Better to select and disconnect than deal with the day-to-day disgruntled gloom of various rejected art boys, or the fallout of random flirtations, unsolicited feelings, and the inevitable disintegration of both. As far as my heart was concerned, he'd barely existed.

There had only ever been three friends who mattered to me, who let me breathe and feel and be myself; who loved that self beyond the measure of my hands. Who exploded from the woods each summer in a frenzy of shrieks and laughter and open arms, eager to sweep me up and make us all whole again.

There had only ever been one boy.

And as I followed my mother down the carved oak staircase, properly freshened and powdered back to blank, I set about draining my nerves to match. The hollow inside me filled with sleet as that last day clawed its way to the surface, no longer willing to sleep.

The table was polished to its glossiest cherry shine, set with Grandma's embroidered linen runner and silver charger plates beneath the nice company china. A step down from formal, but more than the usual day-to-day comfort of the kitchen table. They almost never used the dining room.

It had to be a family dinner. Fuck my life.

"That was Madeleine on the phone, dear," Grandma chirped, bustling in from the kitchen, drying her hands on a rooster-red dish towel. The downstairs rooms were warm and bright, as if waiting to welcome me in every way. "They're having a bit of trouble getting Benny in the car. He's not feeling much up to a visit, she says."

"Good," I answered, slouching against the wall. "I can do without a visit from *Benny*."

"You'll be happy enough to see each other once the smoke clears," Grandpa said, taking half the entire summer to navigate his frail frame around the intricate dining chair arms. "A year's time enough for whatever's eating at you two to die down. In the meantime, we can do some eating of our own."

"God, can anyone just listen to me for once? I don't want to see Ben, okay? I don't. I won't."

"Well, okay, then." Grandpa shuffled back and forth, finally settled into the seat, poured a glass of sun tea from the pitcher next to his place setting. "If it's that big a deal, you can fix a plate for upstairs, and wait till you both cool off some. Maybe in a day or so—"

"No." My mother's voice was a sharpened ax, chopping off his words like a limb. Stilling the helpless fidget of my grandmother's hands. "We will all eat together, like any normal family. You will sit with us and say your hellos, and you and your cousin will act right, or so help me, Amy. I will not tolerate tantrums at your age, especially in your grandparents' home. Am I clear?"

"Yes, Mom." My breath was the edge of a whisper, the words filtered through a haze of cotton batting.

"Yes, *ma'am*."

"Yes, ma'am."

"Thank you, honey." Grandma crossed to me, voice soothing the cuts left by my mother's. Her fingers reached to smooth a strand of my hair, a soft, affectionate gesture ending in the same gentle tug one would give a dog's leash. I waited, but she held tight until I looked up. "It's for the good of the family. This is what we do."

His blurred reflection leaped across the windowpane, scarring my view of the yard—the crooked trees and jagged rocks, our path a hole in the familiar, looming thicket. Our childhood playground, backlit by a flash of sun. I cast a glare over my shoulder, met its twin in the bitter angles of his face.

My cousin leaned against the parlor doorframe, his whole demeanor honed slick and sharp. The boy version of me, staring back from hardened eyes.

He looked older than last year, startlingly so. His hair, though shorter, was still long for River Run. Still white-blond and impeccable, blunt cut right below his cheekbones and slicked back from his face. His hands were larger, his limbs longer, and he was finally as tall as me, grown into the broad, arrogant slope of his father's shoulders. A sudden ache sliced through my throat—a bone-deep longing for us, the way we'd always been: the three of us bound as one, inseparable until that final, awful day.

"Seriously?" I spat as Ben dragged his sneer from my hair to my shoes. "I thought you'd stay home."

"I was the first one in the door," he drawled. "Wanted to see if you had the sack to show your face."

"Because I'm the fuckup in this scenario? Benjamin. Please."

"Please whatever. You're the one who said we were done. And that's without mentioning the elephant in the room—or, more accurately, the elephant who is decidedly *not* in this particular room."

"I'm aware of the elephant."

"Good, then you'll recall the elephant was also a huge asshole, right? Or did you totally block out his part in this?"

"I 'recall' everything—and as I *recall,* you started it. You're the one who ruined us."

I turned back to the window, stared through our reflected faces, focused on the empty mouth of the path. Winced at the involuntary catch in my voice. He'd sense that weakness and fall upon it like a jackal, lock his jaws the second he hit bone. He always did.

"*You started it,*" he mimicked. "Like I'm letting either one of you put this on me."

"It was your fault, Ben."

"Not all of it. I know I fucked up, but so did he. And you sure did do your part, Ames, so fucking own it. Don't hole away upstairs, or hide out in the sitting room, crying at the trees."

"I'm not crying." I whipped back around to face him, smeared a fist across my stinging eyes. Officially undid my mother's attempt at makeup repair. Pathetic. "*Or* hiding."

"Oh really? Guess that's for the best. Far as I can tell, nobody's trying too hard to seek."

His grin widened at my gasp, flexed open and bit down, feeding on my pain. His laughter followed me as I stalked past him, steeling myself to face our family.

D inner was always going to be a shit show—a Langston family gathering, especially one including my mother, was a guaranteed runaway train, poised to crash before it even left the station. Add in Aunt Mattie and Uncle Peter, their usual veneer of clenched smiles, cued laughter, and default small talk, and there was nothing to do but sit pretty and hang on tight.

Seven people at a setting for eight, the gaps between us packed edge to edge with unspoken tension and decorative bowls, elaborately folded napkins and edible distractions—platters of carved roast beef and spiral ham; chunks of red potato fried in bacon grease, tossed with garlic and fresh rosemary; sliced tomatoes with salt; green beans from the garden, stewed in smoked pork; corn bread and yeast rolls both, waiting to be split and slathered. I had to bite back a giggle at my mother's resigned sigh as she settled into the chair across from mine, accepting the temporary abandonment of her usual carb-free lifestyle.

Grandpa sat between us at the head of the table, smiled at Grandma's ecstatic face at the other end. Aunt Mattie's gaze swiveled between them, reflecting their siphoned joy. Uncle Peter towered quietly to her right, sent over an apologetic little nod when he reached for his napkin, grazing my shoulder with the crisp crease of his shirtsleeve. Ben was last to the table, of course, sliding in next to my mother with an air of disgruntlement and barely restrained douchebaggery. The chair between him and Grandma, occupied in years previous by my father, stood empty.

The chewing was always the best part of these gatherings. Mouths packed with food, hands busy with utensils and serving spoons. Senses focused and sated. Silent.

Of course, eventually, everyone had to swallow.

"Amy, honey, we've just missed you so much."

Grandma was the one to break the silence this year, which was enough to shock Ben and me into a moment of involuntary eye contact. If there'd ever been an occasion when someone had beaten Aunt Mattie to the punch, it existed in a time line outside our shared memory.

"I missed you too, Grandma. It's good to be back."

"Summer always goes too fast," she sighed. "I feel like I could look out the window any moment and see you and those boys tearing up that trail, you looking all but like a boy yourself. All three of you, covered in mud and banging on the screen door for Popsicles. And here you are now—a young lady. It's like I have no idea where the years went. You just mean the world to us—you always have. Especially to Benny."

It had been true at one point—maybe even as recently as a year ago. But if ever a bullshit statement had been uttered at that table, I knew it and Ben knew it. My mother's sudden cough around a mouthful of wine indicated she wasn't exactly clueless. Grandma's eyes were bright, though, above the soft clasp of hands that wanted nothing more than to gather us both and press us back together.

"I'm almost afraid to blink anymore," she continued, "in case I up and miss everything. He'll be a senior this fall, you know."

"Oh, I can hardly wait," Aunt Mattie gushed. "So many plans and traditions, so many exciting milestones. He'll be homecoming king, of course. He's been on the court every year since he started at that school—I can't think of anyone more suitable."

"*If* he keeps his grades up through Christmas." Uncle Peter chuckled. "But we know he'll make a fine king, just like his old man. Right, Benny?"

"What? Oh. Sure, Dad."

"Oh, Benny's grades are fine, Peter," Aunt Mattie tinkled. "Lord knows he doesn't need top honors to run your rock quarry."

My mother's snort was more than audible, her follow-up coughing fit impossible to ignore. Uncle Peter's jaw clenched tight around the silence that followed. He returned to his plate, chewing and swallowing, repurposing his mouth. My aunt's eyes darted around the table, skipping over Ben's hunched shoulders and Grandpa's silence, before snaring themselves on me.

"I expect you'll be busy as well, won't you, Amy?" she continued, her voice a light and even lie. "The arts aren't for everyone, of course, but Eleanor tells me you're quite the talent."

"Her talent isn't the issue." My mother drained her glass, sloshed a refill from the rapidly emptying bottle. She was already drunk as hell. "More her reluctance to push beyond the bare minimum. If she doesn't get her priorities in line, she'll—well, social festivities are the least of her worries. The goal is to stay *out* of River Run, not eliminate all other options."

I shoved half a roll into my mouth as their eyes met across the table, though I knew neither expected a reply. This conversation had never been about me.

Aunt Mattie answered my mother's sardonic grin with an amused little smile, shiny gaze chilling to frost.

"There's always the family land, Ellie. Amy's inheritance still stands, even if it's not to *your* liking."

"The land wasn't the problem for me, Mattie. More the lack of options—speaking in terms both general and excruciatingly specific."

"Well, it should stay in the bloodline, either way. If Amy doesn't want it, we can add it to Benny's." The smile erupted into teeth. "*That* plot likely would've been yours, too, if there hadn't been that mess with—"

"Girls."

Grandma's voice was a slap across both their mouths. My mother's face corrected first, undid its snarls and smoothed its lines. She propped her elbows on the table and leaned forward, swung her head slowly right. Zeroed in on Ben, and his polite, crumbling smile.

"So. *Senior year.* Any big plans? Beyond homecoming king, of course."

"Not really, ma'am. Might take a year off after graduation. U of Kentucky has a couple programs that could help my future in the business, but it's kind of far."

"You can't be serious. Lexington's less than an hour."

"Well, kind of far to drive every day, anyway. Mom doesn't want me leaving town just yet. You know. It's a big change."

"Sometimes a big change can be just the thing." She swirled her wine, the long-absent River Run drawl sneaking past a tiny smirk as her gaze shifted between my aunt and uncle. "I'm sure *you* won't mind a disruption in the routine. So to speak."

"Oh, we certainly plan to keep busy, wherever Benny is,"

Aunt Mattie chirped. "In the meantime, there's plenty of—"

"I wasn't talking to you, Madeleine."

Uncle Peter's knife skittered on his plate, a bone china screech that set my teeth on edge. He swallowed his mouthful of food, blinked at my mother with eyes like bright blue glass.

"I'm sure I'll make do either way," he said slowly, "so long as Benjamin finds his place in the world. Right, son?"

"Sure, Dad," Ben muttered into his plate.

"Only so many 'places' in a small pond." Mom aimed that smirk at my cousin once more, waiting for him to squirm. "Time to swim, little fish."

"Oh, it's just so good to have us all together at the table again," Grandma broke in, gesturing wildly past my father's empty chair. "Such a blessing to have everybody home."

"Oh, isn't it?" Aunt Mattie latched on to that one like a lifeline, let it drag her back to surface normal. She caught Grandma's hand in her own, stretched her other across the table toward Ben. He stared at it a beat too long before surrendering his palm to her grasp. "Nothing is more important than family."

"Hear, hear," Grandpa piped up. His hand on my shoulder was a strange and crooked claw, foreign as his voice in a conversation as he turned to my mother, fixed an unblinking stare on her bleary eyes. "Family. Right, Eleanor?"

"Oh, certainly, Papa. Hear, hear, indeed."

I forced a smile on my face, then lowered my eyes a blink at a time until they reached my fork. I focused on my food, on spearing it and chewing it, swallowing without a sound. Doing my best to make it disappear.

CHAPTER 4
SUMMER 2019

My heart sank along with the sun. Night settled in over the trees and the land and the wide stone patio steps, still warm beneath my thighs. The kitchen light flicked on behind me, splashing its bright window frame square across the grass. The path beyond it was a pitch-black, toothless grin.

It was official. Teddy was a no-show.

That Ben had called it was the worst part, by far. He'd tried to warn me—he and my mother and everyone goddamn else on earth had foreseen this as inevitable. Not that him swaggering into the yard right now would realistically be any better, what with said mother still hanging around. Arguing was one thing; open defiance quite another. She'd raised me better than that for damn sure, whether I liked it or not.

Yet here I sat, like an asshole, teeth clenched and eyes on the trees, as if wishing would pluck Teddy from the ether and deposit him onto the grass. I'd spent the entire year since last summer making wishes, wanting nothing more than to return and find him waiting for me, the way he'd sworn he would. Like I'd waited for him, in a loop of endless, futile seasons.

I sensed it before I heard it—a rustle of underbrush, the crunch of twigs. Careful footsteps drawing closer, trying too hard to be quiet. I rose slowly from my perch on the steps, shoulders tensing at the sudden snap of a branch. It wouldn't be Ben; I'd seen him leave myself, glared at the back of his blond head through the rear window of Uncle Peter's truck as it wound its way up the hill, away from us. And Teddy wouldn't be caught dead fumbling around in the dark—even if he *had* decided to rush over here last minute, he'd have brought a flashlight.

Still, though. What if.

"Teddy?" It came out raw, too low and soft for human ears. I cleared my throat, and the footsteps stopped. Sweat prickled at my temples, gathered cold along the lines of my neck. I had to force the word from my throat. "Hello?"

"Amy?"

"Oh my God, seriously? Nat?"

She burst from the trees in a blur of mist and moonlight, streaming hair and long, pale limbs. Little Nat. A skinny, bright-eyed battering ram slamming through the world. Her silhouette bounded toward me, pulling up short a few feet away, dropping a worn canvas backpack on the ground—Teddy's old pack, scuffed at the corners and threadbare at the seams.

"Hi," she squeaked, right before she leaped.

I had to catch her. Had to laugh, even as her forehead butted my chin and I stumbled backward, locked in her sweet, enthusiastic hug. I absolutely had to return that hug, with every bit of my heart.

"Look at you," I finally breathed, holding her at arm's length. Taking in that grin and those cheekbones, the knobby knees and wide blue eyes. Teddy's baseball cap was jammed down over her head; her ponytail sprouted from the hole in the back like a chaotic sunbeam, ending just above her hips. "You got *so* tall."

"I'm ten now," she said, grinning. "Double digits. Bear says I'll be tall as him, soon enough."

"I bet you will. Did he . . ." I couldn't help but check the space behind her, as if he'd be crouched behind a tree or ducking into the bushes. As if he'd bothered to make the trip in the first place. "I mean, he's not—"

"He's at home," she said, sparing me the effort of coherent speech. "Mom went out and left him in charge."

"And he let you come over here alone?" Her nonanswer was answer enough, even without the shifty pucker of her mouth. "You *snuck out?*"

"I didn't *sneak*. He put on a movie for us but fell asleep on the couch right at the beginning. So I just left."

"That's sneaking, Natasha."

"Is not. Not if he never knows I'm gone. He'll sleep the whole night, I bet. He was real down today. Real tired, too."

"I wouldn't know." I bit the edge of my tongue, too late to stem the bitterness. "I haven't seen him."

"I know. He felt bad about that, but—well, that's why I'm here. To figure it out."

"Good luck with that," I muttered, half wincing at her scowl. Nat had never been the thundercloud type before, but what the hell did I know. Everything was upside down. "It's sort of a mess."

"I *know* it's a mess. It's a mess that *sucks*. And now that you're back, you need to fix it."

"Yeah. Not happening."

I reclaimed my seat on the steps, patted the space beside me. She settled into it and sat facing me. Her nose was scrunched, her eyes fierce under stern brows that rearranged themselves into uncertainty as she unconsciously gnawed her lower lip—stubborn but nervous, inching toward scared. Determined to find an answer in the worst possible place.

"Please, Amy. *Please*. How could you let this get so bad?"

"I didn't 'let' anything—know what? You need to talk to your brother."

"I *can't*," she wailed. "It's all ruined. Benny won't even come down anymore—hasn't been over to the house since you left last year, and dumb old Bear won't tell me why. No one will tell me *shit*."

"I can't help that, Nat. It's not my place to tell you his business."

"I don't get it. You were there, right? So it's your business too."

"Some of it." I looked away, skin heating at the memory of Ben's words: *Fucking own it*. "I did my part, yes. But whatever you hear, it should be from Teddy. The last thing I want to do is make it worse."

"This is so stupid. Are you still friends with him or not?"

"I don't know."

There it was—the truth. A year's worth of blame and hope and bitter dread, finally falling from my mouth. I'd tried. I'd stalked his mostly quiet social media like it was my life's true calling. I'd sent him more than a month's worth of increasingly, embarrassingly plaintive DMs, all of which had gone unanswered. I'd pummeled him with my fears and my feelings, turned on my fucking read receipts, twisted my panic into ultimatums, and still, silence. It was an utter mind fuck, how he could so easily ghost me after our last moment together, but I sure could take a hint. He'd proven he could move on; I was trying my best to do the same.

I'd just always been so very bad at letting him go.

I centered myself with a breath, packed my nerves down deep beneath my skin. Slammed the door on those thoughts before they devoured me.

"But . . . am *I* still your friend?" Nat's voice wavered, damp with unexpected tears. "Are you mad at me too?"

"Oh God. No. Nat, no. Come here."

Her cap brim nearly took the skin off my face. She flung herself into my outstretched arms, let me gather her close. She really was taller—so angular and gangly, so much bigger than she'd been the last time I'd seen her. Still, a little girl.

"I need to go," she finally sniffed, drawing back and sitting up. She ground a fist into each eye, smearing her cheeks with tears and sweat. "I don't want to get Bear in trouble."

"I can walk you back if you want, in case June's home. I'll tell her I came down to get you, so it's not technically sneaking out."

"Oh. Nooo, that . . . would not be good."

"Goddamn it, Nat. You're supposed to be grounded, aren't you?"

"Only till two more days from now. But I did extra chores today, so Mom will probably let me off tomorrow."

"If she does, come up and see me around lunchtime. We can hang out, maybe go down to the cove. Bring a picnic. Have some girl time."

"Really? Even though you're still fighting with—"

"Absolutely."

"Oh wow. I can't wait." She hopped off the step and unzipped her pack, dragged a gigantic silver flashlight from its depths, and flicked it on, hitching the pack over her shoulder. "Best day ever."

She trotted back toward the path. I watched her go, then rose and followed, chasing down the one bright moment in my dreary day.

"Nat?" She paused at the edge of the woods, cocked her head my way as I caught up. I tugged on her mess of a ponytail, pulled her in for one last hug. Felt her grin against my shoulder. "We'll always be friends, okay? No matter what kind of shit the boys pull."

"Promise?"

"World without end."

She squeezed me tighter at that, then scurried away in a burst of giggles that followed her down the path. The night swallowed her quickly—first her form, then her footfalls, blotting her out bit by bit. Soon, only her light was visible, bouncing brightly as it lit her way. Flitting through the trees like a tiny, happy ghost.

CHAPTER 5

SUMMER 2018—THE FIRST DAY

on't be silly, Eleanor. If you have time for a drink at the airport, you have time for a chat with your poor old mama. Amy, the boys came tearing over here a couple hours ago, eager as can be. They're waiting on you down at the riverbank."

My mother's mouth pulled into its usual pucker. You wouldn't think someone with a next-level case of chronic resting bitch face could manage to look even more unpleasant; somehow, she had it down.

"I hope this isn't a precedent for this trip, young lady. When I was your age—"

Grandma waved her hand, swiping the rest of my mother's thought into dust.

"When you were her age, you were running through those woods to the Franklin place and back every time I turned around. Go on, Amy. Go catch up with them."

"I also didn't have a series of assignments to complete before August." She squinted at her phone, holding it high to search for a signal. "Ugh. Never mind, I don't have time for this. Come kiss me goodbye, Amy. Try not to waste the entire summer, if at all possible."

Such an even, light tone with an audience, as if she was only joking. As if even a single block of white space in my sketchbook wouldn't be taken out on me in a million tiny ways. I suffered through her air kiss, waved her into the house, and felt a small, strange stir of pride at the void in my chest.

She'd left me in River Run every summer since I was old enough to be left, completely ignorant that three months away from her meant relief—meant three months without her criticism and scrutiny and hovering shadow. It had taken fifteen years, but that soft, needy part of me that craved her approval had finally scabbed. It did no good to mourn what you never had in the first place.

I set off for the cove on a path I could walk in my sleep, the unchecked trees and ancient boulders enfolding me in their sameness as my thoughts turned to him, like they did every summer before we reunited. Like they did over and over again every season in between.

And every time, my mind would eat itself, wondering if I'd imagined a different slant to his gaze, or whether I'd ever see a return on the years of patient hope; whether he'd ever thought of us as more than childhood friends. Wondering what he'd say, how he'd look. How he'd look at me.

The path broke at the riverbank, opened to the wide, calm cove, tree-ringed and perfect for swimming. I rounded the boulder, and there they were.

My boys.

Ben crouched beneath a tree, lighting a cigarette in his cupped hands and fiddling with the Zippo as he inhaled, sparking then dousing the flame over and over. My cousin was all angles—shoulders and brow, chin and jaw, pale and thin with hair to match. He'd grown it out almost to his collarbone, tucked the ends behind his ears in careless swoops. Teddy leaned against the trunk behind him, wiping his forehead on the hem of his worn T-shirt. Leaf shadows scattered across his skin, played over the dips and swells of his hip bones. Brushed the angles of his sunburned arms, leaner than last year and defined in ways that made my breath go short, then catch, as he shook his hair back from his face.

I'd sketched that face so many times. I'd traced those lips and shaded those cheekbones, captured the shadows of his eyes over and over on countless sketchbook pages. I'd run my fingers over that jaw and neck, smoothed down the dark fan of his hair, blending it past his ears, past his collar, over his shoulders until it matched my memories. Even with every relentless hour at my desk—every drop of talent and training bled from my hands onto rough-toothed paper—none of it came close. None of it prepared me for him.

"Holy shiiiiiiit," Ben suddenly screamed, flinging his cigarette aside. A wild laugh ripped from my throat as he ran at me and caught me in a hug, hopping up and down in crazy circles. "Amy, you're taller than me. Teddy, the girl is taller than me. She might even be taller than you. Goddamn, child, I missed you."

"I missed you too. So much." I meant to match his shriek, but a sudden rush of emotion dropped it to a whisper. Ben's hugs always felt like home.

The approach of Teddy's footsteps at my back tugged at my limbs and heart; the quiet words that followed curled through me like a breath of smoke.

"There's my city girl."

His voice was lower than I remembered. I spun directly from Ben's arms to his, pulling him closer than I'd ever dared. If I'd had any doubts, they dissolved as he enfolded me. I wasn't imagining the tremble in my eyelids, or the barely audible rasp of his inhale. I wasn't inventing the slight tilt of his head, or the brush of his lips against my jaw as he spoke.

"How about me? Did you miss me, Ames?"

"Only every single day."

"Yeah, that sounds about right." He drew back, taking me in from the ground up. "Damn. Benny, you called it. Girl went and grew up on us, all at once."

"Hopefully to your satisfaction."

Something unfamiliar, almost wicked, flared in his eyes.

"No complaints here." He pulled me in again, one hand drifting over my back, the other sneaking into my hair. I dropped my forehead to his shoulder, squeezed my eyes shut at the rise and fall of his chest.

Ben wandered back to the riverbank and bent over, scouring the ground. He reached down, plucked his still-lit cigarette from the dirt, and took a drag, standing straight then bending backward to exhale into the sky. I barely noticed his follow-up sigh, or the way he turned toward the river, fixed his eyes on the flow of the current.

Too much was happening beneath my skin. Everything was suddenly real.

Hours later, we huddled around our bonfire, formed as always by our own years-old ritual: I gathered exactly fifteen smooth, fist-size river rocks and arranged them in a circle in the center of the clearing. Teddy scoured the surrounding woods for dead branches, stockpiling enough to sustain a blaze long into the night. Ben gathered and prepared kindling scraps, then lit the fire itself.

He'd done four years of Boy Scouts proud with the perfect little bundle of sticks and dried grass, but his big production fell flat when he held the lighter to the kindling and thumbed the flint wheel. It didn't even spark.

Teddy dropped his head in his hands as Ben shook the Zippo, tried a second time, and came up empty.

"Again, Benny? I told you to quit fucking around with it about a thousand times."

"Don't tell me it came as a shock when I ignored you." Ben flicked the wheel another couple times before giving up. "Well, what now? Don't you have your own shitty lighter? Or did you come out here prepared to bum off mine, like usual?"

"Since when do I count on your slack ass, Benny?" Teddy grinned, producing a plastic Bic and making quick work of the kindling. "Happy now?"

"Very. You're a credit to us all, Theo. To your family, your legacy, and River Run itself."

"Don't call me Theo, bitch."

"Bitch, I'll call you whatever I want." He glanced at me, then cracked up, smacking Teddy's shoulder. "Oh shit, dude, look at her face. I always forget the introductory adjustment period."

"Every year, Amy." Teddy shook his head. "You show up and act all shocked, like you haven't heard us do this a million times. Like you forgot all about us."

"Can you blame me? You guys are horrible. Like, why are we even friends?"

"Eh, whatever, Ames." Teddy smirked, unfurling from his hunch and stretching on the ground like a snake, tapping his knuckles to Ben's extended fist. "You can't get enough of us."

I didn't answer. Of course I hadn't forgotten their unfiltered dynamic—how they constantly dragged each other, launched profanity and insults and snark through the air like skipping stones, passed them off as jokes before they left a mark. Of course I hadn't forgotten *them*. But I did do my best to sweep them away each year, bury them alongside everything I missed too much—eleven summers, countless memories. A load too heavy to lug with me through winter.

"Guys, look." Ben's hushed voice drew our eyes. He lay on his back, gaze fixed overhead, lit by the fire and the fading day. Teddy dropped down next to him and I stretched out the opposite way, my head resting between both of theirs.

The treetops formed a frame around the sky, around that slow, immeasurable shift from bruise-purple dusk to deep, limitless night. Stars winked into view, clusters bursting into layers, closer, then far, then farthest. Infinite.

"It never gets old, does it?" Teddy's voice brushed against my ear and I turned my head his way, falling into his gentle, upside-down smile. "I'm glad you came back to us."

"I'll always come back to you, Teddy."

The words rode out on my heart, vacating my mouth before I thought to close it. I snapped my eyes to the sky, fixing them desperately on the moon. Dreading his reply.

Silence. Nothing but slow, even breathing. I marinated in humiliation, hoping Ben hadn't heard, wondering how long they'd string this one out. They'd make it last the season, no doubt, rag on me until the words lost even their most basic meaning.

Teddy's fingers touched my cheek. My breath stuttered as they slid to my chin, tilting my face back toward him. Firelight stroked shadows over his features, turned his eyes to candle flame. They drew mine in, caught and held, in a way they never had before.

"Careful what you wish for, Ames. If I had my way, you'd never leave me again."

CHAPTER 6

SUMMER 2019

The doorbell dragged me from a haze of clasping hands and running feet, swirls of sky and sun and river green. Our world in watercolor, splashed beneath my sleeping eyelids. I opened my eyes to the ceiling, then squinted at the antique clock on the nightstand. Shook myself awake at the angle of the hands: almost three in the afternoon already. I hadn't meant to nap so long.

I hadn't meant to nap at all, actually—hadn't done more than set my pencils down and stretch out on the bed, flex the tension from my fingers and arms and back. At least I'd gotten some good stuff done before my accidental slumber. I stretched and yawned, closed the sketchbook on images my instructors would never see: Ben as an ersatz Loki, bound but defiant, trickster grin staring down a hissing serpent; Teddy's form sprouting from the riverbed rocks like a half-carved statue, chisel in hand, chipping himself free; an updated version of Nat: a Neverland refugee tougher than any Lost Boy, last summer's flower-petal wings swapped out for shredded cobwebs, pointed elf ears, and a wicked, lovely smile; the four of us, each depicted as an element—earth, air, fire, and water, separate but inseparable. Each miserable without the rest.

As for my actual assigned work, I'd officially completed sixteen thumbnail sketches—sixteen out of the daily goal of fifty. My mother was going to kill me.

The day had been a long and lonely slog mostly spent holed up in my room, listening for the riding mower and forbidding myself from approaching the window. I still hadn't seen Teddy, but no way would I let his first glimpse of me be my face peeking around a curtain, staring at him like a goddamn stalker.

I hated that he worked for us. I fucking hated it.

The deal at Grandma's was a pretty good one, all things considered—River Run's employment opportunities that didn't involve either Uncle Peter's limestone quarry or freelance meth production were limited even for adults, let alone a teenager with no car. But Teddy was one person, wrangling a property that would've been a bitch for a professional landscaping crew, and Grandma was a cheapskate in the way old people are, maintaining willful ignorance of inflation and the wage gap, treating the arrangement like he was supplementing his allowance instead of supporting his family. Assuming what she paid was plenty because he was seventeen and too proud to ask for more.

I'd spent the past two summers watching my best friend bust his ass in the sun, working for a pittance that was one late payment away from literally going right back to my grandparents for rent and utilities on the trailer. June's employment history was succinctly defined as erratic; she managed to keep the lights on and the water running, feed her children and herself, but anything beyond that was a perpetual maybe, tricked out of spare change and odd jobs.

Still, I'd never heard him complain. He arrived at his scheduled time and cycled through his tasks like a machine, refusing to leave before the day's agenda was complete. He was on the riding mower two days a week. The flowerbeds took up a day on their own, including weeding, mulching, and transplanting. Edging, raking, and pruning took up the other two days. Assorted heavy labor, such as branch removal, brush clearing, rock hauling, or general repairs happened as needed, sometimes adding a sixth day to his schedule, which he worked without comment. Tackled, even, with a dedication that masked the truth of its own frustration. As if the constant flame of my ambition hadn't long ago recognized in him its own determined twin.

I dragged ass all the way downstairs as the doorbell chimed a third time, not bothering to check what I knew was a groggy, tousled reflection in the foyer mirror. Decidedly unprepared to face the person waiting on the far side of the doorway.

He was still in his work clothes, the usual jeans and T-shirt streaked with grass stains, heavy with sweat and dirt. His hair was long and loose, tucked behind his ears. His eyes widened as they met mine, then moved over me, took me in. Lingered on my limbs and lips, my wide, rapt gaze. Drank the curves of my body in a single, swooping gulp.

"Hey, City Girl."

Sparks surged beneath my skin, woken by the drawl of that voice. All the times I'd imagined this moment—all the words I'd planned, the practiced scowls and scornful dismissals—those things burned away like mist in sunlight. And as we stood there, me on one side of the threshold, him on the other, I stopped caring about the details and the anger, and the finer points of my resentful broken heart. In that moment, it just didn't matter.

He was here.

"I waited for you." It came out softer, needier than I wanted. Stronger by far than the sudden melt of my bones. I faltered, then rallied, made myself call him out before I lost my nerve. "Yesterday, I mean—you never showed up. You never answered my e-mails. You could have messaged me, at least, or picked up a phone at some point in the last year. I thought—"

"I know. I wanted to stop by, but I figured Ben—I knew he'd get dragged down here at some point, and I didn't want to start that shit all over again. I just wanted to see you." He stepped closer, holding my eyes. His hand twitched, like he wanted to reach for me, but wasn't sure if it was a good idea. "And the DMs, the e-mails—I know you're pissed. I get it; I'd be pissed too. Things have been—shit." He searched my face, shoulders sagging as he took in my measured, unblinking stare. "Yeah, I should just go. If you want."

"Oh my God, shut up." It only took a step to cross the distance between us. We filled that space with each other—with unasked questions and impatient hearts. I pressed my face against his neck, breathing in the mess of him. "Don't you go anywhere. Ever again."

"I won't." His lips moved against my hair, gently, like I'd break. Or like he would. "Amy, you don't even know. I missed you so much, every single day."

The words flowed through me like an echo, familiar and wistful. Winding inevitably into my heart. He was sweaty and dirty, and ruining my shirt. He was all the things I needed in the world.

"I missed you too. I have to tell you something, though." I paused, every second ticking us closer to the inevitable confession— the winter I'd spent at someone else's side. "Can we talk?"

"We need to," he answered, voice shifting almost imperceptibly. "Ames, this past year . . . well, it's complicated."

"That doesn't sound as benign as you think it does, Teddy," I muttered, drawing away from him. Stepping back until my heels grazed the threshold. Complicated. A word said through half a smile, when you need to sand the edges off things you don't really want to say. "Should *I* just go back inside, or . . . ?"

"It's not like that. There's just a lot to sort out—expectations versus reality, I guess. Can you come back with me?"

"To your place?"

"If that's okay. I told Mom I'd bring her home, but after that, I'm yours." He craned his neck, peered over my shoulder to the foyer behind me. "Is she here?"

"What? I don't think so." I glanced at the coatrack. Grandma's purse was gone, along with Grandpa's cap and cane, and my mother's bag. "No, I guess she's still out. I was drawing, and I fell asleep, and—"

"You fell asleep? She just took off, without telling you?"

"They left around noon, with my mom. Does she owe you a check? She might've put it on the counter."

"Wait. Who are you talking about?"

"Um, my grandmother? Your employer, who lives here? Who are *you* talking about?"

"Jesus." He shook his head, rubbing a hand over his eyes. "Nat, Amy. I'm looking for Nat. She's not here?"

"I haven't seen her today," I said. And I hadn't—she'd never shown up for girl time. "I assumed she was still grounded."

"But—if she's not here—" His eyes roamed across the porch,

over the lawn, stopping at the edge of the woods, then swung back to me. "How did you know she'd been grounded?"

"Oh." Shit. "Yeah, you fell asleep during the movie last night, and she came to see me. Don't be mad."

"She snuck out?" His mouth puckered, wavered between a snarl and a smile. "Goddamn. That'll teach me, huh? Need to put a bell on that girl. Like a cat."

"She made it home, right? Before June got back?"

"I woke up during the credits and she was right next to me, getting chip crumbs all over the couch. Sent her to bed myself. Not sure when Mom got in, but they were both up when I left this morning. She was all excited about coming over here." I watched him sort through his thoughts, watched those thoughts etch themselves across his brow in worried lines. "She really never showed?"

"No, but it was tentative. She didn't know if she'd be allowed out. We were supposed to have lunch down at the cove, but I told her to meet me at the house. Would she even go near the water on her own?"

"Has done a couple of times. Worth a look to know for sure."

It was instinct as much as anything, the way we turned as one toward the path. The way our footfalls synced, pacing each other as I fell into step beside him. I didn't realize I'd forgotten my shoes until I stumbled on a protruding root. Teddy heard my gasp and reached for my hand, drew me closer as we reached the clearing.

"Well, she was here at some point." He nodded at the blue-striped beach towel sitting bright and blameless at the base of the giant oak. "We must've just missed her."

"Wouldn't she have come to the house?"

"She probably did. You said you were sleeping, right? Maybe you didn't hear the doorbell."

"Maybe." I glanced down at our hands, still entwined from when he'd steadied me. So natural and right, I'd forgotten to let go. "Either she went there, or back to your place. Where she also might be, at this very moment."

It was like I'd run out of words. The conversation was happening on its own, making the same nonsensical loop over the same obvious, already stated suggestions, until I didn't know if I was parroting him or myself. Dear God, was I a mess. If I didn't gather my shit together, I was going to ruin everything.

I squeezed my eyes shut, frantically sorting my thoughts from my heartbeats, and when I opened them, his gaze was waiting to meld with mine. His smile untwisted, reformed into something softer. Still, he held himself back, even as I stepped closer. Even as his free hand rose to brush a leaf from my shoulder, then lingered, fingertips barely grazing my collarbone. I could see what it cost to keep himself at bay, though I could hardly fault him. We both knew exactly how useless we'd be to Nat or anyone else once we let ourselves sink beneath that surface.

We had time. We had a summer's worth of moments to make it perfect.

"Come on," he whispered. "I'll check in with Mom, make sure Nat's settled, and we can take a walk, if you want. Maybe hang out on the porch, or at the firepit."

"Or in your room."

The words fell on him as heavy as I wanted, all the questions and answers between us resolved with the meaning of their weight.

His eyes flashed and darkened, thunderclouds promising a violent, lovely squall.

That look. That goddamn look that had crushed too many to count, leveled at me full force. Wrenching me in two, as his brow grazed mine.

"Or that. Let's go."

I gulped a jittery breath as he walked away from me, headed for Nat's things.

"Should we check the rest of the woods first?" I asked, hating the shrill timbre of my own voice. Hating even more the space between us, and the way it widened with every step.

"My money's on her being home. She leaves her towels and shit out here all the time. Might as well grab them now, save her a trip back." His words ended in a laugh as he lifted the folded towel, shook it out, and draped it over his arm, revealing the package of Nutter Butters underneath. "Son of a bitch. Looks like I need to have a chat with Miss Natasha about going through my room."

"You hide cookies in your room?"

"I do if I want to get my share. She'll inhale a sleeve of these in no—huh. That's weird."

"What is it?"

"Her shoes are still here. Her clothes too. Everything." He picked up the baseball cap, pushed aside the dirt-streaked beach cover-up, polka-dotted pink and neatly folded, resting atop the neon-green flip-flops. A water canteen and Teddy's pack lay side by side at the bottom of the stack. "Is she just like, wandering around in her bathing suit?"

I turned away from him, scanning the trees for a flash of color or a hint of movement. Cocked my head, listened for footsteps or a stifled giggle. The woods were quiet, though—as quiet as they ever got, anyway, what with the rustle of trees and brush, the occasional bird twitter, the steady swoosh of the river. No sign of Nat or anyone else.

"She wouldn't have gone home barefoot." Teddy's face was drawn and wary, visibly fighting a sudden rising tide of panic. It washed over me all at once, chilling me to my toes. "The trail goes to gravel about a hundred feet from the yard, cuts your feet up bad. She knows better."

"I'll go back to the house. We could have crossed paths and missed each other."

"Look for any sign of her—maybe she's in the garden. Or went to the back door." He slung the towel and her pack over his shoulder, scooped the food and clothes and shoes into a frantic jumble against his chest. "Maybe she—check everywhere, Ames, and call—oh God. I have to go."

And he was gone, cutting across the cove and disappearing into the trees, headed down the path to his home, and I was already fleeing, ignoring the rocks and twigs shredding my soles as I raced back up the hill. Trying as hard as I could not to think of her abandoned things, nestled in the roots at the water's edge.

"Nothing yet, Millie. They're getting a search together, back down the hill."

Grandpa's voice drifted out low, a resigned, downtrodden murmur creeping through the doorway. Grandma raised her head from her folded hands, her silent prayer cut short as I crossed the threshold; crossed from the orderly gleam of parquet to the cool, smooth stone of the kitchen floor. Both of them eyed me, slowing my feet to a stop halfway to the table.

Well over an hour had passed since I'd burst out of the woods and scrambled to find my shoes in the still-empty house. Instead of waiting around on my ass, I'd doubled back and searched everywhere I could think to search—the shed, my mother's old playhouse. The expanse of gardens and freshly mown grass, all the way to the property line. Never mind that Teddy had spent his morning out there; it wouldn't have been the first time Nat had roped us into hide-and-seek, giggling from the shadows as we combed the woods, unknowing participants in a game we hadn't agreed to play.

She wasn't there. She wasn't anywhere.

I'd returned to the house breathless and frantic, catapulted through the foyer and past the bewildered faces of my family, just returned from town, to answer my grandparents' ringing landline. My mother had listened to my half of the babbled conversation with a set jaw, something like fear creeping into her eyes, and calmly taken the receiver from my hand. After a brief exchange with June, she'd hung up, then put in a call to Aunt Mattie, waving me away. Taking over.

Now, I watched her from the doorway as she set a plate of cheese and crackers on the table and poured herself a coffee, ran a dish towel over the granite countertop, brushed away nonexistent crumbs from the stove. Grandpa's jaws worked around a wad of tobacco in slow, rhythmic contrast to his trembling hands.

"Oh Jonas, this is just terrible," Grandma murmured. "Oh Lord, poor June. I can't imagine how I'd feel if my child went missing. I just can't."

"You really think she's—*missing*? As in *lost*?" A waking, numbing horror overtook my confusion as the words settled, sowed themselves, rooted in my mind. My grandfather blinked at me, eyes bloodshot and sad. "Grandpa. Tell me."

"Well now, Amy, you know how kids tend to wander. Could be she's off somewhere, taking her time to get home. Could be holed up in a hiding spot, or off with a friend. Wouldn't be the first—" He cut off at the gentle weight of my mother's hand on his shoulder, her fingers pressing indentations into his shirt. "Anyhow, so far as we know, there ain't been no sign of her—she's gone. Vanished into thin air."

Grandpa kept talking, but his words went fuzzy, circling my head and drifting past unheard as I spiraled away. A single syllable breaking off from the fray, screaming itself raw over and over again.

Gone.

"I'll put together a casserole for June," Grandma said, rising from her chair and crossing to the counter. "She'll need to eat, keep her strength up. You and Benny can take it down the hill. And—yes, I should do one for Madeleine, too."

"What's Aunt Mattie got to do with it?"

Her hand fluttered toward the dish towel, lost its way in an absent pause. Drifted back to her side, unclean.

"What, honey? Oh . . . well, you know how close Peter was with Sam, still is with June, how he looks after those kids—they're worried to death. Madeleine's been making calls, and—well, I'm sure they haven't had time to cook. Get the door, will you, Amy? I think I hear them now."

My fingers trembled as I crossed to the foyer, every tremor tugging me toward action—toward anything that wasn't helpless inertia.

Instead I opened the heavy door to find the Hansen family radiating shocked despair, lined up on the porch by height like a set of fucked-up nesting dolls. Instead I was bulldozed forward by five foot, three inches of Grandma, who all but swung me into Uncle Peter's lumberjack-large embrace.

"Hey, kiddo," he kept saying, monotone, blank and restrained as my own set jaw. "Hey, kiddo, hey." He let me go and swooped in on Grandma. "Hey, Mama Langston."

I reeled away from their weird emotions, only to get swept up by Aunt Mattie and her flurry of tissues and tears and trembling hands, her wails matching those of my grandmother. I managed to slip free of her arms as my mother appeared, an ice floe sliding through a warm salt sea. Aunt Mattie released me to do their bullshit little air kisses, and I pushed past them, past Ben, and took the porch steps two at a time.

Their voices faded as I walked, determined to remove myself from the scene—to end up far away, as if I could ever escape their entanglement of absurd gloom. As if anyone aside from Ben and me considered Nat part of the family or knew her beyond the fond familiarity adults reserve for the children of longtime friends.

The front door slammed on their cacophony with a decisive bang as I headed for the woods.

CHAPTER 7

SUMMER 2019

S o."

Ben's voice dragged me out of the void, back to the ache of my grinding teeth and burning eyes, the rough bite of tree bark through my shirt. A twig snapped beneath his leg as he settled next to me and leaned against the trunk. We watched the shadows play over the lawn, brush long, dark fingers over the shed and the house. I hadn't gone far; just a few trees deep onto the path. There was no point trying to hide from my cousin on the family land. No point walking away from Ben Hansen at all when he didn't want you to leave.

"So," he said again. "This is fucked; we both know that. And far be it from me to overstep, but we might want to cut the shit and focus on what happens next, for her sake. And his."

I let my silence tighten around his hunched shoulders. When I finally spoke, my words emerged in my mother's voice, all frostbite and bitch, wrapped in a year's worth of repressed anger, hurt, and a glacier's worth of icy guilt.

"I'd say 'fucked' is an understatement. I saw Nat last night. She told me exactly how fucked things have been since I left last year."

"Which should barely be news to you."

"Trust me, I'm hardly surprised. But if she's really gone—if this is as bad as it seems—he's going to need both of us, and if you go over there and start up again after—"

"You honestly think I would?" He took a swipe at the grass, his face hard and dark as the thoughts in my head. "It's insane. Dad said Teddy found her stuff on the riverbank, down at the cove. Shoes, cover-up, all that."

"I'm aware, Benjamin. I was there."

He started at that little detail, visibly quashing the urge to pick it apart.

"So, you know what they're saying, then."

"What who's saying? No one's told me anything since I got back. I've just been sitting around, waiting, and—I mean seriously, what the *fuck*? What *happened* to her?"

"Well, Amy, the official knee-jerk police theory, according to what June told Dad, is she might have been sucked underwater. During a *swim*."

His words hung in the air, a benign jumble of letters and sounds that formed suddenly into fact and crashed through me like a fist.

"What?"

"Like she just stripped down to her bathing suit and dove on in. It can't be right. Are you sure there was no other sign of her?"

"Only her clothes and her towel sitting under the oak. Folded up, even. She'd brought stuff for the picnic, too, and her pack and water—" Tears pricked the corners of my eyes. "This is my fault, Ben. I should've gone down to get her, but—"

"Stop. Did you say 'folded'?" Ben stared into the middle distance, something unknown and dangerous creeping across his face. "Amy, never mind swimming on her own—when was the last time

eva v. gibson

Natasha Fox folded any damn thing on the face of the earth?"

He was right. It didn't make sense—not for chaotic, messy Nat, who could barely stand to get her ears wet. Nat, who'd been caught in a current four years before and swept out of the shallows where we'd been playing, gotten her foot wedged in the river rocks and been trapped underwater; who'd nearly died in front of us that long-ago day before Ben and Teddy pulled her out. Nat, who'd subsequently never learned to swim—she'd sooner eat a live spider than casually dive into deep water, let alone bother to fold her clothes before doing so.

I blinked at him, questions shredding against the edges of my mind. Bits and pieces fluttering, reforming, then bursting, before the craziest one, the only one that mattered, fought its way through to my throat.

"Then who did?"

"My best guess?" He turned away from me, his eyes fixed on the slow, green sway of the river. "Whoever took her."

The downhill hike to Teddy's was easy enough on a good day, but with the cove blocked off by the cops, and hampered as we were by the casserole Grandma all but shoved into my hands, there was no question that we'd eschew it in favor of Ben's car.

"What happened to the Dodge?" I asked, as he slid into the driver's seat of the unfamiliar black Mustang parked haphazardly on the front lawn.

"The Ram or the Challenger?"

"I don't know, whichever one you were driving last year."

"The Challenger. Nothing, it's up at my place. In the garage. Would you prefer—"

"I don't care. Just wondering."

We followed the paved drive down the steep slope of the hill, past the woods on the right, and the Hansens' now-empty stables and acres of fenced pasture on the left, until we reached the turnoff to Teddy's: the gravel lane, marked by a bank of mailboxes.

We crunched along, Ben's foot noticeably lighter on the gas pedal. At the last quarter mile, the trees closed in again, then broke open to a clearing on the riverbank, where the single-wide trailer squatted on cinderblock haunches. The yard was an unkempt mess of people, scattered lawn chairs, and hastily parked police cruisers, none of which were doing any favors for the already patchy grass. A basket of still-damp laundry moldered away next to a step stool. A mason jar of clothespins lay on its side, contents strewn and stepped on, ground into the red clay earth beneath the clothesline.

Ben parked without incident, made it out of the car just fine, but hung back as we approached the porch stairs, the telltale eye twitch a familiar, wearisome warning.

"Oh God," he muttered. "I can't do this."

"This is absolutely *not* the time for your issues, Benjamin. Take a cleansing breath and get your ass up here."

"I'm serious, Amy. I can't see him now, not after—"

I rose to my full height, significant even when I wasn't standing two steps higher on a flight of stairs. I tucked away the quiver in my throat and fell away from myself, reaching for that hollow calm. I froze my nerves. I became my mother's girl.

"Know what? Right now I don't care about your anxiety, or how badly you fucked things up last summer—for once, it's not *about* you. You will pull yourself together, you will walk in there with me, and you will be there for him. However he needs."

It was as horrible as it was effective. Beneath his fear lurked a hint of relief, a part of him that welcomed my familiar tone—the one that absolved him of authority and took the decision from his hands. That relief, and his silent, acquiescing nod, made me sick.

The already-cramped trailer was packed, wall-to-wall people woven through with quiet murmurs and the low, feral wail of June Barrett. I caught sight of her bowed blond head, of her thin elbows, clutched on either side by rough, rawboned men whose lips moved together as they prayed. The family had always been secular, but after Sam Fox's sudden death, June had gone off the deep end and embraced a backwoods congregation that made the most heated televangelists look downright reasonable. Teddy couldn't stand them; he wouldn't be anywhere near that mess of a prayer circle.

I set Grandma's casserole on the kitchen counter and strode straight past them, down the narrow hallway with its needlepoint hangings and family portraits, its wall sconces of frayed silk flowers, age-worn and threaded with cobwebs.

Teddy sat slumped on the floor beside his unmade bed, eyes squeezed shut, lips bitten raw. He was surrounded by a scattering of photographs: Him and Nat grinning and hugging on some long-ago Christmas; a tween version of Teddy replacing his bike chain, brow furrowed in concentration, Nat sneaking up behind him with an active garden hose; and a more recent snapshot—him slouched in a kitchen chair as she braided ribbons into his dark hair, her own blond braids, apple cheeks, and bright-eyed grin the antithesis to his resigned, heavy-browed irritation.

His eyes cracked open at the click of the closing door, then widened, taking us in as I knelt beside him, and I didn't see anything after that. His arms crushed me, his face pressed against my neck as I kissed his hair and cheek and forehead, one leg twisted beneath me, my rib cage at painful odds with my spine.

It didn't matter—not the ache or the awkwardness, nor any bitterness that lingered from before. I'd have sat there until every last bone snapped and splintered if that was what he needed.

"Oh man," he said into my shoulder. "I meant to call you back, but I—"

"Oh my God, Teddy, don't. I'm here. We're here for you."

"We'll find her, dude." Ben was wired and restless, pacing a groove between the bed and the window. "Tell me what you need, and I'll get it done. Anything."

"I don't know what I need, Benny. I don't. It's unreal. It's just so—" The thin walls failed to block the loud "AMEN" emanating from the living room. Teddy moaned and rocked to his feet, catching me off guard. "God, I can't. I can't sit here anymore. I have to find her. Come with me? Both of you?"

"Hell yes." Ben was already headed for the door. He'd never done well in narrow enclosures, even under non-horrible circumstances. "Let's do this."

CHAPTER 8

SUMMER 2018

She launched herself straight at my head, lit the world with her sweet, familiar grin. I caught the flurry of sunburned limbs and wild, summer-light hair, and hugged it close. Little Nat, who never waited for my knock before bursting through the door.

"AMY." She reared her head backward, still hanging on to my neck. "Did you see it?"

"See what?" I stepped through the front door into the dark, cool living room, and set her on her feet, made a show of studying her face: June's cheekbones and nose and delicate, arched brows in miniature, set off by fair, freckled skin. Her jaw and chin, still childishly round. Crooked, smiling lips, pink and sticky with glitter gloss. "Hmmm. Let me guess. Your hair is pink? Your eyes are green instead of blue?"

"Aaaaaamyyyyyy. Nooo. Look CLOSER."

"Oh. My. God." I put my hands to my face in mock surprise, setting off her giggles. "Nat, are you wearing sparkly lip gloss?"

"She sure is," Teddy said, appearing in the doorway of his bedroom. "The finest Walmart has to offer."

His voice flowed over me, winding through my veins as I met his smile. That same smile from the previous night's bonfire, curving slow and shy at me from across the room. His T-shirt was dark gray and tight across his chest, his hair loose on his shoulders. I couldn't stop staring.

"Hey, Ames. Long time, no see."

"Oh definitely. A whole twelve hours."

"Always time enough to miss you." His wink sucked the wind from my lungs; the crook of his smile gave it back. "And I always do."

"Um. Bear?"

Our eyes jerked apart, refocused on Nat's fidgeting hands and the hesitant furrow of her face.

"What's up? You okay?"

"I'm okay." She was quiet for a breath, then exploded in a flurry of bouncing hair and pleading puppy eyes. "Can I come with you? I'll be good and I won't complain, and I'll do whatever you say. Please."

"It's fine by me, Bug," Teddy said, "but Mom said you have to stay in until your room gets clean. I'll bring you something from town, okay? We won't be long."

She slouched off, face scrunched around her sparkly pout. Teddy shook his head and held the door for me, slipped out at my heels. He followed me down the steps to where Ben waited, engine running, music riding out on a wave of air-conditioning and cigarette smoke.

"Finally." He lowered the music and flicked the cigarette butt onto the driveway as I climbed in the back and Teddy slid into the passenger seat. "You in there jerking it, or what? If you need to finish off real quick, we can wait."

"Yeah, I'm all set, thanks. I actually started to earlier, but then I pictured your mom and the urge disappeared."

"I get that," Ben said. "Same thing happens to me when I picture June, only the opposite."

"Bet you're not the only Hansen with that burning thirst. Though he'd have to fish his balls out of Mattie's purse before he takes the chance."

"Nah, she keeps those in the wine cellar. Stable temperature, less humidity. Longer shelf life, in case he wants to rub one out sometime in the next decade."

"Guys, no," I groaned, as they both burst into laughter. When Ben and Teddy got started on the Your Mom jokes, boundaries were theoretical at best, and mostly nonexistent. This wouldn't end until one of them caved. "That is like, all the facets of gross."

"Aw, you're no fun." Teddy smirked. "It's like you don't even want to *hear* about your uncle's dusty old nutsa—"

"Oh my *God*, shut up—those are your *parents*. You're both disgusting."

"But we're not wrong, Ames," Ben cackled. "We have high MILF standards here in River Run. Like everyone in this car wouldn't dive down on one over the other, no contest."

"*Whoa.* Okay, okay, Benny," Teddy said, ceding victory with a repulsed shudder. "Truce. You win."

"June's got that ass is what makes the difference," Ben continued, unfazed. "Like this one time, she was out here hanging the laundry in these cute little cutoff shorts, and I—"

"WHAT THE FUCK, DUDE. STOP."

"Guys. Look at that."

They followed my finger to the porch where Nat stood, clutching the strap of her Descendants purse. She'd swiped on another layer of lip gloss and brushed her hair, swept it back with a ladybug clip from her nervous, hopeful eyes.

"Christ." Ben met my eyes in the rearview. "She's not coming with?"

"Teddy told her no."

"Dude, come on. We can't leave her here when she got all fixed up."

Teddy shook his head, rubbing a hand over his face.

"Yeah, I know. I'll get my ass handed to me later, but whatever." He crawled between the bucket seats into the back, then leaned over the console and into Ben's smirk. "But if you mention my mom, I'll punch you right in the fucking teeth."

"I would never do that," Ben huffed. "Unless, of course, I decide I want you to get a little rough, in which case—"

"Goddamn it, Benny, you can't say that shit around her. She's just a kid. She doesn't—"

"Calm down, Theo. I promise I won't talk about your mom's sweet ass in front of your sister, okay? God." He ignored Teddy's splutters and uncoiled from his seat, leaning his entire body out the window. "Girl, get your butt down into this car before I drive away and leave you here."

"Really?"

"Don't make me take my foot off the brake, Natasha."

Nat squealed down the steps and dove into the car. Ben reached across to help with her seat belt and threw a lurid wink at Teddy as he settled next to me.

"You guys cozy? Maybe Ames can help get your mind off old Auntie Madeleine."

"JESUS. So much for promises, huh?"

"Devil's in the details, man. I never said MY mom was off the table."

The roar of the engine drowned out Teddy's profane reply as Ben stomped the gas, peeling out of the driveway and up the lane in a spray of gravel. His foot got heavier the farther we went, and we all but burst from the trees, narrowly missing the postal truck parked in front of the mailboxes. Ben cranked the music louder as the wind rushed in, stealing any possibility of words.

Nat waved to the mailman as we swung past. Before he could lift a hand in return, we were gone.

River Run was nothing if not a decrepit hole in the earth, and in no part of town was that more apparent than the historic district. It sprouted from the soil in a tired slouch of gothic revival homes and empty brownstone storefronts, everything mismatched and trying to look like someplace else. We almost never bothered with it, save for when Ben got a craving for baklava from the one decent coffee shop in twenty miles.

After loading up on sugar and caffeine, we wandered down the cobblestones toward the park, where Ben and Teddy ran for the biggest tree in the place. Usually Nat would be right behind them, but she hung back, settled next to me on the grass, leaned against the trunk as the boys disappeared into the branches above us. Pulled her lip gloss from her purse and rolled it between her hands, frowning at the label.

"Can you help me with this, Amy? I feel like I'm doing it wrong."

"Didn't your mom show you how to use it?"

"Yes, but I think she does it wrong too."

I had to bite back a grin at that; June did apply her makeup with a Kentucky-heavy hand. I unscrewed the wand and dragged it against the rim of the tube, scraping off as much gloss as possible. It was really fucking pink.

"You only need the tiniest bit on the tip of your finger. Like this." I scooped a dab onto my pinky and spread it thin and even across her lips, dug in my purse for my compact mirror. "See?"

"I love it," she said, tilting her chin to catch the light, admiring herself from every angle. She watched me tuck away the compact and zipped her gloss back into her purse before tapping her finger on my bag. "Can I see? Please?"

"Oh. I don't know. I'm not working on anything special right now."

"Pleeeeeeease? I just want to see them. Just for a second."

"Fine." She wasn't going to stop, so I pulled out my Moleskine. "Don't wrinkle the pages."

"These are so good." Nat browsed through the pages, studied the still-life assignments and thumbnail sketches before handing it back to me with a tiny grin. "Now, let me see the real one."

Unlike many of my classmates, I didn't have to worry about my mother tossing my room on the regular, snooping through my things, looking for reasons to pry further into my life. Eleanor Larsen was a lot of things, but not needlessly nosy—her controlling tendencies didn't extend past monitoring my assignments, public image, and general manners. So as long as I kept my real sketchbook zipped into the inner pocket of my purse, she'd never know how many hours I spent on art unrelated to my formal studies.

Nat, however, was all about going through my stuff. She'd discovered my secret years ago.

"Okay, you can see the real one," I said with a sigh, glancing into the tree before handing it over. Ben and Teddy were high above us, too far up to peek even if they tried. "The best stuff is toward the front."

Her giggles turned to squeals as she delved into the pages, delighting in the mandrakes and naiads, the gnomes and harpies and bumpy toads; at her own face on a series of fae folk, tiny and laughing, each with wings formed by the petals of different flowers. At Ben sporting antlers and a forked serpent tongue. I hovered; she glanced up, caught my nervous gaze, her own eyes lit with curiosity, then understanding, and I made a grab for it, but she rolled out of reach, flipping past a big chunk of pages to land somewhere near the back.

Before I could stop her, she was staring at her brother's face—sketch after sketch of Teddy, born in black and white from every angle. I clenched my jaw as she studied the drawings, steeled against the giggles and taunts I knew were seconds away. The typical teasing words that fell just short of hurtful.

She didn't laugh, though. She didn't even smile. Instead, she closed the sketchbook carefully and held it out to me, shifted to lean against my side.

"It looks exactly like him. I wish—never mind."

"What do you wish, Nat?"

"Nothing. I'm not supposed to." She scratched the corner of her mouth, frowned at the thin crescent of gloss under her fingernail. "Crap. I didn't mean to do that."

"Nat."

"I wish this was your home. I wish you'd come for the summer and stay forever. Bear says I shouldn't say things like that. He says you're better off where you are."

"It's complicated." I faltered, the twist of an uncertain half-truth lurking behind every syllable. She picked at a flake of glitter on her finger, head down. Leaned away from my hand on her arm. "Hey. It's okay. I always come back."

"Yeah, but one day you won't. You'll go, and it'll be the last time. I won't ever see you again." Her slim hand crept over to mine, finger tracing my bones knuckle to wrist and back again. Lingering on the tough, callused edge of my finger. "Bear's wrong, Amy. You're better off here."

I dropped my eyes, a million replies locked behind my lips. Home. The cove and the woods and the bright snake of the river. Grandma and Grandpa, and their unchanging maze of a house, every crack and creak and familiar, worn-smooth surface. Ben. Nat herself. Teddy. Everyone I loved most in the world.

They were the constants. They were the ones left behind at the end of the summer, and they were the ones waiting every time I found my way back. If River Run didn't qualify as home, nowhere did—but where did that leave me?

A long whoop smashed through my reverie, sent my thoughts scattering. Ben landed next to me, followed by Teddy, who over-balanced, knocking us both over.

We were the same as we'd always been, closer to perfect than anything I knew—steady and real, eyes teary with laughter and the relentless heat of the sun. Forever tangled up in one another.

My boys and me, dreaming breathlessly into the sky.

CHAPTER 9

SUMMER 2019

Our determined strides would have carried us straight into the woods were it not for the unexpected surge of people blocking the porch stairs. I had to hand it to them—we'd found Nat's stuff only a few hours before, but River Run already had its shit sorted on the search-party front. Organizers passed out bottled water and Lance crackers, directed people into parties, sent them splintering off into the trees and up the driveway on foot. Some of them stopped to shake Teddy's hand, squeeze his shoulder, offer low words of support; most walked right on by. A green-eyed girl with wild black hair detached herself from a group and wrapped him in a too-long hug. Pressed her lips against his cheek, then his collarbone, leaving smeary, plum-stained imprints.

"I'm here if you need me," she whispered, fading out as fast as she'd leaped in, without throwing so much as a side-eye my way. Teddy stared after her, then turned toward me. Turned away just as quickly from the blaze of my face.

"Well." I had to work to keep my voice steady, fully aware how shitty it was to harp on him under the circumstances. Fully ashamed of my pettiness, even as the words left my mouth. "I guess that's what you meant by 'complicated.'"

"She's just a friend," he told the ground.

"No doubt. I'm well aware how far you're able to stretch that word."

"Amy, don't. You know it's not like that with—"

"This is a goddamn mess." Ben wedged his way in between us, slung a heavy bicep over my shoulder. Nudged a warning into my upper arm. "The median IQ around here is dropping by the second."

A cluster of uniformed cops broke off from the throng and huddled nearby, surveying the scene. The sun glinted off their badges, coaxed sweat from their temples and brows and troubled upper lips.

"She wouldn't have got far on foot without her shoes," one said, his eyes fixed on the bramble-laced underbrush of the woods, the scattered gravel of the path and driveway, and the deep, sucking mud of the riverbank. The others murmured in agreement, squinted into the trees.

Ben blinked at them for a split second, then pushed past Teddy and strode over, butting right into their circle. Their official conversation devolved from there as he drilled them on the search and rescue team's credentials, Amber Alerts, and every other thing, until one of them silenced him with a firm but sympathetic hand on his shoulder.

"We're putting our best men on this, son," the officer said, shaking his head at Ben's protest. The sunlight wove through his thinning thatch of bright red hair, turning his scalp to flame. "The squad is vetted and legit—we know these men. They're good people, trained professionals. Got their K-9s, even, if need be. As for an Amber Alert, we'd need a confirmed abduction to issue one, plus certain criteria met, none of which we have. Right now, it's a standard lost-child case, and the family will be the first to know if that changes."

My eyes crept over to Teddy, who stared past the crowded yard at the bloated green river. A driftwood log surged past, tossed and battered then overwhelmed by the current, out of sight before I finished a breath. Sunk and swallowed far too fast.

"I'm about to drive over these bitches," Ben muttered, reappearing at our side. "This is some hard-core amateur horseshit, is it not? Brilliant, shoe-centric observations aside, of course."

"At least they're trying," I said. "I don't know what more you expect."

"I expect more than this merry band of yokels and small-town protocol, that's what. I expect a SWAT team, and bloodhounds, and HELICOPTERS IN THE GODDAMN SKY, THAT'S WHAT."

He screamed that last bit over his shoulder at the cops, who barely glanced up, much less acknowledged his raised middle finger. The community as a whole was well acquainted with Ben, both in theory and in practice. Three-quarters of the region earned a living from Hansen, Inc.—the owner's son was as prominent a fixture in River Run as the quarry itself. Anyone else would be facedown in handcuffs.

"Ben," I said, "your Xanax is in the car."

"I don't need a Xanax, Amy, I need the cops to stop treating this like a novelty and do their goddamn jobs instead of jerking off in the yard like a bunch of—holy shit, what is that smell?"

It hit me a split second after he spoke—a wild animal stench of adrenaline, filthy hair, and sour, sweaty clothes, all wrapped around the ice pick of a man who'd appeared at our side. Ben gave him the up and down, revulsion dripping from his sneer.

"And who the fuck are you supposed to be?"

"Benny." Teddy stepped in front of Ben, extended his hand to the man. "Sorry, Mr. Calhoun. It's been a rough day."

"Apology accepted, son. Not many things on earth worse than what's happened here." He accepted the handshake, rocked backward on his heels, craned his neck to eye the cops over my shoulder. Angled his stance so we blocked him from their view. "Your sister sure is a pretty little thing. Gonna be a fine woman someday, just like Sister Barrett. Mark my words."

"Yes, sir. She does take after the Barrett side."

"Very much so. Two or three years and she'll be real sweet. Give some lucky boy all the trouble he can handle."

His words slithered up my neck, squirmed their way across Teddy's uneasy smile, landed squarely in the pursed corners of Ben's sour mouth. Two or three years. Christ.

"But we have to find her first." He shook off his dreamy tone and clapped Teddy on the shoulder with his free hand, all business. "Your mama asked me to fetch you in, young man. Wants you to join our circle, lift your voice in prayer. Ask the Lord to bring Natasha home."

"Oh. No, thank you. I'm not really the praying type."

"Well, now, I understand. I weren't much for it myself before I came to know Christ as my personal Savior." He tightened his grip on Teddy's hand, stepped in way too close. "Have your mama witness, have her bring you out to our service. Bring your friends, too— hear for yourself the true Word. He died on the cross for *you*, to erase all that came before. Everything dirty in your soul comes out *clean* on the other side."

"Yes, Mr. Calhoun. Thank you. I appreciate it, but—"

"Your mama said go inside, boy." His voice dropped low, a whiff of brimstone cloaked in warning. "Exodus 20:12. Learn up on that one first, I think, before you—"

"'We are men of action, sir,'" Ben quoted, clasping both hands over Calhoun's and forcing it off Teddy's into a double douchebag handshake of his own. Stepped between them and tightened his grip until he got the wince he was going for. "Please tell June I'll return her son once we finish searching for her daughter."

Teddy was already halfway across the yard, falling into step with a group of volunteers headed for the downhill trail. I caught up to him, reached for his hand, faltered at the downturn of his face.

"You okay?"

"I hear enough of that shit when Mom has a few too many. Crying about her unclean spirit, asking us to forgive her sins, whatever those are. You'd think she killed someone." We stepped onto the path together, forced closer by the encroaching trees. "That's her thing, I get that. But if we want to bring Nat home, we need to do more than shout at the sky."

"Time to move, you two." Ben's voice crashed against our backs followed by the actual crash of his hands slapping down to grip my shoulders. "We need to get going before it's too late."

"Too late?" Teddy stopped cold and turned, met Ben's blaze with a bewildered frown. "Meaning what, exactly?"

"Too late to keep her out of the windowless van, Teddy. They could be selling her to some pervert kiddie porn ring as we speak." Ben blinked back and forth at us, then clutched his head. "Jesus God, am I the only one who watches *CSI*?"

"Dude, what are you talking about? You think someone took her?"

"I think that's a more likely reality than Nat diving right on into the river, and both of you know I'm right. Every news report, every true-crime show—they all say the same thing. Every hour a kid is missing, the chance of finding them alive drops by some fucked-up crazy percent. After a day or so, you're not doing much more than looking for a corpse."

"Ben!" I shoved him away from Teddy, almost all the way off the path. "You'd better shut your mouth, I swear to God."

"Fuck that noise, Ames. We need to check everywhere—ponds, ditches, abandoned barns. The cave system out by the quarry. Every second we stand here is another second wasted. If you can't handle that—"

"He's right."

Teddy's voice stopped us both. A look passed between them, blotting out the world. Sweeping away a year of silence in a single, indecipherable moment.

"You're right, Benny. We have to find her." He swallowed hard, lips pressed together over innumerable unsaid horrors. "Let's move."

Ben's mouth twitched at the corners, then drew into a flat, determined line.

"Both of you, follow me," he barked. "This is a search party, not a goddamn nature walk."

As it turned out, though, the search for Nat *was* a nature walk of sorts—an evening stroll across a woodsy swath of hell. To call the group amateur was a kindness; it was incompetence in human form on a long, fruitless march toward nothing.

Ben was hyper focused, lost in his own obsessive scan of the landscape. I was going through the motions, soldiering on despite having detached my brain from the world about three minutes into the journey—we might have left Teddy behind entirely if I hadn't heard him retch. He veered off the path and bent double at the base of a tree, waved us away from the splash of vomit at his feet.

"Don't. I'm okay."

"Dude, the word 'okay' applies to nothing about this situation." Ben handed him a half-full water bottle, squinting after the rest of the volunteers as they disappeared into the thicket. "Even *with* her shoes, she'd never wander this far."

"You're right. We're wasting time." He spat on the ground, shook the last drops of water into his mouth, let the empty bottle fall from his hand into the dirt. Ben blinked at it, swiped it back up with a scowl.

"What the fuck, Teddy? You can't leave that lying around out here."

"Since when do you care?"

"Since the whole damn town started combing the woods for any sign of Nat, that's when. Do you really want the cops picking up a bottle covered in both our fingerprints? Use your head."

"I didn't even think of it like that. God." Teddy scrubbed a hand over his eyes, cast a wild glance at our surroundings. "Half the people out here were dropping wrappers and stuff all up and down the trails."

"So you're saying they've been casually fucking things up from the word 'go.' Never would have guessed."

The sun hung low by the time we made it back. The cops and most of the volunteers were gone; the yard was a trodden mess of footprints and debris—bottle lids, more snack wrappers. Someone's left-behind sunglasses. Ben kicked an empty Ale-8-One soda can clear from the driveway to the far side of the clothesline.

"Goddamn, these people are feral. Tell June not to sweat this—I'll have Dad send someone over to clean up."

Teddy didn't answer. His eyes jumped from the path behind us to the one ahead, to the snarls of rocks and trees and undergrowth, the malachite depths of the river. Ben stared at his profile, took in his set jaw and tangled hair, the uncontrolled quiver of his lips.

"Hey. We'll find her, okay? We'll hire people, take out ads. I'll get the FBI involved if we have to. We'll bring her home."

"Thank you."

Ben turned away at the tremor in those words, grief and determination clouding his face like a sickness. My eyes slid past him, fixed on the sky's slow fade to sunset. I tried not to picture Nat, wherever she was. Tried not to picture those same shadows collecting on her skin, drawing her into the landscape of night.

Pictured her anyway, lost in the gathering dusk.

CHAPTER 10
SUMMER 2019

I t was no one's fault, really. River Run was a quiet town, blindsided by a panic too big for its borders—the rally was destined to be an oil-and-water disaster zone no matter what.

The property was a carnival of madness, a swarm of people clamoring for answers. The media descended upon us in a stream of endless questions and hyperbole. They shoved cameras in Teddy's face, ran alongside the human shield of June's congregation, which surrounded her on the walk from the trailer to the Hansens' lower pastures, delivering her safely to the makeshift stage. People clustered earnestly in prayer; others compared search-party stories, criticized the cops, discussed their own theories concerning Nat's fate. Most stood in groups and pairs, soaking up the drama and spinning themselves into the story. Someone had brought a fucking cooler.

My mother had elbowed her way into the crush of reporters, wielding her own camera like a shield. Aunt Mattie commandeered the podium, imploring the television cameras for Nat's safe return. Uncle Peter was a shell-shocked mess behind her, staring into nothing as June wept openly at his side. Teddy, Ben, and I stood in the crowd at the lip of the stage, close enough to see the tears on June's cheeks. Far enough from the sound system speakers to catch the conversation at our backs.

"It's so sad for the family, but folks really pulled together, huh? Peter Hansen is the picture of Christian charity, organizing all this on a day's notice."

"Oh, no doubt. It's real nice, him taking an interest in the less fortunate. I'm sure the Hansen boy is a lovely influence on the young folks, too. A pillar of the community, I hear."

I blinked rapidly at that wildly inaccurate statement, cast a side-eye at said Hansen boy. His eyes flicked to mine, equally confused.

"My girls are in school with the brother, you know. He's a little wild—rough around the edges, like both the parents, but no police record." The *yet* hung from her teeth like syrup. "Does okay in class. Not headed for college anytime soon, of course."

"Y'all know college ain't for everybody—he'll find him a job and a good wife, settle down, take care of his mama. I hear he's a workhorse, like Sam was."

"Oh sure. Sam Fox was a good man, bless his heart, but he never did do right by those kids. Near twenty years with June and wouldn't even take her down to the courthouse."

"Well, can you blame him?" Their chuckles snuck out past the useless barrier of their hands. "You can't tie down to trash like that. June ain't never been reliable, not with him or her kids, neither—and look how that's turned out."

Their words crept over me, ate away at my skin. Teddy was a scribble of pain at my side, round-shouldered and dead-eyed, lips a bitten mess. He'd heard them. He'd heard every hateful word.

Unfortunately for them, so had Ben.

"I beg your pardon, ma'am." Ben turned to face them, flashing the best, most dangerous version of his golden-boy smile. "I'd like to thank you both for taking the time to come on out today. I have to say, though—I couldn't help but notice you're talking an awful lot of shit for being here to show support."

His words stopped the world, rang loud and clear, shocking Aunt Mattie's scripted pleas to silence. She cleared her throat and fumbled her notes at the podium. Tried to defuse things, as if Ben had been listening even before he was sidetracked.

"Benny, come on up here and help me finish, honey," she said. "I'm sure everyone is here for a reason."

"Y'all are throwing more stones than you got in your stockpile," Ben continued, ignoring his mother. He leaned into his usually refined Kentucky drawl, bloating every word in mockery of theirs. "The only march your man ever took to the courthouse, Mrs. Baxter Parker, involved a shotgun in the back. Faced with the option, I myself would've took the shell."

"Ben," I muttered, hyper aware of the TV cameras and dozens of smartphones aimed our way. "You have an audience."

"And you." He swung his focus to his second victim. "Tabitha Morgan Hayes. Your daughters *do* in fact go to school with Teddy— both of us know them *quite* well. As do most young men who don't mind standing in a real long line."

The words spread through the crowd in whispers, each gasp and chuckle piercing me like tiny, vicious stings. Leaving a taste in my mouth as bitter and gross as Ben's sneer. I couldn't help but cringe for those girls, who were likely in the crowd—and who, in this very public moment, were *unlikely* to challenge Ben Hansen, whether what he'd said was true or not. That they or any other girl in River Run would risk *that* confrontation was doubtful at best, even without a legion of cameras aimed their way. Beside me, Teddy's eyes squeezed shut. He cupped a hand over his grimacing mouth, ducked his head until his hair swung forward to cover his face.

"How dare you," hissed Tabitha Morgan Hayes. "I never seen such—who do you think you are, boy?"

"I'm a pillar of the community, bitch. And you're no longer welcome on my land."

Ben lifted a hand, caught the eye of the hired security guard, and gestured to the women with a flourish. He'd turned his back on them before the crowd drew a breath, nodding to his mother to continue her speech.

It hit the Internet in minutes. By the end of the day, Ben was more notorious than ever.

The rally had derailed after that little scene, to the surprise of exactly no one, and we'd resumed searching on foot. The three of us had broken off from the main groups, crisscrossing the property over and over, staring at our surroundings in a stupid, desperate haze, as if we'd catch a sudden glimpse of Nat strolling through the trees, unaware of her own disappearance a full goddamn day after it occurred. I'd shut down before we'd even left the pastures—detached from the chaos of the crowd; back-burnered Ben's outburst and all it implied; put the task of finding Nat above my shallow, bitter gloom. Let my mind empty out and wall itself away until everything hurt just a little bit less.

By the time we returned to the trailer, the sky was a dark hollow, poised to fill with stars. I waited while the last of the volunteers returned and departed, then sank onto the bottom step of the porch to process the day's events, working my palm against the sharpest edge of the wood. Working my way back to the world, one splinter at a time.

"Fuck those people," Ben said, sprawling across the hood of the Mustang, the lone car left in the previously packed yard. Teddy stood with his back to us, watching the last taillights disappear up the driveway. "Pull up that video again, Ames—I'm about to FaceTime the whole town and hit play. Remind folks what happens when you come for my friends."

"Pull it up yourself," I snapped, the reminder scraping the scab from my anger. "You're lucky that video doesn't include certain 'folks' smacking you right across the mouth."

"What? Why?" Ben sneered at my scornful glare. "Are you, like, offended on their behalf? Give me a fucking break."

"So you're fine trashing some old hookups of yours on what was basically a live feed because their mom pissed you off? Awesome. Love to be a girl in River Run, where apparently that's an okay thing. Along with getting called 'bitch' all day—which is also super fun, if misogyny's your kink."

"*Misogyny?* Ames, since when have I ever held back on trashing *anyone*? I'd have gone just as hard on that lady—that *bitch,* regardless of whether I banged her daughter."

"Way to prove my point, because no, you wouldn't have—and you *especially* wouldn't have gone that hard if she'd been a man and big enough to beat your ass. And you know it."

"Oh my God, are you serious? Fine—we'll go with *jerk off.* As in 'You are being a pedantic fucking jerk off, Amy Larsen, transcending both gender and the patriarchy.' Does that work for you?"

"Benjamin—"

"Yeah, 'Benjamin' whatever. From a politically neutral stand-point, none of it was any worse than the shit that left her mouth." Ben held my eyes, let his chill and narrow to match his grin. "And not a single *word* I said was a lie."

"Benny."

Teddy's voice broke into our standoff. He'd appeared at the railing beside me, head down, shoulders hunched.

"Benny," he said again, "you really had my back today. I won't forget that, and I owe you big-time. But could you let this one go? Just this once? Please."

I tensed, ready to fly in between them, take whatever barbs my cousin hurled and send them back a thousand-fold. But Ben stared at him, took in his pinched face and downcast eyes, then nodded. Actually nodded, without a shred of resistance.

"Know what? Yes. For you, today, I will let it go."

"You—" Teddy cleared his throat, visibly caught off guard. That he'd in no way expected Ben to cave without a fight was starkly, wincingly obvious. "Thank you. Thanks, Ben. For real."

"World without end. You go on and get to bed. And don't worry, I'm sure I'll live to regret the whole scene tonight once Mom rips into me. But hey, between her and Amy at least I'll have a shiny new asshole to show off when next we meet."

"I can hardly wait."

"You can't get enough of me. Hang back, Ames—I need to blaze up before facing the wrath of a publicly humiliated Mattie Hansen."

Teddy waited until Ben was in the car, waited until the stink of weed wafted our way before facing me.

"How's it going, City Girl?"

"I'm fine." I didn't miss the wince my frost-edged voice inspired. I blinked hard, forcing my lips into a tiny, grim smile. Struggled to be pleasant—and present—one word at a time. "Sorry. I should be asking you that question."

"I'm still here, you know? Pulling through. It's just—" The words snagged on a catch in his throat. He took a breath, swallowed them down. "It's fucked up. Surreal like you wouldn't believe."

He brushed past me without further comment, made his way up the steps, disappeared inside without looking back. The screen door slammed itself automatically, but the inner door drifted to a stop a good six inches from the doorjamb. I stared at it, waiting for Teddy to reappear and finish the job, but there it stayed.

"All done." Ben slid out his open window like a jack-in-the-box, made his way toward me on markedly relaxed legs. "Climb on in, unless you're still pissed enough that walking sounds like fun."

"I think I should stay, actually. Make sure he gets settled."

I steeled myself for the usual thundercloud sneer, one of many indicators of an imminent Hansen tantrum. His nod of approval was as unexpected as his rally outburst, and almost as unsettling.

"I'll pick you up at Grandma's tomorrow at seven, okay? I don't know what the cops have planned, but I'm not about to wait for a squadron of competent fucking people to burst from the foliage. We'll start early, drive out past town and search on our own. Catch the son of a bitch who took Nat and bring her home."

"Hush." I glanced over my shoulder at the screen door, a rectangle of light I couldn't see past. "We don't *know* if she was taken."

"Doesn't matter. Worst-case scenario, we're looking for a shallow grave." He shook his head at my gasp, clamped a heavy hand on my shoulder. Pulled me in for the first hug he'd offered since I arrived. "I know—'Fuck you, Benny,' right? But we can't rule it out."

My arms rose automatically, then hesitated, then wrapped around him, let him squeeze me back to earth. Back to myself.

"Ben—"

"It doesn't matter. None of it matters until we know she's safe." He released me, walked backward to the car, and climbed in through the window. "Get your shit together, Ames. Go take care of him."

Teddy started as the screen door opened, blinked at me as I crossed the threshold and closed both doors quietly behind me. He sat slumped in a kitchen chair, elbows resting on the cluttered table-top. Numerous containers and covered dishes took up every inch of counter space. Muffled sobs drifted through June's closed bedroom door like a heartbroken mist, cloaking everything in sight.

"We'll head out again first thing tomorrow," I hedged. "Ben wants to drive out farther into town, check a couple spots in the countryside. You should get some rest."

"Like I could sleep right now." He rubbed a hand over his face, let it drop, listless, back to the tabletop. "It's fine, Ames. You can go ahead on home, if you want."

I could feel my heart receding once more; feel the hole in my head expand to swallow the churning tide of worry, the exhaustion mixed with longing, the guilt that clung to it all like dust. I stood there, blinking at him in typical Amy form—the sociopathic stare, silent and helpless. The blank detachment, which protected and soothed me, while simultaneously rendering me useless. Before last summer, Teddy and I had barely exchanged harsh words; we'd never faced anything remotely like this.

I wanted to gather him to me, brush the hair from those eyes and the sorrow from that face. I wanted to unwind the day; change everything I'd done since the moment I arrived in River Run: Skip the stupid family dinner. Pick up the phone instead of pining away on the back steps. Walk my ass down the hill to see him on my terms, instead of holing up in my room to sulk. Facing him in those first awkward moments would've been infinitely better than the sequence of events that had led us to this hellish end. And now he sat in front of me, close enough to touch, and still I balked at the thought of taking his grief and fear and worry onto my own shoulders. I couldn't imagine navigating past the remains of that afternoon. I didn't know how to make it better.

I sucked at emotions. I really did.

I damn sure was well-versed in efficient coping mechanisms, however. So instead of speaking or fleeing, I got to work.

The plates and cutlery were easy enough to locate. Finding serving utensils took a bit longer, but I still had a warmed-up plate of pulled pork, greens, honeyed biscuits, and sweet potato casserole on the table in under five minutes. I added a glass of milk and a dish of pineapple upside-down cake to the spread, then grabbed the broom from the tiny utility closet. By the time he picked up his fork, the floor was clean, and I'd moved on to the counters. I divvied up the food between refrigerator and freezer, did the dishes, wiped the surfaces. Tackled the living room next, vacuumed up tracked-in dirt, gathered the various cans and bottles left by well-meaning visitors whose helpfulness had apparently stopped just short of cleaning up their goddamn collective mess.

I couldn't bring myself to touch the coffee table. It wasn't my place to clear away Nat's macramé set—to sweep the bright jumble of beads and half-knotted string into its box and tuck it out of sight; to collect her scattered comic books, or her fuzzy purple slippers, erasing the last traces of her from the room. A low wail swelled inside me like an ocean wave. I choked it down, then heard its twin at my back, too broken to be a sob.

It wasn't at all difficult to go to him then. To lead him by the hand or settle next to him on the couch, sit with my arms around his shaking form and hold him—not in the way I'd wanted to for so long, but as the friend he'd always been, since I was old enough to remember having friends at all. I let him drift off with his head in my lap, watched his face relax and his limbs go slack as he escaped from that long, awful day.

It was easy as anything to close my eyes and follow.

"Where have you been?"

My mother's voice made me miss a step on my way up the stairs. I backtracked to where she waited in the kitchen doorway, stomach dropping at the curl of her lip. The lights were off all over the house; I'd had no idea she was lying in wait. My grandparents' cordless phone hung from her hand, Aunt Mattie's squawks drifting from the speaker holes.

"Mom? Why are you up?"

Why was she still here at all was a better question—I couldn't remember the last time she'd stayed more than a single night in River Run. Last year she'd barely bothered with a cup of coffee before heading back to the airport in the same car she'd rented not two hours previous. And here she was in the middle of the night, still dressed in the designer suit she'd worn to the rally. Her makeup was smudged, and she was barefoot, her hair a loose, pale spill over rigid shoulders. Her eyes blazed at me across the room as she raised the phone to her ear.

"Yes, she's here. Just walked in the door. You too." She hung up without saying goodbye, barely got the receiver on the base in her rush to get to me. I stood there, stiff and still, as her hands ran over my arms and shoulders, brushed my clothes, combed through my hair, as if checking for bumps or bruises or an exit wound. As if my late return guaranteed some fresh trauma that would've been warded off by daylight. Finally, apparently satisfied with my condition, she let go and paced the room, fear shifting to anger as she hid her face.

"It's after midnight. I woke your aunt just now. If you hadn't shown up when you did, I'd be dialing the police."

"Seriously? I never even left the property. What's the worst that could happen—Ben holding me hostage, until I let him win at *Mario Kart*?"

"That's not funny. You have no idea the things that can go wrong in these woods at night." Her eyes were wide and haunted, gleaming with fury and unshed tears. "Goddamn it, Amy. One missing child isn't enough, is that it?"

"I wasn't *missing*—I was down at Teddy's. I was helping him out after the rally, and I fell asleep. Feel free to call off the manhunt whenever."

"You fell asleep? I've been out of my mind with worry—and you're out there in the dead of night, doing God knows what with that boy? I was this close to hiking through those woods myself to look for you, and you fell asleep."

"Kind of unclear on why you're still here at all."

She stared at me, then stepped forward, crossing into a slice of moonlight. It fell along the lines of her face, lighting every crease and tremor.

"*Unclear?* You don't think I'd be scared to death for you, what with everything that's going on?"

"I'm sure you were terrified. Lord knows June Barrett's living room is a dark and dreadful place."

"Don't take that tone with me. You don't know." Her fingers closed around my wrist, firm but steady, never rough enough to hurt. "How am I supposed to leave you here now, knowing you just wander in and out any time of the night? If something happens to you—you *have* to be more careful. You have to promise me you'll keep yourself safe."

I almost laughed. Not that it was funny, but if what passed for our mother-daughter bond had led us here—to a place where her concern sparked mirth rather than contrition—well, she could hardly expect me to shoulder the blame.

I'd held her at bay for years with omissions and half-truths, kept my summers secret in the locked box behind my heart. Taken up my pencils on command and worn them to nubs. Worn myself to shreds on the edges of her words until they blurred and bled, trickled through the cracks and fell away. Let myself fall between the lines and angles until the day my mind withdrew on its own.

I'd more than perfected the art of shutting her out.

And now she stood there in the foyer with eyes like grease on fire, mouth a knot of anger and frustration, and yes—actual, visceral fear that sent a twinge of guilt through my chest. I hadn't meant to make her worry; what with decidedly more pressing matters at hand, I hadn't actually given her or her feelings a second thought. She held my gaze, waiting for my reassurance. She was my mother, begging me to be okay.

Where the hell had *this* been all my life—this raw, unshrouded version of her love? And what did she expect me to do—indulge it with apologies, or empty, placating words? Siphon it into my own hollow chest, waking all that lay dormant after so many years spent fasting?

It was all I wanted—to collapse into the past and find her waiting, let her scoop me up in the safety of her arms. Shrink down until she soothed rather than scoffed at my troubles. Curl into my tiny bed as she settled next to me, stroked my hair in rhythm with her calm and steady breath. That version of her was all but lost to time, but it *had* been real; she'd *been* that mother, long ago—she'd more than had the capacity to hold me in her heart.

I remembered just enough to rip me into bitter, spiteful shreds. And what she offered now—it was nowhere near a compensation.

"I'm sure it won't be an issue," I finally said, watching her flinch away from my icy voice. Stifling the impulse that howled for the comfort of my mom. "Say bye to Dad for me."

I yanked my arm from her grip, cut myself off from the tips of her fingers and the roots of my heart. Ignored the hitch of her breath as I walked away.

She left in the morning. Silver linings.

CHAPTER 11

SUMMER 2018

I peeked from beneath my hat brim as they passed, saw his eyes follow the obvious swing of her barely covered backside. The swish of the sliding glass door setting my jaw in a hard line as they disappeared into the pool house.

I'd been sitting there for ages, watching her flirt her way through every boy at Ben's poolside gathering, lingering long after most guests had taken off, at which point she'd conspicuously shifted her focus. For someone who hadn't given him half a glance all day, Dana had certainly leaped at the chance to help Teddy carry some goddamn drinks.

"I see you, Amy."

I slid a glare in the direction of the tiny stream of giggles, which only increased when I shushed her. Nat's grin stretched wide beneath her ridiculous oversize heart sunglasses as she adjusted her legs to mirror mine—one knee bent, the other extended the length of the chaise longue, purple-painted toenails sparkling in the sunlight.

"You're watching him," she continued. "You and Bear—always watching, never seeing. So dumb."

"That was insightful as fuck, Nat," Ben called from the opposite end of the pool. He flipped on his stomach, hung a hand off the edge of his oversize raft. "'Always watching, never seeing.' It's exactly how they are."

"Daddy used to say that all the time. Said Bear was just like him—so wrapped up in life's big picture he wouldn't know he was snakebit until the poison reached his heart. He never notices something till it's right in his face."

"Hear that, Ames? You'll need to get right up in his face. Show him your big picture."

"And maybe your butt," Nat whispered, sending Ben into a fit of cackles.

"Oh my God, will you two shut up?" I craned my neck toward the pool house, watched Teddy's oblivious, sun-darkened back through the glass door as he rummaged through the refrigerator. "How are you even hearing this from over there, Ben?"

"The acoustics out here are fucking sweet—you can hear everything. And she's right about your ass, by the way. I'm sure he wouldn't mind a peek."

"Seriously? What is wrong with you?"

"Don't be nasty. It's an observation. A strictly objective standpoint, based on conventional aesthetics."

"That's what I said," Nat crowed. "An objective standpoint. It's like, a fact, not an opinion."

"Ugh. Stop talking about my ass, Natasha."

"I feel like I suddenly want in on this conversation." Of course Teddy would reappear at that very second, drinks in hand, Dana in tow. Of course he would. "What exactly are we saying about Amy's ass?"

"Nothing important," Ben said. "Her big picture, now—THAT is a conversation piece."

"Benjamin, I swear to God I will strangle you in your sleep."

"Let me know if I can lend a hand with that, Ames." Teddy winked as he handed me an Evian, that teasing half grin curving the corner of his mouth. I cut my eyes at him, hoping the sudden heat in my cheeks could pass as sun flush.

"You can't get enough of me," Ben called. "But while you're at it, dude, make sure you 'lend a hand' with that ass."

The two of them cracked up, Ben waving off my glare. Dana gave a pointed huff, and when Teddy didn't turn, when he caught my gaze and held it way past the point of normal, fingers still wrapped around my water bottle, she nudged his arm.

"Can I talk to you for a minute? Alone?"

"Yeah, sure. Lead the way."

He followed her past the pool house and around the privacy hedges to the edge of the garden. I sat there, condensation dripping down my fingers onto my leg, then slammed the Evian onto the side table and yanked off my hat, shook my hair back, and jumped into the pool. I swam underwater without pausing until I reached the deep end, emerging alongside Ben's raft. Whether I had the technical right to object was moot; I was decidedly not okay with Teddy disappearing behind a tall hedge accompanied by a girl who wasn't me.

"Did you seriously pull me out here to discuss this *again*?" His voice rose and fell, pulsating with impatience. "That wasn't even a date. Can we move on, or are you married to the whole clingy psycho act?"

"This is some shit, huh?" Ben muttered, a wide smile eating up his face as I shushed him. "Nothing like a little drama to add flavor to my life."

"What is she, his ex?"

"Dana? Hell no. They probably sealed the deal at some point, and now she's after another piece. This happens on the regular." He chuckled, rubbing his hands together as I shoved his face away from my ear. "Never gets old."

"You think you can lead me on and I won't call you out on it? Someone like you?" Dana's voice rose over Teddy's. "Nope. Not happening."

"I didn't lead you on. And what the fuck does that mean, someone like me?"

"You're not exactly selective. I'm not exactly desperate. You think I can't do better?"

"Yeah, whatever. Don't let me stop you." He turned and headed back our way. She followed, glaring at the back of his head. I ducked underwater, pushing off the wall and gliding back toward the shallow end, holding my breath as long as I could stand before gasping to the surface.

"The purple. The purple is definitely the best," Ben boomed. "The glitter catches the light better than the pink."

"That's what I thought, too," Nat yelled back, making a show of examining her nails. "I'm just worried it makes me look all yellowy."

"Nah, it's good. You have pink undertones, you can wear it fine." He smirked at Dana's retreating back as she stomped barefoot toward her car, arms loaded down with her stuff. "Aw, Dana—leaving so soon?"

"Fuck you, Ben."

"I'm a little sluggish this late in the day. Rain check?" His answer was a raised middle finger over her shoulder. He waved at it, unconcerned. "That's right, girl, you know how I like it."

"Okay, she's gone, you guys can stop," Teddy said, lowering himself into the pool.

"She was pretty mad, Bear." Nat left the chaise and sat carefully on the topmost pool step, flinching as the water swished against her tiny waist. "Either she really likes you or she got the wrong idea when she saw you looking at her butt."

The entire world froze in its tracks for a long, horrifying moment. Nat peered at us over the rim of her sunglasses, innocence too thick to be authentic painted across her face.

"I wasn't," Teddy stammered, his mouth a dropped-jaw inversion of Ben's maniacal grin.

"Holy shit, you so were." Ben thumped his head backward on the raft pillow, shaking with mirth. "You reap what you sow, dude. You can't hit it and quit it without catching some fallout."

"I didn't hit it and—look, we hung out once, like six months ago, and didn't even hook up. Then today she made a move on me and got pissed when I blew her off. That's the entire basis for whatever thing she thinks we have going on." He ducked underwater and came up streaming, slicked his hair back as if washing away the thought. Ben smirked at the sour twist of his mouth.

"Sounds like you dodged quite the bullet, my friend." He rolled off the raft and splashed his way toward us. "Hey Nat, want to practice floating? I have earplugs."

"Really? Yes!"

Ben disappeared into the pool house and returned with a set of silicone plugs. He helped Nat fit them in place before lifting her off the steps and moving to deeper water, supporting her with steady hands as she stretched on her back.

"Benny? Are you out here?" Aunt Mattie's voice carried clear across the patio as she stepped outside. "I picked up your medicine, and the dry cleaning. It's on the chair in your—oh. Hello, kids."

"Hi, Ms. Mattie," Nat called, waving from her prone position. "Benny's teaching me to float."

"Is he? That's nice of him." Her eyes swept over the patio, taking in our crumpled towels and strewn shoes. She fixated on Ben's T-shirt, draped over a potted hydrangea, picked it up and shook it out, rubbed at a speck of dirt. "Is everyone okay out here? Have you all eaten?"

"No, ma'am," Ben said. "I didn't want to track water into your kitchen."

"Well, that's very considerate, but you shouldn't skip lunch. I'll fix you all a tray, and—"

Aunt Mattie's small smile turned to a pinch as her eyes fell on the bar, on the messy ashtray askew on its surface. The shirt sagged in her hand, half-folded. She dropped it absently on a nearby chaise and turned to Ben. Her face closed off and clouded over, darkened to the edge of a threatening sky.

"Benjamin Hansen. Were you kids smoking?"

"I think they're Dad's," Ben lied. "They were there when we came out here, in any case."

"Typical. I have asked that man, time and again, to clean up after himself. To stop leaving his trash around where everyone can see—where I have to look at it, and deal with it. Nothing. Ever. Changes."

She picked up the ashtray and clacked her way to the pool house, skirting our mess.

"Dude," Teddy began. Ben shook his head, resumed Nat's floating lesson in silence. I made my way back to the chaise, grabbed the sunscreen off the side table, slathered it on my already pink shoulders. We went about our leisure, subdued and alert, our movements slow and calm in the static air.

My eyes wandered, though, through the glass doors to where Aunt Mattie stood, scrubbing the ashtray beneath the kitchen tap. She held it up to the light, rubbing a single spot over and over. Brought it down hard on the rim of the sink in a sudden, violent arc. The ashtray blew apart, scattering across the counter in a shimmering spray of fragments.

"Fuck," Ben muttered, turning his back on the pool house. "That was Waterford."

Aunt Mattie swept up the shards, tipped them into the trash can, wiped the sink with brisk, steady hands. We waited until she'd crossed the patio and disappeared into the main house before daring to breathe. Teddy slid through the water toward Ben.

"You okay, man? We can take off if you need us gone."

"Nah, it's fine, she's not mad at me. We can stay out here all day and she won't care. I'd bet money she's in there right now making us that snack tray."

"If not, just say the word. Or if you want to come home with us." He clapped Ben on the shoulder, the crack of skin on wet skin gunshot clear. "It's not much, but there's an air mattress at my place with your name on it."

Ben didn't answer beyond a nod, but I caught a glimpse of his face, sad and grateful and wistful. Humiliated.

I scooped up my hat and pulled it into place, hiding my own

blank face at the sound of the patio door. At Aunt Mattie's cheerful footsteps as she placed an identical crystal ashtray on the gleaming bar and returned to the house without a word. The door whooshed shut behind her, the lingering tension in Ben's back the only sign she'd ever been outside at all.

CHAPTER 12

SUMMER 2019

W̲e all crumbled in our own ways in the week following my mother's departure—fell to bits piece by tiny
piece as the sun rode high and hot in the sky, turned
its harsh spotlight on the absolute absence of news, and sank back
down again on the same steadfast nothing.

June took to her bed full time after the rally, left Teddy to hold it
together and deal with her congregation and the search party updates.
I'd withdrawn into the backdrop without complaint, acutely aware
that the question of us had no place in the cacophony of worry and
grief and frantic, desperate fear that consumed him. He spent his
days in the woods or by the phone, forgot to eat, refused to rest.
Stared out the windows long after dusk, as if his vigil would summon
Nat from the shadows—a sister formed of rocks and trees and earth,
bound with river whispers and wisps of moonlight.

The reality was far bleaker than his wild and futile hope. Her
sweet, smiling face blared from every screen, splashed across every
front page, local and beyond, and she might as well have been dead
the way they framed it: a lamentation. A tragic loss. A girl all but
reclassified from missing to gone before the dogs forgot her scent.
Grandma banned the news trucks from the property, sparing Teddy
and June from all but the most aggressive cold callers, but Uncle

Peter was fair game every time he crossed onto public land. He and Aunt Mattie fielded endless questions about their involvement with the search effort, their reward money, their friendship with June. Their son's friendship with Teddy and Nat. Their son's very public outburst.

Ironically, that outburst extended the search effort far beyond the reach of any local media outlet. Ben was the goddamn prince of River Run, and his subjects rose to the occasion. The video, ceremoniously tagged #YouBenTold, went viral in under a day, much to his unending delight. He didn't even catch heat from Aunt Mattie—a rare flash of spine on Uncle Peter's part had saved Ben from an old-school taste of her backhand, emboldening him further. The candlelight vigil he organized drew four times the anticipated crowd. #FindNatNow trended all over the state. His three hundred custom flyers plastered the buildings and utility poles of every town in an hour's radius.

I hovered at the fringes of usefulness as the days melted into one another, kept my mind contained and my heart steeled, waiting to be needed. Waiting for any opportunity to be more than an extra pair of busy hands. I spent my mornings on the search-party circuit, Ben at my side. Afternoons were spent bustling around my grandparents' house, helping Grandma assemble casseroles and stews for June and Teddy, sandwich platters for the volunteers, and haphazard afterthought meals for me, Grandpa, and herself, though none of us did much more than pick at the results. I dusted figurines and polished spotless surfaces. Swept floors I'd already swept. I even attempted to wrangle the riding mower, managing a couple crooked laps around the side yard before Grandpa put a stop to that nonsense.

"A few inches of grass ain't worth the strain on my nerves, honey," he called, tottering his way across the porch after watching me nearly clip the corner of the shed while trying to avoid annihilating Grandma's day lilies. "Come on inside and take a break. You're worn out, is all—don't let me catch you out in this heat again until you've had some rest."

I'd followed him into the relief of central air-conditioning and headed upstairs, rattled by the glimpse of my own reflection thrown back by the foyer mirror—hair wild, skin flushed, hands like rigid, skittish claws. A grim face framing bloodshot, desperate eyes. Grandpa wasn't wrong—I *needed* rest. I needed *something*.

After a shower that did little to calm my nerves, I slid into the chair at my mother's old desk, sketchbook open on its smooth surface, determined to grind this restless energy into something worthwhile. I sharpened my charcoals, rolled my shoulders, turned to a fresh, blank page, and set to work on my thumbnail sketches, waiting for the knots in my middle to relax and realign. Waiting to lose myself in the flow of creation, even if only for a short reprieve.

The results themselves were fine. The technique was on point; the ideas translated from mind to paper with minimal effort, but that was all it was—minimal. Barely an effort at all, as if a portcullis had closed off the channel between my hands and my heart, admitting images as precise and hollow as textbook diagrams. Trapping anything that transcended the technicalities of a filled-in space.

Twelve sketches in and my insides were knots. Another five, and the page was a blur. The pencil fell from my fingers, rolled off the side of the desk and onto the floor. I pressed my hands to my eyes, counted backward from twenty over and over until the world receded. When I raised my face, I was calm and empty, straight-spined and steady-handed. Ready to push through.

The pencil lay on the carpet, closer to the wall than the chair. I crawled beneath the desk to retrieve it, then backed out a little too quickly, catching my head on a sharp corner—the bottom edge of the desk drawer, jutting two inches lower than the area of the desk where my head had been. Stupid antique furniture.

I flipped onto my back and scooted carefully forward, eyeing the underside of the desk to avoid any more unexpected obstacles. A tiny white triangle caught my eye—the corner of an envelope, sticking out from the back of the drawer.

I cleared the desk, got to my feet, and settled back into the chair, gave the drawer's brass knob a half-hearted tug. It stuck; I couldn't remember the last time I'd used it, if I ever had. I worked it open, bit by bit, until it gave.

The envelope was in the very back, tucked between a Lisa Frank day planner and a cream-colored stationery set, my mother's initials, *EAL*, embossed at the top of each page. I pulled the corner free of the drawer and lifted the unsealed flap, expecting an unsent letter—maybe a forgotten thank-you note, or an invitation withheld at the zero hour. Some old love poem better tucked away forever than read by its intended recipient.

Instead I found a blank sheet of that same fancy stationery folded around a thin stack of printed photographs. A cold, unfamiliar prickle snaked through my rib cage, pulled tight around my lungs; I'd spent my childhood in this room. The windows, the wallpaper, the furniture and hidey-holes, even the scent—they'd been mine, as far back as I could remember. These pictures—their contents, their concealment, that they existed at all—undid that certainty in the space of a blink.

The boy knelt in the light-specked shadows of the cove—a slight, dark-haired teen in cargo shorts and a Pantera T-shirt, eyes as soft and friendly as the eyes of the muddy-pawed yellow Labrador at his side. Their smiles were wide and natural, formed and captured before they'd registered the presence of a camera.

I flipped to the second picture, then the third. The dog had bounded into the background and was nothing but a golden splotch, happily swimming in the river. The boy's smile was wider, more vulnerable; it turned to a self-conscious laugh in the fourth image, which captured him moving closer, one playful hand raised to block the camera even as he appeared captivated by the lens—or, more likely, by the person taking the picture. In the fifth and final snapshot, he peeked from behind the head of a girl my age with summer-tan skin and bluebell-colored eyes, hair like tangled springtime sun. His arms circled her from behind, drawing her close as she held the camera facing inward in her outstretched hands, so they both fit in the frame—a selfie, from before selfies were a thing. His chin rested on her shoulder; her cheekbone grazed his as she leaned in to him. All vulnerability and hesitation had fled from their faces—they emanated contentment, each, apparently, exactly where they fit the best.

My mother, gazing out from a long-ago moment. Smiling like she'd never known the sting of tears.

A dull pressure gathered in my throat, swelling and shifting as I studied her face—the peaceful curve of lips and chin; the lively, laughing eyes; the effortless delight. She'd cast her own light in that cove, loved a bashful boy with riverbed eyes who'd clearly returned that love. Was he the reason she was so quick to dismiss the possibility, or even the thought, of me falling for a River Run boy of my own? What had happened in the years between then and me to cut the glow from that bright and happy heart?

"AMES. YOU IN THERE?"

Ben's voice preceded the crash of the door against the wall by two entire seconds. I nearly left my skin. The pictures flew from my hands, three landing on the desk, the others drifting to the floor. I swiped a hand over my stinging eyes, hurried to collect them before he could get his bearings, but he was too quick. He swooped in and snatched the last one up right before my fingers grazed it, and of course it was the one featuring my mother, front and center and blissfully smitten. Of course it was.

"Come on, Ben. Give it back."

"Holy God, is that Aunt Ellie? Man, it's *super* creepy how much she looked like you." He squinted at the image, nose wrinkling above his smirk. "Who the fuck is that kid low-key trying to feel up her shirt?"

"No idea. I've never seen these before today." I plucked it from his fingers and slid it back into the envelope with the rest of the photos. Ben had a way of scraping the shine off anything approaching sentimental, no matter how potentially sacred. "Found them stuck in the back of the drawer just now."

"Well, stick them back in there and come on. We're about to take a little drive."

Ben's idea of a little drive, it turned out, involved an in-depth scouring of a different side of River Run—the sketchy, isolated edges of the town. We passed the quarry and kept on going, passed broken fences and dilapidated barns. Passed a junkyard and an impound lot, which Ben said were monitored and therefore classified as last resorts for our purposes. He'd finally turned down a narrow dirt road that bottomed out about a mile in at a tiny, fern-ringed clearing.

We emerged from the car into the sweltering afternoon, Ben ignoring my questions as he led the way along a barely visible foot path, through trees that closed in on us the further we walked; soon enough, we were hemmed in on all sides by clusters of jagged rocks and thick, overgrown foliage. I followed him reluctantly, more nervous about breaking an ankle on the terrain than the possibility of getting caught—we'd barely made it out here as it was. There was no way to follow us unnoticed, no place to hide a vehicle or lie in wait. Definitely no way to sneak up behind us on foot and take us by surprise.

The path reached an end at the base of a stone plateau. The cave didn't look like the caves in the movies—it wasn't a yawning mouth, or a half-moon arch. It was more like a chipped tooth; a shard knocked loose from the earth itself. I crouched low and peered inside, found nothing beyond a solid wall of darkness.

"Ben? What is this?"

Instead of explaining, he gestured to the opening with a grand, sweeping flourish and a bow, which would have come off as mocking if he hadn't looked as inexplicably scared shitless as I'd ever seen him look.

"After you, Ames."

"After me? Are you—no. *Hell* no. I'm not crawling into some unmapped hole in the ground."

"It's hardly unmapped. This is where you go when you want to fuck around hard-core and not get caught. Check it out." He knelt beside me and shone his phone flashlight through the opening, revealing a ledge of rock jutting benchlike from the wall opposite the entrance. The ground around it was a clutter of beer cans and used needles, discarded condoms, cigarette butts, and broken glass. "What can I say? It's a quiet town. Folks get bored."

"Fascinating. And we're out here staring at all this shit because . . . ?" The obvious answer flashed in my brain before my mouth finished asking the question. "Benjamin Hansen. You are not serious."

"We've looked everywhere else, haven't we? People have been coming out here for years, but you best believe no one's mentioned it to the cops. As soon as I realized that, I knew we had to at least check." He tilted his light up at my face, making me wince. "The whole town is already searching all the most obvious spots—for a *missing* kid, who disappeared by accident. Who's lost somewhere, or hurt, waiting to be rescued. And no one wants to talk about how many spaces in this world are small enough to stash a kid who's never coming home."

"Ben."

"We have to," he hissed. "We *have* to think it, because maybe someone else already did. And that might be the difference between finding her or not." The flashlight swooped away from me and back into the cave, scanned the low ceiling, sliced through the stifling dark. "There's a reason I didn't bring Teddy, you know. If she's tucked away in here, or the junkyard, or one of those barns—"

"STOP."

It was a word that built to a shriek—a long, wordless cry that echoed off the rocks around us. Ben took it without flinching, not even moving to cover his ears, as if he knew it was better for me to let it loose as far from home as we could get. Better to leave it to rot in these thick and distant woods than keep it bottled up until I no longer could.

"Why," I finally gasped. "Why did you bring me out to the ass end of nowhere without so much as a warning?"

"I knew if I told you where we were headed, you wouldn't go," he sighed. "It was the only way to get you here."

"Fuck you, Ben. What the hell did you think would happen— that I'd follow you out here and skip right on into that hole, no problem, since we'd already come all this way?"

"I know, Ames. I hate it too. And I'm so fucking sorry—but I had to bring you. I need you here with me, because *I can't do this on my own.*" His outstretched hand appeared between us, waiting. As if he hadn't known exactly what I'd do, when faced with a split-second choice. My cousin, who'd learned long ago just how far he could push me before I really, truly snapped. "Please."

His sigh of relief, when my palm met his, was the motivation I needed. I had to duck to make it through. Once inside, I was able to stand up straight, but just barely. Ben's phone-light beam bounced off the too-close walls as he appeared at my side. The entrance opened into a small, circular room littered with more junk. A tunnel sloped away to the left, emptying into darkness.

We faced it together, arms pressed tight from palms to shoulders. Set off into the deepest hole in River Run, step by halting, fearful step.

· · ·

We didn't find her. We didn't find a single trace, not of Nat. Not of any sign of violence or its aftermath. Once we'd exhausted the tunnel's possibilities, Ben and I made our way back to the opening and emerged quietly back into daylight, muted by grief, choked with guilt. Weak with relief that the cave had been empty.

It had been too long since she'd last been seen. Time had chipped away bit by bit at my remaining optimism, leaving nothing but dread at what might remain to be recovered. It clawed at my heart, that truth, as we combed through three barns and a deserted farmhouse before returning home empty-handed. It only dug deeper the longer we looked.

It ate up our lives, but we kept on searching, kept on hoping. As if our wishes would twist the fabric of the world until it shook her loose. As if the force of our hearts would lift her from wherever she'd landed and carry her home to us.

CHAPTER 13
SUMMER 2019

The sixth day bore down hot on my head, blistered my scalp even through Ben's baseball cap. Our land ended at the main road, but the water wound on, and we'd followed it over and over: combed through the woods, across a clearing, over the old, abandoned Franklin property. Past a nature preserve. Beyond the borders of River Run. The group broke up into twos and threes, split off and left the path, combed the underbrush for an unnamed horror that haunted our steps. Every footfall was a risk that ended in relief when shoes met dirt instead of flesh.

No one actually said it—no one flat-out told us to watch for the crawl of insects toward her still, blue feet, or scan the tall grass for the bright knots of her hair. No one told us to double-check that those snapping twigs weren't bones, or press our fingers into the soaked-dark ground and hope they didn't come back red.

We did those things anyway, silent and careful. Our hopes flagging to nothing when nothing was exactly what we found.

Ben had soldiered on beside me all morning, shared his water, forced his sweaty hat on my head to save my sunburned face. Stopped to wait when I lagged behind without a breath of complaint. We returned home in a fog of unsurprised gloom, split up with plans to reconvene at Teddy's, though I'd have been perfectly content to let a much-needed nap swallow the afternoon.

I arrived at the trailer first, found June pacing the hallway, lost in a haze of cigarette smog and frayed nerves. Teddy slouched alone at the kitchen table, head resting on his folded arms. He looked up as I sat beside him, squinted at me through eyes swollen down to slits.

"Amy." My name slipped dead and tasteless from his mouth. "Any luck today?"

"No. Sorry."

"Figured as much. It's early still, maybe—"

The phone shrieked through the kitchen, slamming his voice to dust in his rush to answer. I rose slowly, trekked across a suddenly endless room. Waded through air like mud, each step a fight against the dread building in my middle as June hurried to grab the receiver from his outstretched hand.

"Hello? Pete? What is it? Is there—"

Her voice spilled out, ran dry, fell to her feet along with the phone and her cigarette as she turned and left the kitchen, brushing past as if I wasn't there. Making it halfway to her bedroom before a shoulder on the wall became a slide to the floor, and there she stayed. There she stared. There she heaved suddenly to life and expelled a surge of vomit through her shaking, listless hands.

I turned to Teddy, who'd scooped up the phone again and was speaking into it, his mouth moving and twisting, but I couldn't hear a thing over June's wail—a sudden blade, long and loud and ageless. Rending the world into Before and After.

My head swung back and forth between them: June's miserable, sick-soaked hunch. The void of Teddy, that blank, confused hollow disguised as my best friend. That empty boy, whose hand still clutched the disconnected phone.

"What happened?" His deep, shuddering breath dropped in my stomach like stones; dread slid through my veins on an arctic belly. "Teddy, please. Did they find her?"

"Yeah."

That was all he said. A single word choked off by a hacking sob, then silence—a hideous nothing screeching between us, clearer and more horrible than any sound I'd ever heard.

The living room was a muffled blur of their voices, June's unchecked tears rising and falling, blending with Uncle Peter's hushed, heart-broken whispers, all drifting to us through Nat's bedroom door.

When he arrived, I was in the bathroom, wringing out a cold cloth. By the time I emerged, Teddy was gone. June sobbed against my uncle's shoulder, devastated beyond my help. I'd set the cloth on the floor beside them, wove my way down the hall on unsteady feet.

I'd found them in pieces. Ben was a mess of tics and wild, wide eyes; his vacant gaze roamed the room, landing on everything except the broken boy beside him. The boy who trembled silently until he saw my face. I knelt and enfolded him, let his splintered moans work their way into my skin. Let his tears burn through my shirt, each one a needle pricking my sunburned shoulder. Each a brand I gladly bore.

Ben's arms bracketed our grief, stripped away last summer's words and walls and resentment. Left us mangled and adrift, anchored only to one another.

We ended up in a row on the floor, surrounded by everything she'd left behind—her tiny slice of the world, stuttered to a stop. A dog-eared book, forever waiting for the turn of a page. Nat grinned at us from glitter-framed photographs, peeked at us from the blue ribbon hair clip in the corner, whirled her way into our senses like a fog. Choked the air with the specter of her laugh. She was everywhere and nowhere, and it was worse than anything we'd known.

Our Nat. A sudden, permanent hole in the future.

We heard the tap of those high heels on the porch steps before she reached the door. Ben's head jerked up; his eyes met mine, a reflection of bewilderment and shattered nerves.

"Peter. I've been looking for you."

Aunt Mattie's voice was a crisp, cold chill, seeping suddenly through the walls. Teddy's fingers gripped mine harder as we turned to stare down the door, as if expecting it to buckle and implode, blow inward and splinter at our feet. Uncle Peter's answer skated a hard path, acceptance and defiance twined with sorrow.

"Well, looks like you found me. You always know which stone to turn, I guess."

"Don't you take that tone with me. If you—"

"Shut up. She's dead." His low growl sent a shiver over my scalp, coaxed another fractured cry from June. "We found her not two hours ago, so my tone is the least of my worries."

"Oh. Oh good Lord. I'm—I didn't know. Can they tell—do they know what happened to her?"

"Drowned, it looks like. Washed up downriver, past the preserve."

"God save us. I—where's Benny?"

"He's in the back, consoling his grieving friend. Wouldn't hurt you to take a page from him, you know."

"Of course." Her words slipped out lower, sugar soft and sprinkled with contrition. "She was a very sweet girl, June. It's terrible, what happened. I can't imagine. Your family is in my prayers."

June's reply was muffled, inaudible, and the conversation dropped to mirror it. Ben's shoulders quivered, shedding flakes of tension in each deep, controlled breath, releasing them to die in the air as his muscles relaxed in practiced increments.

Until Uncle Peter's voice cut through the murmur, hard and dangerous as a rusty blade.

"Will you leave off that already, Mattie? You're upset, I understand, but I was with the search party all morning. Forgive me if your schedule slipped my mind."

"Did our appointment also 'slip your mind'? I sat in that office for over an hour, waiting. For you."

The silence hung thick in the air, ebbed through the room and under the door. It slid around us, wrapped and squeezed and stole our breath until he spoke again.

"I found her, Madeleine. I found that child's body. Your priorities are hardly—"

"Pete, don't." June's weary voice overrode his snarl. "I appreciate it, but this is not what I need right now. Go on home, okay?"

"Junie, please. You know I'm here for you always. I promised Sam I'd look out for you, and I—"

"Oh shut up, Pete. Just shut up for once and get yourself on out of here. Your *wife* needs you."

Aunt Mattie gave a single sharp laugh, more bite than bark, killing off any pretense of civility.

"If you have a shred of conscience left in your bones, Peter Hansen, you'll stand on your feet this moment and follow me out the door. It's a very sad thing, what happened to Natasha, but you're needed in *our* life. For you to sit here and try to make this about Sam—to spend your attention on June, when I can't get you to tend to *your* family—"

We didn't see June leap to her feet, of course, but we heard it. Heard Aunt Mattie's strangled gasp. Heard Uncle Peter beg June to sit back down, to stay calm, to let go of Mattie and get ahold of herself. He might as well have been on his way up the hill already for all the difference he made.

"My baby's dead," June shrieked. "Do you think I give a shit about your appointments, or his attention, or your sick joke of a marriage?"

Both my boys went still, flanking me like silent statues. Ben's eyes and face were blank, his lower lip paralyzed between his teeth. My hand crept over to his, and he damn near crushed my bones to dust as Teddy shifted closer. His eyes were hooded and wet, bloodshot reflections of his mother's wails, and they hooked into mine for an instant before leaping away to land on Ben.

"Benny," he whispered, "we need to clear out of here. If your mom—"

He bit the end off his sentence at Ben's raised hand, his frantic gesture begging us for silence as June's voice once again rose over those of his parents.

"Get out. Both of you get out. I don't *want* you here, Pete, if this is what you bring to my door."

"June, just give me a moment, and we'll talk this out, okay? Mattie, will you *please,* for fuck's *sake,* go wait in the car. I'll get Benny, we'll all go home together. I'll—"

June's laughter was harsh and raw and heartbreaking. Nowhere near amused.

"That's right, Pete, go on. Go on, Mattie, hook that leash on and drag him up the hill before I throw you out on your ass. The only way you ever could keep him home was to chain him down."

The air was a slice of hell, heavy with a horrible pause. The world tilted, then, as Nat's door banged open, smashing against the wall, and Ben was in his mother's grip, as if he'd never outgrown her hands. She hauled him by the collar, dragged him through the doorway and the living room, past Uncle Peter and his shattered, pleading voice. Ben's thin cry pierced me through the throat, then Teddy was on his feet, and my breath was gone, my hands grasping at air as I realized his intent—he was going after Aunt Mattie. He was rushing forward to rescue Ben for real, finally big enough to shield him like we never could as kids. I scrambled to my feet and raced after Teddy, crashed against his back as he pulled up short at the sound of flesh on flesh. Pushed past him expecting to find Ben cowering beneath my aunt's wrath. Instead I only saw the screen door slam itself behind him. Instead I saw Uncle Peter rock backward, shocked off balance by June's open hand.

"June."

It was a pitiful thing, that word—that small, weak syllable, barely escaping his mouth as he reached for her. A surge of desperation, cut off by a second slap.

"Get *out*, Pete. Go on back to your family."

"You're my family too, Junie—you've always been. You're my best friend—you and Sam, the kids—June, please. You're the—"

"NO," she wailed. "That's not what I am to you, Peter Hansen. You have *no* family here."

He reared away as her words, violent as any set of hands, shoved him backward onto the porch. His face was in ruins, eyes wide and horrified, as June slammed the door in his face, slammed her fist against the door, slammed her forehead and foot and knee and palms against his sobs. Aunt Mattie's unintelligible screeches pulled those sobs down the steps and across the yard. Pulled them into her car and cut them off, leaving June's to ride out on a broken moan as she slid to the floor.

Teddy's arm, which he'd automatically raised in front of me like a shield, drifted back to his side, an afterthought in the wake of everything. My eyes burned at the sag of his shoulders; at the low, strangled catch of his breath. At the way he turned and brushed past me, retreating to his room. Not bothering to go to June, as if he knew there was no point. As if he'd left off seeking comfort from her long before this day.

I followed like I always did, found him back on the floor beside his bed, head down, hands clasped at the back of his neck. I took my place beside him, let his fingers clench my shirt and his tears streak my face. Let his grief wash over me like water until it overwhelmed us both.

CHAPTER 14

SUMMER 2019

Uncle Peter paid for the funeral without question or solicitation, as he'd paid for Sam's funeral four years before. Consequently, Nat's send-off was a shit show of Aunt Mattie's gross ostentation wrapped in June's stark, Jesus-freak brimstone. The cracks started showing after Nat's former kindergarten teacher arrived, brushing past Teddy's rumpled dress shirt and dark hair and offering Ben her sincerest condolences. Blinking between them in confused silence at Ben's gentle correction. By the time members of June's congregation started chanting their own skewed prayers over the pastor's memorial sermon, not ten minutes into the closed-casket service, Teddy was done. I followed him out the double doors of the funeral parlor, sat on the stoop beside him as he smoked and cried in intervals, my palm steady on the small of his back. My own tears locked within my hollow, red-rimmed eyes.

The morning passed in a blur of lamentation and surreal flashes of unity—the subtle press of Ben's hand against Teddy's shoulder as he guided him away from a circle of Grandma's friends. The open-air furnace of the cemetery. Uncle Peter's vacancy, his gaze roaming aimless and empty and strung. The curve of Aunt Mattie's arm, a weird snake around June's inconsolable shoulders as Nat's small, shell-pink coffin disappeared into the ground.

It was just short of an utter mess—a horrible day held together with the steel-cable stitches of manners and upbringing and practiced company faces. Even so, the snags were minor. It wasn't until later that everything came undone.

Ben and I rode home with his parents, him and Grandma in the middle row of Uncle Peter's SUV, me crammed in between Grandpa and a floral arrangement in the fold-down back seats. Instead of following the procession of cars from the gravesite to the trailer, however, we continued up the drive to Ben's house.

"Why are we here?" Ben leaned between the seats as the car drew to a stop. "We told Teddy we'd see him at his place."

"We should take a moment, Benny." Aunt Mattie dabbed a tissue beneath each eye, checked herself in the visor mirror before opening the passenger door. "Collect ourselves. Give poor June a chance to catch her breath before we intrude."

"Christ, Mom, really? Whatever, I'll walk. Amy and I will meet you down there."

"Don't be silly; she'll ruin her shoes. We'll drive down as a family once we freshen up."

She ushered us into the cool, dark house, steered my grandparents and uncle into the formal sitting room. Ben and I attempted an escape, but Aunt Mattie swooped in before we made it to the stairs, hustled us back to join the others.

"Better to share our grief, not bottle it up—bottling never did anyone a bit of good, did it? You kids just let it all out now, and don't be ashamed. There's no shame in honest tears. Have a good cry if you need to, and don't mind the furniture."

"Mom." Ben's voice cut through her rambling, drew a ruddy

slash of dismay across her mouth that vanished as soon as it appeared. "We're ready to go when you are."

"Of course, Benny. Oh, but we should eat something first—we shouldn't impose ourselves on June's hospitality during a difficult time, when we're blessed with a full larder of our own. She has so little as it is. Let me put together something quick, and we'll be on our way."

She tapped off to the kitchen, words trailing behind her. Before we could properly settle on the stiff, silk-upholstered chairs, she was back bearing a loaded tray, pressing a plate into my bewildered hands: a jumble of cold ham slices and deviled eggs, a roll wrapped in a napkin. A skewerless cob of corn. A fried chicken drumstick, half-buried under a scoop of macaroni salad, celery-studded, mayonnaise-thick. Put together quick, my ass—it was fresh and homemade, obviously prepared and arranged by the housekeeper in our absence and garnished with goddamn parsley moments before we'd arrived. The chicken alone, still hot from the fryer, negated the lie that the meal was in any way impromptu. The sight of it—the pooling grease, alongside the iridescent sheen of the ham—made my throat close.

It was all such bullshit.

Never mind that none of Nat's actual family members were anywhere near the living room—Aunt Mattie wasn't about to let a mere technicality drop the curtain on her Display of Grief. Nat had grown up on my grandparents' land, even if only in the trailer, which was no reason to judge someone, didn't we know? We were like one big family, really, and ". . . it's been so good for all of us, that bond. Natasha came from good people, such good, hardworking folks. Why, Sam stuck around to raise those kids, married or not, and it was so sad when he had the stroke, but he was there till the end, and that's commendable. You never know how those situations will end up."

On and on she went, until my nerves screamed raw beneath my skin, and Ben's fingers were white around his glass. As if we should smile and nod along, calmly enable his mother's ridiculous private reception. She pulled that brand of shit on the regular— had done so for decades, and not one person called her out on it. No one ever called her out on anything, apart from the single incident, long ago, when she'd chased me with one of my sandals, intent on spanking me for some childhood naughtiness I no longer recalled. It was the only time I'd ever seen my mother lay hands on anyone. It was the last time Aunt Mattie so much as frowned in my direction, no matter what I'd done.

It used to take so much for me to stay quiet. Now, after too many years of reprimands, punishments that began with time-outs and escalated into lectures and groundings and the confiscation of everything but my art supplies, I'd finally learned to shut up and shut down. Now, it was second nature to sit in silence and nod along, twist my anger into acquiescence that might coax from my relatives the too-fleeting concepts of normalcy and peace. Not that we dared speak a word to the lack of either. The whole family made me sick.

". . . and Teddy's a good boy either way, such a good boy, such a good friend to Benny and to little Amy. Such a good brother to Natasha, and wasn't she sweet? Such a pretty little girl, and this is God's will, of course, but so terrible. Her poor mother. Her poor,

poor mother. I can't imagine how she feels. I can't. I—"

"So don't."

Ben was suddenly animated, suddenly on his feet. Aunt Mattie swiveled slowly toward him, jaw listing open like a broken door.

"What was that, Benny?"

"I said, 'don't.' Don't imagine it—go over there and see June, why don't you, and ask her yourself how it felt to put her kid in the dirt."

"Now, Benny, that's enough." Uncle Peter's voice bubbled out in restrained tremors as he stepped between Ben and Aunt Mattie's rapidly reddening face. "I know you're upset, son, but—"

"No, go on. Go take June a plate, why don't you? After all, they're *practically family*, and this is such a tragedy! A tragedy, Mom! It'll be amazing. 'Are you *okaaay*, Junie? It's such a sad loss—God's will, of course, but I can't *imagine*! Have you eaten? Have you eaten? Have you EATEN, JUNE?'"

His full plate shattered against the wall, china shards and ham shrapnel ricocheting past my head. I didn't even flinch. My eyes slid closed as the room exploded, their rising voices overlapping like ocean waves.

"BENJAMIN. You sit down now, son, and apologize to your mother, or I'll—"

"OR YOU'LL WHAT? YOU WON'T DO SHIT TO ME, DAD. YOU CAN'T FORM A THOUGHT IN YOUR HEAD WITHOUT RUNNING IT BY HER."

"Don't you dare speak to me that way. You—"

"Benny, what did I do? What did I dooooooo?"

"SHUT UP, MOM. JUST SHUT UP. I WILL LITERALLY

KILL MYSELF IF YOU DON'T. FUCKING. STOP."

That did it. Aunt Mattie's wails broke off into nothing at his words; I opened my eyes in time to watch her face collapse into sudden, furious sorrow. Tears glittered at her lash line, just above her makeup.

"Don't you *ever* say that," she hissed. "I am your mother. Do you know what it does to me, to hear—no. You don't know. You can't fathom."

Her guilt trip had the opposite effect. Ben's eyes darkened, a cruel shadow of their usual open gleam. Far from the boy who'd been collared and yanked away from us only days before.

"Oh, so you *can* empathize with June. Got it. Because that's who this is about, Mom—June Barrett, who we should be supporting right now, instead of listening to you talk about Nat like she's *yours*. It's about June. Not you."

"It's always about me when it comes to my son. What will I have left if something happens to you?"

"What will you *have*?" His flailing arms indicated the whole of the house, sweeping over marble and glass, tooled Italian leather and hand-carved teak. Indicating every bulb and bauble that comprised their lovely world. "All this shit, for starters. Dad's fucking wallet. Dad himself, not that I expect you to give a flying—"

"Oh *Dad. Dad*, he says. And *money. Things.* All worth nothing if you're gone." The tears escaped, cutting two perfect, glistening trails over her cheekbones. "When my time is up, what else will I have done with my life that amounts to anything at all?"

She was crumbling in front of us. Ben's outburst had torn open her carefully constructed world, shattered its fragile, spun-glass ideals. I still sat frozen, eyes flicking back and forth between them. Grandma stood behind the wingback chair, her hands steady on Grandpa's crooked shoulders. Uncle Peter was a six-and-a-half-foot void, choking on the truth of Aunt Mattie's words. Ben, however, was a forest on fire.

"There it is again, Mom—*your* family name. *Your* life. *Your* feelings. Always you. You don't give a shit about Nat, or Dad, or even *me*. You don't give a shit about anything that doesn't feed your purpose. It's fucking *sick*."

"You *are* me, Benjamin. Everything I've done since you were born has been for your benefit. *Everything*. You just have *no* idea. The things I've given up—for you—for—"

Her tears compounded; her fingers reached across the coffee table to touch his face, smooth away a lock of his hair. He flinched out of reach, breaking what remained of her composure.

Aunt Mattie was bad at emotions in general, worse at dealing with the fallout of her own. If she couldn't ignore a situation—if it called for anything more than smoothing out a moment with a plate of food or a practiced smile—she could be counted on to do one of two things: shut down or come apart. Neither option was a pretty sight.

Every now and then, she did both at once.

The room was a silent nightmare as she fled, each footfall a thump on my cousin's sagging shoulders. Grandpa, who'd barely blinked since we'd arrived, struggled to his feet and knelt in the mess, scraped bits of ham into a pile. Lost half of it in the process to his trembling hands. A sliver of plate slipped against his finger, the well of blood sudden and startling. He rose slowly, tottered to the kitchen on quiet feet. Tears stung my eyes at the sight of his abandoned napkin, small and crumpled, flecked red.

I set my plate on the coffee table and stood, left that room and that house on my own without shifting so much as a muscle in my tranquil face. Made my own way down the driveway, feet raw and blistered in shoes that were never meant for walking.

Okay, everyone out. You guys have enough water and stuff in case you have to wait? Have to take those branches down today, so work might run over." Teddy lowered the tailgate of my uncle's truck so I could jump out of the bed. "Amy, you need a hand?"

"I'm fine, just help me with the tubes."

"Toss 'em here, City Girl."

I chucked them out, one by one. Teddy caught the first and deflected the other. It bounced past Ben and rolled onto the path. We waited; he stared back at us, unmoving. Teddy rolled his eyes and went after the tube, flung it back toward the truck.

"Jesus, Ben," I said. "He's not your manservant."

"Whatever. If I felt like being self-sufficient, I'd leave you both at home."

"It's okay, Benny." Teddy threw a mock punch, which Ben easily blocked, then snaked his open hand past both their arms to pat Ben's sun-pink cheek. "I know you can't get enough of me."

"Yeah, yeah. Lead the way, pretty boy."

We lugged the supplies down to the cove, leaving the truck in Grandma's driveway. Teddy and I had hiked the hill to Ben's place that morning and helped him load up our tubing gear and Uncle

Peter's chain saw. The day was muggy and sweltering; he'd long ago unzipped the top of his full-body coveralls, shedding the sweaty upper half and letting the empty sleeves dangle.

I'd trailed behind him on the path, fixating on the undulations of his back, the sweat-damp hair sticking to his shoulders, and felt a twinge of conscience when we reached the clearing. While Ben and I spent the day doing literally nothing but floating downriver, Teddy would be covered neck to ankle, breaking down trees beneath the hellish sun.

"It sucks you can't go," I said, zipping up the backpack that held our shoes and towels so I wouldn't have to look at him.

"Thanks, Ames, but I wouldn't go tubing with a gun to my head. I'll see you guys at the landing, okay?"

"You're too, too good to us, darling," Ben crooned, batting his eyes. "We'd be simply lost without you."

"Someone has to take care of your useless ass." Teddy winged his hat at Ben, who swatted it out of the air. "No one else can stand you, so I guess it's me by default."

"You can't get enough of me."

Teddy headed for the path as Ben and I dragged the tubes into the shallows, stopping knee-deep to strip off and soak our T-shirts, wringing the water over our necks and shoulders. Ben waded deeper into the current and I slung my shirt over my arm, prepared to follow, when his sunscreen floated past me, headed for the shore.

"Grab that, will you, Ames? You're closer."

"And you're lazy." I turned and snagged the bottle, glanced up, and froze, halfway to standing.

Teddy crouched in the clearing, hand outstretched, reaching for his forgotten hat. I stood slowly and his eyes lowered; instead of turning away, he fixed them on the water and let them roam their way up, over my miles of legs, over my cutoffs and river-damp hips, my bikini top and my sunburned mouth, until they hooked themselves on mine.

And for once, I didn't look away. For once, I didn't duck my head in a flash of awkward shame or hide my blushing face; I raised my chin and matched his measured stare directly, let him see me for the first time as his equal. Let him see me, seeing him as mine.

"Hey, what's the holdup? Oh Jesus." Ben's eyeroll was audible. "Close your mouth, dude, it's just my cousin."

Teddy blinked at him, a spot of color bursting bright on each cheekbone.

"Yeah. Sorry about that, man."

He stood quickly, strode back toward the path. My neck nearly snapped off my shoulders as I whirled to face Ben's smirk. I slapped the sunscreen into his waiting hand and shouldered past him, hoisting myself into my tube.

"You'd better damn well not say a word, Benjamin. Not a single one."

He chuckled, radiant with smug amusement.

"Wouldn't dream of it, Ames."

"So. Sooooo. You've had the Talk, right? I know sweet Aunt Ellie probably didn't think to cover whatever the hell *that* was back there, but still."

Of course he started in on me before we were even ten minutes downstream. Of course he did.

"Oh my God. Can we please discuss literally anything else?"

"Sure. Or we can skip over the chitchat and go straight to the part where you agree to dial back the whole zero-chill thing. I could do without watching the two of you eye-fuck each other beneath the shadows of a woodsy cove."

A flash of humiliation burst warm in my body, then prickled cold, dancing down my spine on stinging feet before flaring into a different glow beneath my skin. I bit my lip, breath catching at the memory of Teddy, and what had passed between us back at the shore—something so obvious and real, even Ben had pulled himself out of his own ass long enough to take note, though what he'd seen clearly wasn't sitting well. His impatience seethed around us, like he was waiting on an apology, or a confession. Like I owed him either.

"We have not been doing that at all, thank you very much," I said, my voice a squeak above nonchalance. I slapped a mosquito into bloody oblivion and cupped my hands in the water, trying to create enough of a drag to put some much-needed distance between me and my cousin. The current didn't give a shit. "I don't even think of him like that."

Ben threw me a side-eye, eyebrows migrating toward his hairline. "Amy. Please. It's so obvious it makes my skin crawl."

There was no real answer that wouldn't sound like bullshit, so I didn't bother arguing. This conversation had always been pending—that it had taken him this long to call me on it was the real surprise.

We floated along in heavy silence. Ben swished a hand through the water, changing his course until he drifted close enough to catch the handle of my tube. His eyes were bright but guarded. Confusing.

"Look," he began. "Aside from the fact that your mom would

shit kittens, you have to know this is a bad idea. Girls have been obsessing over Teddy since we were eleven—dude gets around like you wouldn't believe."

The words gathered on my heart like frost, dousing any hint of a spark.

"Because I was so very unaware of that." I drew a hand across my eyes, too weary to argue. "I for sure don't need the details, if it's all the same to you. And leave my mother out of it, unless you want me having a Ben-centric version of the fucking Talk with my own sweet auntie."

"You wouldn't."

"I won't, as long as you mind your business. You don't really think this is new information, do you? Trust me, I am *very* aware of all things Teddy, both good and—well, questionable."

Ben's exhale was audible. His hand relaxed, white-knuckle grip flushing back to pink.

"That's exactly my point. I knew this would be an issue eventually, especially with your whole bad-boy thing, but what I do *not* want to do is spend all goddamn summer sweeping up the shards of your shattered heart."

"Whatever. It sucks, but at least I know not to expect anything long-term."

When he didn't answer I glanced his way, then blinked at his stricken expression: frustration and disbelief and helplessness, a smear of anger shading everything right down the middle.

"Holy shit. That is not what I thought would be the takeaway from this."

"Like I'd turn him down over this if I actually got the chance?

Not to be desperate, but when it comes to him, I'm happy to take what I can get, however badly it ends."

"You're—*what*? Do you need an annotated list of all the ways that would suck for you, or are you good with a general warning?"

"I don't need a warning concerning my best friend." I rolled my eyes at his wide eyes and gaping mouth, the overly dramatic flush of his face. "Plus, you know. I have that thing for bad boys. You said it yourself."

"I was hoping you also have a thing for good decisions, but I guess I can add that to the pile of broken dreams. He won't be the friend you think he is, Ames. Not once you cross that line."

"God, don't worry so much. I won't make things weird, okay? But—"

Ben's hand came down on the rubber tube, a solid, angry crack that echoed off the water.

"I fail to see," he said, his voice a low, even snarl, "how you and Teddy hooking up wouldn't be the very definition of 'making things weird.' There's too much history. It could—no, it *would*. It would ruin absolutely everything."

"Maybe. Maybe not."

I turned away from him, fixed my eyes on the riverbank. The trees were sparse along the water's edge; a few brave stragglers grew from the rocks, a branch trembling here and there beneath the weight of unseen creatures. Behind them, the cliffs rose sheer and striated, fully impassable. If something went wrong on this stretch of river, we'd be trapped in the water, forced to keep swimming until rock gave way to shoreline.

Ben let go of my tube and shoved away, drifted ahead of me on a rogue current. I didn't try to catch up.

CHAPTER 16

SUMMER 2019

L ife without Nat spiraled on into a cowardly streak of long
silences and awkward semicircles, all of us overcompensat-
ing, trying to fill the empty space she'd left. Each morning
was a fresh reminder of her absence; each hour, an exercise in bleak
acceptance.

To his credit, Teddy pulled it together hard core, putting on
the bravest of brave faces, as if he'd buried his sorrow alongside his
sister. I still saw it, though: in the too-bright spark of his eyes, and
the disciplined tension of his shoulders, squared where they'd once
casually slouched. Lurking in the tight corners of his smile, darker
and more vacant than I'd ever drawn it—not that I'd drawn anything
at all since the day she disappeared.

The work itself didn't matter—the assignments were boring
and rote, nothing more than technical practice designed to keep me
sharp over vacation and appease my mother upon my return. I'd
have to bust ass come August but would have no problem knocking
those out before my lessons resumed. I couldn't create, though. I
couldn't lose myself in lines and shadows or blend the world into
charcoal smudges.

It was my own fault. I'd left it too long, and gone absolutely
dry—my mother's prophecy, realized in stiffened fingers and wasted

stares. I muddled through it anyway, desperate to lose myself. Strained my senses raw reaching for that familiar, synchronic flow of mind and heart.

Nothing helped.

Meanwhile, Ben had gone to ground. His car stayed parked on the hilltop, at the same skewed, sloppy angle he'd last left it. His parents came and went as usual, falling back into their respective, separate routines. Grandma resumed her orbit around the household, tended to Grandpa and his schedule, and his increasingly complicated health. My cousin, however, had seemingly disappeared—until he barged into my room one morning, eight days after the funeral, a leather messenger bag bumping against one slim hip as he waved a dismissive hand at the scattered charcoals and blank sketchbook on the desk and rolled his eyes at my half-present sideways glance.

"Put that shit away, Ames, and get your head clear. We need to focus."

"You need to open a window," I retorted, fanning the air as I swiveled in my chair to face him. "Did you smoke your whole stash on the way up the stairs, or is that just how you smell all the time now?"

"I hotboxed on the drive down. Now shut up and listen. The first thing we have to do is retrace her steps."

"What are you talking about? What steps?"

"And here I thought you were the smart one. So much for Mama's perfect girl." Ben sighed, dropping wearily onto the bed. "I'm talking about Nat. If we can figure out everything she did that last day, we can figure out what happened to her."

"Seriously? We know what happened to her—she died. She was

supposed to come and see me, went to the cove instead for some unknown reason, and drowned in the river. The news story said—"

"The news story echoed what I'm sure is a totally accurate and not at all half-assed police report. Look, you saw her stuff—you know she wasn't the one who left it like that. I've spent all week going over this, and I need your help, Amy." He leaned forward, a week's worth of isolation and agitation evidenced in his bloodshot eyes. "Please."

"Hey. Calm down, okay? Breathe." His face wavered, folded inward as he fought down a panic attack. I looked away. When he was trending toward normal, I reached over and squeezed his arm, shoving past the moment as best I could. "Help with what, exactly?"

I expected him to start rattling off random details, maybe launch into a finger-ticking session of bullet points and half-formed theories—yet another trip down the well-worn and overshared path of his thought process. Instead he took a final deep breath, opened his messenger bag, and pulled out a thick spiral notebook, flipped to an already ink-covered page.

"A notebook, Ben? How vintage."

"Analog is the only way to keep a secret. You really want this shit in the home network, where my parents can access it?"

"They actually care what you do online?"

"Bet your ass. Mom randomly checks my phone *and* monitors my laptop activity. I can't even look at porn."

"Like I yearned for that information."

"Whatever. I don't care if they see me on TikTok or something, but I don't want them involved in this. Can I talk now, or would you care to critique my fucking penmanship?" He waited, eyebrows raised, until I waved him on. "So as I was saying, we need to put ourselves in Nat's shoes. June said she left the house sometime that morning after ten but before noon. Said she was going to see you, and maybe go swimming."

"Which, for Nat, means wading in up to her ankles and lying around in the shallows."

Ben glanced up, nodded approvingly. The pool was one thing, but we both knew knee-deep was as far as Nat ever would go in the river.

"Exactly. Now, apparently she had a thing lately where she loved getting the mail. She was supposed to go do that and bring it back down before heading over. June watched her walk up the driveway in the direction of the mailboxes. That was the last time anyone saw her."

"That we know of."

"Yeah, that we know of." He blinked, caught off guard by his own theory leaving someone else's mouth. "Fuck."

"What next?" I pressed, determined to soldier past the thought before it crashed down and buried us both. He shook it off and refocused.

"When Nat didn't come back, June figured either there was no mail that day or it hadn't run yet. Since it's closer to take the main drive from there to Grandma's, she assumed Nat went up that way to meet you. Say hi to Teddy, or whatever, then ring the bell."

"And obviously he never saw her."

"Nah, he was on the mower, all over the back end of the hill. You can't see the road from there, or the trail. He knocked off around two thirty, went home, and when they realized she'd been gone all that time, he went back up to Grandma's." He was quiet for a moment, fingers pressed into his temples, as if he could squeeze images out, siphon answers in. "So. Anyway. You were there for the next part— you confirmed Nat never showed. You went with him down to the cove and found her stuff."

"Stop it." I couldn't think about Nat's things at the base of that tree—couldn't bear the memory of Teddy's face, the budding seeds of panic bursting into full-blown bloom as his mind wrapped around their meaning.

"I know it sucks, okay? Makes me sick to even contemplate. But hear me out. You and Teddy split up then, he went home, and June called the cops. Teddy called me, like, six times, but I was out with this girl and had my phone turned off. I didn't even see I'd missed his calls until I was home."

"And you didn't go straight over to check on him? Of course you didn't. You're an asshole, Ben."

"Sure, okay—I'm the asshole who made exactly one stop along the way, and that was to collect your sorry ass. Obviously I could have run straight down there on my own, but I figured he'd need us both, and—"

"Wait, back up. Earlier you said Teddy went straight home after work. Wouldn't he have seen Nat's things when he cut through the cove?"

"That's what I thought, too. Apparently Dad stopped by Grandma's to pick up his tools right when Teddy was finishing up. He offered him a ride back, dropped him off at the top of the drive, then turned around and headed back to our place. Otherwise, yeah." He paused, frowned at a point somewhere past my head. "Though it's weird Teddy didn't see the stuff on the way back up, don't you think?"

"Not really. It was all on the far side of the tree, closer to the water than the trail. Coming from his place, they'd be out of the line of sight."

"Yeah, that makes sense. And you know what happened next— we wasted days on that travesty of a search when it was already too late. Seems like everything is, after this." Ben's gaze strayed past me again, a glow sparked deep in his eyes. "I had this whole plan for my life, you know? Where I'd live, what I'd do, who I had to be—now it all seems like bullshit. If someone like Nat can just be *gone*, then—"

"—none of the other stuff matters. I know."

"Exactly. She deserves more than this, Ames. Those volunteers weren't exactly treating the area like a crime scene—even Teddy didn't think twice about dropping his water bottle. He took her stuff home from the cove, too, which fucked up any chance at using it for evidence. So nice work ruining that right off the bat, before we even knew she was gone."

"We didn't *think* of it as a crime scene," I said slowly. "No one did. Even now they're calling it an accident, because—"

"Because they didn't know her. We did. We *know* she didn't just swim out too far and drown. If she ended up in the water, it's because someone put her there."

"Oh my God. You're right. Ben, if there's even a chance—but what can we do? Everyone's going to think we've lost our minds. As far as this town's concerned, the case is closed."

"That," he said, "is exactly why it's up to us to solve it."

We cornered Teddy at home, caught him doing a half-assed job of hanging laundry—tossing bath towels over the shitty clothesline, not bothering with clothespin anchors. He gave us a half grin as we approached, abandoned his task, and crossed the overgrown lawn to meet us. Lost that grin in increments when Ben began to speak.

"Holy shit, Ben," he broke in, once Ben's words painted a picture too clear to deny. "Are you for real? I mean, do you seriously think—who? Who would do that?"

"Could have been anyone. Everyone knows everyone around here; everyone knew Nat. It wouldn't take much for her to go with someone she trusted."

"But she never left the property—we don't have many rules in my house, but that was the big one. She never broke it."

"Maybe she didn't," I said, crossing to him. Hovering a hand over his rigid back, not quite daring to touch. "Maybe she was out by the pastures or the mailboxes, and someone saw her from the main road. Called her over, drove onto the land. Talked her into showing him the woods."

"The point is, we don't know," Ben interrupted, brow creased, eyes focused on something past my head. "But the official story just doesn't *sit* right. We need to put ourselves in the moment—figure out the final scene. I keep wondering what it was like for her. Was it a blink, or a slow fade out? Did she have time to think, or to feel fear? What did she see—the sky? Someone's face? Did it hurt, or—oh. Shit." He grimaced at Teddy, who gaped at him, his drained-white face a twist of horror and disbelief. "Sorry, man."

"Someone's *face*? Jesus fuck, Benny, is that supposed to make it better?" Teddy turned to me, eyes wide and frantic, pleading for an answer we couldn't give. "The idea that someone she trusted, who I've maybe actually met? That this someone took her, then—what? Then *what*, Amy?"

Ben butted in before I could speak. Of course he did.

"That's what we need to figure out. The news report says she hit her head, got tossed around and banged up on the rocks, but the cause of death was straight-up drowning. She wasn't beaten up, or strangled, or some shit like that. There's no murder weapon, no evidence of a struggle. She wasn't—" Ben gulped down the end of his thought. "I mean, no one . . . messed with her."

"Ben, that is *enough*." My words were sharp, too late to stop his. Too late to stop them landing full force on Teddy.

"Christ." He backed away from us, putting distance between himself and the absolute worst hypothetical. "Jesus Christ. Is this a fact, Ben? Are they sure that didn't happen to her?"

"No way they'd be treating the case like an accident if there were signs of that. Someone her age, they'd have to investigate it. So at least that's something."

"Yeah, it's really something. Someone might have murdered my ten-year-old sister, but at least no one fucked her beforehand, right?

There's that bright side." He slid to his hands and knees in the dirt, heaving deep, erratic breaths. "God. I can't deal with this. I—"

He choked on his grief, lost the rest of his words in a splatter of vomit. I knelt beside him and pulled my fingers through his hair, gathered it away from his face, like my mother used to do to mine when I was sick. Soft, soothing sounds rose from some long-neglected abyss inside me, even as my mind recoiled from his stark and unchecked pain. What I wouldn't give to be better at feeling.

Ben ran off and returned a few minutes later, holding out an icy glass and a damp dish towel.

"I'm sorry, dude, I shouldn't have said anything. You have enough to worry about."

Teddy didn't answer. His eyes were fixed on the river, its slow, green surface barely rippling, beautiful and benign. Savage.

"I'm glad you did," he finally said. His face was grim, but something stronger and stubborn flared behind the pain. "If you're right—if there's even a *chance* you might be right—we have to know. So, what do we do first?"

We waited. The room was a mess of dingy filing cabinets, overflowing desk trays, and faux-wood paneling; the cop, a sweaty, overboiled ham, sat crammed into a too-small chair. Officer Martin Darrow gazed out the window in silence, a full minute after he'd gestured to the seats in front of his desk. Ben, reveling in spokesperson capacity, remained standing, his mouth pursing and puckering, flattening down to a resentful line. My cousin had never craved invisibility. He certainly hadn't made the trek downtown to River Run's overstaffed and underwhelmed police station to be treated like any average citizen.

"Thank you for taking the time out of your busy day to meet with us," he finally boomed, shaking Darrow out of his trance. "My name is Benjamin Hansen."

"I know who you are, son. Hansen. Hansen, Inc."

"Correct. Peter Hansen is my father."

"Imagine that." The cop glanced his way, flipped open a notebook, painstakingly wrote Ben's name at the top of a page. "What can I do you for, 'Benjamin Hansen'?"

"We wanted to speak to you about the possibility of an investigation," Teddy said. I reached over and took his hand, hardly wincing at the furious pressure of his grip. "Into my sister's death."

"I see. And who's your sister, son? If you don't mind my asking, of course."

"Natasha Fox."

Darrow perked up.

"You mean that little girl, what warshed up from the river? That was *your* sister? Must have missed meeting you at the search party efforts." His eyes narrowed. "Come to recall, though, I *have* seen you out and about, not a few months back. Last spring, it was. Think I caught you out of school, if I'm not mistaken."

"Pardon?" Ben cut in, cheeks flushing red, eyes darting to Teddy's fixed, unblinking face. "Is that somehow relevant to our inquiry?"

"Not as such," Darrow sneered, "but I sure do remember this young man throwing his cup of Pepsi through my cruiser window. I did have a time of it, cleaning that mess—but we can talk further about that little incident after you finish up your 'inquiry.'"

"Or maybe we can get to the fucking point?"

I closed my mouth too late, startled as anyone by the blare of my voice leaping unbidden into the world. Teddy's eyes bugged, his hand practically crushing mine to dust. Ben's mouth pulled in at the corners with barely restrained glee, a far friendlier sight than the cop's sneer, which swung toward me, puckering his already crimson face.

"Now you listen here, little miss. That is no way for a young lady to speak to—"

"Sweet Lord in Heaven, give me strength. Callahan? Again? We don't spend enough time together in the thirty-eight seconds it takes to pour my morning coffee, and now I have to walk in here and see you stinking up my chair cushion?"

The voice was heavy and Midwestern, a jaded, no-bullshit twang layered with sarcasm. The source of said voice stood at our backs, tall and solid as he was pale and freckled—the same redheaded officer who'd talked Ben down from his Amber Alert rant a thousand years ago, the day Nat died.

Officer Apparently-Not-Darrow started in the chair, blanched, then blushed. Color engulfed his neck and chin, spread north in a slow, guilty tide.

"Oh, there you are, Marty. I was just—"

"You were just hauling your hind end through my doorframe in the manner of an exit, thank you. If I catch you in my office again, I'll be filling out the formal complaint paperwork. And if I have to fill out paperwork, it'll unleash a darkness in me previously unseen by the fine folks of River Run."

"You're *not* Officer Darrow?" Ben came to life, mirth disintegrating as the cop bumped his way out from behind the desk. "Should I even ask why you were trying—and failing—to do his job? Or why you're stuck on bullying my grieving friend?"

"Well now, listen, son. I—"

"No, *you* listen, *Officer Callahan.* As soon as Officer Darrow green lights this investigation, I'll be requesting your badge number and the name of your direct superior. We can have ourselves a little sit-down about your cruiser, or whatever else is eating at you. Unless you'd prefer I take it up with *his* boss the next time he and his wife join my parents for supper."

"Better late than never, asshole," I muttered, shooting Ben a look. He'd damn sure taken long enough to play the Hansen card. Teddy was as still as one of my sketches, his face a drawn, humiliated pinch. I tightened my grip on his hand.

Darrow settled at his desk as Callahan scurried out.

"Don't worry, son, I'll handle him personally once we're done here. Now, tell me: What's this you say about an investigation?"

"Hey. You okay?"

I leaned against the police station's weathered Greek revival column as Teddy lit a cigarette with shaking hands. He gazed out at the empty street beyond the station steps, watched a MoonPie wrapper travel from sidewalk to gutter on a hot sigh of wind. The hair at my temples was already damp.

"I'll be fine. I get it—you know, Ben was with me the day I cut school, when I threw that Pepsi. Hell, he *bought* me the Pepsi, *and* he yelled at the cop to kiss his sweet Kentucky ass. Practically dared him to cuff us. But no one's saying shit to old Hansen, Inc. Not then, and not today."

"No one ever does," I sighed. "It's like, the structural framework of his charming personality."

That drew a laugh from him, at least—a harsh veneer over the pain in his voice.

"You're not wrong." He turned a sweet, shy smile my way, catching me in his eyes. "Thank you, Amy."

I almost kissed him right there on the steps. I almost told him I loved him. The words hovered in my mouth, tapping against my teeth in search of a weak spot, on the verge of restarting everything from where we'd left it last summer. Never mind that it was inappropriate and inopportune, and decidedly not the fucking time—all I wanted was to be the thing that held him together. To console us both with all that might have been.

Then Ben was there, butting in between us all pale and self-important, as per forever.

"That was some crazy shit in there, was it not? I had to name-drop my dad a couple more times, but the real Darrow agreed to get on board with the case. Oh, and I got the other asshole's badge number—as soon I get bored enough to bother, I'll dismantle his life from the inside out. You guys want to get a Frappuccino? It's hot as balls out here."

Teddy stared at him openmouthed, then collapsed on the station steps, laughing so hard he had to gasp for breath.

"Goddamn," he finally wheezed, wiping his eyes. "I think I'd die without you guys in my corner. I really think I would."

"We've got your back, man. World without end."

We reached out together and grasped Teddy's hands as he stood, pulling him to his feet.

CHAPTER 18

SUMMER 2018

The sun slid between the leaves and branches, grasping at us with too-hot fingers. I watched it sweep across the cove and over Teddy's face, swipe a morning-bright streak across his squint as he ducked his head. Nat giggled and yanked the lock of hair she held, tugging his chin back to center.

"Hold still, Bear. We're not done yet."

"Yeah, well, I sure as hell am."

He swatted at her hands and she shrieked, smacking playfully at him until he tipped over and landed in my lap. I felt him relax for an instant, felt him submit and rest against my heartbeat as he peered at me from the beautiful mess we'd made of his hair—a riot of braids and twists, woven with white clover and dandelions and river reeds. His gaze strung me up and held me fast, and I died and lived and died again in those eyes. I chose that end a thousand times rather than look away.

Then he rolled off me and stretched on the ground next to my legs, fending off Nat's renewed attempts at decoration. I clenched my fingers, squeezed them bloodless white as the world snapped back into focus. Rubbed a hand over my face, hoping he hadn't felt the shiver running through my limbs.

"Ten minutes," Teddy said, squinting up at us. "It's almost

noon—if he hasn't shown by then, we go get his lazy ass."

"You know he's not showing up in the next ten minutes," I sighed. "Or twenty. Or probably ever."

"Yeah, you're right. I bet he's still asleep. Or just plain forgot our plans, and is up there lying by the pool, wondering why we haven't called."

"The pool sounds pretty good to me, actually. Better than here."

"Let's go now, Bear." Nat's sweaty face split around a yawn, then curled into a pout. "I'm hot. And hungry. And Benny takes too damn long."

"Watch it, Bug. Mom heard you cuss the other day and ripped me a new one. She won't let you hang out with us anymore if you don't clean up that talk."

Nat's answer was a half-hearted middle finger. Teddy swatted at it and rolled to his feet, clawed at the braids and flowers, shook his head until his hair hung loose around his face in a mess of tangles.

"Get ready to walk, you two. We're going up the hill."

Up the hill. Such a simple, benign way to describe the ascent into a strange and backward hell. The woods were humid and still; we were winded before the halfway point. Teddy gave into Nat's lamentations on the final leg, carried her piggyback the rest of the way, and by the time he deposited her onto Hansen property, even she was too exhausted to waste breath on complaints.

We slogged across the lawn to the house by force of will, the promise of air-conditioning worth the final few steps. The blacktop driveway soaked up the sun and spilled it back at us, relentless. Aunt Mattie's daylilies wilted in the beds. The porch fan spun in slow, lazy circles, drawing in pockets of misery and blowing them back unchanged.

I pushed open the front door, taking their screams right in the face.

The fight rose and fell, swelled and burst, wove its way through the prisms of the hallway chandelier. I felt Teddy's hand close around mine, knew without looking he was an ally, not a hindrance, at my side—we were moving together, walking straight into the worst fight I'd ever heard, even as Nat backed away. I didn't blame her—I'd have turned and headed right on out the door myself, if there were any way to know Ben wasn't trapped in the middle of his parents' mess. It was only the thought of his safety that let my voice ring loud and strong as I called his name.

The living room went dead silent.

Aunt Mattie's face around the doorjamb was a jolt even to me. Her eyes bulged at the sight of me and Teddy, then went dark with unchecked rage as they landed on Nat. I followed that glare, turned in time to see the accent table wobble at the bump of her hip. Just in time to watch the china vase tip casually off its surface, meet the floor, and blow apart.

Teddy's soft curse was quashed by the thin, high wail that spun from Nat's mouth, and then Uncle Peter was there, advancing on her tiny, shaking form, a mess of corded arms and bloodshot eyes. She covered her mouth and shrank against the table as he knelt before her. The veins in his neck stood out beneath an angry set of scratches; his cheek was a familiar blotch of palm and fingers, the same hand-print I'd seen on Ben far too many times to count.

"It's okay. It's okay, Natasha, it's just a vase. You know that, right?" My uncle's big hands closed over her upper arms, squeezed a fresh flare of panic into her eyes. "Now, honey, don't you worry. It's fine. It's going to be fine. We'll get this cleared up, and it'll be like it never happened, and—"

"Peter, let go of her." Aunt Mattie's voice looped around his neck, choking off his words.

He stood slowly and turned, shoulders bowed, face like a summer storm ready to split the sky. "It's just a vase, Madeleine."

"Lower your voice."

"Make no mistake. There are lines, and you are crossing those lines, and I *will not have that.* Do you hear me?"

"Leave it." Her eyes cut past him, narrow and clouded, filled with disdain. "You're scaring her."

He blinked at that, mouth working around a response before he swiveled back toward Nat, boot heels grinding china into dust.

"Oh. No, don't be scared." He reached for her again, recoiled as she flinched away. "Don't. I didn't—I'm—"

"Kids, have you eaten? Come on and have a snack." Aunt Mattie sidestepped him easily, swept Nat away, herded the three of us around the debris and toward the kitchen. Away from Uncle Peter, who stood in the middle of the broken mess, staring at the space where the vase had been.

"I didn't mean to," Nat whispered, miserable and leaking tears. "I'm sorry, Ms. Mattie."

"I know you are." Her words were clipped but calm. Resigned. "It's done, though—no need to dwell on what we can't fix."

"Aunt Mattie? Where's Ben?"

She blinked at me a beat too long, as if she'd forgotten who Ben was. As if she hadn't quite arrived at the idea that we'd appeared in her home with the purpose of fetching her son, like we'd be here for any other reason on earth. Like I'd have ventured anywhere near the place if I'd had a clue what we'd find.

"No, I guess he's not with you, is he?" she finally said. "Must still be upstairs. Go on up and bring him down, honey. I'll fix you both a plate."

Sure enough, Ben was in his room, a strangely fragile creature surrounded by antique mahogany and Ralph Lauren linens. He lounged on his unmade bed, MacBook open, AirPods jammed in place. I aimed a kick at his footboard, and he jumped a mile, the panic draining from his face when he focused on mine.

"Shit. You scared me, Ames." He pulled the AirPods from his ears and closed his laptop, slid down his pillow into a prone position. "What are you doing here?"

"Oh, you know me—can't get enough Hansen domestic bliss."

"God. Are they still—"

"Not since we walked into the middle of it. Why are you here and not down at the cove like you said you'd be?"

"Why do you think? I'm not above hiding up here like a little bitch when the alternative is walking into one of their brawls."

"Well, they're settled now. They're sweeping up the Wedgwood as we speak."

"The Wedgwood? Not the one with the—"

"Butterflies. Yep."

"Damn." He ran a hand through his hair, tugging absently at the ends. "So much for the nice, matched set."

"Go ahead and apply that thought to every single thing in this family, Ben," I said, flopping across the foot of his bed. "Oh, and bonus: Teddy and Nat got front-row seats. Nat freaked out and accidentally broke the vase, and now your mom's busting out the snacks."

"Of course she is." He heaved himself up and headed for the door, motioning for me to follow with a jerk of his chin. "Might as well get in on that while we can. I've been trapped up here all morning."

"Are you serious? What could they possibly have to fight about for that long?"

"How the fuck would I know? Earbuds were invented specifically so I don't have to listen to that shit. I'm sure you can relate."

I shrugged as we started downstairs, conceding his point, though it had been a good few years since I'd heard my own parents fight— mostly because a fight usually required both parties to be in the same room for longer than ten-second stretches.

Uncle Peter stared out at the cliffs through the sliding glass door, which led from the enormous kitchen to the second-story deck. His left cheek was damp and pink; a baggie of crushed ice hung half-forgotten from his hand.

Teddy and Nat perched on stools at the breakfast bar, a captive audience to their hostess, who'd pulled out half the damn pantry and lined it up in a neat, blameless row: homemade shortbread cookies and store-bought cheese straws. Spiced pecans in a Blue Willow dish. A platter of sliced fruit—peaches and plums, tart red cherries. A pile of blackberries, juicy and swollen. Perfect square-cut brownies, thick with walnuts and dark chocolate chunks.

"Go on, kids, dig in. There's plenty for everyone." She added more berries to Nat's rapidly emptying plate and set a glass of milk in front of Teddy's untouched food and wide, apprehensive eyes. "Benny, Amy, sit down before Miss Natasha here eats up the whole house. They do feed you at home, don't they, honey?"

"Yes, ma'am." Nat smiled up at her as Ben and I slid onto bar-stools. "This is really good, though. Thank you."

"Well, bless your heart, you're very welcome. Your mama's rais-ing you up nice, isn't she? You'll be a real pretty girl someday, just like her, and you got your daddy's sweetness on top of it all. It'll be real interesting to see how you turn out, won't it? I bet—"

Uncle Peter's fist smashed against the wall—once, twice. He turned and threw the ice pack as hard as he could. Its contents blew through the plastic, splattered the mantel, skittered across the stone hearth of the fireplace beneath. His boot lashed out, caught a chair off-balance; he threw open the sliding door and burst through it onto the deck, a near-smothered flame seeking new air. My uncle, gone to splinters in the space of a breath.

Poor Nat squeaked out a whimper and cringed against me, but Ben didn't flinch. He scrolled through his phone, elbows calm on the countertop, jaw working over his food. Teddy was a blank-faced sculpture, hands folded in his lap. His eyes sought mine, blinking and desperate—I let them swallow me for a heartbeat, shifted my gaze past him, watched a slurry of water and ice gather at the lip of the hearth. Watched it swell and rise and spill over, soak into the edge of the floor runner. I rubbed my finger through a smear of chocolate and brought it to my mouth. Let it melt on my tongue, sharp and rich and bitter.

Aunt Mattie ignored the puddle, focused instead on her hus-band's broad, defeated back as he gripped the deck railing. Her face skidded up against the moment, listed to the side; the one beneath it was a mangled twist, furious and deeply wounded. Then she gathered the pieces and tucked them behind her teeth. She went to work slicing a block of cheddar, empty-eyed over the bright bend of her smile.

"Don't you worry about him; he's in one of his moods. No telling what that man will do once he goes on a tear. Isn't that right, Benny?"

She stared at Ben until he met her gaze; his head bobbed once, less an agreement than an acknowledgment. Then she turned to the counter, stacked brownies like building blocks in a Tupperware container, added berries and cookies and cheese and nuts. Popped a cherry into her mouth, puckered for an instant around its bite before her lips smoothed back to normal. Smiled at Nat, whose wide, scared eyes glistened with new tears. The puddle disappeared into the rug.

"Have whatever you like, Natasha—take some home. You're skin and bones, you lucky girl. Thin enough to float away."

CHAPTER 19

SUMMER 2019

It was too hot to sit by the pool, so Ben and I sprawled across his bedroom floor. The AC kicked on, scattering the chaotic sea of papers, sending them drifting past our empty Perrier bottles and crumpled Grippo's bags. The rest of the house was placid and empty, the tranquil silence broken only by our discouraged sighs; the air between us buzzing with helpless, desperate hope.

"I'm not sure how wide to cast the net," Ben fretted, shuffling his notes. "Who did she know? Do I draw the line at school officials, or go down the rabbit hole and start looking for a trafficking ring?"

"Sure, let's go with that one. Just to simplify things." I sighed. "If it was a case of trafficking, she'd still be missing—and probably alive. And as for who she knew—why cast the net at all? It's River Run. Who *didn't* she know?"

"Waiting for names whenever you're ready, Ames. I'll add them to the e-mail I'm composing for Darrow."

"Christ. If that man hasn't blocked you, it's only out of a sense of civic duty."

"Well, these details are important. He won't let me see the files, so—"

"No. Please tell me you didn't ask the police for confidential case records. Please, at least tell me that."

"Why? Are you worried he'll be even more useless if I piss him off? Let me assure you, that ship has sailed. That ship has sunk to the bottom of the goddamn sea."

"Awesome. You realize he doesn't actually give a shit, right? As far as the cops are concerned, Nat's no longer their problem. One less underprivileged kid sucking up the tax dollars."

"Yeah, I'm aware—I'm the one who had to threaten a sit-down with the lawyers just to get him halfway to a yes." Ben jumped up and threw himself back into his desk chair. "I'm starting a new list: everyone who's set foot on this land in the last year. Plumbers, the bug guy, my parents' landscaping crew, the pool guy. Who else?"

"I don't live here, Ben. I have literally nothing to contribute."

"Know how you *can* contribute? By selecting one from this fine assortment of pens, sitting your ass down in front of the notebook, and transcribing my words."

"Transcribe them yourself. There're tons of people on the property all the time; any one of whom could've fixated on her." I rubbed my face, racked my brain. Unearthed nothing but the most generic options. "Family friends? The mailman? Someone from June's congregation?"

"You know what? I can actually see that last one being a real thing," Ben mused. "They'd have access, and Nat would've trusted June's friends. And they all came over here after she went missing—returning to the scene. That's like, Serial Killer 101. Holy God, it makes perfect sense."

"I don't know about *that,* but it's a start, at least. Teddy would know names. He'd remember who came by often, especially the weird ones."

"Well, that's a mile-long list. They're a bunch of fucking creeps out there—snake handling, speaking in tongues, all kinds of crazy shit. Teddy told me a while back about this one dude who's like, fully obsessed with June. Rags on her all the time about her out-of-wedlock kids, says all women are sinners at heart who need the firm hand of a godly husband, or some shit like that."

"Are you kidding me? Why am I not reading a dossier on that guy this very minute, Ben?"

"Because I don't give a rat's ass about him in general, much less have his contact info? I forgot he existed until you brought up the church. Goddamn it, I wish Teddy had a cell phone."

"He's mowing today. We can try to catch him on a break."

"Get off your ass and let's go, then. This is good, Amy. This is a fucking *direction*."

Teddy was circling the front lawn when we pulled up to Grandma's. He waved and shut off the mower, wiped his face on the shoulder of his T-shirt as he jogged toward us.

"Hey, guys. Everything okay?"

Ben filled him in on the gist of our theory, for once treading carefully around the subject. Teddy listened quietly, gnawing on his thumbnail.

"The more I think about it, the more convinced I am," Ben concluded. "Did any of those guys ever come to the house, spend enough time here to learn the property? Nat would've trusted someone who was over a lot, right? I mean, that kid fucking loved everyone."

"Yeah. She did." Teddy stared past us, unblinking, thinking, barely holding it together on the heels of that reminder. "It's mostly women who come to the house, but the pastor's been over plenty. Then there are two who keep showing up at the same time and like, talking over each other, trying to get Mom's attention. Offering to drive her to the prayer circles, like that'll get them laid. It's pitiful."

"What about that one Men's Rights guy you told me about, who low-key wants to be your new dad?"

"That guy? No way, she'd never let him near us. As far as I know he never laid eyes on Nat."

"Got it. And the ones who did? Do you know their names?"

"The pastor is . . . his last name is Henley; can't remember his first. Isaac or Isaiah, something biblical. Don't know if that's his real name or his born-again one. Some of them do that—pick a new name when they get saved."

"What about the two who want to double up on your mom?"

"Gary Gray and John Paul Jennings. And dude, come on. Gross."

"Sorry. This is good, though. I'm not saying any of them killed her, but they should at least be checked for alibis or whatever. Don't ask me; Darrow can handle that shit."

"I don't know. I think you're stretching a little bit here, Benny. I mean, before they found her, you thought she'd been sold on the black market." He was quiet for a moment. "There is one guy, though. Luke Calhoun? From the search party?"

"*That* guy? The pedo freak who smelled like unwashed ass?"

"Yeah, he's been up here a few times. Always brought things for Nat. Colored pencils, bookmarks. Weird tract comics, little stuff like that. Hair clips once, I think. God." He looked at Ben. "Do you really think there's something to this?"

"I don't know, man. But it's the best idea we've had so far, and it's way more than we had this morning." He stood, tucking his notepad into his back pocket. "I'll run over there right now, see if anyone knows where this Luke Calhoun guy lives."

"To the church? Dude, you can't just go over there."

"The fuck I can't—it's a free country. You in?"

The question dithered in the air, turned over and over itself as we waited for an answer. Teddy's face closed; his expression hardened. Shifted to some unknown, unseen depth.

"Wait here."

We lingered in the car while he put the mower up, left a note for Grandma. Disappeared into Grandpa's shed, emerging with his pack slung over his left shoulder, Grandpa's .22 rifle propped on his right. He strode toward the car, hair pulled back, mouth pulled tight. Way too many possibilities spooled out from that grimace, none of them promising any good thing.

"Oh my actual living—no. No way in hell." I leaned between the front seats and slapped my cousin's shoulder. "Ben, make him put it back."

"Put what back?" Ben leaned across the center console, hair falling across his face as he peered out the window. "Oh nice. Good thinking."

"Good *thinking*?" I snapped as Teddy climbed into the passenger seat and laid the goddamn thing right across his lap. "Teddy, what are you *doing*?"

"Taking precautions," he answered. "Can't be the only one there empty-handed—better to have it and not need it than the other way around."

"You're telling me we might literally get shot? At your mom's church?"

He didn't answer. He didn't need to—it was River Run, Kentucky, land of the casually wielded firearm. Fuck my life.

"Who can say for sure?" Ben grinned, throwing the car into reverse before Teddy even got the door closed. "For all we know it could end in a hostage situation, but fuck it—that's part of the fun."

"Remind me to stay home next time." When they didn't respond, I kicked the back of Teddy's seat. He caught my eyes in the rearview, held them a second too long without blinking. "If you get me killed, I swear I'll find a way to beat your ass."

"Calm down, Ames. It's mostly for show, okay? Like, fifty-nine percent, mostly."

"Thirty," Ben said.

"Right. Fifteen percent for show, I promise. If we find him, and he thinks his ass is on the line, he'll be more likely to talk."

"Oh, he'll talk," Ben drawled. "And if he happens to say a bit too much? Well, let him try to run before the cops get there. He won't get far without his kneecaps."

"To hell with that. If we're right—if this is the guy who killed my sister, and he straight-up spills? We won't bother the cops."

"Damn right we won't." He drew to a stop at the property line, put the car in idle as they both turned to face me, amped with adrenaline, buoyed with anticipation. "Last chance to bail, Ames."

I slouched in my seat, glared between their fierce, determined faces. Let Ben's wild grin and Teddy's slow, predatory smirk overtake the world as they anticipated my answer.

As if it was even a question. I'd sooner stare down a gun myself than send those boys off on their own to confront whatever waited at that creepy church.

"Goddamn it. You know I'm with you."

"World without end." Ben threw the car into gear. His hands gripped the wheel and his foot hit the floor. "Hang on tight."

"Well, Google isn't telling me a damn thing on this guy—not even a River Run address. Which means we'll have to smoke him out ourselves." My cousin pocketed his phone, unbuckled his seat belt, and slid from the car into the heat. "Brace yourselves, guys—we're going in."

Ben had been blessedly quiet on the drive, a condition that evaporated the moment he fishtailed to a stop in a cloud of dust. The church balanced at the end of an unpaved, mile-long driveway, presiding over a parking lot of red-clay dirt and half-dead grass. The building itself, a battered one-room chapel, barely supported the decrepit tin roof and empty, collapsing bell tower. No signs, no letter boards; nothing but a black-painted cross above the double doors and a shitty lean-to built onto one side.

"This is it? Are you sure, Ben?"

"Positive." Teddy answered for him, speaking for the first time since we'd left the property. "Been here more than once, unfortunately."

"I think we should leave." They ignored me, climbed out of the car without so much as hesitating. Of course they did. "Come on, guys. There's no one here."

"Won't know till we check, City Girl." Teddy cocked his head toward the far end of the building, spoke to Ben over my protests and my head. "Around back?"

"Scope it out, dude. I'll try the doors."

Teddy shouldered the rifle and stalked off, disappeared around the corner of the building before I'd managed to climb over the seats. Ben was no help, busy as he was with the task of peering into the church windows. I left the passenger door open in my rush to grab him as he moved on to the entrance.

"Get away from there. Goddamn it, Ben—"

"Language, Amy, please. This is a house of worship." He knocked, grimacing as his knuckles came back coated in flecks of white paint. "Christ, this place is a piece of shit. You think the locks work? I bet they don't."

"Don't you dare open that door. I'm serious, you'd better—"

The pump of a shotgun behind us froze his hand on the knob, froze my words in the air and the breath in my lungs.

"The hell y'all kids doing out here?"

I saw Ben go pale from the corner of my eye, saw the flash of fear and shock contort his features. His eyelids blinked and twitched; his jaw worked over grinding teeth. If he went into panic mode, we were so fucked.

"You hear me, boy? You got till a two-count to about-face and start talking. One."

I spun on my heel immediately, blinked at the man behind the gun. He was a compact mess of scars and suspicion, ropy arms destroyed by sunburn and ugly, faded tattoos. He squinted at me through round, smudged glasses, above a beard as full and white as the wild overgrowth on his head. I heard Ben's long, slow breath, felt the tension rolling off his arms as he fought for control.

He was a different boy by the time he turned around—a sunburst of confident shoulders and Hansen charm, beaming with the bright detachment of Aunt Mattie's company face.

"Good afternoon, sir. Are you the proprietor of this establishment?"

"I'm Pastor Henley, if that's what you mean. Who all are you?"

"Pleasure to meet you, Pastor Henley. My name is Benjamin Hansen, and this young lady is my cousin Amy. How are you enjoying this fine summer day?"

The pastor's scowl took a nasty turn; I had to fight to keep my own face still. Ben was going to get us both killed.

"I don't much care for horseshit, son, so if you'll state your business—"

"*Our* business."

It might have been the sudden voice at his back—the one that sent a chill from my scalp to my fingertips, cool and slow as a sip of water—it might have been that voice that drained the color from Henley's face. More likely, it was the rifle muzzle pressed against his ear.

Teddy stepped into view at the far end of the stock. He sent a wink at me straight down the sight, answered my glare with a wicked smile that doubled my pulse.

"Our business," he said again. "Go on, get it on the ground."

The shotgun swung down slowly until the muzzle met the dirt. I felt Ben sigh with relief, stepped away as he shook the fear out of his limbs and squared up to his full height. Henley's gaze skittered wildly between the three of us as we closed in on him, widening in recognition when they landed on Teddy.

"You're Sister Barrett's boy."

"Yes, sir. Good to see you again. And sorry about the trouble—we'll be out of your hair pretty soon."

"Lord above, son, you scared the shit outta me." He coughed out a wet chuckle, sized us up with a sweeping, bewildered glance. "Can I help you kids with something, or—"

"I sure do hope you can. We're looking for Luke Calhoun."

The pastor's face changed at the name, rolling from rain cloud to thunderstorm, moments from cracking open. His eyes flicked back and forth from the gun to Teddy's set face.

"What you want with Luke?"

"We had the *immense* pleasure of speaking with him a while back." Ben leaned forward, grin stretching far past grotesque. His voice honed itself to an edge. "Told us to stop by and hear for ourselves the true Word of God. Well, turns out we need to have a word with good old Luke *himself*, and—"

It wasn't even a lie, but it had the opposite effect of Ben's intent—he found himself nose to nose with Henley before the thought reached completion.

"Y'all stay clear of him, hear? Man's got trouble enough on his own without young folk poking around."

"I beg your pardon? I'm not sure what you—"

"Move on along, son. All three of you, get on out." He shouldered his shotgun and turned away, started a slow, uneven gait toward the lean-to. "Brother Calhoun is a godly man, but he's a sinner, much as any one of us. You want to keep your distance when the devil takes his heart."

"I'm sorry, I think there's been a misunderstanding," Teddy

pressed, lowering the rifle. "Can you tell us where to find Luke Calhoun or not?"

Henley faced us, his mouth ground down to a thin line. The sun flashed bright across his glasses, hiding his eyes.

"I ain't seen him here since your mama's girl went lost. And I wouldn't tell you where he was even if I could."

studied the string of embellished *X* marks on the map, blue and purple slashes extending the length of our family's land. The papers scattered over Teddy's bedspread had been in some semblance of order when I arrived, but I'd neglected to stack one set properly, then Teddy knocked another onto the floor. Now, the bed was a shit storm of unfinished lists, half-formed ideas, and scribbled, incoherent margins.

The AC window unit kicked on, sending a shiver over my already chilly skin. I wobbled on the edge of my own mind, overwhelmed by the rustle of paper, the scratch of pens. Ben's habitual throat clearing. Teddy's frustrated sighs. The drum of rain on the roof and windows, punctuated by low snarls of thunder. All barely incidental on their own—all building on one another, overlapping into a tooth-grinding din. I blinked hard and shook myself back, doubled my focus on the page.

"These don't make sense to me," I said, nudging Ben with my foot. "What are they supposed to be, exactly?"

"Possible points of entrance." He abandoned his notebook and knelt beside me on the floor, tracing his finger over the hastily drawn map. "Working on the assumption that Nat never left the property, of course."

"What do you mean?"

Teddy leaned over both of us from his spot on the bed. His hair swung forward, tickling my cheek.

"Where she went in," he muttered, his words a soft-focus lens over their horrible meaning. "*X* marks the spot. Right, Benny?"

"Exactly. Here." Ben pointed to the largest *X*. "This is the cove, where she supposedly went 'swimming.' These two along the way down to the trailer are those little clearings, and that's the old boat launch. And this *X*—"

"That doesn't remotely look like those things," I said. "It's not even to scale, Ben."

"Excuse me for not being the hotter reincarnation of Leonardo goddamn da Vinci. Feel free to put your extensive training to work on a new version. Now, as I was saying, this *X* is Teddy's yard, which would make sense as a crime scene if June hadn't been home all day. She'd have seen something."

"And the purple ones? Where are those? Why are they purple?"

"My blue pen ran out."

"Way to go, dude," Teddy scoffed. "Very professional."

"Whatever, not everything has some deep meaning attached. That one is the lower cliff face on Grandma's land. These three ascending points go from there on up. And this"—he tapped the topmost *X*—"this is the very top of the cliff, outside my house. The highest point of the property."

"That seems unlikely," I said, mostly to myself.

Teddy sat back on the bed, swiped a hand angrily through the notes.

"So does the rest of it," he said, frustration edging his voice.

"You can look at the details all you want, but they don't make any sense. Too many big pieces are missing—like which fucking *X* is the right one. If you go by the accident theory, like the cops are saying, it's most likely the cove, right? Her clothes were there, and it's the easiest place to wade in. But as a crime scene? It doesn't *fit*. No one outside our families would know about it. You have to take trails from the houses to even get there."

"Teddy," I said, a dark, sick hollow opening in my heart, "that's actually the most obvious of the missing pieces: whoever killed her wouldn't have had to know on his own. If Ben's main theory holds true—if Nat was approached by and went with someone she knew, she could've shown him the cove long before that day."

"Oh God, you're right," Ben breathed. "There wouldn't have been time to take her somewhere else, then sneak back and plant her stuff. Not with Teddy working, and Grandma and our parents all over the place. My mom went between the houses at least twice that morning before I even finished my damn breakfast. She'd have noticed a strange car going up and down the drive, no question. That means he must've killed Nat almost immediately."

"Do we know that for a fact? That she was dead by the time we realized she was gone?"

"Yep. They couldn't nail down an exact time, but it was within a window of a few hours that same day. And we know she washed up pretty soon after she went in."

"Seriously?" My heart sank at the idea of Nat lying dead for so long, beneath the cycle of sun and stars, empty eyes fixed on night after endless night.

"Yeah, she'd have made it way down into the next county

otherwise. The search took as long as it did because she ended up in this remote fishing hole that's practically invisible unless you know it's there. They only found her because they were looking for her, and they barely managed to get that right. It'd been too long, by then—think of all the evidence that washed off, or decayed, or—"

Teddy's sock-clad foot came down between us, trampling the map. Our eyes followed him as he stalked out of the room, nearly ripped the door off its hinges on his way. It bounced off the shitty doorstop as I swung my head slowly back to face my cousin.

"Don't give me that look, Ames," he sneered as I opened my mouth to unload on him. "You need to acknowledge him as a part of this, and—no, shut up and listen, okay? We loved Nat, but he's her brother. This whole situation is *his*. Not mine. Not yours."

"I know you mean well," I began, breathing through a flare of irritation. "I know you do. But if you hurt him again—"

"He's already hurting. I'm trying to *help* him, and the only way I know to do that is to solve this fucking case. You're welcome to get on board, and if he needs you to pick up the pieces after, you can damn well do that too. But for fuck's sake, stop babying him."

"Let's go."

Teddy had reappeared in the doorway without warning, boots on, fists balled. I studied him, expecting tear tracks and sniffles, a tremor in his hands or chin. Found instead a set brow and stubborn jaw, eyes dark and dry over a twisted mouth. If he'd slept a full night since Nat disappeared, it didn't show.

"Go?" Ben glanced from him to the storm-streaked window, and back again. "Where?"

"You're right. We can't know what happened to her without considering everything. Luke Calhoun's in the wind, which means we're stalled on that, but if we're wrong about him—if it really *was* an accident, we can at least narrow down the options by going through it. Step-by-step—"

"—*X* by *X*."

It was uncanny the way their faces changed. Brows furrowed, chins tilted downward, the same angle at the same second. Lips pulled into the same tight-lipped grimace. Two sides of the same trick coin, identical in every way that mattered. Ben reached out a hand, let Teddy pull him to standing. Met his questioning gaze with a single sure nod, and I saw them—my boys, as they'd been before: wild and reckless, utterly untouchable. River Run, from the roots on up.

Teddy let his eyes slide past Ben and land on me, grin flickering, rearranging into a nervous, wordless inquiry that would've convinced me on its own if his outstretched hand hadn't already done so. At least they weren't bringing the rifle.

"I'm in."

"That's my girl." He grasped my left hand, Ben grabbed my right, and I was on my feet in less than a breath. "Follow me."

The air was sludge and threats, fat black clouds and steely sky. The trees spared us the worst of the storm; still, the rain snuck through the branches, drenched us gradually until it was just one of many things that no longer mattered. The clearings between the trailer and the cove were long untouched—one was flooded out entirely, the other choked with river reeds and poison oak. The boat launch was empty save for Sam Fox's old canoe, lashed to a tree, resting on its side a few feet clear of the water. Teddy and Ben poked around it half-heartedly, expecting little and finding less. We skipped the cove entirely—it'd been thoroughly combed through weeks ago, purged of all but memories. The lower cliff face on Grandma's land was essentially a root-studded slope, edged with an unbroken tangle of thorny hedges, and not one of the already iffy clearings on the uphill trek was more than thick underbrush and poorly maintained footpaths. Even the main trail was overgrown.

By the time the woods broke open onto Hansen land, I was a husk of smudged mascara and soggy, exhausted nerves, squishing along behind an equally bedraggled Ben. Teddy strode ahead—past the tree line, over the pristine lawn, straight to the waist-high, piled stone wall edging the cliff. Ben and I shared a look, doubled our pace as Teddy hoisted himself up, balanced on the narrow, uneven rocks, and leaned out, staring down at the river. Rainwater streamed from his sodden hair, traced the frustrated lines of his face.

"Well, here we are—the final *X*." His voice, already head and shoulders above us, nearly lost itself in a sudden swoosh of rain on its way to our ears. "And a wasted afternoon."

"I know it was my idea, but honestly? This spot makes zero sense." Ben spoke the thought as it formed in my head. "Why the hell would she climb the entire hill, let alone the retaining wall? Looking for Amy?"

"We were supposed to meet at Grandma's," I said. "Anyway, she knew you and I weren't speaking. She wouldn't look for me here."

"Hence, un-fucking-likely," Ben said. "Can we maybe get out of the rain now, Teddy, or are you staking out a goddamn campsite up there?"

"I'm good, Benny—just checking out the view. Step-by-step."

He dislodged a fist-size stone with his boot and kicked it free, sent it over the edge. We were too far up to hear the splash. Ben flinched along with me, straightened up, and assumed Hansen damage control mode. Clenched his teeth in a futile attempt to quell the twitch starting up in his eyelid.

"We couldn't even find *Nat* when she was right downriver," Teddy continued. "How're we supposed to find whoever killed her? They're either right in front of us, or they went on the run—and that's if they even exist."

"Maybe that's the next step. Check around, see if anyone else we know left town."

"Yeah. That won't be awkward at all." Teddy nudged another loose stone with his boot, braced himself against a gust of wind. "Did you guys know that like, half the atoms in our bodies came from outer space?"

Ben kicked my ankle, interrupting me mid-nod. Met my glare with a meaningful frown as he answered.

"No shit, huh? Where'd you hear that?"

"I read it. Or saw it on TV, I can't remember. Stardust, blown to Earth from somewhere outside the solar system. Intergalactic winds, moving in exactly the right way, and that's the only reason we exist." He pivoted in place, paced back over his own steps. Wobbled as the wall shifted beneath his boots. "And here we are. And it's all for nothing."

He faced the horizon and leaned out farther, peered down and down and down. Fixed his eyes on the feral, churning water. The wind kicked up again, ran muggy fingers through our dripping hair.

"You know, Benny, I keep thinking about what you said earlier, way back when this first started—what did that last moment look like? Did she scream? Did she feel pain? Did everything just go dark, or could she see the sky, all distant and watery-looking, from the bottom of the river? Or maybe someone's face, grinning while he held her down."

"Holy shit, dude. Don't."

"I didn't, *dude*—these are *your* thoughts."

"Yeah, well, you can't possibly imagine how many of my 'thoughts' originate in my own ass." I heard the hiss of air through Ben's teeth at the sudden, audible shift of rocks. Teddy leaned out further, daring the storm to take him. "Come on, man. Please."

"If we're following her—really getting down in there, like we said—shouldn't we go all the way? Don't we need to at least dive in, to see how it feels to drown?"

"Teddy, be careful."

He kept on as if he hadn't heard my plea, and maybe he hadn't. He heard my scream in the next second, though, when the careless pivot of his boot heel rolled a stone from its setting, sent it tumbling over the edge as he turned to face us. His foot slipped after it and he stumbled and followed, flailing, tilting backward. Falling away from us before it even hit the water.

B en was cracking up so hard he couldn't even stay on his own feet, much less pull anyone out of the river. A rescue mission for Nat's shoe had ended with Teddy's ass on the slick rocks of the riverbed, kept down by the drag of the same strong current that claimed the shoe in the first place. Ever the copycat, Nat had dropped to roll on the ground beside Ben, howling with laughter.

"You're a real pal, asshole." Teddy tried in vain to stand and slipped again, sending Ben further into gleeful spasms. "I'm so glad you're around to set an example for my sister."

"Oh God. Oh Jesus God, I can't. I can't with this at all, dude, I'm sorry. It's too much."

"You two need help, Benjamin." I set aside my charcoals, kicked off my shoes, and waded in, stepping carefully on the mossy rocks until I reached a sodden, resigned Teddy. "Watch out, it's slippery. Like you don't know that."

"I also know who has my back around here." He grasped my hands, pulled himself carefully to standing, caught my hips to steady me in turn as the river clawed at our legs. Water streamed from his clothes, dripped from his hair onto my arms and shoulders. "Not surprised it's you, Ames."

"World without end," I teased. His smile snared me; his low laugh sent a warm prickle across the back of my neck.

Something was happening that summer—everything was shifting, in tiny ways I didn't understand. We moved through the days together, a subtle, relentless progression toward an unknown end. Making contact in unconscious, impulsive gestures too frequent to be entirely accidental—his hands finding my shoulders, brushing the small of my back. Mine landing on his arm or knee, reaching for his fingers over and over without thought. The best moments were deliberate: when he hugged me goodbye or pushed my bangs out of my eyes. When I played with his hair or wiped a smudge from his face with my thumb. When we stood in the river, holding each other upright against a powerful current.

"I guess we need to detour by my place before the festival," he said as we slowly made our way back to the bank. "Don't think Benny will want me in his car all muddy and—whoa, careful. Just a few more yards to safety."

"My hero. What would I ever do without you?"

"You know you can't get enough of me."

We collected Ben and Nat from the ground and headed back to the trailer. Teddy stripped off his wet shirt in the yard, flung it over the clothesline, and pulled down a clean towel, taking the porch steps two at a time.

"Eyes to the front, Ames," Ben muttered as he passed me, slamming his shoulder into mine. I shoved him and he stomped a foot backward, stepping on my toes without even turning his head. A wave of real irritation surged through me, compounded by his casually raised middle finger.

He'd been a real asshole ever since our tubing excursion, gone out of his way to drop scornful remarks and slap me with side-eyes at every opportunity. Not that asshole behavior was a new development for Ben. He'd spent our childhood flying into snits over the finer points of game rules, stomping off when he didn't get his way. Crying to Grandma or Aunt Mattie when he felt slighted or ignored, regardless of our actual level of Ben focus. And apparently he had yet to grow out of it—my dismissal of his so-called warning still ate at him, shone clearly in his narrowed eyes; in his knuckles, white around the gearshift. In the clench of his jaw, around words that held a sharper, subtler edge, each phrase honed so precisely you wouldn't know you'd been cut until your fingers came back bloody.

"Make yourselves at home," Teddy said as we filed inside. The welcome blast of the window unit cooled my sweaty face, soothed the irate prickle of my mood. "I need to hop in the shower. Won't be ten minutes."

"Let me know if you need a hand, hot stuff," Ben said, kicking back in the recliner.

"No worries; your mom said she'd be right over."

They both cracked up, Teddy slapping Ben's high five as he passed by on his way to the hall. I settled in for the long wait, all too aware how long "ten minutes" could stretch in this aspect of Teddy's world.

Ben and I lapsed into a drowsy silence as Nat disappeared into June's room, reappeared and flitted from distraction to distraction, art supplies to TV to glittery nail polish. She ate two Popsicles, then Ben grabbed one for himself and passed her a third, and we could still hear Teddy in the bathroom. The splash of the shower wore on

eva v. gibson

my already strung nerves; the thought of him beneath the spray, just on the far side of the wall, set my nerves on edge.

"Well, he's apparently never coming out of there," Ben finally sighed, resting his bare Popsicle stick in the ashtray. "We should've gone home and changed instead of following him down here to sit on our collective ass."

"It's a bit late for bright ideas, Benny."

"Whatever, bitch. I'll go get the car while he makes himself pretty." He heaved himself out of the recliner and ruffled Nat's hair as he headed for the door. She slurped down the last of her Popsicle and jumped up, swooped after him like a manic sparrow. "Come on, Bug. I'm sure Ames won't mind helping him out."

"Thought that was your mom's job," I muttered.

"That's what she said." Nat giggled, skipping backward toward the door.

Ben stopped on the entryway rug, turning himself into a Nat barrier. She ran straight into him, nearly slamming him into the wall. He stared down at her wide grin for a beat, then erupted into howls of laughter.

"This kid," he gasped, yanking open the door. "She's my greatest achievement. The pinnacle of—" Ben pushed open the screen without looking, practically mowing down Uncle Peter, who stood on the tiny porch, confused, paper bag in hand. "Dad. What are you doing here?"

"I might ask you the same thing. I myself drove down to drop off the firecrackers. Saw your car at your grandparents'. Figured you kids were down at the cove."

"We were, but Bear fell in the river." Nat poked her head around

Ben, grinning at my uncle with red-stained teeth. "Hi, Mr. Pete. Happy Fourth of July!"

"Happy Fourth to you too, Little Miss Nat. Can you guess what I brought for you?"

"Hmmm." Nat scrunched her face, pretending to think. I had to bite down on a giggle as Ben rolled his eyes and made a wanking motion down by his leg. They did the same routine every single year. "Is it something purple?"

"Could very well be purple in there."

"Is it something pretty?"

"Not as pretty as Natasha Fox."

"Can I light it on fire?"

"That you can."

"Is it my VERY FAVORITE SPECIAL PURPLE SPARKLERS?"

"Yes, ma'am, it is!" She snatched them from his extended hand and ran in a screaming circle, waving them in the air. "Is your mama home?"

"She's getting ready for a daaaaaate."

Uncle Peter blinked at Nat, blank for a split second, as if he'd forgotten what a date was. As if he'd forgotten Sam had been gone for years.

"That right? Anyone I know?"

"Goddamn, Nat, settle down. It's not a date." Teddy walked up behind us in fresh shorts and a short-sleeved button-down, buttons undone. "She's headed to a barbecue at the church. They invited all three of us, but Nat and I have plans. Right, Bug?"

"Big plans! Best plans ever!"

"You kids close that door; you're letting out the AC." June's voice cut through the living room as she walked up behind us, fastening a silver hoop earring. Her blond hair lay in an intricate braid over one thin shoulder alongside the strap of her sundress. "What are you all—oh, hi there, Pete."

It was only a split second, but the next beat turned to one of those weird pauses where everything falls silent and expands outward, engulfing the room in a momentary fear of movement. Even Nat went quiet, though it was only to draw breath before whooping again, effectively restarting the world.

"Well, come on in, get out of that god-awful heat," June said. "You all want a cold drink?"

"We were just leaving, Mom."

"We were just LEAVING," Nat sang, twirling around the room. "And we are riding RIDES, and eating ICE CREAM, and having FUN. And when we get back? SPARKLERS."

"You let her have a Popsicle, didn't you, Teddy?"

"Three Popsicles, Mama." Nat giggled.

"Well, you're your brother's problem tonight. You're sure you'll be okay with her on your own? I can take you kids myself, like usual, if you—"

"We'll be fine. She'll behave, won't you, Bug?"

"We'll be *fine*," Nat repeated, batting her eyes.

"Lord help us." June shook her head, the twin to Nat's wide grin flashing sweet on her still-young face. She caught Nat and gave her a kiss on each cheek, then stood on tiptoe to leave one on Teddy's forehead. "Drive safe, have fun, and stick together. Don't keep her out too late. And not too much ice cream, Natasha, hear?"

"Bye, June," Ben said, jumping from the porch to the ground

in a single leap. I waved and ducked out the door, turning back to wait for Teddy, who was wrapped up in arguing with Nat, listing off a slew of reasons why it was a bad idea to bring her sparklers to the festival.

"Hold on, Benny, I'll drive y'all back up." Uncle Pete passed his grocery bag to June. It was stuffed full, filled to the brim with the borderline illegal firecrackers he casually provided each year. "Brought these for the kids. Have to keep up tradition."

"Well, thank you. I'm sure they'll have as much fun as always." She smiled again, this time tight-lipped, not quite as wide. "You and Mattie coming down?"

"Mattie's got me roped into an event this evening. Might stop by after. Around ten, if that's okay."

"You're both welcome. It's always nice to see the kids enjoy themselves."

Teddy hustled Nat down the steps, boosting her and then me into the bed of Uncle Peter's truck. Ben already slouched against the rear window, fiddling with his lighter. Teddy hopped up and settled next to me, casting an aggravated glare at his sister's smug grin.

"She brought the sparklers, didn't she," I whispered, jumping at the bang of the trailer door as it swung shut behind Uncle Peter. Teddy sighed, gathered his still-damp hair into its usual ponytail.

"Of course she brought the fucking sparklers."

"Shouldn't have given her that third Popsicle."

"Ben gave her the third Popsicle, didn't he?"

"Of course he did." I collapsed into laughter as he leaned against my shoulder. His scent wove into my senses—the warm spice of cinnamon toothpaste and June's homemade clove soap. He was so close.

I caught the barb of Ben's eyes from the corner of my own, automatically fixed my gaze on him. He held it for a moment, then looked away, his lips a bitter slit. I stared at him all the way up the driveway, tried to catch his gaze as we turned on to the main road. Tried to coax a word from him with the force of my thoughts.

It didn't work. He didn't look at me again.

We arrived at the fairgrounds only to run straight into a pack of Ben and Teddy's school friends—a collection of striking, quick-witted boys and gleaming girls, wide-eyed and small-town pretty, peeking out around shiny swaths of hair. Ben's already-bright star went supernova as he fell into his element, laughing and flicking back his own long hair. The other boys hung on his words and clambered for high fives and fist bumps, talking over one another to catch his ear. The girls smirked and giggled, eyes constantly sliding to Teddy. He stood deliberately apart, his hooded looks and slow laughter designed to ensnare and taunt, suggesting everything, promising nothing. Teddy and Ben assumed their roles without hesitation, holding court with a practiced air that contradicted everything I knew about both of them.

The day wore on; the bright sky turned to dusk, then dark, then sparked bright again with fireworks. I held it together, smiled and laughed and celebrated on cue, but inside I was slipping, fighting a mental retreat from the press of the crowd, the cacophony of sounds and scents and colors, and the crushing clamor of patriotism. It was too close, Teddy's unfamiliar, unfettered world. Too heartbreaking to watch the way his eyes slid over hips and legs, met gazes with winks and smirks, avoiding my own furtive, pathetically frequent glances. Avoiding me.

Everything—all of it—was too much.

Back in the car I let my head drop to the headrest, closed my eyes through the horns and headlights of parking lot traffic. Nat crashed before we'd gone fifty feet, conquered by the whirlwind of midway games and carnival rides and fireworks. She slumped sideways against the passenger window, her frantic claim on shotgun utterly wasted. The world faded to background buzz as Ben turned from the fairgrounds onto the dark stretch of country road.

"You okay?" Teddy's voice barely made it to my ears over the rush of wind, but his hand grazed, then settled, over mine. I rolled my head his way; he was closer than I'd thought, a collection of bright eyes and beautiful shadows riding through the night beside me. A world away from the intoxicating stranger who'd hijacked his face that afternoon.

"I don't know." I sighed. "It was sort of a bad—long. It was sort of a long day. Interesting, though. I got to watch my best friend turn into a different person right in front of my eyes."

"Oh. Yeah, that was weird for you, I guess. You've never really met our friends. Not that group, anyway. Guess the festival's different without our parents there, huh?"

"'Different' is applicable, sure. Accurate, yet somehow insufficient."

"Uh . . . okay." He studied me in the slip-slide of moonlight and shade, found more than plenty to give him pause. "You *sure* you're all right?"

I let my throat close over the impending surge of words, all grudge-sour and borderline accusatory, none of which would change a thing. My face softened into neutral until my pout was a tiny smile.

My disquiet, my weariness, my bitter heart—all would have to pass unspoken. I couldn't let it be more than incidental.

"I'm good," I said, forcing the smile into my voice. "Just glad to have you back."

"I'll always come back to you, Ames."

The dash lights caught his teasing grin as he echoed my own line back to me, the humiliating slipup he'd apparently carried with him from the summer's first bonfire to that very moment. My vexation vanished, swallowed whole by a surge of hope as that confident, sexy gaze turned vulnerable. If he meant those words even a fraction as much as I had, it was good enough for me.

"Yeah, well," I whispered. "If I had my way . . . you know the rest."

His fingers threaded with mine; his grip on my hand tightened, a different kind of pressure than his usual friendly touch. The air between us sparked and crackled, thickened with anticipation as he leaned in.

"HOME SWEET HOME," Ben screamed, fishtailing onto the property. Nat woke with a triumphant yell, as pumped and alert as if she'd never been asleep.

We jerked apart. Teddy's hand left mine, drawing away as he faded into the shadows. I looked out my window and tucked my hands into my lap, where he couldn't touch them.

Uncle Peter's truck was already parked alongside June's old beater of a Chevy. They sat side by side in camping chairs around a bonfire, chatting and working through a six-pack. Aunt Mattie, unsurprisingly, appeared to have declined her invitation.

"You're here early," Ben said as we poured out of the car.

"No, you're here late, son. It's nearly ten thirty."

"It is?" He turned to me. "I thought we left the fairgrounds right after the fireworks."

"We would have if you hadn't spent half an hour bidding farewell to your entourage."

"Huh. I guess you're right. Sorry about that, June. I didn't mean to keep Nat out."

"It's no trouble, Benny," June said, shaking her head at Nat's impatient bouncing. "A late night every now and then never hurt anyone. Go on and help her light those damn sparklers before she has a conniption."

I settled on the still-warm hood of the Dodge, teeth clenched. Ben and Nat headed for the sack of explosives, but Teddy hung back, lurking around my edges like a moth. Empathy flared across his features and he stepped closer, but I stared him down, glaring and unblinking. Mad at him for making me feel.

He knew how close we'd been to a kiss; how we'd toed that last uncrossed line between our solid friendship and the looming unknown of something more, and what it meant to take things even that far. He knew. And he'd pulled away.

Ben was right. I was going to ruin everything.

"It's okay," I lied as Teddy drew breath to speak. "Don't worry about it."

"Don't do that, Amy. Don't—"

"Don't what?" Ben appeared at my elbow and slid onto the hood next to me. "What are we talking about?"

"Nothing," I said. "We were talking about nothing, Benjamin."

Ben raised his eyebrows and looked away, pretending to focus on the sky. Teddy stared at me for another beat, then stalked off, grabbed the fireworks bag, and headed toward the river. Past the bonfire and past Nat, who swirled her sparklers in blazing figure eights around her head.

"Spin me, Mr. Pete," she yelled. "Spin me up high."

Uncle Peter laughed and rose from his chair, bent down to scoop her up.

"Pete."

The single syllable from June stopped him cold. He raised his head slowly, a sudden, sad resignation stealing over his face as June shook her head, almost imperceptibly. He straightened up, leaving Nat on the ground.

"Better not, honey," he said. "These old bones can't take that sort of roughhousing anymore."

"You're too big for shoulder rides, Nat." June waved off her protests. "Finish up with those things and go help your brother."

Uncle Peter stood where he'd been left, watching Nat barrel away. She crouched on the riverbank beside Teddy, who was busy prepping a row of bottle rockets for launch. June, in turn, watched my uncle, her face a flicker of shadows in the firelight.

"I miss him," she said, drawing his eyes back to her. "It's hard this time of year."

"He always did love those sparklers, didn't he? Damn near set himself on fire, and not just the once. I miss him, too." He picked his way around the bonfire and settled back in his chair. Their heads turned to Nat and Teddy as if moved by the same neck. "Girl's just like her daddy."

"They both are. Just alike." She turned back to stare into the fire, lips tight around a sad, strained smile.

"The hell was that about?" I whispered to Ben in the ensuing stillness.

"Sam used to do that, remember? Put us all up on his shoulders with our sparklers, one by one, and spin us in circles."

"That's right." A long-buried memory tapped its way through the ice, a sensation of twirling high above the ground, dizzy and laughing and free, fingers stung by errant, snapping sparks. "I'd forgotten all about that."

"Doesn't sound like Dad and June have. The three of them grew up together, just like you, Teddy, and me. That must suck shit, huh? Being left behind."

I slipped an arm around his waist, giving him a sideways hug. We looked as one to Teddy, as if making sure he was still whole, still here. Still ours. He saw us watching and lifted his hand in a wave, then turned back to help Nat, guiding her fingers around the lighter to touch flame to fuse. The rocket sparked and launched, whizzed its way into the air, detonating in a sudden flash. The burned remains drifted back to earth and were swept away, swallowed silently by the slow, dark water.

n my head, I saw it: the way it almost went.

Teddy didn't scream—didn't cry out for help, or loose a wordless, terrified shriek on the way down. He fell, silent, and if his body made a noise when he hit the rocks, I couldn't hear it over Ben's wretched wail.

We reached the wall as the river took him, saw it pitch his crooked, broken limbs against the cliff face, until the current sucked him under. Until the sky split open, bathing us in light. He was gone before my voice ran out.

That's how it could've happened, had my cousin been even one step farther from the wall.

Ben was a blur of adrenaline and reaching hands, catching fistfuls of Teddy's shirt. He lost his grip almost instantly, rocked backward onto his ass. I tripped over him, scrambled the rest of the way on my knees as Teddy fell sideways instead of backward. He landed hard on top of the wall, and I caught his arm, pulled with all my strength, anchoring him as he clung to the rocks. Barely registered Ben beside me once more, hauling him the rest of the way to safety.

We lay in a pile at the foot of the wall; me on my back, Teddy's shoulder digging into my ribs, one of Ben's legs crushing my arm. Teddy sat up slowly, taking inventory of his injuries—bruised palms and skinned elbows, forearms scraped raw and bloody. T-shirt speckled red, too, from a long, nasty scrape across his torso. His face was wild, eyes wide, skin drenched in rain. Still breathing.

Still here.

"Fuck, that'll hurt in the morning." It came out as a laugh, twisted and torn. Profane in a way unrelated to the word itself. "Everyone okay?"

"*Okay?* I should throw you over that goddamn wall myself." Ben clambered to his knees, fingers crooked and clawing at his own flushed face. "You trying to get killed up there?"

"Nah, I'm solid. Good thing you work out, though, Benny. If Ames had grabbed me, I'd probably have dragged her right off the edge."

"You're *joking* now. *Fuck* you." And that was the swan song of Ben's coherency as he hunched forward, braced his hands against the marshy earth. Gasped for air through the wind and rain, bent double in the grip of a full-blown panic attack. Something caught in my gut like a fishhook, slammed the hatch on my heart and spun the wheel, locking down the threat of tears. Smoothed my features into tranquil brushstrokes as if there was nothing wrong at all.

God, but we were broken.

Teddy scraped himself off the grass, crawled over my prone form. He was on his knees, hands on Ben's hands, then on his shoulders, lifting him upright. Pulling him out of the mud and out of his head.

"Hey. It's okay, man. You're okay. Count it out."

He nodded along with the rise and fall of Ben's chest, counting to three over and over. Ben regained composure long enough to smack his hand away.

"Get off me. You need your fucking head checked, dude."

"It was an accident, okay? And anyway, look at that water—this is the deepest part of the river for miles in both directions. Even if I had gone in, worst case I'd swim until the shoreline starts and crawl out there."

"No—worst case, you'd die. You'd die, and then what?"

"Ben, stop," I said, putting myself in between their familiar glares—the same fury of that day last summer etched across both their faces. As if we'd returned to the cove to find that moment lying on the ground, picked it up and polished it off, carried it up the hill to start the scene again, exactly where it ended. I shook the hair out of my eyes, tried to make my voice louder than the wind. "He's okay—it's fine. Everything will be—"

"It's not fine. In fact, I'd say it's pretty damn far from fine, wouldn't you, Teddy? What do you think would happen to Amy if she lost you? What do you think would happen to me?"

"To *you*? If *I* died? Christ." He sat back on his heels. "There's not a damn thing on earth you can't somehow make all about Benny, is there?"

"It's not about *me*," Ben howled. "It's *not*, don't you get it, asshole? It's always, always been—"

His words ran into wheezes once more, but this time he didn't double over. Instead, his fist flew in a wide arc, catching Teddy on the shoulder. Instead, he scrambled up and took off, heading for the house—my cousin, bent and shattered. Rushing away from us in a gust of rain.

I didn't realize how drenched I was until I stood. My shorts were muddy, my hoodie soaked through. My hair was string plastered to my cheeks. Teddy was still on his knees, looking even more bedraggled than I felt. He stared into the distance—not at Ben's retreating form, but past the wall, over the river. His mouth worked at the corners, fixed itself into a neutral line as he climbed to his feet.

"We'd better get back."

He motioned to me to tag along, picked his way across the lawn and into the woods. I followed in a daze, ground my knuckles into my stinging eyes, wanting nothing more than to scratch away the almost—Teddy, slipping from Ben's grip. Tilting backward instead of forward. Disappearing and dying, over and over, no matter how I tried to push it down.

What if. What if.

My feet drifted off the path, stumbled over the roots of a gnarled oak tree. I pressed my shaking palms against the trunk, letting the rough, soggy bark dig into my flesh. His footsteps paused, then doubled back.

"Ames, you okay? Oh God. Don't cry."

"No, I'm not fucking 'okay.' You can't keep doing this shit like nothing matters."

"I know. I'm sorry." His arms crept around my rigid form from behind and pulled me into a soft, careful hug. I sagged against him, felt his grip tighten, like he couldn't draw me close enough. "It's fine, City Girl. I'm safe."

My sigh chased the shiver that raced across my skin. I turned in his arms to face him, reaching up to tuck a string of soggy hair behind his ear. Wondering how the world had managed to get so utterly fucked.

"You'd better be—I need you to be safe, Teddy. I need *you*."

"Amy."

My name was an anvil, flat and heavy, iron cold. His arms went slack then fell away, leaving me to stand on my own.

I hadn't meant that the way it sounded. I'd meant to reassure him, at most. Let him know that he was important, and I was here—that he didn't have to claw through hell alone. Instead I'd flayed the skin from my own facade, in a way that opened the worst of his wounds. To even acknowledge my own wishes at this point was unthinkable.

"Never mind," I said, wincing at the sting of heat across my rain-chilled face. "What I meant, was—"

"I think we need to . . . move past all that."

I blinked up at him, realization rushing in, tugging me off my feet. Dragging me beneath the surface of his careful gaze. His eyes shifted past me, drained down to a deliberate blankness. My mouth opened and closed, seeking words that never managed to form. I backed up until my shoulder blades met the tree trunk, then slipped past him and stalked away so he couldn't see my face collapse. He followed, of course, stepped into my path, his hands on my shoulders stilling my feet.

"Ames, wait. You're my best friend. That's the only thing that matters anymore." He grimaced around the words, squeezed his eyes shut and breathed through a surge of grief. "You're all I have. If we try for more and it falls apart, or if Ben blows up again—didn't you hear what he said up there? That goes all the way around the circle. I can't lose you guys, not now. You can't ask me to take that chance."

"I *wasn't* asking you to." I fixed my gaze on his, determined to be what he needed. To bleed, if I had to, as long as we were okay. "It came out wrong, is all, and I just—"

"It doesn't matter. I won't risk it."

Silence pulled between us, heavy and long, broken by the steady spatter of rain on leaves. A damp wind stirred the branches overhead, lifted wisps of his hair, stung my nose with the sharp, green bite of mangled grass. We'd all but buried what we'd had. My eyes burned at the thought of sifting through the broken bits, scavenging a future from the wreck of what we'd become.

"So there's *no* chance, ever," I said, resenting the flat, hollow thud that was my voice. Hating every word that left my mouth. "Even after everything that happened before."

. A question that wasn't a question. It flexed its claws and hooked in, refusing to pass unanswered. A bitter laugh escaped him, scattered at our feet like broken glass.

"My sister was alive before."

And that was it, really—the starting point, for the rest of forever. That irreversible shift of the world. How selfish was I, to let even an accidental flutter in my heart manifest in real time? How pitiful, to ask anything of him, or think for a second I was more than a blur in his periphery.

A raindrop fell from his nose, landed on my lips, and I drew back, let the storm blow into the space between us. He gave my shoulder a final, perfunctory squeeze as he brushed past me, resuming his trek downhill. It should've been easy enough to retreat—to sever myself from that voice and that heart, and the way it never stopped working its way into mine. It should've been so simple to just keep breathing.

"If you don't want me, I'm not about to beg," I burst out, throwing the last fuck I had to give straight into the blustering wind. "I just need to know—is this really how it is now, Teddy?"

My words stopped him. I didn't turn around but saw him anyway: saw his shoulders tense and square; saw his head drop and his hands clench into fists. I steeled myself, then pivoted, took a step toward him as he turned back, his face a puzzle of regret and affection, pain and defeat. The edge of the universe lay sharp beneath my toes; one misplaced step or careless word would send us both hurtling over it, falling away from each other into nothing.

If he let me, I knew I could catch him. If he reached for me, I'd never, ever let him go.

"I don't know how it is," he finally said, voice breaking. Sweeping me over that edge as it dropped to a mutter. "Unfortunately, falling short of expectations is sort of my thing."

I watched him leave me, took in the contrast of his bare arms against the soft, worn white of his shirt; the wet strands of dark hair, the way they clung to his work-hardened shoulders. Not one of the banal, well-heeled boys at school would ever look like that. No gilt-edged prodigy would ever map his life by the lines of his body, or tear open my world with a glance.

I stayed where I was and listened to him walk away, every step a boot print on my own crumbling heart.

CHAPTER 23

SUMMER 2019

was eleven years old when everything changed.

It was a day too much like the one on the cliffs: the morning's blue skies blotted out by sudden clouds; sunshine lost to rain; wind that swept in from nowhere, catching us knee-deep in a quest for treasure—chunks of quartz, shards of shiny pyrite, maybe even a fossil—nestled in the riverbed beneath our toes. Treasure for Ben, sick in bed with a summer cold.

After an hour of searching, Teddy had hit the jackpot—a palm-size geode, split clean down the middle. He'd dug it out of the mud, placed it reverently in my cupped hands. Marveled at our luck as we watched the sun wink off its jagged, glittering innards.

"He'll love it."

I don't remember who said it. Maybe no one did—maybe it was no more than a whisper in my head, or an unspoken smile between us. I do know it was the last thought that crossed my mind before lightning lit the world.

Thunder growled at our heels as we made for the shore, tugged on our shoes, fled the cove hand in hand. We raced the darkening clouds, taking the faster downhill path to Teddy's place. The geode slipped from my grasp along the way.

We reached the trailer as the first drops fell, only to have our hopes dashed by a locked door and empty driveway. The air crackled, the sky cracked, and Teddy dragged me across the lawn to the laundry shed, slipped inside behind me, and slammed the door on a whoosh of rain. The power was out, or maybe only the bulb, but either way the shed was dark and cramped, stuffy with the smell of ozone and mud and river and soap. I was jumping at every sound, shivering with nervous energy.

But I was okay. I had my friend.

I heard him breathing, sensed his smile; felt that smile like the tug of a tide carrying me to a place beyond fear as his fingers tightened carefully around mine. We sat close together, hands linked, hearts light. We didn't let go for a very long time.

We never did find Ben's geode.

That was our beginning: reaching for each other beneath a broken sky. Never thinking to look for anyone else.

As if those kids we'd been had a clue of the clusterfuck in store.

I'd meant it when I said I wouldn't beg. I'd slogged my way back to Grandma's, soggy but dry-eyed, determined to narrow my focus. I had one job: to be the friend he needed while he coped with his sister's death, and so that was what I'd do. I'd sort through facts and dig up clues. I'd listen, even when he struggled for words. I'd shut the fuck up and help him go on in the wake of his loss. Lamentation was a waste of time.

Still, it was absurd, the way we clawed at normalcy. Failed, time and again, to return to what we'd been.

His plan to protect our friendship by refusing any possibility of more had, thus voiced, produced ass-backward results. We sat on opposite sides of everything, eyes meeting and skittering away. I interjected sounds into the ether, answered words with other, impersonal words. Detached from him and from myself, and if he saw my buried heart surface in the days that followed—if he felt its weight in my too-brief glances, or caught it peeking from the tension in my neck—he was kind enough to look away. We struggled forward together, ever wary of my cousin's too-sharp gaze.

Not that Ben gave an actual damn. Of course he didn't. He'd blown off his own breakdown in typical fashion, throwing himself headlong into the investigation. He spent all his spare hours online at the library, searching statewide crime reports, compiling lists of possible suspects. I was his reluctant secretary, transcribing his ramblings verbatim in the spiral notebook.

"The problem," he said one morning from his sprawl on the poolside chaise, "is very simple. The answer lies not in what we know, but in what we don't."

My pen drifted to a stop. He deigned to throw me a sideways glance, lips pursed, eyes bright over the rims of his sunglasses.

"Everything okay, Amy?"

"If this is you at your best, I'm taking a break. It's way too hot for statements that asinine."

"I know," he said, sighing. "My game is off. I could use a dip, but—"

"—he needs his space."

"Yeah."

I reached across the gap between our chairs, closed my fingers over his balled fist. Turned my gaze to follow his. Watched Teddy swim the length of the pool, push off the wall and continue his relentless, circular path over and over, only surfacing to gasp for breath.

"Ben. You're doing all you can."

"It's not enough. It won't be enough until he can sleep again."

The buzz of Ben's phone roused us both. He squinted at the caller ID, and gave an impatient huff. Tapped the voice-to-text button and yelled into the mic.

"He doesn't have one. Try subtlety; this is getting sad AF J/K LOL." He hit send. "Not kidding, actually. Write *this* down, Ames— as soon as the case is wrapped, I'm finding whoever gave this girl my number, and beating the shit out of them."

"How the hell are you texting? This property is a goddamn cellular black hole."

"Down at Grandma's, yeah, but I get a signal all over the hill. Hey, T." He snapped his fingers at Teddy, who'd emerged in the shallow end. "What should I tell Mia? She wants your number. And your dick, apparently."

"Tell her I don't have a cell. It's not even a lie."

"I did. Denial is a bitch." He thumbed the screen, chuckled at the reply. "I can close the deal for you right now, if you're down—all you need to do is sit tight."

"Know what, Benny? Thanks, but no thanks." Teddy hauled himself out of the pool and dripped his way across the flagstone patio, stretched out on the chaise next to mine. Slung a forearm over his eyes to block the sun. "There's enough going on right now without chick drama."

"Truer fucking words. I'll send her a rain check." His phone buzzed; he squinted at it, pushed himself off the chaise, and headed for the house. "Be right back, you guys. She is *not* letting up."

The world was livid, a midsummer blare of sunlight, far-off bird-calls, and the dark seethe of my breath. It was one thing to respect his emotional needs, but to sit silently by and watch him regress to his allegedly former fuckboy ways? Neutrality was all well and good until it was impossible.

"You can have her over, you know," I grumbled at his ennui. "Don't let me stop you."

"You're not stopping me," he said, still blinded by his arm. "If I wanted to, I would."

"I don't know *what* you'd do. Don't really care. As long as there's no 'chick drama,' right?" I shook my head, disdain sparring with humiliation as I tossed Ben's notebook to the foot of my chaise and shifted my way to sitting, winced as my feet touched the hot patio. Pretended to scan the ground for my sandals so I didn't have to look at him. "Please."

"Amy." He sighed and sat up, swung his legs over the edge so we were knee-to-knee. His hand crept over to mine, fingertips grazing my knuckles.

It was the first time we'd touched since the day he walked away. His hands no longer landed softly on my shoulders and waist or sought mine between the front and back seats of the car. My fingers no longer absently combed through his hair, or impulsively twirled it into braids. We laughed too little; paused too long between bursts of benign words that shaved away the corners of his smile, siphoned another drop of light from his skies—a sip here, a mouthful there. Draining him hollow, bit by bit.

There was so little left of who he'd been, and not enough of me to compensate. Going back was hardly an option, *that* was perfectly fucking clear, but what was there left to salvage if our roots had gone to dust? This careful trek around the Nat-shaped hole in our summer—was it the first of countless tiny stitches that could let us heal? Or the breaking point of everything we'd been?

What had happened to us?

"This sucks," he finally said. "I thought it would be easier, you know—to cut each other off. But it's making things worse. I need us to be okay. I need *us*, Amy, no matter what. But there's a lot to unpack, you know?"

"I know. I have . . . a few things to unpack too." My cheeks flared at the memory of last winter's unanswered messages, and the way they'd morphed from tears to rage to delicate musician hands. I met his questioning gaze with defiance, daring him, of all people, to pass judgment. "It's complicated."

"Well, exactly," he said, completely missing everything I hadn't said. "We should talk—*really* talk. Get everything out and see where it goes."

"Now?"

"Might as well, right? Find the same page, try to move forward. At least try to move closer back to *normal*."

Back to normal. Christ. I rubbed my damp palms on my knees, aching to tiptoe quietly past this step of the moving forward thing. But he'd said the words—he'd chosen this. I'd told myself I'd follow his lead, and if he was determined to unpack our shit poolside, so be it. I had a whole carousel of baggage to lay out on this particular chaise longue.

"Okay," I began, forcing my face into its vaguest shade of blank. "When we left off last summer, everything was a mess. The fight, the

Ben situation—but after what you said, I thought at least *we'd* make it, right? You and me—we'd be okay. But I went home, and that was it. You totally cut me off."

"I know," he said. "I know, and I'm sorry. I—there's no good reason, really. You were just gone again, like every year. Back in your art scene, and your social life—this whole huge world I can never be part of. I couldn't even explain it—every time I tried, it just looked stupid as fuck all typed out. I always ended up deleting it, thinking I'd deal with it when I found the right words. But I never did."

"But you never did. And I *tried* to include you—I wrote to you for weeks. I told you about my gallery showing, my new instructor, and it was like I was fucking talking to myself. You didn't *want* to be part of my life. And then I met a guy who did, and—"

"You—*what*?" I might as well have kicked him off the chaise. Had it been possible he might have rocketed straight up into the sky. "You *met a guy*? Wow. Fucking wow, Amy." He sat back and shook his head, raked me with a glare that left my body edged in frost. "So much for promises, huh? So much for not forgetting everything we said."

"Okay, well, another thing I haven't forgotten is the extended lapse into silence on your end. Or the six thousand pathetic, needy messages I sent—the last of which, if I recall, was basically an ultimatum to reply or we were done. So no, *I* didn't forget. Did *you*?"

"It was complicated on my end too, okay?" He caught himself right before his words became a yell, braced his palms against his knees, as if physically holding himself in place. "Completely fucked in ways you won't ever understand. And that you went ahead and hooked up with some DC pretty boy while I was back here dealing with it is even more fucked."

"Oh, was it? More than ghosting me completely when I was literally begging you to answer me? You don't get to play victim now, not when you left me on read since September."

"What's his name?"

"Why do you care?" I challenged, a flare of resentment warming my cheeks. "You sure didn't give a fuck at the time, or we wouldn't even be having this conversation."

"No, tell me. Is it Chad? Please tell me it's Chad. Or Weatherby. Stanford—Stanford Junior. Stanford the Third. No, wait—Preston." His eyes widened at my startled blink. "Holy shit, *is* it Preston?"

"It actually is. Last name, none of your goddamn business." Like I was giving him that opening. He'd be online in no time, stalking the social media of everyone I'd ever met. Gleefully commandeering one of Ben's many troll accounts and shit-posting into oblivion at a boy who didn't know he existed. How the hell had he even guessed that name?

"Oh my *God*. Seriously, Ames? Preston. *Wow.* Trust fund?" His laugh was short and harsh; his eyes spit bitter sparks at my silent, grudging nod. "Trust fund. Of course. Eighteen-karat dick? Or was it new-money gold-plate?"

"*I* wouldn't know," I huffed. "Not that it's your business. Besides, for you? To call *me* out for seeing someone else? That takes balls for days, Teddy."

"Yeah, whatever. I bet he went over like gangbusters at home, huh? She must have been like a pig in shit, seeing you level up like that. One step closer to being her perfect little—"

"Don't," I snarled. "Don't you fucking dare."

I saw it in his eyes—the spark of comprehension. The wary

blink as the memory of what had happened last time he'd made that comparison cut through his impulsive anger. He swallowed the rest of his words and sat back, mouth forming something between a sneer and a pout—the same sulky face he'd made as a kid when things didn't go his way. The same face we still saw on Ben every other day, in fact.

It was enough to make me grind my teeth to dust. For all Teddy had tried to play it cool, insisting we needed to move on after disappearing from my life for so many months, he himself hadn't moved on from one damn bit of it. What a fucking liar.

I turned away from his thundercloud stare, looked up in time to catch Ben at the sliding door. He didn't bother closing it after him, just strode toward us on a blast of wasted AC.

"Get dressed, guys. We have to go see about a thing."

Teddy sighed, dropped his face into his waiting hand.

"Dude, if this 'thing' involves you trying to get me laid, I swear to God—"

"Nah, I shut that down. You should get back out there at some point, though—I heard it's been a long dry spell." He tossed his phone on the bar and scooped his T-shirt up from where it lay on the flagstones. "For real, though, we have to hurry—I just now set in motion a sequence of events that could take our investigation to the next level."

"I can't. I have work in an hour."

"What? Come on, man, this is big. Work'll wait."

"Bills won't, Benny."

Ben's side-eye was sullen, his standard response to an encounter with the word *no*. Teddy gave it right back, though, matching his glare from behind a stringy fall of hair. I ignored them both and stood, pulled my cutoffs over my bikini bottoms. Swiped a finger beneath each eye. Bit down hard on the edge of my lower lip.

"Fine," Ben pouted. "But Amy and I are going. I'll drop you off at yours."

The drive down was a silent howl of stifled glares and unsaid words, crowding and overlapping with every breath until we reached the trailer. I climbed over the console from the back to the passenger seat, pulled the door closed as soon as Teddy was clear. His eyes lit for a split second as they met mine, blinked their way back to neutral as he turned and jogged across the lawn, tugging his shirt off and chucking it in the laundry shed. I took in his shoulders, the curve of his calves, the suntanned planes of his back. Rubbed a hand over my stinging eyes as he climbed the steps of his trailer and disappeared inside. The door had barely shut behind him before I turned on Ben.

"Seriously? 'You should get back out there'? What the actual hell is wrong with you?"

"You've been holding that one in this whole time, huh? Whatever. The boy needs a distraction." He narrowed his eyes at my glare. "You aren't still planning to hit that, are you? Won't want to piss off your prodigy."

"What the fuck?" My eyes bugged, only enhancing his already-gleeful smirk. "How do you even know about him?"

"Are you kidding me? Your mom called Grandma the second you guys met. Grandma told my mom, and it was all they talked about for like a month. They practically shat themselves with glee—a *pianist*. How *refined*." He slid an evil grin my way, chuckling at the furious set of my face. "And since Teddy looks like someone just pissed in his protein shake, I take it he's been informed. I'd have told him myself, but—well, you know. The fight and all."

"Jesus. Drive away, Benjamin. Just go."

Ben peeled out of his three-point turn in a spray of gravel, disturbing the stack of true-crime novels cluttering the floorboard. I grabbed the thickest and skimmed the pages, focused on the photos of exhumed bones and pooled blood, grainy mug shots and young, smiling victims—all marginally preferable to the sight of my cousin's smug profile.

"Thumb through those, will you?" he said. "Dog-ear anything related to child murder."

"Yeah, no thanks. Why are you reading this garbage?"

"To get in the killer's head." Ben's smirk faded into a sigh as we turned past the mailboxes and made our way to the main road. "I'm at a disadvantage now because I'm not a fucking psychopath, but the more I understand about the type of person who'd drown a kid, the better chance I'll have of sniffing him out on a local level."

"Christ, Ben. You'll lose your mind dwelling on all this."

"Like I'm not halfway there already. You should see the stuff I found on personality disorders—holy fuck, does it read like a Langston family reunion."

"I can only imagine. My mom could inspire a whole trilogy just on her own."

"Throw in mine, and you have a five-season Netflix series, bare minimum. Source material for days before you even scratch the surface."

"You win," I said, wincing at memories I'd long ago buried to rot—my cousin's red-rimmed eyes and fading sniffles; fresh, pink strap welts across thighs too small to run away. The blotch of hand-prints on summer-flushed cheeks. "Of course, I'm pretty sure mine broke my brain, but that's one of those invisible afflictions."

"What's wrong with your brain?" He took his eyes off the road a second too long, startled back to attention at the horn blast of a passing car. "Loaded question, I know."

"I'm not sure, really—Mom's always going on about her sacrifices, the things she's given up for my future, but in a way that makes it shitty. Like that's all I am to her—an investment. So when she starts in on me, I fade out. She's still there, but everything slips away except my work. But fuck her, you know? My art is mine no matter what she does." I stared out the window at the neat black fences, the swoops of perfect bluegrass sprinkled with horses. "It's kind of nice, actually. By this point, I can do it without trying whenever I need to get away."

"That's fucked up, Amy."

"Whatever. My instructor digs it. Says he admires my mother's involvement in my process, the way she pushes me to exceed my potential. Says it's a sign of love."

A memory surfaced unexpectedly at the word, sending an ache through my chest—my mother in the foyer, eyes brimming with anger and fear, overflowing with love of a softer sort. I opened his glove box and sifted through the clutter of orange pharmacy bottles, half-empty cigarette boxes, loose cash, and rolling papers. Not a Kleenex in sight, of course. Ben swatted my hand away, head swiveling back and forth between the road and my pinched face as he plucked a pack of gum from the mess and offered me a piece.

"Where's Uncle Jake during all this bullshit?"

"Oh, he's gone almost all the time now." I shoved the gum in my mouth, wincing at the first overwhelming burst of spearmint. "Up in Manhattan at least two weeks a month, sometimes more. Pretty sure he's only sticking around at this point for their work. And because she'd clean him out."

"And because of you, right? Right, Ames?"

"Probably not."

Ben went quiet at that. Our silence filled the car, mixing with the warm waft of wildflowers and mown hay. His jaw clenched and strained in sync with the flex of his fingers on the wheel.

"Well, that sucks," he finally said, "but I can't say it doesn't explain a lot." He mimed slitting his own throat. "Genetics, man. No escape."

"Not necessarily. Kids turn out different from their parents all the time. Grandma's awesome, yet here we are."

"Good point. June too—she grew up in this boring, perfectly normal, middle-class Irish-Catholic family. Her folks are both dead now, but they disowned her when she moved in with Sam and got knocked up, and now she goes home to the trailer after jerking off a rattlesnake, or whatever they do out at that backwoods cult. *Her* kids are nothing like her either."

"Teddy's a miniature Sam, though. Genetics got him, but he caught a lucky break. As for Nat—" I swallowed that unanswerable thought, stared out the window at the iron-bright slice of sky. "Well. Who knows."

"Yeah, but Sam's parents were assholes too. They shunned him for years. Last I heard they moved down to Tennessee after Sam died, and no one's heard from them since—not even when Nat went missing."

"So Teddy *really* dodged one, is what you're saying. You and I, however, are basically screwed."

"Whatever. I still can't believe your mom is actually somewhat on par with mine. It's like I don't know what's real anymore."

"Yeah, well, this morning I smudged the shit out of my allegedly smudge-proof eyeliner. The world is lies on top of lies."

You guys are nothing but chickenshit," I yelled down at them, leaning over the rotten planks. "It's not even that high."

"Yeah, it's not too high when you're like, seven feet tall, Ames," Ben said. "If you fall, you can just reach one of those pogo stick legs out. It'll be, like, a two-inch drop."

Both boys cackled at that, squinting up at me through the sunlit branches. Ben stood beneath me by the ladder, compulsively jiggling one of the rungs, yet making no move to climb his ass up it to join me. On second thought, adding his weight to the platform would probably send us both crashing down in a hail of splinters. The house portion of the old tree house had fallen prey to the boys' antics long ago, and what was left was barely big enough to hold me, my satchel, and my sketchbook.

I studied them from my bird's-eye view, putting the cove to paper from a new perspective. Nat crouched at the shoreline just out of earshot, scooping water and dirt into her plastic bucket. Teddy wasn't even trying to care about the tree house. He slouched against a nearby tree, shirtless, hair half covering his face as he fiddled absently with his lighter. A barely smoked cigarette, bummed from Ben, hung loose between his fingers. My sketchbook seethed with the crook of his thumb, the curve of his lip, the shadows of his downcast eyes. The smooth jut of his hip bone, softened and blurred by the wish of my fingertips.

"What do you guys know about Sweden?" he asked out of nowhere, tapping ashes against the tree trunk.

"It gets very cold," Ben mused. "Lots of blonds, many of whom are lucky enough to look like me. Good pancakes. Viking shit. Ikea. Skarsgårds. I don't know, dude; it's Sweden. Why are you even asking?"

"Saw an article about Scandinavian hiking tours in one of Mom's travel magazines. It looks nice. Wouldn't mind checking it out at some point. Visit Stockholm, head over to Norway, see some fjords. Stuff like that."

"I'm in," I said. "Planning starts now if you want company. You can drop me off in Paris on your way back."

"Hell yes. What say you, Ben?" Teddy took a final puff on the cigarette and ground it out, folding it into a foil gum wrapper and tucking it into his pocket. "We've got to get you out of this town one way or another, right?"

"Nah, it's not so bad here." Ben's words caught on the contradictory twitch of his jaw. "I might take a road trip or a gap year, hike the Appalachian Trail or whatever the kids are doing these days. Beyond that, what's the point? Everything I care about is here."

"What's the *point*?" Teddy pushed himself off the tree, spreading his arms. "All your money, and you choose *this*? How can you not want more? How can you not want to see everything there is to see?"

"That's a statistical impossibility, dude."

"Don't be an asshole. What about seeking your destiny? Finding your place, man, what about that? Finding your people?"

"You *are* my people."

His quiet words cut the air, tugging the grin from Teddy's face. The sun shifted through the branches, stung the backs of my legs. Wrapped us in a gust of muggy wind that lifted the hair from my temples as the look between the boys stretched into a dark, heavy silence. The pencil slipped from my fingers, dropping from tree to ground as Teddy finally spoke.

"Benny, you're like my brother. But if you stick around this dump just to watch me bust rocks at your dad's quarry and mow your grandma's lawn to save up for Natasha's fucking school supplies, I might have to ditch our friendship for your own good."

"Well, that's not very neighborly of you." Ben's light tone belied the hesitance in his eyes, the soft, guarded upturn of his lips. "Sounds like I wouldn't be missing out on much when you put it that way."

"You really wouldn't be. You won't find what you need here, man."

"You sure about that, Teddy?"

The words slid out low and earnest, almost desperate. Teddy watched him with wary eyes, mouth parting on the verge of a plea. Blinked at him, then past him, focused on the space between my cousin and the rest of the world.

"Yeah, I am, actually. Trust me."

"Bear!" Nat's happy shriek dispelled the building pressure, drawing our attention to the riverbank. She clutched a bizarre brown creature in both hands, holding it aloft as it waved its spiny, kicking legs in the air. "Amy, Benny, come here! Look what I found!"

"What the fuck is that thing?" Teddy kicked his shoes off and jogged toward the water. I swung down from the tree house in one clumsy swoop, landing next to Ben, who stood where he'd been left, mouth tight, gaze fixed ahead on nothing.

"You okay?"

"He's never going to Sweden, Ames. You know that, right?"

"Well, not now, of course. But—"

"Probably not ever. Can't decide whether it's crueler to clue him in or let him keep his hopes up."

"Don't be like that. If Teddy wants to go to Sweden, he'll find a way. Who knows, maybe he'll forget all about it in a couple weeks. Maybe he'll see an article on Saskatchewan or something."

"Nah, he tends to fixate. He might get distracted once in a while, but he always holds out for that one big dream, no matter how far-fetched." We both turned to look at Teddy, watched him push his hair behind his ears and beckon to us before crouching to inspect Nat's find. "One of the many traits he and I have in common."

"Benny? Is everything okay?"

"Hm? Oh. Yeah. Life is damn near perfect, Ames. Go on." He motioned to the water. "He's waiting for you."

I stared at his unmoving profile for a moment, then took off fast, the weird, desperate tension snapping at my heels. I blew through the shallows, past Teddy and Nat, momentum carrying me hip deep before I dove under, let the river swallow me in its green embrace. It was safer under there, where I didn't have to decipher the dulling edge of Ben's smile.

"Hey. Hey!" Teddy's voice greeted me with barely restrained panic when I broke the surface. Ever since that day Nat went under, he'd kept a paranoid eye on me, on constant watch even though I could swim circles around him. "Amy, come on. Come back."

"I'm fine." I waded over to him, picking at my sodden clothes. "This is what normal people do in rivers, you know—swimming, not standing around knee-deep or screwing with innocent crayfish."

"Oh, you want to swim, do you? I'll show you swimming, City Girl."

I shrieked as he scooped me up and spun me around, flipping me over his arm and into the current. Nat chucked the crayfish and screamed with laughter as I surfaced, flinging water from her bucket at Teddy's defenseless back.

"Real Kentucky-style swimmin' hole swimmin'," he howled, his drawl contorted and twanged to a horrible, fake caricature. "This here's why ol' Benny won't leave River Run—this here fine Kentucky swimmin' hole. You won't find swimmin' holes like this in Norway, you bet yer sweet ass. Nothin' but fjords and shit up in Norway, or so I heard tell."

"Fjords and shit," parroted Nat. "What's a fjord, Bear?"

Still gasping, exhilarated, breathless with laughter, I sent an armful of water his way, then another. He kicked a splash into my face and one of my legs swung out, an ankle hooking accidentally around Nat's, toppling her backward. I saw her arms flail, saw her hands fly up to cover her ears in a flash of panic. I reached out, grabbed her elbow before she went under. Teddy was there in an instant, catching her other arm, steadying her.

"I've got you, Little Bug," I said, brushing a wet string of hair off her forehead. She blinked at me, her eyes a contradiction of gratitude, fear, and bashful apology.

"Up you go." Teddy set Nat on her feet and plopped back next to me as she took off for shore. His shoulder bumped against mine and our eyes hooked, sending a jolt straight to my heart. I reached up to pluck a blade of river grass from his hair, twirling the strand around my finger.

"You okay, Teddy?"

"I am now."

His smile crept over me slowly, saying all manner of new things. My hand went rogue, dropped from his hair to his shoulder before I could think, smoothing across the bare skin. He reached out to tuck my hair behind my ear, erasing my remaining doubt and denial as his fingers continued their slow, deliberate path down my neck.

I was in it, all right, whatever "it" was. There was nothing Ben or my mother or anyone else could say to undo what we'd already begun.

We were too close, too dangerous. I had to turn away. I made a show of searching for Ben, found him still tucked in the shadows beneath the tree, that same tiny smile on his face—an alien look, somehow all wrong. I waved, but he shifted his focus just over my shoulder, as if he'd been looking at the far bank all along.

As if he hadn't been watching us at all.

SUMMER 2019

T he old Franklin place was a weary Victorian, a haphazard jumble of missing pieces and rotten angles. The owner was long dead; his son lived out of state and had clearly forgotten to add "give a rat's ass about Dad's old place" to his agenda. The porch steps were gone, the boarded windows plastered with official notices—condemnation, trespassing, zoning.

But the place was half a mile off the main road. No one was around to enforce any kind of sign.

Ben parked around back, plucked his messenger bag from the Mustang's trunk, and marched through the patches of grass and gravel to the front driveway. We climbed onto the porch and creaked carefully across the hole-riddled floorboards to the looming mass of the front door. I had an insane urge to knock, alert whatever haunts held up the walls, send spiders scattering away from the doorframes before I walked beneath them.

"How is this place remotely linked to our purposes?"

"All will be revealed, Ames. Stand back."

"Oh Christ. Where did you get a crowbar, and what the hell are you doing with it?"

"Opening the door—I'm not about to wait out here in this heat. Figured I'll pop the pins out of the hinges, and we can get in that way."

"The hinges are on the inside, Ben."

He opened his mouth, then closed it again, stared hard at the door where the hinges weren't.

"Well. Shit. Now what?"

I pushed past him, ascertaining after approximately two seconds that the knob was long gone, along with the lock and latch. I put my shoulder against the door and leaned hard, inching it past the jamb, until it swung open in a puff of dust and mold spores.

Ben stormed past me and crouched in a slice of light near the far wall, brandishing a middle finger at my smirk as he unloaded his MacBook, the spiral notebook, and a three-ring binder from his bag. I felt a wave of fresh annoyance at the sight of his cowlick, the glimpse of pale scalp at the center practically glowing in what little sunlight filtered through the boarded-up windows.

"What happened to analog only?"

"I might need you to take notes faster than usual, depending on how this goes," he answered vaguely. "We can print a hard copy at the library, then delete it before heading home. I have a full charge. It should be enough for what we need."

"Awesome," I muttered, turning away from him. Taking in our surroundings, as my eyes adjusted to the dimness.

The main room was a large, open space, wallpapered in moldy, blue-flowered silk. To the left was a staircase flanked by a pair of doors. The room was empty apart from a stained mattress tossed in one corner. A cracked camping lantern and a gnawed-up roll of toilet paper sat on the wooden milk crate upturned beside it.

"Um, Ben? You don't, like, live here on the side or something, do you?"

The words had barely left my mouth when a floorboard creaked somewhere above us. I closed my hand around his sleeve as he cocked his head, listening, eyes on the ceiling.

"It's probably just the house settling," he said. "I think it'll be okay." Another creak, a short scuffle, a thump. Blood rushed onto my tongue as I bit through my own lip. "Okay, screw this. Let's go."

We didn't stop or look back at the bang of a door behind us, or the sound of feet on gravel—we ran hard until we were at least four trees deep in the thicket, backs to the trunk of a giant maple, facing away from the house.

"Ben," I squeaked, "we need to get out of here right now."

"We can't go now—we'd have to cut back across the property and past the house to the car. Whoever the hell is out there could be lying in wait."

"For all we know he's about to lean around from the other side of this tree."

"Don't say shit like that." He clutched at his hair, seethed out a string of short, shaky gasps. "This is why we should've brought Teddy. He's way better in an emergency."

"You'd better hold it together, Benjamin. What about the path back to our property?"

"On the other side, right next to the car. Shit. Amy, I'm sorry. I had no idea someone was squatting in there, or I'd have never—" We both jumped at the crunch of approaching tires. Ben peeked around the tree, then relaxed and stood, smoothing down the wreck of his hair. "Oh, thank Christ. He's here."

"Who's here?" I leaned around him in time to see Darrow climbing out of his squad car. "What the hell is going on?"

He shook off my hand and strode toward the yard, apparently no longer concerned by whoever was creaking around in the house.

"Good afternoon, Officer Darrow. You made it."

Darrow didn't whirl around so much as leap in a half circle, eyes wild and wily. He smacked a hand on the hood of his cruiser when he saw us.

"Goddamn it, son, don't do that! I might have pulled my gun on you. Go on home; you kids shouldn't be out here."

"I can be here any time I want. My father owns this place."

"Seriously?" I glared at his nonchalant profile. "Since when?"

Ben shrugged. "A year, maybe? It's my graduation present. After renovations, of course."

"You're getting a *house* for graduation? Jesus, Ben."

"Not a shabby deal," Darrow said, "but that doesn't explain why you're hanging around out here. I got a call, said someone was trespassing, and I—"

"Yeah, that was me," Ben drawled. "And it's funny because I made that part up to get you out here, but it turns out someone might actually be in the house right this second. Ironic, huh? Also, I left my stuff in there, so if you don't mind."

"You made it up? Are you trying to make me start drinking again?"

"Not intentionally, but you're welcome. I wanted to meet someplace private to discuss the investigation. The Natasha Fox investigation, specifically."

"I know which damn investigation you mean. Why are you dragging me out to your daddy's condemned house instead of calling the station and speaking to me like anyone else under God's blue canopy would do?"

"Oh, so calling the station *is* an actual option?" Ben's sneer slit the air between them. "Because every single message I've left you in the past week has mysteriously failed to net a return call. I'm optimistic enough to believe they never made it to your desk, and not assume you're simply neglecting to answer them."

"I *haven't* gotten any messages from you, as a matter of fact," Darrow said, drawing a weary hand across his eyes. "To which officers have you spoken?"

"Okay," I said, an invisible, irritated third wheel. "I know your phone messages are thrilling and important, Ben, but we have a more pressing issue at hand. Sir, could you maybe—"

"Hold up, missy," Darrow muttered, distracted, fishing a pen out his shirt pocket. "I'll get to you in a minute."

"Yeah, *missy*," Ben echoed, grinning at the furious clench of my jaw. "Calm your shit. Let a man get a word in."

"'Missy'? Seriously? *You* dragged *me* out here to your little secret meeting, Benjamin. If I'm in the way, I can head out right now and let you handle it your own damn self."

"Now, now, settle down. She likes to get right to the point, huh?" Darrow shifted his attention to Ben, pen poised over his notepad. I aimed both middle fingers at Darrow's back, making sure my cousin got a nice, clear view of his own. "So, you say there's someone in the house, son?"

"We heard noises upstairs. It sounded like someone ran out after us, but we didn't see anyone. Might still be inside."

"All right, I'll check it out. You kids wait here. Don't do anything stupid like follow me."

Darrow went into cop mode, sweeping the grounds and then

the house, handily flushing a fat raccoon out the front door. It barely glanced at us as it scrabbled across the porch, leaped into the yard, and disappeared into the woods. Darrow reappeared a moment later, dusty but nonchalant, not even pissed when he saw us sitting on the hood of his cruiser.

"No one here—apart from an abundance of brown recluse spiders."

"But we heard someone," I protested. "There were footsteps right above our heads—and not raccoon footsteps, either."

"Well, sometimes the ears play tricks, especially in older houses. Could've been a transient, but my best guess is that critter, paired with a healthy imagination."

"Thank you for taking care of that for us, sir," Ben said. "Now, about the investigation. I wanted to share my own findings, if you'd like to have a look."

Darrow, to his credit, didn't laugh at Ben or tell him to run on home to his mama. He took the binder and notebook and joined us on the hood, flipping through the maps and notes.

"You've clearly done your homework, son," he said. "Rest assured, I haven't been entirely idle myself. I'm going through the official databases on my own time, some online, and then in the library, looking at the newspapers, the old microfiche. It seems like—"

"What's microfiche?" I butted in. "And why newspapers? Wouldn't all that be archived online?" Of course this tiny, shitty town would be decades behind modern technology. I shouldn't even have asked.

"Not necessarily." Ben's brow furrowed as he slid a glance my way. "Smaller, local papers—not all of them bother posting every single back issue, especially the really old stuff. Stuff that happened a long time ago, before there was an 'online.'"

"Why is that relevant?"

"Because, Ames. If there's a precedent to all this, something that happened a long time ago that looks a little too close to what happened to Nat could indicate a pattern. Which means it might be happening again."

Darrow opened his mouth, and as soon as he did, I wished he would close it, forget all the words he'd planned to say, forget we'd ever asked him to help us with this awful, morbid quest.

The fear rushed in like it had never left, and I squeezed my eyes closed as tight as they would shut.

But not before I saw him nod.

CHAPTER 26

SUMMER 2019

While Teddy guided the mower in never-ending rows through Grandma's yard, Ben and I hunkered down in my room, shuffling through his notes and maps, intermittently discussing the details of Darrow's research and bitching about the lack of Wi-Fi. We'd stuffed everything under the bed when we heard the mower shut down, both guilty and glad for the opportunity to leave it be. June had left at dawn for an all-day church event, which meant Teddy would build a fire in their pit whether Ben and I showed up or not—as if we'd pass up the promise of an unsupervised evening, even in the midst of our weird, unspoken half truce. More than that, the anticipation of a bonfire sparked a strange sense of normalcy, a familiarity we hadn't experienced since my return. A chance to recapture a sliver of what we'd lost.

The Fourth of July had passed without mention, and without a sign of Teddy. Even Ben had known better, for once, than to barge onto the property and make demands. We also hadn't been to the cove all summer, apart from scurrying through it in the pouring rain—not since we'd found Nat's things in a neat pile beneath the tree. So when Teddy led the way into the woods, Ben and I hesitated, balking at the idea of setting foot in that unchanged place. Though the police had canvassed the area, they hadn't done any lasting damage—the real danger was in the sameness, calm and welcoming, bearing no sign of the dead girl whose footprints had been forever scuffed to nothing. The girl who'd slipped from its banks into deadly water.

That sameness, so deceptively benign. No fit place for our wrecked remains.

We'd followed him anyway. Of course we had.

"Is he going to be okay, Ben?" I whispered as we walked. "He's barely said two words."

"This isn't so bad, actually," Ben said in a low voice. "Should have seen him last week after we met with Darrow. I told him about the old articles—the ones Darrow found that sound like Nat's case? Dude almost had a mental break. I doubt he's slept all summer."

"I think you're right. I don't want to say he looks like shit, but—"

"Oh, he definitely looks like shit. That's not even up for debate." He waved off my attempted retort. "Not now. It'll only piss him off."

I scrunched my face at that, let my words reform into a huff. Wished I could expel my frustration along with my breath. Instead I fixated on Teddy, took in his long, deliberate strides and squared shoulders. Worried over his rigid back, the dirty, fraying hem of his shirt, the barely combed mess of his ponytail. He was coming apart. Everything was.

"This isn't right," I muttered about thirty seconds later, tugging on Ben's sleeve like an impatient kid. "We have to do something."

"Jesus Christ, Amy, can you stop? Let him—let *us* have a goddamn break, okay? Just for tonight."

"I'm not taking a break from being his friend, Benjamin."

"I know." Ben sighed. As if he'd had a hope in hell I'd drop the subject. "Not sure what to tell you, though. We can't expect him to just move on, but how much worse can we let him get? He's not even trying."

"He's not deaf, either." Teddy stopped in his tracks and turned on us. A sudden burn of guilt washed through my chest at the fury in his eyes. "So if you want to talk shit behind his back, Benny, next time make sure to whisper."

"Don't yell at him, Teddy," I said. "We're worried about you. We don't want you to—"

"Sure you are. Since when do you worry about me, Amy? Since when do either of you worry about *me*, for real, unrelated to your-selves?"

"You can't be serious," Ben scoffed. "When does Ames do any-thing *except* worry about your dumb ass? She's so obsessed with being your *friend*, she—"

"Oh my God, Ben," I yelled, drawing glares from them both. "Is this really the time?"

"Oh whatever. This is such bullshit. This whole world is nothing but lies and bullshit, and people looking the other way. Makes me fucking sick."

"Lies and bullshit, huh Benny? Yeah, you'd know all about that." Teddy's laugh was vicious. "Must be tough, being you."

Ben stared at him, stone still, then moved in all at once—got right in his face, and my breath was gone. I braced for the fight I could see forming in the lines of Ben's tense shoulders, in the dark blaze of Teddy's eyes; in their fingers, balling into fists. Too much and too familiar. I couldn't speak.

Ben folded first. He stepped past Teddy, deliberately slamming him out of the way with his shoulder. Teddy spun fast, and I snapped out of my paralysis just in time to catch the arm that shot out to grab Ben's collar, just tall enough to act as barrier between his rage and Ben's eventual, inevitable ass-kicking. As soon as I felt Teddy withdraw, I turned on him.

"What the fuck is your problem? He's busting his ass to help you with all this."

"Help me? Do you have any idea how much shit I deal with on my own, with work and Mom and—you know what? You wouldn't. You and Ben don't have a clue what kind of help I need."

"How are we supposed to *get* a clue when you won't talk to us? Ask us for anything—*tell* us what you need. All we want in the world is to help you, but none of that matters if you keep shutting us down every time we try."

"What good would talking do? You get to escape this fucking hellhole whenever you want, right, Amy? Don't act like you have a stake in what actually happens once you go." He strode off, storming down the path without looking back. I followed him anyway, because what choice did I have? "You wouldn't understand if I wrote it in the sky."

We reached the cove and he kept right on going, lifting his head and crossing the clearing as if it were just another leg of the journey. Stalking past Ben, who had stalled at the giant oak, his Zippo flaring and dousing in practiced rhythm. Ben focused on the flame, eyebrow raised, chin tilted, and threw that shitty Hansen smirk at Teddy's retreating back.

"Told you it would piss him off."

"Benjamin, I swear to God—"

"Yeah, I know, I'm the literal worst. Let's go before he drinks all the booze."

My cousin waited for me to catch up, clapped me on the back like I'd seen both boys do to each other a million times—a violent gesture of affection that only incensed where it was supposed to placate.

The trail wasn't long enough to walk off our anger. Ben and I were greeted by the thumps of carelessly hurled firewood, crashing and sparking in the already too-high flames. Teddy's face was a soot-streaked shadow. He returned Ben's raised middle finger with one hand, chucked a final split log onto the bonfire with the other, then disappeared into the trailer. Materialized a moment later with a half-empty bottle of Ten High bourbon, flung himself into the lawn chair, and raised it our way.

"Cheers."

"What the shit is that?" Ben scoffed. "Ten High? Really?"

"Feeds my white-trash soul, Benny. Don't judge till you try it."

And so the tone was set for the evening—silence and side-eyes, Ben's languid sneers. Teddy's sullen eyes lingering a beat too long on mine, fingers deliberately brushing my palm as he passed me the bottle. We worked our way through the Ten High and a twelve-pack of June's Old Milwaukee, and we were beyond the realm of good ideas. Then Ben's flask appeared, and he wandered off to the river-bank, stretched out on the flat rock and lay there, staring up at the sky. Leaving us alone.

My eyes followed Teddy's movements, seeking the quirk of his lips and the tilt of his jaw. Collecting them from the shadows that stained his face and storing them away for later, to dredge up and scatter through the shapeless solace of my bedroom. He barely dodged the fire's absent flicker, face half-hidden behind bottle after bottle, his unconscious sigh catching and reversing as I shifted and stretched. Everything blurry and spinning, stark and magnified all at once as his eyes landed on mine. Everything hungry.

It wasn't a question of whether I wanted him. It was how far I'd let that wanting take us—if what we could become was enough to conquer the fear and anger, the fights and insecurities, the crushing weight of past and future. How willing I was to scuff my feet over lines that couldn't be uncrossed.

All valid concerns. All meaningless to ponder when he looked at me like that.

There had only ever been one real answer.

So, when he held my gaze, raised his eyebrow in that lazy, almost mocking way of his, I raised mine right back, meeting his challenge. Gesturing with my chin to the ground between my feet, an indication and invitation I knew he'd never refuse.

He didn't even hesitate. He slid from his chair, dropped to his knees in front of me. My hands went immediately to his hair, tugging it loose from its ponytail, tugging a moan from his throat as my fingers wove against his scalp. He leaned into my touch, eyes falling shut as our foreheads met.

We were so skittish. We'd always been that way—spent our adolescence protecting our childhood, prolonging the shift from maybe to always that promised to upend everything we were. Now I was reckless and hot-blooded, tired of chasing fading days. Sick to death of always being so very, very careful.

"What are we doing, Ames?"

"Ruining our friendship." I leaned in and let my nose graze his, drew back before he could close the distance. Made him wait until it hurt. "Again."

"Fucking destroying it. All those years down the drain. Remind me why I'm not more upset."

"Because you're an asshole."

His laugh was raw and soft, stripped of its earlier sullen edge. Charged with a need beyond the visceral. He opened his eyes and let them fuse with mine, pushing us forever past our inhibitions.

"Yeah, that's probably it. But you dig that about me."

It wasn't our first kiss. It wasn't even our second. It was a continuation—a flame we'd tamped to ash, sparked and fanned and reignited. His fingers gripped my calves, slid slowly upward, teasing the edge of my shorts. Skimming my hips. Slipping under then tugging open my shirt as I leaned into everything, let my lips drag across his jaw to his neck. He was the embodiment of the forbidden—every rebellion and atonement; every tender, wicked thought. There was no way to pull him closer without tipping over the chair. There was no stopping point.

We were lost in our grudge and in each other, drunk beyond sense, oblivious to the fade of the sky from twilit blue to dusk-purple to deep, star-pricked black. Oblivious to Ben and his whereabouts. Oblivious to June's car, or her approaching footsteps. Unaware of her presence until she spoke.

"Theo. Samuel. Fox."

"Shiiiiit." Teddy jerked away from me and twisted around, tipping over sideways, scattering the row of empty beer bottles as he landed on his ass in the dirt. I stared up at June, my eyes wide

and hazy, fingers fumbling over my undone buttons. Her hair was skinned into a messy bun, her bare face drawn and wan. She looked years older. She looked like hell. "Mom. I thought—"

"Obviously you thought I wouldn't be home till much later from the look of things. Is it just you two?" Her eyes scanned the property, landing on Ben as he shook the last drops from the flask over his open mouth and rolled off the rock. "Oh, there he is. That it? Nothing happening inside my home I should know about before I walk in on it?"

"No, ma'am. Just the three of us. I'm sorry. I'm—"

"I'll save the big lecture for your hangover, but right now . . . I don't have the strength God gave a newborn rabbit, Teddy. I don't. My bathroom, third drawer down. I'm too young to be a grand-mother."

"Holy shit. Mom, it's not like that. We were just—"

"Watch your mouth. Don't you wake me when you're done out here, understand? It's been a long, long day."

"Christ," he whispered as she dragged herself up the steps and into the trailer. "I am so screwed."

"She didn't seem that mad," I slurred, gathering my senses, failing to project even the appearance of having my shit together. What were we doing? What the hell had we just done? "Did Benny see?"

"Did Benny see what?" Ben staggered over, blinking in the fire-light as Teddy dragged himself upright on the arm of the lawn chair. "Oh shit, is that June's car? Ames, we should head back. Let Teddy get bitched out in peace."

"You're a true friend, Ben." Teddy sighed.

"You can't get enough of me. You grounded?"

"Breadwinners don't get grounded. She'll definitely ream my ass, though, so that should be fun."

"Must be tough, being you." Ben swayed on his feet, shook his head fast, like a wet dog. "Catch up, Ames."

Teddy watched him amble off, waited until he saw the beam of Ben's phone flashlight bobbing up the driveway before reaching down to pull me to my feet. I swayed on the spot and hooked my fingers through his belt loops, kissed the mark I'd left right beneath his ear. Reveled in his answering moan and the way his arms snaked around my waist, nowhere near ready to stop what we'd begun.

"Yeah, this friendship is toast. I—" I kissed him again, turning his words to a dark, dangerous hiss. "You're about to get carried up those steps, girl."

"I'm sure it's a well-worn path."

"I'm sure I'm not the first to make the offer." His hands slid over my hips, anchoring me. Daring me to pull away. "The question is, am I the first to make you want it this bad?"

"Keep dwelling on the Preston thing, Teddy," I said, my words a low warning against his skin. "I'd make a list of all the reasons you can go fuck your*self*, but I doubt even you know all their names."

"Goddamn it, Amy." His teasing voice went dull all at once, blurred and slurred past banter as he pulled me closer, suddenly gentle. His forehead hit my shoulder, slid along the line of my neck. "There's no one else for me, don't you get that? Hasn't been since before last summer."

"Too bad we're such good friends, then, or I might be dumb enough to stay."

I shoved him off me, hard enough to send him stumbling,

turned my back before he could answer. Felt his eyes on the sway of my hips as I walked away.

Ben and I went around by way of the road, neither of us exactly aching to pass through the cove after dark. The walk did its part to sober us up, but he still staggered when we reached the porch; my limbs still dangled loose and heavy, face flushing and cooling in cycles as we eased the kitchen door open and crept upstairs. My senses still whirled with memories of Teddy, and the premonition that what had happened would be far, far more crucial once the sky gave way to daylight. What the fuck had I been thinking, letting him get that close? Why had I walked away at all when even now his touch still buzzed along my skin?

"We should talk," Ben whispered as my bedroom door shut behind us. "I had some seriously intense thoughts about the case I need to write down now before I pass out and forget this entire night even happened."

He went straight for his binder, ripped out a fresh sheet of paper, and went to town on it with a blue Sharpie.

"Here's the thing," he said, squinting at his own hand, as if the force of his concentration would steady it. "I've been approaching this from the wrong angle—*where* she was. *What* happened to her. *How* she ended up in the river. But shouldn't we wonder more about the *who*? *Who* was on the property? *Who* knew about the cove? Answer the WHO, and everything else will be clear."

"None of this is clear," I said into my hands, trying to rub feeling into my cheeks. My mind was far away, in a fireside camping chair, wrapped around a warm, solid body. "Anyway, we already checked into that, remember? You almost got us killed in a church parking lot."

"But I didn't *actually* get us killed, Ames, and that's what matters. Hold on."

Ben bore down with the Sharpie, doubling his efforts.

"Get focused and check this out," he said a moment later. "These are all the people in town who—for an absolute, undeniable fact—knew Nat and this property equally well, and had unrestricted access to both. Tell me what you think of this."

The list he handed me was sloppily numbered, a road into madness paved with names:

1. Jonas Langston
2. Amelia Lee Langston
3. Peter Hansen
4. Madeleine Hansen
5. June Barrett

"What the actual fuck, Ben?" I slammed the paper onto the bed, ignoring his frantic shushing. "Are you joking?"

"Look, I'm not saying any of them actually *did* it. I'm trying to start with the basics here."

"Oh my God. Okay, I'll play. Grandpa." I picked up the Sharpie and drew a confident line through his name. "He can't even get down a flight of stairs, much less down to the cove."

"That's exactly right, and exactly why I made this list: to narrow this shit down." Ben wobbled a bit getting to his knees, slapped his own face to clear away the remaining haze. "Grandpa is officially not a suspect. What about Grandma?"

"How drunk are you? She hasn't been in the woods for years.

Besides, why would she kill Nat?" I snatched the paper from him, rested it on the binder, and wrote a single word across the top in huge block letters: *MOTIVE*. "She didn't wake up one morning and decide out of nowhere to murder a child."

"Okay, I can dig it. Grandma's out. Wait—your mom was still around, wasn't she?"

"Oh, she was so very much around. She spent all morning climbing up my ass, then drove the grandparents to the doctor. Wasn't more than a room away from me until she literally left the house."

"So that's a solid no. I'm going to go ahead and skip June, too, for obvious reasons."

"Good, because I think you're missing the big picture. The question is not who had an *opportunity* to kill her—it's who would *want* to, and why. Suspecting someone of murder because they happen to be around is insane."

"I hear what you're saying, but we have to start somewhere. The most logical things to consider first are proximity and accessibility. Now, who's left on the list?"

"Both *your* parents, Ben."

"Oh." That brought him up short. "Well, it's only fair to give them the same consideration. Mom is a wash. She barely ever saw Nat and was always perfectly nice when she did. I mean, she can be a bitch, but she's not dangerous."

"That's not my version of reality," I said. "She used to hit you all the time. Probably still would, if you weren't practically twice her size now."

"Oh sure, I always got the belt. And the wooden spoon. And the extension cord, for special occasions." He sighed, waving away my huff of disgust. "But she's never been *violent* violent."

217

"It's *all* violence." I stared him down, watched his hackles rise even as he refused to meet my gaze. "How bad does it have to hurt before it counts? Or is it all okay because she's your mom?"

My words, made possible by the blur of my brain and the burning in my bones, pelted him, wearing down the line between upbringing and unhinged. Forcing him to contemplate the beginning and ending points of both. That distinction and any discussion of it—it was more than off the table in our family. Even acknowledging it was unthinkable.

"You know it's not the same," he finally muttered, eyes fixed on the paper. "She was old school about punishment back then, and she only really went off when I was being a little shit—which, as you know, was often. It's how things are around here. Practically a rite of passage."

"Not for everyone."

"Yeah, well, congratulations to Teddy for being the only kid in River Run history who never had to pick his own switch. Shit, both *our* moms were raised like that, and they turned out fine."

"If there's one thing our moms have in common, Benjamin, it's that they're seriously far from 'fine,' in any sense whatsoever."

"You know what I meant. And anyway, to get back to the actual point, none of that means anything in relation to the discussion at hand, motives or otherwise. Mom was barely home that day—she had some event over at the equestrian complex and was on and off the property all morning. I passed her on the way out when I left, as she was coming up the drive for like, the fifth time. Waved and everything, with a smile on her face."

"Told you this was a stupid idea." I started gathering the papers, tapping them into a rectangle. "Anything to say about Uncle Peter—the only one not of the 'bloodline,' as your mother would say, hence possibly the least fucked-up person in our entire fucked-up family? Or are we done here?"

"That's a pretty low bar to clear, Ames. But . . . he's the one who knew Nat best." The shift in Ben's voice caught my attention. He stared at the names, a crease between his suddenly sober eyes. "He's been friends with June and Sam since before any of us were born—practically helped raise both their kids from day one. He's out on those trails as much as we are, knows the woods backward and forward. He's a man, so that sends him to the top of the list, statistically. Physically, he's the strongest—he could overpower any one of us. He was even there at just the right moment that day, offering Teddy a ride. Keeping him out of the cove."

"Will you listen to yourself? Do you honestly think your dad had a thing in the world to do with any of this?"

He blinked at my incredulous face, then laughed, a short, humorless bark that morphed into real giggles as he shook his head.

"No. No, I don't. Holy shit, can you imagine? Peter Hansen: Entrepreneur. CEO. Killer of children." He cackled, then covered his own mouth, shushed himself louder than the laugh. Tapped the word *MOTIVE* with his pen, circling it over and over again, as if the motion could tease an answer from the ink itself. "But you're right. None of this means anything without the one missing piece, and I can't think of a single reason why Dad would want Nat dead. I can't think of a motive for *anyone*. It's a completely illogical, completely insane thought."

"It was your thought, Ben."

"It was the bourbon's thought." He sighed, tucking his list into the binder pocket. "Going to hit the couch now before I think or say any more dumb shit."

"Good night, Benjamin."

I swept the binder off the bed as he slouched out the door, passing out on top of the covers before I even heard it close behind him.

We crouched behind the tree trunk, her summer-sweet blond hair tickling my nose. Teddy stalked the forest around us, made a show of searching beneath the underbrush and circling every tree but ours, an exaggerated dance he'd repeat until Nat got tired of hiding. He knew exactly where we were—he'd even caught my eye at one point, dropped a flirtatious wink on me before resuming the hunt. Nat leaned against my arm, quivering with stifled giggles.

"Sweet fucking Christ, can we hurry it up?" Ben called from his crouch at the foot of the giant oak—our official home base, as dictated by Nat. He went along with the game to a point, but mostly let himself get caught immediately so he could bitch and smoke in peace. "What are you even doing on the ground, dude?"

"Looking for the little bug. She's around here somewhere, Benny, I just know it."

"Lord. Well, find them already, and then make yourself useful and find my smokes. And Amy's sketchbook, so I don't have to hear about the goddamn thing anymore."

Nat pressed both hands over her mouth at my annoyed huff and peeked around the tree trunk, cracked up all over again at the sight of her brother peering under rocks and twigs.

"I HEARD THAT," he yelled, scrambling to his feet. "I heard you, and I'm coming after you!"

I leaped from behind the tree, running away from home base, and he crashed after me, deliberately ignoring Nat. As soon as he passed her, she took off, screeching in triumph. Ben high-fived her as she collapsed beside him, panting and victorious, swatting at his hand as it darted out to ruffle her hair.

Teddy chased me up the trail and out of the clearing, following our usual pattern—the same game we'd played over and over, every summer since Nat could form the words to ask. We'd been running that hide-and-seek path for years, and here I was again—fleeing not from him but from the cove itself. Moving away from Ben and from Nat, hoping he'd follow. Hoping like hell I'd be caught.

Soon enough, his arm looped my waist from behind, pulling me off my feet as we spun to a stop—pulling me closer, as if he'd forgotten how to let go. I leaned into him, struggled for a breath that skipped just out of reach. His hands moved slowly across my middle, dragging a shiver through my body.

We never did have our post–Fourth of July chat about the "nothing" that hadn't occurred in the back seat of Ben's car. Instead we'd scurried past it and resumed circling the fringes, touching then retreating—ignoring the moments when teasing turned sincere; when flirtation turned to intention. Everything in me returning again and again to things left unsaid.

"Tag. I win."

"Wrong game, Teddy."

"Eh, fuck hide-and-seek. You're it."

I laughed, turning to face him. He kept me close, thumbs braced on my hip bones, that smile I'd loved so long way too close to mine. A deliberate proximity I'd only ever dreamed, finally made real.

"Oh really?" I breathed. "I'm it?"

"Is that a problem?"

"No." I raised my eyes to his, let myself fall into them as his hand slipped around my fingers. He pressed a soft kiss to my knuckles, then my palm, sighing as I brushed my thumb over his skin. "Not for me."

"Good," he whispered. "There's no one else I want to catch."

"Really?"

"Never has been, Ames." He was suddenly closer, leaning in, searching my eyes for any trace of uncertainty. Finding nothing of the sort.

It was every wish I'd ever made.

His hands moved to cup my face as I returned the kiss, all hesitation dissipating. All doubt and fear and insecurity picked up and blown away by a passing breeze, until all that remained was him.

We stayed close on the path back, the default gap between us forever narrowed, the secret glow in my heart forever fanned to flame. Our eyes caught and broke and caught again, little glances darting back and forth like fish; our hands brushed and clasped, grasping tight. Withdrawing when we heard their voices.

Ben and Nat waited beneath the home-base tree, both hunched over his cupped palms, squandering yet another store of lighter fluid. Their brows furrowed together, his thumb guiding hers on the flint wheel of the long-suffering Zippo.

"I can't do it." Nat rolled the wheel in a useless circle. "Help me again, Benny."

"Here. Push your thumb really hard against the ridges, then snap it down. Snap. See? Easy."

"Great job, Ben," I said. "You're an upstanding example to future smokers and arsonists everywhere."

"Gotta do my part, Ames." Ben's grin shone up at me, but wavered suddenly, eyes flicking back and forth between Teddy and me. "You guys were gone awhile."

"Took me a while to catch her."

"Right." He stood, brushing dirt off his shorts. Nat barely noticed; she was focused on the Zippo, tongue poking from the corner of her mouth, eyes bright at the sparks she'd finally managed to coax from the eyelet. "Hey, Teddy, got a minute?"

"Sure, man. Everything okay?"

They faded off together, retreating a few yards back up the path. I watched them carefully, wondering how obvious we'd been. Had Ben picked up on it, and was he pissed? Or worse, was he over there scoffing at my inexperience, mocking my flushed cheeks and delighted vulnerability? Was Teddy stonewalling an interrogation— or was he grinning triumphantly, returning a fist bump, accepting a nice big bro-pat on the back? Was he laughing at me too?

Nat sparked the lighter a couple more times, then chucked it aside.

"I'm bored with that. Can we play more hide-and-seek?"

"Sure," I said, careful not to let my worries weigh on my tone. Though Nat was still a kid, she could be cagey as hell. The last thing I wanted was to drag her down the path of my self-doubt. "Do you want me to seek this time?"

"You're better at hiding, Amy. Besides, I like it when—"

"No, YOU look, motherfucker." Ben's voice carried, sharp and sudden, drawing our eyes. He stood rigid, arms crossed, head shaking back and forth. Teddy's arms were at his sides, but his hands were fisted, entire body strung and waiting for Ben's next move. "I *told* you—"

"You okay?" I asked, shifting so I blocked her view of them.

Nat threw me one of Ben's loaded side-eyes, way too jaded and sarcastic on a nine-year-old face, then lifted one shoulder in a noncommittal shrug that was pure Teddy. She stood and stretched, swung her arms, looked away from me toward the river. It ran high and fast, its usually lazy current swollen and bumpy and deep.

"They always go off like this and leave me. I'll go home when I get tired of it, as usual."

"Seriously? They've done this before?" I got to my feet at her reluctant nod, brushed my hands off on my shorts. "Wait here."

"It's not up to you, Benny," I heard Teddy say as I approached. "Leave off it and mind your business."

"Don't you tell me my business. This affects all of us, and you can't just—"

The boys fell silent as I breached their weird tension bubble— that specific intensity that builds when two people who've known each other way too long start butting heads. Ben swore under his breath then turned to me, a benign mask slipping over his anger as if I hadn't known him my entire life. As if I wouldn't instantly recognize the unique waft of his bullshit.

"Hey, Ames. What's up? Did you find your sketchbook?"

"'What's up?' Seriously? How about what's up with you guys ditching us to yell at each other? How about what's up with Nat having an actual plan of exit because that's how often it's been happening lately?"

"She said that? Shit. I'd better check on her." Teddy turned and headed for his sister, avoiding my eyes as he brushed past. Ben's face blazed after him, fury rising in his eyes and voice.

"Hey, we're not done here."

"Know what? I think I am done, actually." He raised a middle finger over his shoulder. Ben returned fire twofold, aimed both of his at Teddy's retreating back.

"I'll remember who walked away first, dude. I'll fucking remember, I swear to God."

"Go right ahead. At least I know exactly where I'm headed, Benny."

Ben's mouth opened and closed, crumpled and shrank. Twisted into a soundless wail as he spun away from me, slammed his fists into his head once, twice. His shoulders sagged; he slumped against a tree and slid to the ground, the fight draining from his body in a long, shuddering sigh.

I'd seen my cousin throw more tantrums than I could count on all our fingers. I'd seen him rage and stomp, shriek and rant. When we were very small, I'd seen him cry. But I'd never seen him break like his heart had gone sideways, driving him to a place beyond anger or frustration. Something was very, very wrong.

"Ben, are you all right? What the hell is going on?"

"Amy, please." His voice rode a wobbly edge. "I can't talk about this right now. I literally can't put it into words. Just give me a minute. Please."

"Okay, if you're sure . . . but you know I'm here for you, right? You can talk to me."

I knelt beside him, rubbed my hand over his back. Planted a kiss on the swirl of his cowlick before starting back toward the clearing. I was only a few feet away when I heard his voice, strained and thick, barely hanging on to the dry side of tears.

"God. I wish I could, Ames. You have no idea."

CHAPTER 28
SUMMER 2019

swear to Christ, Teddy, I will never forgive you for this. This is a literal waste of my life."

"Blame your grandma—or better yet, your dad. He's the one who bought a fixer-upper." Teddy tied the top closed on yet another trash bag, swinging it off the porch toward the rental dumpster. "Anyway, if you didn't stop to bitch at me every thirty seconds, we'd have been done hours ago."

"Thirty seconds." Ben swiped a cobweb out of his hair. "You're lucky I haven't walked. This is some fresh version of hell, is it not? Ninety-seven degrees out, and no AC in this dump. I've got swamp balls like you wouldn't believe."

"DUDE. No one wants to hear about your balls, okay? This is *your* house—shut up and do your part or go take a break if you can't bear another moment of actual work. Just STOP."

After our meeting with Darrow at the old Franklin place, Ben had mentioned the property to his parents in passing, lighting a sudden, unexplained fire under my uncle's ass. He had the place tented and fumigated, then hired Teddy—apparently our family's go-to for cheap manual labor—to clear out the inside. When Teddy mentioned the job might be too big for a single person, Grandma was quick to volunteer Ben and me. Typical Grandma, tickled to death at the idea of us doing what she called an honest day of work.

"It was quite a lovely home when the girls were young," she'd said. "Eleanor was down there all the time playing with little Noah. He was a good friend. Lots of good memories. It'll be nice to see that old place rustled into shape again."

Easy for her to say when it was us doing the rustling. Uncle Peter had promptly agreed, smiling even wider when Grandma waved away his offer of monetary compensation. Ben's face when he learned of his involvement in the cleanup was eclipsed in hilarious tragedy only by his face when he learned he'd be doing it for free.

As it turned out, there was a lot more crap in that house than we'd anticipated. Furniture and trash, dust and debris, animal droppings, cigarette butts, arachnid corpses. We worked our way from room to room, emptying each one, clearing the corners and closets and cabinets. Sweeping up a storm of cobwebs, uncovering now lifeless insect colonies that sent Ben shuddering out of a room more than once. To his credit, he'd actually toned down his initial attitude, interjecting only the occasional bitter comment. Which was really more than I'd expected given the circumstances.

In the week since the bonfire, we three had fallen into a sullen limbo. Ben had bullied my hungover ass into the Mustang the morning after, driven down to the trailer, and let himself inside, reappearing ten minutes later with a squinting, suffering Teddy. We'd ended up at a shitty diner, where the two of them devoured plates of eggs and home fries and assorted breakfast meats, biscuits and coffee and juice, cinnamon rolls as big as my hand. I'd scarfed down half an egg white omelet, puked it up in the bathroom, then forced myself to finish the other half when my empty stomach threatened inversion. The rest of the day was a long, silent drive through the backcountry, past horse farms and distilleries and the green bends of the river.

We didn't argue, and we didn't talk. We didn't apologize or hug, or even smile, and the last I'd seen of Teddy before we'd ended up working side by side in a stuffy, filthy house was a regretful half grimace over his shoulder when we dropped him off that afternoon, as if an apology was what I needed.

As if there was any backtracking from the way we'd collided.

Ben, for his part, had glommed on to the "who" question sparked by his drunken epiphany, and appeared ready to worry it to rags. He'd dedicated every spare moment to his research, brainstorming and highlighting and exhausting me with minutiae. Purging the Franklin house was, in fact, a welcome break from that misery— from mental images that dragged me gasping from dreams of drowning, my own face caught just short of the surface. The world a blur through wide-open, water-filmed eyes.

It was already past dinnertime on the third day—Grandma's honest "day" of work had damn sure managed to extend itself quite efficiently—when we hauled the last of the bags out to the dumpster, then stretched out on the Mustang's hood to rehydrate and catch our breath. Teddy was wiping the grime from his face when he glanced up at the house and froze, his weary relief dissolving into weary resignation.

"Oh. God. Dammit. Benny, take a look at the house and tell me what you see."

"I see a huge pain in my ass, is what I see—oh. Oh God, no. Oh fuck *me*. I see an attic window, am I right? *Shit.*"

"You see an attic window. A window in an attic our dumb asses missed entirely." Teddy threw his empty water bottle at the house and climbed back onto the porch. "Hope you didn't trash your gloves."

"We could skip it," Ben said hopefully. "We could pretend like we never saw that window, and if Dad asks—"

"Dude, we were hired to do a job. We need to finish the job."

"*You* were hired. I was thrown to the wolves by my goddamn grandma." Ben clambered into the rental dumpster to fish out his work gloves, his words echoing off the metal walls. "You and your work ethic can kiss my ass, Teddy."

"Whatever. Let's get this over with so we don't have to come back tomorrow."

As it turned out, we couldn't really fault ourselves for overlooking the attic. It was one of those pull-down staircases, no more than a rectangular hole with a single link where the access chain had been. Our stepladder was too short, of course—I had to stand on Teddy's clasped hands to reach what was left of the handle. I managed to crack it open on the fourth try, drag it low enough for Ben to catch the rim, and pull it down. He clambered up the stairs, disappearing into the ceiling as Teddy lowered me to the ground.

Ben's footfalls echoed above our heads as we faced each other, dirty and disarmed, Teddy's smile sparking a wary hope that burned brighter when his hands rose to rest on my hips. Flared as he drew me closer, then faltered when he stopped, searching my eyes. His own were wary, loaded with fear and questions and too many false starts. We'd spent all three cleaning days skirting around each other, glances meeting over and over, until I thought I'd incinerate every time he brushed past me.

"Is this how it is now, City Girl?"

"It doesn't have to be. Can we talk later?"

"Whatever you want." He brushed a strand of hair from my face, rested his forehead against mine. "Anything, Amy. As long as we're okay."

"Yeah. We're okay."

He leaned in. My heart quickened, sensing his need in the grip of his fingers—an echo of my own longing, real and aching, undeniable. What would it do to us, to sate that longing—to push past the sting of my chilly silence and his heated, jealous stares, wrecking the foundation of our fragile truce? How could we do anything else when every attempt at ordinary led us straight back to each other?

His hand moved through my hair, erasing those thoughts and the distance between us. It no longer mattered. We were flint and steel, and I was lost.

"HURRY UP, YOU GUYS. I AM NOT DOING THIS SHIT BY MYSELF."

The kiss broke off before it began. Teddy withdrew, huffed his way to the stairs, and climbed into the attic without looking back. Left me reeling and intoxicated, too close to undone. I rubbed my face and gathered my wits, shook the shivers from my arms, and followed him upstairs, meekly, my internal groan at the sight that greeted me a silent echo of Ben's quite audible one.

The attic was packed with garbage—bags of scrap cloth, boxes of junk, stacks of old newspapers, sticks of old furniture. There was no way we'd get through it before sundown, and though Uncle Peter had had the power turned on the week before, there was no bulb socket in the attic, no light switch, no lantern. Nothing.

"There goes another day," Ben griped, kicking over a box. File folders slid out of it, scattered across the floor in a puff of mildew. "I swear to God, I don't even want this fucking place enough to deal with this."

"It's a free house, you spoiled prick." Frustration and irritation turned my words to a growl. "You didn't and won't have to do anything else to actually earn it."

"Yeah, I am a spoiled prick. At least I know that. At least I don't act one way in public and another behind closed doors, unlike some people. Oh what?" He scoffed at our matching skeptical side-eyes. "Pretty sure there are glass houses all up in this bitch where that's concerned. Right, Amy?"

"Guys, come on." Teddy's voice was a wary mirror of his face. "It's one more day. Please don't do this again."

Ben glared at me but kept his words in check. Gave the file folders another kick, dislodging a stack of newspaper clippings. They scattered across the floor in a musty fan of smudged ink and children's faces.

"I'm not cleaning up your fucking tantrum," I muttered, picking my way through the mess to check the corners for stray spiders. "Can we please just finish this and go? This heat's making me sick."

"Finishing up sounds pretty damn good to me," Ben said. "Drink some more water, and if you puke, aim for one of the boxes so we don't have to clean the floor. Teddy, where did you leave the pack?"

When Teddy didn't answer, I turned around. He knelt by the clippings, his mouth stretched strange and horrible. I crept over and peered around him, gut twisting at the headlines:

MISSING FAYETTE COUNTY GIRL FOUND DEAD
SEARCH CALLED OFF FOR LEXINGTON YOUTH
THIRD BODY FOUND AT HIGH BRIDGE

With each headline, a picture: all young, all grinning. All bliss-fully unaware of the bleak, bloated sameness of their shared end-ing. My eyes caught and held on a wide, smiling face, beautiful and bright beneath a riot of red curls: Mackenzie Delaine Griggs, forever twelve years old.

"Jesus." I took the stack from his limp hands and shuffled the articles, as if they'd make some kind of twisted sense in a new order—a horrid puzzle waiting for the proper solution. "Who the hell saves stuff like this?"

"I don't know; this guy saved every other fucking thing." Ben indicated the overstuffed attic. "Hoarders, man. Dude had issues."

"Get it away from me." Teddy made his way to the stairs and sat down heavily, pressed his palms to the hollows of his eyes. "I'm serious, you guys—I can't see this right now. Please."

"No problem." Ben crouched beside him, brought a hand down roughly on his shoulder in what passed for a comforting gesture between them. "Hang in there, man. Take a break if you need to. I scattered this crap; I'll deal with it."

We resumed our work in silence, moving as fast as we could against the sun. Teddy was a furious machine, slamming boxes and throwing bags; he'd stayed curled around himself on the stairs for approximately thirty seconds, then soldiered on, delving into the mess with a determination bordering on violence. Ben finished collecting the files and clippings, tossed the bags down the stairs. I dragged an old bourbon barrel out of the corner, revealing a forest of cobwebs and dead recluses. As I ducked to avoid the slope of the eave, my elbow bumped against the wall, dislodging a loose board. It fell to the floor with a short, sharp bang.

"Goddamn it. Ben, I broke your house."

"Have at it. Tear this mess to the ground, I don't care. Might as well have some fun while we're working for free, right?"

"Don't remind me." I tried to shove the board back into place—it fell through the opening, landing out of reach. I ducked down, reached into a hollow much bigger than it seemed from the outside. Scraped my arm against a jagged nail. "Ah, shit. Countdown to tetanus starts now."

"Watch yourself, Ames," Teddy called. "Let me or Benny reach in there. Who knows what's living in a hole like that."

"So you'll volunteer my ass to find out?" Ben shook his head. "I've got your back too, bitch. God."

"You'd rather let her take one for the team? Figures. Move over, Amy, I'll check it out."

"I'm a capable human, and I'm wearing gloves. I'll be fine. Ugh, gross." I reached past a spider egg sac the size of a dwarf star, my fingers finding purchase on a hard, flat surface that moved when I nudged it. "Guys? There's something in here."

"More spiders?" Ben edged toward the stairs. "I'll be in the car."

"It's a box. Some sort of weird kid's thing, with a fucked-up clown on it."

"Ten bucks says it's full of evil spirits." Teddy grinned at Ben's involuntary shudder. "Don't open it. Opening it is like, the first step in bringing that clown's vengeful ghost to life."

"Don't joke about that shit, man," Ben said. "Murder clowns are serious business. I have to live here one day, you know."

I rolled my eyes at them, working my finger along the edge of the rusted metal. It stuck, then squeaked, then gave all at once. The contents registered slowly, filtered through the blurred edges of my mind, their meaning looming half a beat back. I blinked hard, a sick shudder racing over my skin, everything snapping into hectic, sharp focus.

"Oh. Oh God."

"What's up?" Ben looked up from his dustpan, instantly on guard. "You okay?"

"Ben, we need to leave. Now. I mean *right* now, no questions."

"Ames? What is it?"

Teddy's voice was way too close. He moved toward me, eyes gone wide at the fear in mine. The unknown lurked too close to the surface, wormed its way inside him before he even saw its face.

I couldn't show him. I couldn't let him see it.

"Nothing. Go on, let's go."

"Amy. Give me the box."

"I can't." I barely got the words out around the bile rising in my throat. "Please, just go. Ben, get him out of here."

Ben, to his credit, didn't hesitate. He stepped between us, but it was too late. Teddy pushed past him easily, no real feat for even one less determined, wrested the box from me over my rising protests— so I was right there to hear his strangled gasp, there to watch him break as he jerked backward and let it drop, scattering its horrible contents across the floor.

The blue plastic ring. The flat marble, round and smooth as

a skipping stone. The silver clover charm, four-leafed for luck. An ancient pot of lip gloss. Hair clippings. So many hair clippings. Dozens, each preserved in a tiny Ziploc bag, deliberately separated and stored. A hideous treasure trove of keepsakes to be taken out and admired long after their owners had rotted to dust.

A light brown twist. A shiny swatch of black. A bright red curl, instantly familiar.

And right on top, slimmer than my finger but twice as long, twice as pale: the tiny blond braid, curved like a noose, looped and waiting for a long-forgotten neck.

T he air was a swamp of misery, heavy with an ominous, sullen charge that crowded the space between my boys as we neared the top of the hill. I loomed on the fringes of their silence, exhausted and somber, yet secretly riding a high nothing could touch—not my fears or insecurities, not the threat of my mother's inevitable reaction. Not even Ben's bleak mood.

Teddy had kissed me. All was right with the world.

The Hansen home was a shadow of silence and dark windows against the bruise-streaked sky, the fading lawn and empty driveway lit only by the cheerful glow of the porch light. Uncle Peter's truck was gone, along with the garden tools we'd intended to fetch.

"Looks like they left." Ben dug in his pocket, fumbled his key in the lock. "Hold on, you guys, I'll open the garage and drive you back."

"No worries, man. I can walk her home."

The house key jerked almost imperceptibly, a tiny stutter against the dead bolt. "It's cool. It'll only take a minute, once I get this door open."

"I said I'll walk her."

Teddy's voice was a calm contrast to his eyes. They fixed on Ben, who'd gone still in the now-open doorway, ignoring the alarm system's countdown and increasingly frantic beeps. Eight. Seven. Six.

"Um, Ben?" My eyes leaped to his hands, watched them tremble in and out of fists at his sides. "You okay?"

He turned toward us at the one count, locking eyes with Teddy as the siren wailed across the lawn. My hands smashed over my ears, but neither of them flinched. They stared each other down, the house shrieking in protest until Ben reached behind him and punched in four numbers, never breaking eye contact.

"Never been better. See you guys tomorrow."

The door shut in our faces, before I even lowered my hands. We were still standing there when the porch light went off.

"What the hell was that about?"

I figured the question was fair enough, all things considered, but Teddy shrugged, keeping pace with me on the downhill slope toward the woods. I blew an exasperated breath upward, scattering my bangs. "Why does no one tell me anything?"

"It's guy stuff. Nothing you need to worry about. But hey—" His grin flashed white in the rising moon, sending a thrill through my spine as we stepped onto the trail. "Do you have to get back?"

"Not right away. I can make time for—ow." I stumbled over a rock, catching myself on a nearby tree. "Goddamn it. Do you have your flashlight?"

"Yeah, hold on." He fumbled with his key chain, then his face appeared, illuminated by a tiny gleam. "You okay? Come sit with me."

We settled against a tree trunk, closer than we'd have dared a year, or even a week, before. Teddy stuck the penlight in the dirt like a candle, the slim, white beam breaking the shadow between us. His lighter flared, cloaking his face in a sultry orange glow as he lit a cigarette. My breath stuttered, so afraid he'd catch my helpless, hopeless stare with his own. So afraid he wouldn't.

"Are those Ben's?" I asked. He nodded, a cackle escaping his mouth on a cloud of smoke as I shook my head. "That's just wrong. He practically tore apart the cove looking for them."

"Finders keepers. He owes me a pack, anyway—did the exact same shit to me last week. Couldn't find your sketches, though, unfortunately. Want one?"

"You know I don't smoke."

"All for the best if you don't start, really. Shouldn't have even offered."

"I'm not into cancer, thanks. And my mother definitely would not approve."

"Yeah, I'm thinking your mother 'would not approve' of a lot of things." He paused. His eyes slid my way, hesitant and hopeful. "Does that matter?"

The distance between us seemed very small as I made my choice. A smile crept slowly over his face as I shook my head, reached to touch his cheek, neither of us breaking the gaze we'd been putting off all our lives. It held all the answers I'd ever need.

"So," he finally said. "One more day until you leave me."

"One more day. I'll miss you, you know. I always do."

"Yeah." He absorbed that, a tiny crease splitting his brow as he looked away. "Gotta get through another year, I guess. SATs, all that shit. College prep, like college is a thing for me."

"It doesn't have to be, but if that's what you want, there are ways—loans, grants, work study. Academic scholarships."

"Huh. Those. Does it count if my 'academics' are pretty much fucked, or is there a special fund for guys who have to pick between homework and rent money?"

"God. I don't know; it's all different." I studied my fingers, tripping over the edge in his voice. His mood had skidded sideways, soured all at once at the mention of the future. Why was he being like this—why was he determined to shoot down even the faintest suggestions of possibilities? "What they'd require depends on where you go, and your field of study."

"The only field I know anything about is the one I mow. No idea what I'd study even if I did manage to get in somewhere halfway decent."

"Figure it out when you get there," I persisted. "Get a two-year degree first, or find a trade school. Join the army, if it comes to that. Anything to escape."

"Maybe. I mean, someone like me would basically be cannon fodder, but at least I'd die somewhere other than River Run, huh? Progress."

"Don't say things like that."

I fidgeted at his answering silence, clicked the flashlight on and off and on again, dropping it in the dirt when his hand closed over mine. His low voice worked its way across the world to find me.

"I guess it won't be so bad, sticking around. Benny won't be lonely, at the very least."

"You think that'll be enough, when you hate it here? Ben means well, but you can't stick around for his sake."

"I'm not."

His meaning turned from air to water, froze between us, solid and clear. He wasn't staying for Ben. But he wasn't leaving, either.

"That's not your responsibility, Teddy."

"Well, I don't see anyone else around here stepping in to handle shit, so yeah—it is. *She* is."

"For how long, though? She'll finish school, get out on her own, and then what? It'll be too late for you to start from scratch."

"As long as she has a chance, it'll be worth it."

"So that's it? You'll do what—cut my grandma's grass forever? Haul rocks at the quarry? You have to think further ahead than that. You have to—"

"It's not up to me, okay? You have no idea what it's like, doing the same damn thing every day of my life. It's like circling a fucking drain, and never quite making it to the pipe."

"That's exactly why you have to leave," I pressed. "So you have a chance for something better. There's nothing *here* for you."

"There's nothing here for Nat, either. Which is why I can't take the risk." He took a final drag on his cigarette, stubbed out the end, and tipped his head back, sharing his smoke with the sky. "You don't get it, Amy. You're going to art school, for fuck's sake."

"Um, yeah? What's wrong with art school?"

"Nothing. It's everything you want, and there's nothing holding you back. We should all be so lucky, huh?"

Silence followed on the heels of those words, building like bitter fog between us. He wasn't yelling; he wasn't even frowning. Still, I flinched at the resentment in his voice, and the knack he had of making money the center of everything. The way he dismissed even hypothetical success, like he didn't see the point in more than a wish. As for his apparent disdain concerning my schooling—how was I supposed to fix that? Did he expect me to downgrade my goals, or pass up opportunities for the sake of fairness? Was I supposed to settle for less simply because he didn't have more?

I watched him carefully, wondering which of the choice phrases crowding my mouth would best express my feelings without crushing his, and was about to say fuck it and just let loose, when he beat me to the punch.

"I looked up some of those places, you know. The top colleges for the arts—the best of the best. And for what they charge? For your sake, Amy, there'd better *not* be a damn thing wrong with any of them."

"Duly noted," I said, further bristling at his tone. "But if this is going to be a long-term issue, now's the time to get it out. You're right—I have money, and I'm going to art school, and I have the chance to be great, if I can. Taking that chance doesn't make me an asshole, not when you know you'd do the same in my place."

"No, I actually can't say I would—because if I had in my pocket what they want for just a year at that one in Rhode Island? That's an AA degree or vo-tech for me and Nat both, maybe more if we play it right. That's groceries and clothes, and my own car with gas in the tank, which might mean a job that doesn't leave me beat at the end of the day. And after all that I'd still have enough left to pay like, four years' rent on the trailer—four entire *years,* Amy. You really don't get it, do you?"

I glared at him through the flashlight beam, face flushing at his dismissive words. Like I was so far up my own ass I'd just never noticed we had outbuildings bigger than his home? For all Ben's family lorded their status over the region, Uncle Peter's quarry fortune didn't approach my parents' earnings—a point of contention between my mother and aunt that topped the list of verboten dinner conversation topics. My family's wealth was hardly a secret, but Teddy, as much as he'd apparently stewed over the disparities in our lives, had never even left Kentucky—it was hard to imagine him fully grasping the gap between what passed for rich in River Run and the offhand opulence of the DC suburbs, where my upbringing was standard rather than elite. Was he more keenly aware of that imbalance than I'd thought? Or did it hurt him regardless, in ways I'd never guessed?

My teeth clenched over a reckless retort; I swallowed it down and made myself listen for once, instead of biting back. Made myself hear his frustration and his needs, the way they overlapped at the absence of things I'd never had to miss. That he had to consider every dollar spent just to have basics like gas and food had never really sunk in; I'd certainly never been faced with the choice of one over the other. It had never even occurred to me to worry.

"I do get it," I began, voice soft. "I know I've had so much handed to me that you never did, but it takes more than money to get as far as I plan to go—and none if it would matter if I didn't put in the work, so—"

"Work? You mean work like picking weeds out of the dirt, or driving that lawn mower all over hell and back? Tearing down goddamn branches in hundred-degree weather until you puke, then getting up the next day and doing it all again? You never worked like that a day in your life, and you never will—and *that's* what I mean when I say you don't get it. That kind of money would change *everything* about my life. Or, you know. I could go and learn to draw real pretty."

It didn't take much to withdraw from him. He let my hand slip away without a fight, then doubled down, turning his face away like there was something to see in the dark beyond the trees. I sat there like an asshole, blinking hard, burning with the sting of his words. He was right—I'd never known the hardship he saw as normal. But I'd also never judged him, or flaunted my money in his face, so what was up with the personal attack? My art, though clearly something less than vital to him, had been my constant since before we'd met. It had soothed and consumed me, given me purpose and brought me joy. It had kept me going through too many long, lonely years to be so casually mocked by one of the few people I'd thought had understood. And now he sat there glaring into the night, like he was waiting for an apology. Did I owe him one anyway, even after what he said? What was left for me to "get" about his life that I could actually help him fix?

"I'm sorry it's not easier on you," I said, trying like hell to keep my voice level, "but I'm not what's holding you back. Give yourself a chance, at least, before getting mad at me for things that aren't my fault."

"I'm not mad," he muttered, reaching for my hand once more. Waiting until my fingers curled around his before meeting my eyes. "Not at you. And your work . . . I know. I know it's great, and it's everything to you, and I honestly didn't mean to talk shit about it. I'm sorry it came off that way. I think it's awesome you get to live your dream—you'll be amazing, you won't have to worry, and you'll have everything you need. I *want* that for you, Ames."

"I want it for you, too, and that's exactly why I'm on your ass to leave this town. Your life won't change itself, especially around here—and you for damn sure won't get anywhere better if you don't at least try."

245

"Yeah, tell me about it." His laugh was low and hollow. "It's just so much fucking harder than I thought it'd be, watching from the outside. Knowing what you'll accomplish and what your art could mean to people who see it, but also knowing I can't be a part of that. Knowing you *belong* in that perfect world—and I just won't. Ever."

"It won't be perfect. Not if the person I belong with gets left behind."

The words left my mouth before I knew they existed. His hand tightened around mine as he ran his thumb over my knuckles, suddenly soft. Suddenly something.

"Amy—"

My fingers linked with his, answering his unasked question; we began for real in that moment, beyond words, beyond our earlier kisses. Shifted from two to one, almost without thought.

"I tell you, girl," he said, voice caught between a smile and a sigh. "If I did have that money, I'd be out of here on the first flight to anywhere else, as far as I could go. Take you with me, and never look back."

"I'm in. When do we leave?"

"As soon as your grandma pays me that king's ransom she owes me for the lawn work, we should be all set."

The night swelled around us, thick with cricket songs and late summer mist, as the moonlight caught his profile and my breath in the same silver glow. In that moment, I'd have done it. I'd have trampled over every last one of our dreams and disappeared into the night beside him, boarded the plane or train or bus without a thought. Stuck out my thumb alongside his on any road in the world.

"I'll hold you to that, you know," I said, breaking the silence. "If you stay, I stay, and then I'm stuck, too. You'll have to spend your life listening to Ben and me bitch at each other over the proper liquid-to-foam ratio of a latte, or whatever. That's no kind of future."

"Not for you it isn't, Amy." He was still smiling, but the joke was long gone. "You'll be more than fine, no matter what happens to me. The world will love you."

The world will love you, I almost told him. I *love you*, I almost told him. Instead I swallowed hard, biting my lip, enduring the burn behind my eyes.

"I have to say it, though," he continued, careless, as if we weren't stepping off the edge of everything. "I don't think I can ever be your friend again."

"I know." My fingers found the flashlight, clicked it off as I leaned in, losing us both in the darkness. "I don't really want you to be."

He caught me up and pulled me close, pressed his face against my neck. I breathed him, drowned in his warmth and the shudder of his sigh. Let my knees land on either side of his hips as I lowered my face to his, and when his lips found mine, leaving him was the last thought in my head.

Darrow paced the length of the porch as Ben and I talked over each other. He'd taken one look at the box and called for backup; his boss had taken one look at the box and called for more. The property was crawling with cops and packed with squad cars, headlights stretching us to tall, sharp shadows, flinging us against the house.

Teddy stood at the edge of the porch, shoulders straight and squared with desperate tension. Ben and I had huddled behind him as we waited for Darrow, watching his unmoving form fade to dark as the sun set.

". . . and after we found the box, I called you. We left it up there like you said to, but Teddy had already spilled it, so everything is out of order. But the braid was right on top. Right, Ames?"

"It was the first thing I saw. Do you think—"

"Could it be my sister's?" Teddy's question drifted over, finishing my thought. "Do you think it's hers?"

"I have to tell you, son, my first instinct would be to say no," Darrow said. "That box is on the older side, doesn't look to have been disturbed before you found it. But there's a chance . . ." He paused, weighing his words. "This place had its share of trespassers over the years and hasn't exactly been locked up tight, even up to now. Could be someone's used it for more than a place to sleep."

"Was that really necessary?" I snarled as Teddy turned away.

"I'm not here to hold anyone's hand, missy. There were signs of possible occupation in the downstairs the last time you called me out here—that mattress, the supplies. Saw those with my own two eyes. In light of today, I won't pretend they might be incidental to save your feelings."

"That's right," Ben said. "Do you think the mattress is connected to what we found in the attic? Do you think the hair was taken from the kids in those articles we found, or is that a totally separate thing? And are those kids the same ones you found in your research, and do you think there's a connection to—"

"Slow down, son. I wouldn't know *what* to think right now. The three of you did your job a little too well, throwing out all that stuff like you did. The sheriff and his men have to go through every box and bag, drag out the mattress for testing, pick through every last file. It's a goddamn forensic nightmare even without being jumbled up. Could take months to know anything at all."

"But it's possible?"

"Anything's possible. But first things first. Burke," he barked, summoning one of the many cops picking his way across the porch. "I want you on task to locate the previous owner of the house. I need details on occupancy history, date of abandonment, property ownership—find out who just up and left all this garbage behind, for starters."

"Easy enough," Burke said. "This is Gerald Franklin's old place. Had been since before I was born, up until he died . . . oh, about twenty, twenty-five years back? Noah's the son—it passed to him, but he hasn't lived here since we were in high school. I guess it was him sold it to Pete Hansen, but I'll check the property records and confirm."

"Good. Track down this Noah Franklin, if you can. Find out when he was last in town, if he accessed the house, who he talked to—all the usual. I need statements from him, and anyone who saw him."

"Don't know about the house, but he was in town just last month, visiting his mama's grave. Had some beers with me and the boys over at the pool hall."

"Last month? Find out where he stayed, cell records, exact times of arrival and departure. Let him know to sit tight, wherever he is now—we may need to bring him in for questioning, depending on what we find. Get Hansen over here as well."

"I already called my dad," Ben butted in. "He's on his way, but why would you question *him*? He's barely ever been in this house."

"Get your hackles down, son. We wouldn't be doing our jobs if we didn't check every lead. At the very least, we'll confirm the dates of ownership transfer, and find out what he knows about the Franklins. My team will check for files on the kids in those articles, try to match them up against what's in the box. That could end up as county jurisdiction, maybe state—out of my hands either way. But I'm still on point with the Fox case until there's a solid link between the two. I'd say not to get your hopes up, Mr. Hansen, but I'd likely only be talking to myself."

Sure enough, Ben was already only half listening. I could see him accessing his mental notebook, caching details, adding them to his official case binder. He'd be up late, scouring the Internet for any local drowning deaths reported in the past century. Making list upon list, conveniently forgetting Darrow had walked that road in the official investigation ages ago. My heart hurt at the thought of Ben working into the night, relentless and clueless, his own naivete rendering him unstoppable.

Uncle Peter's SUV swung into the yard as if answering the summons. He parked beside the dumpster, strode into the fray, and accosted Darrow; the two of them rattled back and forth, Ben interjecting, darting in like a bird from all sides. I left that whole mess behind and crossed to Teddy. Took his clenched hand in both of mine, leaned my head against his shoulder.

"Are you okay?"

"Nah, not really. Haven't actually been okay for a while now."

He was right, of course, and I had no words. I could only grip his hand harder and hold on tight until Ben's voice piped up behind us.

"Nothing new yet, guys, at least nothing they're telling me about. Darrow has that one cop on the Noah Franklin thing, and of course they have to question my dad since he's the property owner, but that's just a formality. Obviously. The priority is testing Nat's hair for a match to the hair in that box, so they'll know whether they should be looking for an active suspect. Right now they think Old Franklin's likely connected to the other missing kids, but he's been dead for ages."

"And they have exactly zero current theories?" I turned to face him, frowning at the helpless downturn of his mouth. "Figures. The whole planet has had access to this heap for years, yet suddenly no one has a clue. This town is the worst."

"It's all they can do." He shook his head. "This is pretty messed up, huh, Ames? Your mom used to hang out here, for fuck's sake—wasn't she like, besties with Noah Franklin growing up?"

"God. You're right." I fought off a shudder at the thought of her shoes thumping on this same porch, climbing those stairs, crunching through the driveway and yard and untended woods. I'd spent far too much of my summer walking, unknowingly, over her long-faded footprints. "Do you think she knew?"

"Knowing her, she probably helped dump the bodies. Hey, Teddy, if you need to go, you can take my car. They won't be done here for ages."

"You sure? If I have to hang around this place much longer—"

"I get it. Go. Take Amy home, get cleaned up, try to get some sleep. Drive it over to Grandma's tomorrow and I'll pick it up there."

"Thanks, man. Thanks for dealing with all this. I don't think I could handle any of it without you, Benny."

"Dude, no worries. Nat was awesome. There's nothing I wouldn't do for her, or—aw, shit. It's okay, man. Hang in there."

Ben gave Teddy a couple manly thumps on the back, then stood there taking the hug awkwardly, arms at his sides, until he was released. A movement behind him caught my attention—Uncle Peter's head, turning their way, the tiny twitch in his cheek a fault line in his otherwise blank expression. His eyes met mine, held them for a split second before he turned his back, caught a passing cop, and dragged him into a flurry of questions. He looked like shit, my uncle. Like all his meals were eighty proof, and he'd forgotten how to sleep.

A memory snagged on my senses: his name, a dark blue Sharpie scrawl, the drunken block letters formed in his own son's hand. Nat's death had devastated all of us, Uncle Peter included—how could we have made that list in the first place, much less added him to the roster? It was a ludicrous thought—the bourbon's thought, like Ben had said. Both illogical and unthinkable.

Still, I watched him for a full minute, waiting to see if he'd turn. Waiting to see if his eyes would hold questions or challenges, or flit away from mine in a flicker of fear or guilt. But no matter how hard I stared, he kept his shoulders squared, his face forward.

He didn't look at me again.

The drive home was an eons-long journey of open windows and cicada songs, warm air heavy with night blossoms and the faint scent of a faraway storm. My grandparents' house was dark save for the porch light; they routinely went to bed at nine, and it was nearly midnight by the time Teddy pulled into the driveway. We looked at each other over the mile of console between us, neither knowing how to break the smothering silence.

"Don't ask if I'm okay." The words tripped over each other as they left his mouth, half shattered and barely audible. "I won't be anywhere near okay until we find out what happened to her. If that's not her braid, then we still don't know. But if it is, that means whoever put it in that box put her in the river. I honestly don't know which is worse."

"Don't think about that. Darrow said it probably isn't hers, anyway."

"But whose was it, then? God, did you see all that hair? Some sick fuck took those kids, maybe took my sister. Someone held her underwater, cut off a piece of her hair, and stored it in his fucking wall. There is no upside to this."

"What can I do, Teddy? Tell me what I can do to help you. Anything."

"Nothing." He killed the engine, leaving us in darkness. "Come on. I'll walk you up."

His shoulder brushed mine as we made our way to the porch. I turned to face him at the foot of the steps, caught the gleam of the moon in his hooded, shadow-smudged eyes. He looked so tired in a way that went beyond our long, physically demanding day. This exhaustion was a different beast, one that had chewed at him, bit by bit, since the moment we'd found Nat's things.

"Want to sit for a while? It's not late."

"Nah, I should get home. Never saw today coming, did we? I should be with Mom when she hears about this. She'll be—"

I caught him as he crumbled, eased us both down to the lowest step. My hands found the lines of his neck, the planes of his face. Followed a smudged tear track to the corner of his mouth.

"Sorry." His laugh was short and humorless. "It keeps catching me off guard, you know? I thought I was doing better—getting back into a routine, getting my head on straight. Even things with you were finally starting to work out. I know I've been a dick about it, but I just want us to be okay."

"We are," I whispered, leveled by a wave of guilt and sorrow. How could I spend a second worrying about our relationship when his heart was so thoroughly in tatters? "I'm here for you—I'm your friend, always. I'm whatever you need."

"God. You have no idea." He pulled away and dropped his head, fingers raking through his hair as he spoke. "I'm such a piece of shit to even have those thoughts. It makes me sick to think I could be happy again, but it scares the hell out of me that I might *not*. I'll never *not* miss Nat, so this must be it for me—it'll just hurt forever, no matter what. How do I get past it? When does any of it ever stop?"

"I don't know." My voice nearly lost its way to my lips, it was that defeated. "But I *am* here for you—I won't leave you alone in this, no matter what happens with us. We don't have to be together to be okay."

"Like I could ever be okay without you." He sighed. "I need to get going. The way things are now with us—as friends—it's enough, I guess. It has to be."

The kiss landed on my cheekbone, soft and final. A goodbye without words. My heart shuddered at his hollow face, caught in profile as he turned away—as he rose to his feet and started back to the car. Every step he took was a tug, a lovely ache that dulled any sense of doubt.

Without each other, neither one of us would be okay. We would never be more than completely incomplete.

"Hey, Teddy?"

My voice stilled his feet, pulled them a couple unplanned steps back toward me. Pulled his eyes from the ground up, until they found mine.

He caught me without trying. My toes barely brushed the grass between his boots as he lifted me; as he broke and scattered and saved me, hands skimming my bones like a river current slipping over hidden rocks. His lips were salt, his skin a dusty burn. He was mine. He was everything.

"It's *not* enough," I whispered, when I finally let him breathe. "It's you and me. World without end."

"Really?" His voice held a raw edge at those words, a plea to not throw our childish vow at him, unless I wanted it to stick. "Because I can't take another round of the whole on-again, off-again thing. If we fuck this up, I can't go back."

"We'll get through all of it, I swear—we'll get through it together. We won't go back, not this time. Not ever."

"Never, Amy. I'm so in love with you."

His words sparked over my neck and shoulders and arms, thrilling down my back. I felt him shudder, an infectious, electric burst that leaped from his skin to mine as our eyes caught and held.

"Same here. Always and always."

"Do you mean that?"

I couldn't help smiling, even as the question stung my already bruised heart. What did it say about my love that it was so easy for him to doubt it after all these years? What did it say about me that he hadn't seen it all along?

"Seriously? Of course I love you. When the hell have I ever not?"

His laugh filled my senses as I kissed his forehead, cheeks, chin—anywhere I could reach, between my own soft sighs of laughter. He drew me into him then, kissed away my smile as my eyes slid closed around the bright buzz of my veins.

And for that moment, at least, everything wrong between us was right.

CHAPTER 31
SUMMER 2019

The river slid along beside me, a slow, swollen worm on a silent belly. I crossed the cove alone, taking in the morning-dappled rocks, the gnarled branches, the familiar curve of the water's edge, beautiful and unchanged. Undeniably marred. I didn't flee, but I didn't stop, either—I kept moving past the shallow depression of the firepit, past the giant oak, until I reached the path to Teddy's place and let the trees swallow me whole.

He waited on the flat rock by the river's edge, watching the water roll and retreat over the banks. His hair was loose and sweat-damp, his back a lonely hunch tense with worry and anticipation. The boy who loved me, weary with the weight of summer.

We'd lingered on the porch far longer that we'd meant to the night before, let ourselves detach from the horrible day and forget the entire shit show unfolding at the Franklin house. Let ourselves feel, for once, something more than a constant, internal wail. It was sweet and essential, heavy with its own vitality. Still seething in the air between us.

I fumbled in my satchel for my sketchpad and charcoal tin, mind and heart and fingers melding, unbinding for the first time since our world had split and shattered. The paralysis trickled away—a chain dissolving link by link.

Teddy shifted and yawned, crossed his ankles in front of him, then went suddenly still. His head turned my way; his eyes swept up my legs, over my body, paused at my parted lips. Lingered on the sketchpad in my white-knuckled grip. He turned back to profile, tossing his hair away from his face.

"Make it pretty, Ames."

My hands moved without me, pulling him out of the paper line by line. The bend of his elbow. The cords of his neck. The swoop of his spine, sprouting from the rock. I was cross-legged on the ground by the final stroke, wired and breathless, thighs a gravel-pocked mess of red clay and charcoal dust. He screamed from the page, all smirk and brow and long, strong limbs. Incomparable. Beautiful.

"Did you get it?" he teased, reaching to steady me as I climbed onto the rock, trapped his sigh in a kiss cut short by his grin. "Let's see the masterpiece."

That grin fell away. He blinked at himself, then at me. Took in my fingers still clutching a blunted pencil. Wiped a charcoal smudge from the hollow of my cheek.

"This is incredible."

"It's how you look to me." I fumbled the charcoal back into its tin, stashed it in my satchel as I spoke. "It's how you've always looked."

The sketchbook dropped between us. His hands found mine and I leaned in, eyelids falling closed. Creeping open again to his earnest, careful face as he spoke.

"This *is* your dream, isn't it? Art school? It's what you truly want?"

"Yes," I whispered, searching his eyes. "But—"

"Then you have to chase it, Ames. You are way too good not to take this as far as you can. I'll move to a town with a goddamn cell tower, text you every day. Save up my paychecks and visit. I'll—"

"Come with me."

My voice was low but strong, smoothing his into silence. He stared at me, then laughed out loud, too incredulous to be bitter.

"To where? Paris? Yeah, that'll happen."

"To wherever. Maybe Europe, maybe New York—you hate this town. I don't graduate for two more years. We have plenty of time to hash out the details."

"Amy, I can't. I have to work, I have responsibilities—"

"Not anymore."

It was the worst thing to say. The worst kind of truth, terrible and undeniable—the kind that took down doors and tore down walls. A silver lining, straight from hell.

"God," he finally said, voice hollow enough to make me wince. "Guess there's nothing keeping me here now, huh? Time to go live the dream."

"That came out wrong. I didn't mean to—"

"I know you didn't." He rubbed his eyes, fixed them on the river—past the river, on the opposite bank. On the thick barrier of trees and rocks that hid the beyond from our view. "But you're right. I'm free."

"Teddy." He let me reclaim his hand without protest, but it was limp against my palm. "I'm sorry. I—"

And then Ben walked into the middle of it, blew open the trail-head like the juggernaut he was—big and blond, boisterous beneath a thin sheen of sweat. Commanding as the sun.

"There you are. Grandma said you left early. When you weren't at the cove—" He paused, studied our pained faces and still, pinched mouths. Teddy's hands withdrew again, just enough that our fingers barely touched. "Everything okay?"

"We're fine, Benny. What's up?"

Ben plunked his bag between us and climbed up next to it, nudging me until I shifted over. He reeked of coffee and mouthwash and too much cologne.

"I'm glad you asked, dude. Last night was a fucked-up mess for sure, but it ended up being productive as hell. Which it better have been, since we were there till four a.m."

"And you're awake?" I side-eyed his manic, toothy grin. "It's not even nine."

"Dexedrine, my friend. Keeps a spring in my step."

"Dude, come on." Teddy sighed. "Go home, sleep it off."

"I'm perfectly fine, Teddy, thanks for your concern. Now look." He reached into his bag and unloaded the same spiral notebook he'd shown me the day we started the investigation—now a tattered mess of folded corners and page marker tabs, swollen and bent with over-use. "We pulled some crazy shit out of that attic, but the braid is what Darrow sees as the focus. We know for sure it was cut. With scissors, probably—could have been a knife. There were no bits of scalp attached, no blood or follicles, which means—"

"Yeah. I need to go." Teddy slid off the rock, ran his hand through his hair, tugging on the ends. Ben blinked at him, missing my furious glare.

"You're not off today?"

"Chores, man. Laundry. Some other shit. Later."

I tried to follow him. I shoved past Ben and scrambled off the rock. Failed to catch up even with my overlong legs. He'd disappeared inside the trailer before I was halfway across the yard.

Ben was absorbed in his notes, flipping through a folder marked *HOUSE*, so he was caught off guard when I smacked it right out of his hands. A scatter of pages and Post-its, slashed with yellow and pink highlighter pen, drifted to the dirt at our feet.

"The fuck is your problem?"

"Goddamn it, Benjamin. You couldn't just leave off? Not even once?"

"Like that was my fault? This is forensic fact, Amy. Holding back at this point is counterproductive."

"Bits of *scalp*? Really?"

"Okay, point taken, but he's in this *with* us. It's horrible—it's brutal as fuck, right down to the core, and there's no way around it. Believe me, I'm not trying to hurt him."

"I believe it—I've seen what happens when you try."

We stared at each other, the words finally out—that terrible day acknowledged at last.

"I expect that sort of shit from the rest of them," I continued, "but the you I know is better than that. And you destroyed him."

"There is a big difference," he said, voice a low growl that matched mine, "between yelling some stupid shit in anger and deliberately setting out to break him. Don't worry about Teddy and me—I've known him a lot longer than you have, no matter how close you think you are."

It took everything in me not to yell it in his face, tell him exactly how close we'd grown while Ben was off playing detective. But the

eva v. gibson

way Teddy had pulled away from me . . . he was wary of the fallout, and with good reason. A repeat performance of last summer was literally the last thing we needed. So instead of setting Ben straight on my own, I climbed back onto the rock and leaned forward, forced him to meet my eye.

"The least you could do is apologize already. For real, not that half-assed brush-off you two always do."

"Don't judge the brush-off, okay? That's our thing. And I *will* apologize, but there are certain things I need to work out, first." His eyes were bloodshot but sharp, the blend of sorrow, anger, and remorse drawing me in. The defiance daring me to look away. "You know how that feels, right, Amy? Having emotions you're not yet ready to share?"

"Shut up."

"Yep, thought so. Oh, and in case you're interested? I'm pretty sure the whole 'one true love' thing is mutual on his part."

"My God, Ben." I leaned back on my hands, turned my face away. "You can stop anytime."

"Whatever. He's been crazy about you since sixth grade and never said shit. Thought he'd be lucky if you gave him the time of day. Why do you think he's plowed his way through the female half of our peer group?"

"Because you're both pigs?"

"Because he was looking for something he'd already given up on having with you. The impossible dream: finally being good enough for rich, pretty, perfect little Amy Larsen."

"I've never given him a single reason to think he wasn't. You *know* I haven't."

My sketchbook fell to the carpet with a soft thud, pencil rolling after it as I shifted my weight beneath him. The television faded into a background drone; rain drummed at the windows and roof as my fingers, still humming with ideas, traced the angles of his face and shoulders, combed through the lovely mess of his hair. Far from rushing things between us, Teddy had taken things middle-school slow in the two days since we'd put our hearts into the world. His restraint had been its own veiled seduction—the tease of his touch, the flush of his skin. The unspoken boundaries he drew between us, and the way his eyes looked when I crept too close to them.

We'd retreated to his place when the rain began, our post-workday walk ending in a flurry of soggy clothes and towel-dried hair. While Teddy changed out of his coveralls, I'd settled onto the couch in front of the TV and immediately put charcoal to paper, descended into a spiral of lines and shadows until he emerged from his room. He'd put on a random movie we'd both promptly ignored, curled up next to me, and dragged a blanket over us both. I'd let him flip through the sketchbook, heart fluttering at the reverence in his face, how each finished image lit his eyes in a way I hadn't seen since last summer. His smile had dissolved where my lips began; his hand

"Well, plenty of other people have. So do me a favor
sure he knows where you stand. It would go a long way towa
what I fucked up."

"Is that why you're no longer having an aneurysm at
thought? Because of your conscience?"

"It's way more than that," he said, sliding off the rock
the scattered pages. His hair swung forward, hiding the t
face. "When I get that whole articulation thing hammer
be sure to let you know."

My sketchbook fell to the carpet with a soft thud, pencil rolling after it as I shifted my weight beneath him. The television faded into a background drone; rain drummed at the windows and roof as my fingers, still humming with ideas, traced the angles of his face and shoulders, combed through the lovely mess of his hair. Far from rushing things between us, Teddy had taken things middle-school slow in the two days since we'd put our hearts into the world. His restraint had been its own veiled seduction—the tease of his touch, the flush of his skin. The unspoken boundaries he drew between us, and the way his eyes looked when I crept too close to them.

We'd retreated to his place when the rain began, our post-workday walk ending in a flurry of soggy clothes and towel-dried hair. While Teddy changed out of his coveralls, I'd settled onto the couch in front of the TV and immediately put charcoal to paper, descended into a spiral of lines and shadows until he emerged from his room. He'd put on a random movie we'd both promptly ignored, curled up next to me, and dragged a blanket over us both. I'd let him flip through the sketchbook, heart fluttering at the reverence in his face, how each finished image lit his eyes in a way I hadn't seen since last summer. His smile had dissolved where my lips began; his hand

"Well, plenty of other people have. So do me a favor—make sure he knows where you stand. It would go a long way toward fixing what I fucked up."

"Is that why you're no longer having an aneurysm at the mere thought? Because of your conscience?"

"It's way more than that," he said, sliding off the rock to collect the scattered pages. His hair swung forward, hiding the twist of his face. "When I get that whole articulation thing hammered out, I'll be sure to let you know."

cupped the back of my head, pulling me closer as we fell into each other, short of patience and of breath. Closer than we'd even been, and finally, completely, alone. Still moving slower than a lazy river current, as if there wasn't a decade-long fuse on the question of us.

As the angles of his body settled over mine, I was more than ready to light it up. I'd spent far too much time already waiting for his cue.

Before I could begin to verbalize that thought, Teddy bolted upright, blanket falling from his shoulders. He ran one hand frantically through his damp hair, gesturing to my legs with the other one. I blinked down at them as I sat up, tugged my dress hem back into place, confusion flipping to understanding at the slam of a car door outside. I sat up straighter, smoothed my own hair as Teddy fussed with the throw pillows and piled the blanket into a lumpy barricade between us. His hand fumbled for mine, squeezed it once, then detached, disappeared into his folded arms just as the door swung open and a rain-spattered June appeared on the threshold like a bewildered ghost. Her keys dangled from one hand, a plastic bag of groceries from the other.

"Hey, Mom." Teddy's voice was a smooth, neutral contradiction to his flushed cheeks. "Need a hand with that?"

She shut the door with her foot and shook her head, not bothering with more than a glance at us before crossing to the kitchen and hefting the bag onto the table. She blinked at it a few times, like she'd forgotten what it was, or why she'd bothered bringing it inside. Then instead of unpacking it, she turned away, shuffled slowly past us and headed down the hall to her room.

I watched her go, let my eyes slide over to Teddy's set jaw and wide, guilty eyes. Remembered the way those eyes had looked the morning I'd found him by the river, when I'd shown him my drawing; the pride in his voice when he'd praised my work; how his hands had closed so gently over mine. How those same hands had fallen away at my cousin's noisy approach. And now he was shifting sideways on the couch, even though June was no longer in the room and had barely acknowledged us in the first place. It wasn't the distance that bothered me; it was the nervous vibe behind the distance. The unknown something keeping us apart in every way.

I waited until I heard June's door close with a soft click, then turned to him, dreading his answer before the question made it past my lips.

"Teddy? Did I do something wrong?"

"No. God, no, Ames, you're amazing. It's—fuck." He sat back, frustrated, teeth all but grinding over his words. "It's complicated. Mom's been kind of helicopter lately. For her, anyway."

"That's weird." I bit my lip, picturing her vacant, broken gaze. Wondered what the baseline for a helicopter mom looked like in June Barrett's world, and whether it involved anything beyond her physical presence in the house. "Is she still mad about the bonfire, or—"

"Not mad, no. She loves you, don't worry about that. But—" He glanced away from me, at June's closed bedroom door. "She thinks it's bad timing with Nat and all. Thinks I should wait until you're out of school to get serious. Find out where you'll be, what your plans are, how soon we'll need to get the place fixed up for you. Stuff like that."

"Fixed up for *me*? Does she think I'm going to like, move in here or something?"

His shrug was more of a cringe; a reluctant half answer that sent a bolt through my chest. A horrendously clear premonition flashed through my mind: sitting opposite him at the green Formica table, June planted in the seat between us; hanging my laundry on the outdoor line; my shoes on the doormat next to theirs. Aging out of adolescence in the home of someone else's mother.

How about no. How about all the noes in the vast and weary world.

"I thought it was *my* mom we were worried about," I said, eyeing the self-conscious flush staining his cheeks. Let my gaze stray, idiotically, to the door, as if expecting Eleanor Larsen herself to glide through it, summoned by her name and my defiance. "Why was that even a discussion? Even if I did come back for longer than a summer, wouldn't we just get our own place?"

"In River Run? There aren't many options. If you don't have the grades for college and can't afford to leave town or build on your family's property, you're better off splitting rent with whoever has room for you." He kept his gaze fixed on the carpet, every word a halting effort. "I hadn't even thought that far ahead until she brought it up, but that's what a lot of kids do around here after graduation—settle down and get to work. Stick with their parents, make sure everyone's fed. You help with bills, they help with the kids, until it eventually, hopefully, balances out."

"Okay, what the fuck. The *kids?*" I rubbed my face, trying to pinpoint the exact moment we'd veered off the path of rational possibilities and into the land of Absolutely Not. "Is this conversation actually happening?"

"Yeah, I'm not wild about it myself, but she has a point—if we stick this out, we'd be on our own. Your mom's not about to pay for art school if she thinks you'd just end up here anyway. She might even disown you." He shook his head slowly, raised a knowing eyebrow at my startled blink. "Yep, see? You hadn't thought it through either."

"You're talking about me moving in here when we've been together for a little under half a second. Literally I would never have 'thought it through' to this particular conclusion."

"Nothing about this was my idea," he sighed, "but it is my reality. It'll be yours, too, if you settle for the lawn boy. Amy, last year, I—fuck." He ran a hand over his eyes and turned away from me, stared hard at the floor between his feet. "Remember after you went home—when I stopped answering your messages? We were going through some real hard shit. Mom lost her job right as school started. We couldn't make rent. I had to ask your grandma for an extension. Twice. I—" He blinked hard, still refusing to meet my eyes. "It was a low point, is what I'm saying. I didn't want you dragged into it, so. Yeah."

"That's why you blew me off? I don't care about stuff like that, Teddy—I could have helped you—talked to Grandma, or even sent cash. Why didn't you just tell me?"

"*Tell* you? I can barely say it *now*. What happens in five years, or ten, if I still can't provide for my own household? Or if things get worse? The yard work thing won't feed a family, and the way things are going around here with the farmers, the best I can hope for is whatever I can get at the quarry—on my own, without sucking up to your uncle. I'm not about to beg for handouts, Amy. Not from your family, and sure as hell not from you. '*Sent cash.*'" His lip curled into a sneer. "Thanks for the offer, but no fucking way."

I stared at his profile, heart cracking at the weary lines of his brow and barely perceptible quiver of his chin. It was surreal—him stressing over being a provider, whatever *that* meant. He was seventeen. He shouldn't have to provide for *anyone*, much less be the person asking for lenience on bills come due. Especially while Ben wealth-signaled like it was his job, swanned around town in whichever one of his cars best enhanced his fucking shirt, then bitched for days on end about the burden of his free house. How Teddy hadn't punched him in the face long ago was a mystery for the ages.

But was I any better? I didn't care about money because I didn't *have* to care, which made me Ben-adjacent, at the very least. How River Run's dating culture might impact my plans had sure as hell never crossed my mind—and if June's assumptions were any indication, it was no wonder my mom had absconded that fate at the first opportunity, fleeing from the guy in the hidden pictures until he was safely in her past—just another small-town stepping-stone whose devotion hadn't been nearly enough to make her stay.

Was I destined for that same driven, lonely path, no matter who I loved? I'd spent my life ambivalent about money—a mindset that seemed admirably neutral from the outside yet stemmed from privilege foreign to most of the world, let alone River Run. It wasn't just my huge, safe home, or the material things inside it—it was the way the world outside that home lay open to me, free of obstacles or obstructions. The tuition set aside at birth for any college that would have me. The means to live comfortably in any city, regardless of the wage I earned. The option to forgo earning anything at all, if I chose, instead, to focus on my art. The time and funds to invest in the art itself; to have my technique honed by instructors who'd push my talent to the next level; to stockpile the necessary tools and supplies, and never once sweat the cost. To casually wave aside the impact of wealth on that future was an insult to every dime and sacrifice made by the boy whose livelihood rested on the aesthetics of my family's yard. That driven, lovely boy, forever starved for a life beyond his reach.

My post–high school expectations involved lectures and installations and travel abroad, followed by an utter immersion in the art scene of my choice—for all the years I'd spent counting heartbeats over thoughts of Teddy, the reality of "settling down," as he so vaguely and casually put it, was nothing but a possible speck in the far distant future. Did he see me as a speck in *his* future, or a partner in a more immediate, looming reality I'd thoroughly taken for granted? I hadn't considered his expectations at all, nor that the path he'd walk to meet them looked far, far different from mine.

Just last summer he'd been clawing at the edges of River Run, searching for a balance between obligation and escape. Now, when obligation had all but been removed, it was like he'd forgotten how to want *anything*, let alone something more. His determination, his frustration, the fucking fjords—all of that had apparently drifted into nothingness along with Nat. And if he was already projecting that attitude onto our relationship, resigning us to an endgame of poverty, drudge, and growing old alongside his mother, then what the hell were we even doing?

"Are you breaking up with me?" The words slipped out meek and unexpected, as small and sad as the tears stinging my eyes. The hole in my head expanded, bit by incremental bit; I clenched my fingers into fists, pressed my nails into the soft beds of my palms.

Applied the precise amount of pressure needed to drag me back to the world. Still, Teddy's voice seemed far away as he answered.

"No. Christ, no, I'm not breaking up with you—I just need you to understand where my head's at. Maybe tone it down when Mom's around." He paused, grimacing around his next words. "Ben, too. He's been awesome lately, with the case and all, but he's still a wild card. I'm not about to deal with him going off on another fit."

"So we get to do what—sneak around until Ben's feeling less delicate?" I shook my head at his helpless shrug, more than done with that particular glitch in our narrative. "I love my cousin, Teddy, but how many chances should he get before we tell him to fuck off? He almost ruined us for good. When do we get to just be happy?"

"You tell me, Ames. Right now I'll settle for whatever we can get."

It seemed huge, what he was asking—to continue to hide, this time from both our families. Was it worth pushing back, though, if acquiescence made things even the least bit easier on him? Losing Nat had scarred his heart in a way that would likely never heal. There *was* no fast track to making things right; no kiss or promise or word powerful enough to ease that pain.

And here I was, the asshole who wanted to put the misery behind us—to erase the utter horror of the summer, sink into the blissful haze we'd found the year before. Lose ourselves in a love made stronger by distance and time and wanting. To hope he'd set aside his grief for that smacked of a selfishness beyond comparison, breathtaking in both scope and weight.

I couldn't watch him suffer anymore, not for my sake. Definitely not for the sake of some hypothetical, unknown future.

"Okay," I whispered, sliding my hand over his. Nearly weeping with relief when he turned it over to thread his fingers through mine. "We don't have to go public yet. Whatever you want is fine with me."

"It's *not* what I want," he muttered, "but it's probably the right choice, at least for now. Just—know that I love you, Amy. Whatever happens."

His words danced through my veins, clamored and sparked along the edges of my heart as I met his eyes, let myself sink beneath their tidal pull of hope and devotion and stark, helpless fear. It would be enough. It would have to be.

I leaned in over the blanket wall, pressed my lips to his temple, then his jaw, waited until he gave in. Waited until his arms wrapped around me before sagging against him, letting my cheek rest carefully against the thump of his heart. He didn't pull away.

We stayed like that until we heard the soft creak of June's door and drew apart, turning our focus back to the TV as she drifted past us and into the kitchen, barely glancing at our blank faces and brushing hands. I stared straight ahead, throat tight and aching, pretending interest in the denouement of a movie I couldn't name.

CHAPTER 33

SUMMER 2019

Teddy's knuckle trailed along the row of books, tapping absently at spine after spine as he wandered up and down the stacks. I swiped a tired hand across my eyes, wishing I could will away the persistent thudding in my temples. We'd been at the library all afternoon, and a veil of exhaustion hung over my head, a dull contrast to the frenetic hammering of Ben's fingers on the computer keyboard, which had no trouble reaching me from across the main room.

Our agreement hadn't taken long to wear thin, not on my part nor on Teddy's. He'd walked me home after the movie that day and promptly pulled me behind the garden shed, kissed me until my legs were weak and my lungs were empty. Every one of our encounters in the few days since had been sketched in the same secretive ink—I'd promised him I'd go along, and I had. But every furtive glance made it harder to see beyond that summer. How were we supposed to really move forward if each accidental touch ended with us ducking behind trees and buildings and goddamn utility poles, jumping apart at any hint of a noise?

I'd woken that morning to the Mustang's horn, followed by the whirlwind of my cousin barging into my room before my brain shook off the fog of sleep. I'd shoved him back into the hallway and into Grandma's clutches; by the time I joined them in the kitchen, she was stuffing him with guilt and pancakes, scolding him for waking me while simultaneously praising his growing-boy appetite and up-and-at-'em energy.

Unfortunately for said energy, Ben, in his enthusiasm, had neglected to confirm Teddy's availability. He'd spent the next three hours pacing my room, peering impatiently out the window to monitor the progress of the riding mower, and bitching about the rate of summer-season grass growth. I ignored him as best I could, a preferred state of existence made even easier by my rekindled artistic focus. By the time the mower's engine growled to a stop, I'd completed fifty-four thumbnails in my sketchbook, more than enough to meet my mother's expectations, each stroke of my pencils lifting its own tiny, leaden weight from my heart.

Now, six eons later, I was hunched over a table in River Run Public Library's tiny periodicals section, muscles aching, fingertips stained with newsprint ink. I'd been delegated the task of thumbing through the nine million years' worth of old newspapers that hadn't been logged in the online system, searching for any mention of missing or dead children, and jotting names and dates in one of Ben's notebooks. I'd found a surprisingly large number, especially for a rural area, but there was nothing hinting at a connection to the Franklin family or the boxes we'd found. It didn't help that I'd barely glanced at most of the articles in the attic; aside from the red-haired girl, whose face now lived eternally in my mind, I couldn't remember any other details. Still, I thumbed through every brittle page, spurred by a gnawing hope that the names I found would yield more information when typed into a search engine.

Teddy, who'd finished his own far less intensive task ages ago, circled behind me like a shark, slow and silent and restless. His fingertip traced a shiver across the back of my neck as he slid into the seat next to mine.

"Hey, Ames," he murmured, a shade too wistful. His hand drifted toward mine, thoughtlessly and naturally. He caught himself and stopped short, eyes flitting past me to scan the room. His hand wavered awkwardly between us before forming into a high five—an actual high five, palm in the air, waiting for the return like I was goddamn Ben. "Um. Up high?"

"Excuse me?" I tossed my head, dragged snowmelt eyes from his face to the hand and back again, a mocking emulation of his initial, pre-high-fucking-five gaze. "Up *high*?"

The hand disappeared beneath the tabletop. He met my glare with sagging shoulders and a tiny, nervous, smile—a sad, sorry shadow of the one I knew. It broke my heart all over again, watching him balk every time he got too close, avoiding my eyes in front of everyone who mattered, and everyone who didn't.

I glanced at the back of Ben's head, then rose from the table and ducked into the stacks, motioning for Teddy to follow. When we reached the wall at the far end of the shelves, I turned to face him, glancing around to check for eavesdroppers before I spoke.

"Teddy, I'm trying, okay? But really? Mixed signals are not my thing, especially when it comes to you."

"I know. I know, okay? I'm just trying to act natural."

"Since when have you ever come at me with a high five, even before all this? Grabbing my ass would be more natural."

"I mean, I can always go there, if you want," he joked, grin stalling into a grimace at my glare, then reforming into a wicked version of itself. He peeked around the stacks at Ben, who still sat at the computer, back to us. Stepped closer until my shoulder blades brushed the wall. "Say the word, Ames."

"You say the word; this was all your idea. Not that it matters—aside from Ben, who do we even know in here who would see us?"

"I know just about everyone, actually, at least by sight. Small town, remember? Most of them know my mom—and yours." His mouth pulled into a smirk at my skeptical glare. "What, you think River Run forgot Eleanor Langston? She's like, the biggest success story to ever come out of this place. They know her, all right—and they sure as hell know Ben Hansen's East Coast cousin. If little Amy Larsen starts slumming around with the kid from her grandma's trailer? Bet that ass of yours it'd get back to all our parents in under a day."

"So it's not just about Ben or June. We have to hide from everyone because of a bunch of nosy, backwoods—" I bit off the end of the thought, swallowed it down before it pierced the wrong target. "I told you—I'm in if you are. But if this is one of your fuckboy games, you need to tell me now."

"Believe me. We"—he leaned in close again, words shifting to a whisper against my ear—"are anything but a game."

"Well, you're the one playing hide-and-seek with the whole damn town," I whispered back, making no attempt to move away. "And you're the one about to get us caught—standing there giving me that look, probably still thinking about my ass."

"I so am. But you're right. I'm sorry." Teddy sighed. "This is just way harder than I thought. Acting like everything's cool, when all

I want is to disappear, find someplace where it doesn't matter." His cheekbone grazed mine, sent a slow, warm flame twisting through my middle. "Away from everything and everyone but you."

"Hey, Teddy. TEDDY. GET OVER HERE." Ben's shout rang through the stacks, pulling us apart. A half-dozen voices shushed him, overlapping one another before he'd finished speaking. "Okay, okay, sorry. Christ. *Ames*," he stage-whispered, voice no less grating for its lowered volume. *"Where are you?"*

"I'm right here, Ben. God." I ducked out from under Teddy's outstretched arm and hurried down an aisle, following the sound of my cousin's voice. He'd commandeered my table and upturned his messenger bag on the surface. I reached him in time to catch a Sharpie right before it rolled off the edge. "Did you find something?"

"Fuckin'-A right I did. It was Noah Franklin. I'm like, eighty percent positive."

"Dude, for real?" Teddy said, appearing at Ben's shoulder, avoiding my exasperated side-eye. He'd circled the stacks, approached from the opposite direction, making it look like he'd been browsing on his own. For someone who'd been so conflicted moments before, he sure as hell had doubled down on keeping up appearances. "What've you got?"

"This is some wild shit, you guys. Check it out." Ben slammed a stack of printed pages onto the table and snatched the Sharpie from my hand, jabbed the top page with the cap. His cheeks were pink, his hair a tousled mess, like he'd dragged his hands through it over and over. "The house itself was built in 1870 by Amos Allen Franklin. He would have been Noah's great-grandfather, I think. Maybe great-great, but it doesn't matter. It's been passed down through the oldest sons every generation. The dates on the articles we found go from about 1997 all the way back to 1986. Noah's mom died in 1984, so he and Old Gerald were the only ones living there at that point. He would have been a kid then—right around Nat's age, actually. Right around the same ages as all the other the kids who went missing."

"Hold up, Benny," Teddy interrupted. "All the other kids? 1986? How the hell do you know all that?"

"I checked my copies of the articles?" He raised an eyebrow at our puzzled faces. "What, you think I memorized all that shit? I took pictures with my phone while we waited on the cops."

"*That's* what you were doing in there that day?" I said, forgetting to whisper. I'd practically broken my legs getting out of that house, and Teddy had been right at my heels. Ben had emerged several moments after us, but we'd hardly thought to question the delay at the time. "What were you thinking?"

"Really? We're in the middle of a murder investigation. I was *thinking* I'd better get them while I could, before Darrow showed up and started slapping evidence labels on everything. He's been a dick about sharing."

"I just spent how many hours looking all this up by hand, and you've had copies this whole time?"

"Well, you never know. I might have missed one."

"Oh, great thinking. Thanks a lot." I dropped my volume back to a whisper right before it rose beyond library polite. "If Darrow finds out what you did—"

"Whatever, that was *our* discovery. If the cops want to get technical, Dad bought the house as is, and all the contents therein, murder trophies included. Taking pictures of my own property isn't illegal. And if it is, well, can you guess how many fucks I give?"

"Goddamn, Ben," Teddy groaned. "Love to see you tell *that* one to a judge."

"All those articles would've gone straight into the landfill if not for me, so as far as I'm concerned, they should *all* be kissing my ass, hypothetical judges included. Anyway." Ben tapped a finger on the folder, getting back to business. "Noah Franklin left River Run in May 1993, right after Amy's mom took off. They were in the same class, I think—is that right, Ames?"

"Yes, '93. Two years behind Aunt Mattie."

"That's right. Dad and Sam were '91—and wasn't June a couple years younger, Teddy? I know they were all in school together at some point."

"Mom was class of '94, I think," Teddy said. "A freshman when Dad was a senior. So yeah. A year behind Amy's mom."

"And Noah Franklin," Ben added. "He was young, but stranger things have happened. He must know *something*. And there's nothing saying he didn't play a part in the later disappearances."

"So because he was in town back then, he must have been involved?" I said. "Ben, everyone we know was in town—on the same land, even. Our mothers lived right through the woods. Teddy's place is practically the halfway point between the houses."

"That land was nothing but trees and a footpath back then. When my parents got married and everyone caught the fucking hint that your mom was staying gone, Grandpa cleared the site. Dad hired Sam to oversee the stables, and they installed the trailer for him and June. This was all before we were born, but either way, they weren't on the property when shit went down at the Franklin house."

"You're making a lot of assumptions, dude," Teddy said. "We don't know for sure if *anything* went down at the Franklin house. Now you think Noah Franklin was a teenage serial killer who came back decades later and took my sister?"

"They're called deductions, Teddy. Standard investigative technique for any detective."

"Yeah, but detectives base their deductions on facts—actual, confirmed case knowledge, not guessing out of thin air. For all we know, Old Franklin was just one of those true-crime junkies who kept up with all the weird local shit."

"And who also happened to keep boxes of human hair in his wall? Okay, sure, man. Keep telling yourself that. Meanwhile, I'll focus on what we know for certain. You're welcome."

"That's the point—we *don't* know for certain. We don't know anything at all, and until they get results back on that stuff, it's all coincidence. I don't know who the fuck this guy even *is*. He might have been in school with my parents a million years ago, but I sure never met him, or even heard of him before all this started, and neither did Nat. You're out there chasing down your theories when we should be focused on what happened to her."

"Noah Franklin was in that house for the vast majority of those disappearances and was back in town when Nat herself disappeared. I can't find anything current on him now—just an old Facebook with a dog as the profile pic, and it's locked down. No Twitter, no blog, not even a LinkedIn. It's like he's gone into hiding—like he's running from something and doesn't want to be found. But coincidence. Right."

"My God, Ben, lower your voice," I hissed, cringing under the eye of the librarian, who'd poked her head around the corner and aimed a warning glare our way. "We shouldn't be talking about this in here. Or anywhere in public."

"You're right, Ames," Ben said, stowing his printouts in his binder and loading his stuff back into his bag. "Let's head back to my place and really dig into this stuff. And grab a sandwich. You guys hungry? I'm dying for a sub. Maybe some hot wings."

Ben slung his bag strap across his body and stalked toward the exit, motioning with his chin for us to follow. We fell into step behind him as he shoved both double doors open at once, bursting defiantly into a wall of summer heat. Teddy and I caught up to him on the sidewalk, flanking him as he surveyed the afternoon shuffle of pedestrians, pickup trucks, and scattered café tables that was downtown River Run. Frustration pulsed in his jaw, knotting the muscles of his shoulders. He'd gone for the hard sell on the Noah Franklin theory, but Teddy was right—it was still nothing *but* a theory. Realistically, we were no closer to an answer than we'd been that morning.

I could practically hear the suspicions spooling through my cousin's mind—it could be anyone. The man sipping from a Styrofoam coffee cup as he waited for the crosswalk signal. The woman taking the last drag off a cigarette as she strolled past, then tossing the butt in the gutter. A farmer or a banker, or a teacher at the school; a quarry worker on his father's own payroll. Anyone.

A group of boys our age ambled by us, whooped a greeting as they passed. Ben acknowledged them with a sharp nod, then turned and headed for the parking lot, not bothering to look back. I reached for Teddy's hand without thinking, my fingers drawn to his automatically. My heart sinking wearily into my gut when he shied away. His eyes darted to mine, heavy with sorrow and apologies. I looked past him, holding my chin high, emptying my veins of any semblance of hurt or rage or longing. Gathered it all and buried it deep beneath our lie, until it felt like nothing but indifference.

CHAPTER 34

SUMMER 2018—THE LAST DAY

We wandered over our own footprints in awkward, jangly silence, down the hill and through the woods, treading on broken sunbeams. The boys had argued again that morning; not that they'd said a word about it to me, but the unfamiliar tension hung over all three of us, ensnaring me by default.

Teddy's eyes caught mine again and again behind Ben's back, and we walked too close, our fingers closing the space between us. I hooked my pinky with his, felt his intake of breath; he stopped in his tracks, then swept me off the path, backing me against the trunk of a tulip poplar. We were face-to-face, breathing each other, and I knew nothing in those next moments but his hands in my hair, and his mouth on mine, erasing the outside world. Nothing registered but him and the heavy summer air, eviscerated suddenly by Ben's ragged yell.

"Teddy? What the fuck are you *doing*?"

My cousin stood rooted in place, still as the trees. Shadows brushed his face, the soft sway of leaves playing over his fury.

"Benny. Hey, man."

"Benny? Don't you 'Benny' me, you asshole. I told you. Every day of this whole fucking summer, I told you to leave her alone."

Teddy's eyes darted nervously to mine, as if he was hoping I hadn't heard that particular shred of information. Still, he took my hand and let me back onto the path, ready to face Ben's anger head-on.

"Calm down, dude, it's not like that. She's—"

"She's family, that's what she is. You should be looking out for her like you do for Nat, not—"

"Oh bullshit—she's never been a sister to me. You've known that since we were twelve."

"Excuse me!" Both sets of eyes snapped my way, disgruntled and unwelcoming, bordering on accusatory. A look they hadn't given me since I was six when I'd burst unannounced into a meeting of their secret club. "Ben, this has literally nothing to do with you."

"Whatever, Amy, like you know shit. You think he's your friend, but know what? So did the others. So does every other piece of ass that ever crossed his path. Go on, though—go wait and see how good a friend he'll be once you give it up. You'll be lucky to get a sideways glance."

"What the fuck, man?" Teddy's sudden yell cut us off. He dropped my hand, the hard set of his shoulders almost a match for Ben's as they squared off. "This is Amy, Ben. You *know* what she means to me."

"Yeah, I know what she means to you—the ultimate conquest. The be-all and end-all notch on a belt that already looks like a fucking chew toy. You've been obsessed with her so long you've gone sick in the head." Ben barked a laugh, his face twisting into his mother's so completely a chill scrabbled across my skin. "But sure, go ahead and keep telling yourself it's real, I guess. Like you of all people would actually have a shot."

"Oh, *I'm* obsessed?" Teddy scoffed. "You sure you want to go there, dude? You sure you want to talk about who has a shot with who?"

"Stop it, both of you," I yelled, my voice ringing through the space between us. "What the hell is wrong with you guys?"

Ben rounded on me, his face furious, red and vein-riddled, eyes slick with tears.

"What's wrong with ME? You're the one with the big secret. Go ahead and make it official—bring the lawn boy home to meet the parents. Kick off your rebellious phase but good. I'll buy all the tickets to that fucking show."

"*Rebellious* phase? Fuck off, Benny. I'll bring him home whenever I feel like it."

"But you haven't *quite* felt like it yet, have you? You haven't, and you wouldn't, and you won't, because it's not even worth the shit you'd catch. I know your mom has high expectations, but I don't think even she knew how low you'd actually sink."

Ben's snarl wrapped around my throat, squeezed the breath from my lungs and the thoughts from my head. I took a step back, with my feet or maybe my brain—I wasn't sure which, and it didn't matter. I was unraveling. His words stole my voice, snagged the thread, tore a ragged hole in the swatch of my mind.

A short laugh from Teddy then, sharp and humorless. Ben and I turned as one, and my heart burst at the downturn of his mouth, the bleak, unsurprised resignation in his eyes.

"Wow. Thanks, Ben. It's good to finally know where I stand with you. Amy, I—" He took in my dead gaze, and the tilt of my chin. He heard my disconnected, involuntary silence, its implication worse than any litany Ben could conceive. He watched me fade away.

"God," he croaked. "He's right, isn't he? That's what you think of me."

My thoughts pinwheeled, processing the shift in his face as it slipped from question to answer, from shock to fury. Everything in me fought against the current; every nerve strained for the surface, scrabbling toward the light.

"I don't," I stammered, eyes blinking slowly in my blank, frozen face. "I—"

"I'd be a *great* way to piss them off, wouldn't I? Get under Mommy's skin, twist the knife with your small-town fling. Just like Benny said."

It was a knife of its own, that word, stripping the sweetness from every kiss. Did he really see us as nothing but a *fling*, when I'd been falling for him half my life? Had Ben, with his outbursts and attitude and shitty, derisive predictions, so easily dismissed as a spin-off of his usual assholery—had he actually called it in the end?

Teddy's gaze dug into mine, darkened with open disdain—those eyes and that sneer broke through the ice, dragged my anger and my voice into open air.

"Oh, MY fling, Teddy? Because I'M the one who can't keep my pants on? I'm not exactly worried about you meeting my parents— by the time you work your way down the list to me, they'll be dead of old age."

"No, you're right—why worry?" He shook his head, running a hand through his hair. "I don't even rate high enough to BE a fling—you'll keep me tucked away in River Run, then head home to whatever trust-fund douche checks all the boxes on the list. I'm the trash-heap toy you'll cut your teeth on behind your rich-bitch mother's back until you run off to art school and disappear. Until you've got everything you could possibly want, and finally get bored enough to become her clone."

"What the *fuck* did you just say to me?"

"Dude," Ben interjected, face gone pale at my venom-laced voice. "I wouldn't—"

His warning came too late. Teddy ignored him, lips curving up further at the corners as he stared me down, a mockery of the same smirk he'd thrown at countless girls. The one that got him anything he wanted, no matter who it hurt.

"I thought it was different with us, Amy," he said, "but it's just a high-end brand of the same old bullshit. She can yell about your career and your art as loud as she wants, but all your mom really cares about is getting you up the next rung on that ladder. And deep down? You're *exactly* like her."

My hands flew on their own, struck him in the chest, shoved him backward as hard as I could. He'd gone there. He'd reached into my being, siphoned out the darkest, deepest dregs of my fear. Tossed them back in my face like a handful of dirt.

"Say it again," I hissed. "You think you're trash? Keep it up and you won't even be worth that to me. Go on." He absorbed another blow and caught my wrists, trapping my hands between us. "Say I'm like my mother again and you really will be nothing."

It felt like a scream. It felt like a howl to rend the skies, but my voice barely seethed above a whisper. It did hit its target, though. It did do that.

Teddy took my words one by one. His fingers slackened; his face cracked like a dropped glass. He stepped away, catching me in a final, desperate look that finished me off, and then he was a blur.

"Yeah," he muttered, turning his back on us. "I guess everything *is* finally out in the open."

He headed for the path back to his home. Ben started after him, then slowed to a stop, the blood draining from his face.

"Teddy, wait. Hey." Teddy kept walking, the proud lift of his head the only sign he'd heard Ben's voice. What little food I'd eaten lurched in my stomach. "TEDDY. Oh God. Oh my God."

"I hope you're proud of yourself, Benjamin Hansen," I whispered, not caring if he heard me. "This is what you wanted, right? You always get your way in the end, I guess, no matter what."

"Oh God, Amy, no. I didn't want *this*. I didn't mean *any* of it. I'm sorry. I'm so, so sorry."

"Fuck your 'sorry'—you make me sick. I don't want to hear *sorry*, or *please*, or any other words from your mouth. Not ever." I turned away from him, trudging toward the path to Grandma's without looking back. His low cry was a hollow-point blast between my shoulders, cutting through the wail of my heart. Too little and far, far too late. "As far as I'm concerned, we're done."

'd barely slept in the week since my art returned. I was already down a sketchbook and a half, nearly finished with my assignments and wearing my pencils to nubs on memories of Nat. She sprang from the page in spectral form—blinking awake from a long nap in the center of a flower. Riding the crest of an eternal river current, laughing and gleeful, fishtail glistening. Translucence cloaked in sorrow, watching us from a tangle of treetop branches. Clawing her way out of the water, face decayed, eyes dark as puddled blood. Alternately whimsical and morbid. Still wild and fierce and achingly vulnerable. Nearly as lovely as she'd been in life.

My mind flipped back and forth between those and other versions as I gazed out the parlor window, browsing through myriad feelings and infinite unknowns. Occasionally straying to my eternal favorite subject, eyes lingering on the contours of his back and shoulders as he tended the flowerbeds.

"He's not going anywhere, honey."

I leaped back from the window like I'd been yanked, catching my finger between the slammed-shut pages of my sketchbook. When Grandma wore slippers, she moved like a damn ghost.

"Pardon, ma'am?"

"Oh, I think you heard me." She settled on the window seat,

patted the cushion next to her. "He's been here since nine—Lord only knows how long you've been at that window."

"Not the whole time," I muttered, sitting carefully beside her. "Am I in trouble?"

"What? Why on earth would you be in trouble?"

The shock in her voice was a finger under my chin, lifting my eyes to hers. I didn't answer for a good minute; couldn't answer, not without the words coming out all wrong and horrible and damning. I'd been so worried about my mother and Ben, and now June, that the issue of my grandparents hadn't even occurred to me.

"Because it's Teddy. My mother—" I swallowed down the apprehension threatening to choke my words. "She hates everything about River Run. Any boy from here is off the table, no matter how I feel."

"Seems to me you set your own table, whether she likes it or not. And really"—her mouth lifted in that little impish Grandma grin—"she's not here to have a say in the silver pattern, is she?"

"She's not. But—"

"Oh, but nothing. Ellie wasn't always like this, you know—she was a dreamer. A romantic. Ready to settle down with her own River Run boy, make no mistake." She chuckled, gazed past me like the memory was projected on the wall at my back. "Let's just say that girl wasn't running through those woods to the Franklin place every day for the fresh air and exercise."

"*What?*" I blinked at her impish smile, question marks bursting from every corner of my mind. The boy in the pictures—the elfin angles; the shy, dark eyes; the joyful smile—was *that* the face of Ben's prime suspect? "Noah Franklin and—my *mother*? Grandma, are you joking?"

"Not in the least—that child was smitten as could be. He was her entire world, and she was the light in his sky. You don't see a match like that every day, not around here." Her smile faltered at corners; her gaze went distant, as if browsing through a past I'd never truly see. "She went cold on him all at once, right around your age. Came home one night in hysterics—then went and locked herself in the bathroom with the shears and cut off all her hair, right up past her jaw. Short as yours, and then some. It had been real long and pretty, and I couldn't get a thing out of her as to *why* she'd go and do that. My best guess is something to do with Noah—they used to sit on that porch swing when they were small, and he'd comb it out for her like they were in a beauty shop. I always thought it was sweet, how he took to it, even if he was a boy. Maybe she didn't want a reminder of those days after what happened between them."

"Maybe." A strange prickle slipped over the back of my neck. Grandma's oblivious gender stereotypes aside, kids playing beauty shop was hardly alarming. A fixation on hair, however; one that theoretically may have grown alongside those kids into some twisted teenage fetish? Did the contents of that box hint at Noah Franklin's subconscious fascination with my mother—or were they his more deliberate attempt to somehow reclaim the girl he'd lost? "What *did* happen?"

"I certainly don't know. That boy showed up every day for a week, looking a mess and asking to see her, but she wasn't having it. She pulled away from all of us after that, left home as soon as she could after high school, and never said why—and he wouldn't give a reason any more than she would. Madeleine might know, but it's not likely. Even as children those girls were never close."

Grandma's words churned restlessly in my gut. My mother. The Langston family contradiction who'd clawed her way out of Kentucky's unchanged earth. A sought-after socialite who, to my knowledge, hadn't been close to anyone *since* Noah goddamn Franklin. Not to me, anyway; not to her parents or sister, and certain as fuck not to my dad.

"Sounds about right," I finally said. "But let me assure you— Mom has definitely lost that dreamy, romantic edge."

Grandma held the silence that followed until I squirmed. I drew breath to apologize, then released it, words unsaid, as her hand covered mine. Her face was a portrait of nostalgia, sad and wistful, deeply lined. Smudged to beauty by the soft brush of her smile.

"I remember being in love at your age—the whole world opened up yet narrowed down at the same time. Narrowed down to that one boy, until he was all I saw." She gestured to the window. "I assume he feels the same?"

"He does. But—"

"Amy, in this family, we have strict standards for public behavior. There are certain things we do, not because we want to, but because they're proper. Because they're the right things, or the polite things, or because we're obliged."

"Yes, ma'am."

It was all I could manage. I schooled my face into its calm and practiced mask, blinked my eyes bone-dry. I'd been trained too thoroughly. Programmed to fall in line at the whims of my elders, without so much as a contradictory breath.

She could take him from me with a word in the name of propriety, and for all my earnest promises, I wouldn't have the first clue

what to say in protest, much less the voice to say anything at all. Defiance and independence were all well and good with a tree line between us, but when my grandmother spoke, my autonomy dissipated into little more than a vague theory.

"I raised my daughters to be proper ladies," she continued, her gaze steady on my placid face. "Taught them to pass along those values, and for the most part I take pride in the result. Love forced by duty, however, was *not* a lesson taught beneath my roof."

I didn't realize I was crying until she gathered me in her arms, a ridiculous mess of spider-leg limbs and shaking shoulders, every fear and insecurity and conflicting emotion whooshing out at once in a long-stifled wail. I'd almost broken. I'd been on the brink of reflexive obedience, ready to stomp both Teddy's and my heart to splinters rather than toss so much as a pebble into the water beneath my family's ancient, precarious boat. How could I let myself be cowed so easily? What had they done to me that I'd ended up so weak?

"Don't you worry about Eleanor," Grandma crooned. "You'll find your own path, for better or worse. Being poor isn't the end of the world."

"I don't care about his money," I sniffed, rattled right to the bone. "I can make my own living, no matter who I'm with. But *he* cares. He thinks he'll drag me down, or that one day I'll be sorry—that he can't provide what I deserve, and I'll regret settling for the lawn boy, whatever that means. I'm not even thinking about stuff like that—I just want to be with him. But it's like he won't let himself accept that, because of how he was raised. And then Ben—"

I cut myself off, hesitant to toss Ben under the Grandma bus, but she just shook her head. "That Benny," she said, her knowing chuckle drifting into a sigh. "What did he do this time?"

"He thinks Teddy's not good enough for the family," I whispered, the memory rippling hot and cold across my face. "And last summer, he told him so."

"Oh, *did* he?" My grandmother's voice went dark, spooled in stern ribbons from the hard line of her mouth. I watched her eyebrows furrow as the bits and pieces she'd heard of our falling-out fit together and fell into place. "I love your cousin, but he's been spoiled long ago—and he has plenty of his own business to mind before inviting himself into yours. As for you—taking his thoughts on this as gospel, when he's never wanted for a thing in his life? Amy Larsen, you're smarter than that."

"I know. But you know how he is. Him, Aunt Mattie. My mother. Even June thinks it's a bad idea."

"If you let others do your deciding for you, you won't get too far in the world at all—and it would serve you right. Teddy is good and decent and hardworking, which is more than can be said for most folks. Don't ever be ashamed to be seen with him, no matter what people we know might say."

She must have seen the horror on my face, which twisted all over again at those words. It wasn't shame that made us wary—it was fear. Fear of tearing open scabs, upsetting our parents, reopening the rift in our friendship with Ben. Fear of losing whatever remained of our own friendship, if the worst happened and we couldn't make it work. But shame?

From the outside, that's exactly what it looked like.

So many things about me were cloaked in neutrality. I fixed my face and schooled my voice, so often spoke only when prompted.

Completed assignments with measured, monitored precision. I wanted nothing more than a chance at something real—something as messy and cherished as my secret sketchbook, each page shaded with the loveliest bits of my heart. But what good was a heart kept forever tucked in hidden pockets? What chance did Teddy and I have at anything if we were too afraid to speak its name?

"Now, honey, I want you to listen to me." Grandma tipped me upright, dabbing at my cheeks with a linen handkerchief she produced from some hidden pocket. "I'm going into town for a bit, but first I'm going to give your young man the rest of the day off. I want you two to take a nice walk together, have a good chat. See if you can't work things out on your own terms."

"Yes, ma'am. Thank you."

"No need to thank me, sweet girl—your happiness is thanks enough. Now go on, splash your face and change that shirt. There's no excuse for looking rumpled when you have a freshly pressed wardrobe on hand."

She *yoo-hoo*ed out the front door as I headed for the stairs, tucking the last of my tears into a soothing mental pocket. By the time I made it back down again, Teddy was waiting on the porch, his confusion turning to concern when he saw my blotchy skin and red-veined eyes.

"Amy, what happened? Are you—"

I cut him off with a kiss, full on the lips. Let him kiss me back, in plain view of anyone and everyone. Like Grandma, for instance, who cheerfully honked her horn as she drove past. Typical Grandma.

"I'm so sorry," I breathed. "Let's go, right now."

"Go where? Am I high, or did your grandma give me a paid day off so I can make out with you?"

"I doubt she'd phrase it exactly like that, but yeah. Sort of." I gave him an abridged version of the conversation, my voice wobbly and wet and shrill. One crack in the facade, and suddenly I was a fucking mess. "I don't want to hide this anymore. I'm not ashamed of you, not even a little bit."

"Hey. Stop." He caught me as I flung myself at him, nearly knocking him off the porch. "Ames, it's okay. I know I'm not . . . what your family had in mind for you. Trust me, I've come to terms with it."

"Fuck coming to terms. They can disown me and disinherit me, and never speak to me again. Anyone who doesn't like it will have to just deal, and that goes triple for goddamn Ben. I am beyond done."

"Yeah?"

The word slid into my gut, sliced a fresh well of tears from my eyes. A single syllable, small and sad, tiptoeing to the edge of hope. It was my fault he had to sound like that. I was the worst.

And yet, it wasn't entirely my call. Keeping secrets had been his idea.

"Yes. I'm yours, Teddy. I don't care who knows it." I paused, stomach dropping, braced for whatever answer he chose to give. "Do you?"

"I should," he muttered, staring past me. "You're not what my mom had in mind for me, either, you know. I doubt she thinks I'll ever leave town at all, let alone run off with you."

"I'm not asking you to run away. But I understand. If it's too soon—"

"Amy, we started this for her sake—for Ben, for your mom—but it'll always be too soon for some people. We can't keep them happy forever. Not when it's nothing but a lie." He kissed me one last time, winding his fingers deliberately through mine as we stepped off the porch together. "Let's go talk to Ben."

I didn't bother knocking. The house was huge and cool and empty, save for the soft patter of Ben's bare feet on the tiles, the rise of his voice when I called his name.

"In the kitchen, Ames."

My cousin was adrenaline and Abercrombie, a solar flare flashing between the fridge and counter. He looked up as we approached, mild surprise lighting his face at the sight of Teddy at my side.

"Hey, man. No work today?"

"Off early. You got a moment? We need to talk to you."

Ben gave our joined hands a bored glance, flicking a lock of hair out of his eyes.

"Huh, let me guess. You and Amy are hooking up and finally decided to clue in the rest of the world." He turned back to the counter, slapping together two more sandwiches without breaking stride. "Please. I could hear you tapping that from the top of these cliffs, dude."

"Not there yet, *dude*." Teddy rubbed a hand over his eyes as we sat at the bar, likely already preferring Ben's anger to the avalanche of remarks we were destined to endure until the end of time. "And really? That's all you have to say?"

"What do you want, a certificate of achievement? Make her happy, don't fuck it up, and you'll be fine. Also, you'd better get around those bases while you can. She's only here for another month." He slid a Perrier and a plate of food my way, plunked another plate in front of Teddy. "Eat up, both of you. We have some work to do today, and I don't have time to deal with either one of you dragging ass."

"Thanks."

My voice rang empty and distant even to my own ears—the remnants of my earlier upset, still blunting the edges of my thoughts and words. Ben stared, then frowned, then clapped his hands together an inch from my nose.

"Snap out of it, Ames. I need your brain fully present and functional, preferably on planet Earth."

"Leave her alone, man," Teddy interjected. "It's not her fault."

"What did you say?" My eyes darted back and forth between their faces, both suddenly guarded, smoothed into identical portraits of guilt as I zeroed in on my cousin. Telltale defiance lurked in his eyes, answering my question before it was asked. "Ben Hansen, how the fuck does he know what is or isn't my fault regarding—anything?"

"Because I told him. Someone has to watch your back when I'm not around, and I knew you'd never say anything yourself."

"Awesome. Good to know you'll always be around to run your mouth. It's totally my favorite thing about you."

"This isn't some rug-sweep bullshit, okay? This is serious. We love you, and—" Ben grimaced, shooting an apologetic glance at Teddy. "Oops. Sorry, dude, didn't mean to step on your line, there."

"It's good, Benny. She knows how I feel." He leaned over and lifted my chin, made me meet his sad and lovely eyes. "We love you.

We want you to be happy and healthy and safe. What she's done to you, Amy? It's fucked up. It is *so* fucked up."

A surge of profanity bubbled up behind my teeth, sour as bile. I choked it back down, focused on the bar, on the tiny teardrops collecting at the base of my water bottle. Flinched away from Teddy's hand on my arm. Struggled not to disengage further at his frustrated huff.

I couldn't associate my boys with the hole in my head.

I hopped down from the barstool and hauled aside the sliding glass door, left it open as I stormed onto the deck, seething with anger and sorrow, and the remnants of self-loathing, left over from my earlier talk with Grandma. I was so ruined. So cowardly and subservient, rendered inert by triggers I could still barely identify. What was the point of asserting myself at all, when I couldn't keep a grip on my own world?

I leaned my elbows on the railing, stared at the woods and cliffs and river below; at the streaky-pale clouds, gone watercolor soft through my blurry eyes. The door slid closed at my back. Careful footsteps approached, stopping a few feet away.

"Still processing the whole douchebag cousin thing," I said, gaze still on the sky. "So if you came out here to placate me, feel free to go right on back inside."

"Nah, I'm good," Teddy said. "Just worried about you is all."

"I'm perfectly fine. I mean, not really, but whatever." I rubbed my hands over my face, turned to meet his pleading eyes. "I never wanted—you know what? It doesn't matter. I can't talk to you about this."

"Why not?" His hands reached for mine, soothing my shaking

fingers. "So you space out sometimes. You think that's anywhere near enough to make me walk?"

"It happened before. Remember?" I stared him down until he looked away. "Yep, thought so. Do you still think I'm like my mother, or is my human skin suit finally lifelike enough to pass?"

"Don't say that. You know I didn't mean—" He stepped closer, but I flinched away, withdrawing my hands. Breaking something in his eyes. "Goddamn it, don't do this."

"You know the worst part about all this? It worked. I turn off my brain, I push myself as hard as I can for her, and now I'm better than anyone expected. I'm getting everything I want, because it worked. But it broke me." I focused on a spot just past his face, slightly to the left of his pity. "You say you love me, but I'm not the girl you fell for when we were kids, Teddy. I haven't been that girl for years."

He winced at that, scrubbed an arm across his bloodshot eyes. But when he raised his head those eyes were bright and soft and full, reflecting more than a blank, distorted mess. He saw me the way he'd always seen me—how I was now and the way I used to be, before I'd taught myself to fade. He saw me and he loved me beyond my missing pieces.

"Doesn't matter. What was it you said earlier? Fuck coming to terms." He brushed my bangs out of my eyes, his knuckles trailing across my cheekbone. "You are everything I want, broken or whole. Until the end of always."

His words flowed through me like water, quelling the shudder of my fingers and shoulders and lips—tremors gone quiet in the space between his arms and heart. They turned to tears instead, a rush of relief so acute it split my voice. I'd held it all in for so long, and suddenly I was nothing but a mess.

"Guys. Hey. Guys." Ben's voice made us both jump. "Dude, come on, unlatch from my cousin for a fucking nanosecond, and pay attention. I—"

He broke off, eyes bugging at my flushed, wet cheeks. "Holy shit, are you okay? Is this because of what *I* said? Ames, just ignore me, seriously. You know I'm an asshole."

"It's not you," I warbled, wiping my face on Teddy's sleeve. "Believe me, Ben, you're the least of my worries."

"Damn, girl, that's the nicest thing anyone's ever said to me. Come here." His hug was warm and familiar; I held on tight, swallowing newer, happier tears until he released me. "All better? Good, because I have some news. I was texting with Darrow, and—"

"With Darrow?" Teddy said. "How the hell did you get his cell number?"

"Off his business card—which you'd have a copy of, Teddy, if you hadn't smoked it, or washed it in your pocket, or whatever you did to render it lost forever the same day he gave it to you. Now, will you shut up? This investigation—well, we actually need to talk about that."

"That reminds me," I began. "Grandma told me something wild this morning, Ben—you won't even believe it. Apparently, Noah Franklin and—"

"Fuck Noah Franklin," Ben drawled, bulldozing over my words. "While you guys were out here sifting through your feelings, I found some stuff on Luke Calhoun."

"Wait, who?" The name solidified into a memory—the man from the search party who'd creeped us out enough to inspire a whole offshoot of our investigation before effectively vanishing into dust. We'd been so focused on the Franklin house I'd all but forgotten him. "Seriously? I thought you said there was nothing to find."

"Yeah—nothing under *that* name. Remember what you said about those freaks, Teddy? How they rename themselves, or some shit? Took the name 'Luke' out of my search, and up popped a brick-thick stack on Lester Lucas Calhoun, mug shots and all. Solicitation, statutory rape, wrongful imprisonment, domestic disputes, possession—wall-to-wall crazy shit in a bunch of different states. I called Darrow just now, told him to check for an alibi, and sent him the links. But he hasn't responded to my last seven"—he checked his phone—"-teen messages. Probably a dropped signal."

I didn't bother to hide my laughter. Sure, a dropped signal. Why else would anyone cease responding to a seventeen-strong barrage of Ben Hansen entitlement texts? Poor Darrow.

"Anyway, he wants to see us," Ben continued, waving his raised middle finger in my face. "His office. One o'clock."

"This doesn't make sense," Teddy cut in. "You're back on Luke Calhoun, Ben? No one's seen him around for ages. And he's got no connection to that house at all."

"That we know of." Ben's eyes shifted to me. "Right, Amy?"

I plucked the thoughts from his loaded gaze, tossed them in the air. Lost my breath as they fell together, clicked into place one by one: A missing doorknob. A thump on the floor above our heads. A mattress and a milk crate, the sound of feet on gravel, not twenty yards behind us. Dismissed as imaginary.

"You never found his local address, did you? Even under his real name?"

"Nope. For all we know, he doesn't have one. For all we know, he's—what's the word Darrow used that day?"

"A transient. Oh my God. Ben, the path from that house goes—"

"Straight to the trailer. No one would ever know you were there. And not that I'm Noah Franklin's biographer, but from what I gather, he hates that place. Sold it as is to Dad without even showing up for a walkthrough. If someone was squatting in there, it wasn't him, whether he was in town or not."

"Okay, I'm lost," Teddy said. "Amy, what the fuck are you two talking about?"

"I don't know where to start. It might be nothing, but—"

"It *might* be nothing," Ben said. His eyes scanned the trees, the outcropping of the cliff, traced a path on the river's current, still unconvinced. Still searching. "But it could very well be everything."

One o'clock found us lined up like toy soldiers in front of Darrow's desk, Ben and I bookending a shifting, fidgeting Teddy. My hand was lost in his grip; my toes braced against the metal rungs of the folding chair, thighs sticking then sliding on the sweat-slick seat. Darrow shifted in his chair, quiet, studying each of us in turn.

"I appreciate you kids coming in today. Before I start in with the updates, do you have any questions?"

Teddy started at my nudge, blinked at me, and shook his head. I answered in the negative, and Darrow was drawing breath to speak when Ben raised his hand, super obnoxious, the Hansen blowhard douchewater practically spraying from his ears.

"I actually do have a question, sir. I understand you have limited say in the delegation of tasks and orders as pertaining to the investigation of the death of Natasha Fox. What I don't understand is the level of incompetence inherent to this department. Frankly I expected an update long before now. Based on my research, and adding to that the gold mine of evidence we three uncovered *for* you, I believe Nat's death should have been reclassified as a homicide ages ago, or given the proper attention pertaining to manslaughter at the very least. Not that I'm judging you personally—I'm sure you're doing your best—but I'm *not* sure why your fellow officers appear to be having so much trouble incorporating these facets into said investigation, much less doing their jobs to the satisfaction of River Run's tax-paying citizens by fucking solving it already."

I had to hand it to Ben. He had his own set of issues, but talking down to any soul on the planet, authority figure or no, was not among them. He must have been working on that little speech the whole drive over. Darrow stared at him, then slapped his hand down on his desk blotter.

"Son, you are the reason I self-medicate, I swear to Christ. This is not—look, I've seen some things in my day, but I moved out here for a slower pace, not to spend my golden years strung up in a child murder case. Could have stayed in St. Louis for that."

"Sorry to inconvenience you, *Officer*," Ben drawled. Darrow cast a guilty glance at Teddy, who sat still and blank-faced, likely still processing Ben's audacity.

"Apologies, son," he said. "That was out of line. I'm happy to do what I can. Just wish I had more to offer is all. It's a damn shame, it is, how this is shaking out."

"What do you mean?" Teddy leaned forward, bright and pitiful, grasping at his last shred of hope. "Did something happen?"

"Well, here's the thing. We got a partial list of results back from the lab this morning. Most of it's still a mess, but we expedited the work on that box, and as it turns out, we got connections for a number of those trophies—links to different missing and dead kids from all over the county. But not one of them was a match to your sister."

"What? That's impossible. What about the hair? The braid—that *wasn't* her hair?"

"No, sir, it wasn't—like I said from the start, we didn't expect that it would be. That braid hasn't found a match yet. Many of these cases don't have a comparative sample in the first place, and most of the ones that do are so old they're near useless. But we ran comparison analyses against every probable match, and didn't find a single shred of evidence tying Natasha to any of it. Whoever collected that hair—and it's looking more and more like it was the late Gerald Franklin, though that hasn't yet been officially confirmed—did so long before your sister died. I hate to be the one to tell you this, but it looks like we're at the end of the line."

"The end of the line? What does *that* mean?"

"No," Ben cut in, pushing forward in his chair. "Don't you dare sit behind that desk and say to me what I think you're about to say, Officer Darrow. I won't have it."

"Regardless of what you'll *have*, Mr. Hansen, what I'm saying is they're closing the case. Reconfirming it as an accidental drowning. There isn't sufficient evidence of foul play, even with everything we gathered. Look, I've seen it plenty—someone mishandles a bag, doesn't seal it properly, now it's contaminated. Inadmissible garbage. Someone walks all over the crime scene. Someone loses the file, or just a piece or two of the file, maybe leaves it too close to the recycling bin. People get sloppy, protocol falls by the wayside. The possibilities are as endless as folks are stupid, and I'm guessing I don't have to tell you three just how endless that is."

"There has to be something," Teddy pressed. "What about Noah Franklin, or the men from the church? What about Luke Calhoun?"

"*Lester* Calhoun was in police custody in Lexington the night before your sister went missing. Picked up on a drunk and disorderly, slept it off in a holding cell. He was still being processed out when Natasha left your house, wasn't even back in town until after she got called in missing. It's one of the more solid alibis I've seen in my career. As for Noah Franklin, his credit card transactions, GPS activity, and local security camera footage would have cleared him even if we didn't have an eyewitness. Which we do." He turned the pages in his file folder, ran his finger down a form, tapped it twice on a name. "Whereabouts on the day in question confirmed by one Eleanor Larsen."

"What. The *fuck*."

The room went sharp then blurry; I blinked through a burst of adrenaline and nausea, sweat popping out cold along my back. All three of their heads turned toward me at once—Ben's face was stuck somewhere between confusion, revulsion, and repressed cackles. I could practically *see* the "your mom" joke forming on the tip of his tongue. Teddy gaped at me, jaw slack, eyebrows somewhere up in outer space. Darrow just looked annoyed. Not that I could blame him.

My mother's name in this context bordered on satirical—nearly five million people in the Commonwealth of Kentucky, and *she* was the one who'd exonerated Noah Franklin? She'd barely been in town a full day when Nat went missing—and she'd been out with my grandparents, for God's sake. It didn't make *sense*.

Except it maybe sort of did. The past had loomed at our backs all summer, so many seemingly unconnected threads whispering and binding, finding one another without our help. Weaving themselves into patterns that should have been familiar if we'd ever bothered to study their origins. Was Noah Franklin the reason my mother had escaped and now returned to River Run, extended her visit from hours to days? How many more loose ends would we unearth before we gave up trying to untangle this family from its own mess of knots?

"I *beg* your pardon?" Darrow scowled from me to the paper and back again, eyebrow arched. "Am I missing something here?"

"That's my mother," I said. "They used to date when she was my age."

"WHAT??" Ben practically screamed. "Wait—that scrawny dude, in the pictures—was that *him*? Jesus God, Amy, how I am JUST NOW learning this information??"

"I tried to tell you back at the house, Benjamin. I think your exact response was 'Fuck Noah Franklin'; does that sound right? He even had a weird thing for her hair, which I would have *also* told you if you weren't being such a—"

"Hold on now," Darrow said, casting a wary side-eye at Ben. "Eleanor Larsen is *your* mother—*and* has a history with Mr. Franklin? Do I have that straight?"

"Yes, sir." I swallowed hard, shifted uncomfortably in my chair. Returned the gentle squeeze Teddy gave my hand. "I just found out from my grandmother this morning. She said they had a falling-out, and Mom left River Run after high school. As far as I knew, she hadn't seen him since. Except—yeah."

Darrow blinked at me, drew breath as if to speak, then changed his mind. Shook his head slowly as he closed the case file.

"As far as you knew, indeed. Apologies, but I won't touch those implications with a ten-foot pole, except to say her statement checked out. We're still investigating Mr. Franklin's ties to the other cold cases, but he wasn't involved in Natasha's death in any way. Nor

was your mother, nor was anyone else, as far as we've determined."

"But it still doesn't make sense as an accident," Teddy persisted. "It just doesn't. Isn't there someone else we can talk to, someone higher up?"

"Son, believe me, I'd fight this myself if I could, but we've exhausted every lead. We don't have so much as a suspect left to question, let alone enough evidence to make an arrest. I've got orders to start shutting it down. I'm sorry, Mr. Fox. I truly am."

He'd heard enough. Teddy grabbed Ben's car keys off the desk and was halfway out the door before the sentence hung fully in the air. Ben watched him go, then turned back to Darrow, his face sliding from blaze to icecap.

"You know who I am."

"Is that a rhetorical question? Is that even a question, period? Boy, you've been hanging around, badgering me with your phone calls and text messages for weeks. Unfortunately for me, I damn sure do know who you—"

"Then you know who my father is. Peter Hansen. Hansen, Inc. Big house, lots of land. Lots of money. I'm willing to bet that if Natasha Fox was called Natasha Hansen, and lived on that land, in that house, there wouldn't be any shutting down of any goddamn thing. Am I right?"

A born-and-bred local cop such as Callahan might have been pissed. He might have blustered and postured, denying such a ridiculous claim: *How dare you, how dare you question an officer of the law, no respect, none, I'd take you over my knee if you were mine, sonny, and maybe I should haul you in, call your mama to come get your no-good hide, teach you to respect the police, respect your elders, yes, sir*—on and on in righteous, redneck rage, as they tended to do.

Darrow didn't even blink.

"I wouldn't be too much surprised if you're right, Ben Hansen. Look, you kids need to understand something. This town looks nice enough, but once you get inside, it's a butterfly jar. People fly around in circles, pretty as can be, and don't even know the lid's come down. Little girls turned cold-case statistics because their daddies don't shake hands with the right people? That's one of the happier endings I've seen in this career."

"Ben," I said, moving toward the door. "Benny, I have to go. I have to find Teddy."

"Go on, Ames." Ben didn't turn, didn't take his eyes off Darrow. "Go take care of him. He needs you."

His flat, cold voice followed me out the door.

I rage-packed that night, shoved clothes haphazardly into my luggage, every swipe of a zipper a clawed hand across Ben's smirk. Every clench of my fingers a fist aimed at Teddy's face. An accidental glance in the vanity mirror threw back a flushed, seething mess, hard jaw and bitten lips, tangled windstorm hair.

If I hadn't been hoping so hard, despite the raw hole in my heart, I might have missed the birdcall entirely. But I heard it; it drew me to the window in a single, giant step. One glimpse of him and I was off, taking the stairs two at a time, bursting through the back door. Driven by the desperation I hadn't known I'd swallowed until I felt it rise in my throat.

He stood at the edge of the woods, blocking the path to the cove. The night was a crush of fireflies and liquid heat, late summer blossoms, the screams of tree frogs. I pulled up short, stilled my steps before I reached him. Let him close the distance to only a foot before I spoke.

"You're here."

His smile was a travesty. "Yeah. I'm here."

"Why are you here?"

I'd known Teddy my whole life. Laughed with him, talked with him; wanted him long before I realized what disaster wanting him could bring. I'd never seen him break before, though—not really. I'd never seen him cry.

"You think I'd let my City Girl go without a goodbye?" He pressed away a well of tears with the heels of his hands, sucked a breath, pushed the chaos of his hair behind his ears. His eyes worked into mine, sorry and stricken, threaded with anguish. "No way. I—"

"I don't know what to say to you." My voice, flat as my bloodshot gaze, choked his to silence. He looked away over the glistening river. "You or Ben."

"It's fine. It might take a day or two this time, but it'll blow over."

"It's not fine. None of this is fine."

"No. It's not. I mean, you know how we are. He talks shit all the time—we both do—and I never even think about it, but this—God. I don't know."

"Yeah, I get it. You two and your endless 'jokes.' Only he wasn't joking this time, Teddy. And neither were you."

"I'm sorry." His mouth puckered over his next words. "I am so sorry for what I said to you. I didn't mean it, I just—well, maybe Ben has a point."

I stared at his face, still turned away from mine, still deliberately blank. Then he spoke again, and the bottom dropped out of my heart.

"Maybe this was all a mistake, anyway. You and me."

"Are you serious?" A flare of panic broke through my anger, washed frantic chills across my skin. He looked at me then past me, his expression a neutral canvas over miserable eyes. "Teddy, no. He's wrong."

"About what? You know, some crazy shit came out of his mouth, but there was solid truth in every word. I *am* nothing. Nowhere near good enough to deserve you."

"Are you kidding me? Forget him—after our whole lives, can

you really look *me* in the eye and believe that's what I think?"

I let the silence string between us like sap, sharp and sticky, several beats too long. His headshake was minuscule, nearly lost in the shadows, but it happened.

"Good," I finally said, tremors crowding into my voice, "because sometimes when we're caught up in a moment, we say things we don't mean. I mean, I don't actually *think* you're a fucking asshole, but I might just go ahead and say it anyway."

"Yeah, well, I sure can *be* a fucking asshole, so feel free to say it all you like. I'm also basically garbage and totally beneath you, but you knew that. Definitely on a lower ladder rung than Amy Larsen."

"How can you even think that? Don't you know what you mean to me?"

His eyes jerked to mine, sparks of hope crushing my lingering fury. I reached out and ran a thumb along his brow, then his lips, years of unsaid words collecting on my tongue.

"Amy?" Grandma's voice smacked against my shoulder blades. "Honey, are you out there?"

"Yes, Grandma." I forced a smile onto my face and emerged from the trees, Teddy a step behind me. "Teddy's here to say goodbye."

"Oh, that's nice. Hello, dear. Would you like to come inside?"

"No, thank you, ma'am, I have to get back." He was tense beside me, the slight tremble of his crossed arms a contrast to his easy words.

"All right, then. See you on Monday for the lawn." Jesus Christ.

The bang of the screen door drove us farther apart. The porch light flickered on; Grandma's shadow flitted against the curtain, paused, and moved on. We stood there, breathless and still, two halves of a torn photograph.

"So. I'll miss you, Amy. I hope you have a good year."

"Yeah. You too."

A breath, a false start, then he swallowed his words, turned, and melted into the trees. I stood still, watching him go, determined to retain as much dignity as I could, all things considered. Determined not to actually chase him down like the pathetic mess I was.

I lasted around five seconds.

He must have known because he was already turning, ready for me, arms open wide then locked around me as we stumbled together. Our kiss was a lifetime in the making, binding us beyond our rage and heartbreak—beyond that afternoon's devastation, and every time we'd touched before that moment. There was no going back.

He would never be anything less than everything.

"Are you okay?" he asked when we finally parted, his fingers tracing the raw lines of my face. "Are *we* okay?"

"I don't know. I don't know anything except that I lo—"

"Don't." His thumb moved over my lips, brushing away the word. "Please. If you say that, then I'll say it, and I'd be in this forever. And if you change your mind, or act like it never happened? Amy, if I'm not good enough, I need to know now. I can't do this if it isn't real."

"It's real. You and me."

"Then come back to me. Please."

"I'll always come back to you."

My words, the last I'd say to him for almost a year, fell soft against his lips. He gripped me tighter, kissed me one final, perfect time. Then Teddy drew away, turned and walked into the dying daylight. Faded, slowly, from my sight.

CHAPTER 38
SUMMER 2019

I took a cab back to the property and found him where I knew he'd be—in his room, doubled over on the floor by his bed. His body was a knot of tension and grief, fingers lost in his unbound hair.

"Oh God, Teddy, I'm so sorry." I knelt beside him, slid my hands up to cover his, and held on as hard as I could, my face pressed against his arm. "It'll be okay. Things will get better. They have to."

"It won't," he groaned into his lap. "They're giving up."

"We can keep looking. Ben's done so much research, stuff he hasn't even shown you. Maybe if we find something they missed—"

"Maybe what? We don't have a clue. Ben means well, but he was always just guessing. You found that box by pure chance. I accused my mother's friend of murder because he's been to the house, for fuck's sake. I pulled a gun on a pastor—might've *shot* him—could've killed someone. And none of it matters. Nat—" A choked half sob broke through his wavering words. He raised his head, face flushed and broken. "She's gone. My dad's gone. Mom can't even function. You're leaving me, *again*. How much more can I lose before there's nothing left?"

"Nothing? Really?" I let go of his hands. "You still think you'll lose me, after everything? What happened to 'no going back'?"

"There *is* no going back. There never has been, Amy, no matter what we told ourselves. But there's no way forward, either. I mean, how else does this really end? Even if it all worked out, do you honestly want me sitting on my ass in Paris or whatever, tagging along on your amazing future? All I'd do is fuck things up—then I'd be the guy who ruined your dream, and I'd hate myself. Forever."

"Stop it. It ends how we make it end, dream or no dream." I took a deep breath, looking straight into his eyes, my own heavy with unshed tears. "I won't let you give up on us."

"There's no point to 'us' if it drags you down," he whispered. "I won't let *you* give up your life."

It was déjà vu at its very worst—the same insecurities; the same conversation even, mere hours after we'd resolved to make things work. And here he was once more, convinced his love would ruin me, as if that was the only option—to split my heart into halves and weigh their value, toss away whichever came up short. Or worse, to pit desire against ambition, let them rage until they consumed each other and all that burned in me went dark.

Teddy had made his choice years ago—devoted his own heart to his family before he ever thought to wish for more. Would he dare to hope for *anything* now, after this hideous summer? Who would he become, with heart and family both in pieces?

My lips found his hairline, pressed against his cheekbone, his temple, the ridge of his brow, my insides knotting around the specter of that fate—of growing and changing, of breathing without him—young, then old, then nothing. Unthinkable.

It was as simple as anything, once I made the choice—there wouldn't *be* a choice. I'd draw my world the way I wanted, and I'd find a way to make him fit. Whatever happened, I wouldn't leave him behind.

I'd tear this town up by the roots before I let either of us sink beneath its rot.

"I won't give up a single thing," I said. "Not my life, not my dream. Definitely not my stubborn River Run boy."

"You're not about to back down on this, are you?" His sigh turned to a soft chuckle as I shook my head. "And it's really what you want, Amy? You and me?"

"You and me. I love you. Until the end of always."

His smile was a sun shower breaking open the sky. Our kiss began softly, barely as a kiss at all, then turned hard and desperate all at once in a blur of heat and gasps, and he was lifting me to his lap, and I was sighing against his mouth. He was running his hands up my legs, and I was pulling his shirt over his head.

I didn't care. I didn't care what Ben was doing at the station, raising hell in his righteous anger. I didn't care that Darrow had all but abandoned hope. I didn't care about my family, what they would think or say about their perfect little Amy. I didn't care about my mother, or her secrets, or whether she'd accept my love for a forbidden boy who embodied all she'd abandoned, or whether she loved me at all beyond an extension of herself. None of it mattered. This moment—this love—it was mine.

Nothing mattered but him.

We unraveled all of it—every grudge and stretch of silence, every hateful word. Took every doubt and fear and misunderstanding, buried them together, and salted the ground. Rebuilt our world a kiss at a time.

It was an end and a beginning—a different version of us, undone and realigned. Made whole again from the ashes of everything we'd been.

• • •

I was awake, though my eyes were closed, my awareness ebbing in and out on a hazy, blissful tide. Teddy slept with his arms tight around me, his deep, even breath warm across my skin.

"You in here, Ames? I—HOLY GOD, NO. WHAT THE EVER-LOVING FUCK, YOU GUYS? WHY. WHY IS THIS MY LIFE?"

The door slammed on his words as my eyes flew open. Teddy startled awake, blinking and disoriented. The rant continued on the other side of the wall.

"Was that Ben?"

"Yeah, that was Ben. Pretty sure he's out there texting his therapist."

"Sucks. He should learn to knock." His eyes focused on me, sweet and shy. "Hey, you."

"Hey, yourself. Did you—" His kiss cut me off, trailed from my mouth across my jaw to my ear, turned my words into a moan.

"I CAN HEAR THAT SHIT, YOU KNOW," Ben screamed from the living room. "FUCKING GROSS, DUDE."

"I should probably go talk to him." I sighed, reluctantly rolling out of bed as Teddy muffled his laugh in the pillow. "Have you seen my—"

"Right here."

He plucked my discarded shirt from the mess of blankets and passed it to me. I pulled it over my head and gathered the rest of my clothes from the floor, cheeks flushing at his blatant, teasing stare.

"You sure you want me to hang back?" he said once I was decent. "If he has a problem with this, he can say it to us both."

"I think it'll be okay. Can you give us a minute?"

"Take your time, Ames. I'm here if you need me."

My cousin hunched at the tiny kitchen table, head down. I sat next to him, watched his hands fiddle with his perpetually empty Zippo, striking a fruitless spark again and again. My eyes roamed away from him, took in the post-Nat sinkhole of Teddy's world. June's housekeeping had never been of the eat-off-the-floor variety, but she'd always kept the place tidy and relatively clean. Now it was a mess of cluttered counters and stained linoleum, furniture strewn with unfolded laundry. The curtains were perpetually closed; the rooms dark and rank with dust motes, spilled wine, and spoiled garbage. A purple plastic cup, the big yellow *N* sloppily hand painted on the front, sat in a sticky ring on the tabletop. It held a couple inches of Coke, a few cigarette butts marked with June's lipstick. I looked away.

"Well, this is awkward," Ben finally said. "I know I said to take care of him, but did you have to go for the literal interpretation?"

"It's not like we invited you in. What time is it, anyway?" I glanced at the stove clock, did a double take. More than five hours had passed since I'd fled Darrow's office. "Did you get an Uber? Does River Run *have* Uber, or—?"

"I walked. Needed the time to clear my head. I've actually been down at the cove for the past few hours, and . . ." He trailed off, squeezing his eyes shut, his entire face screwed into a crunch of pain and fear.

"Hey. Are you okay?"

He shook his head, then nodded, then shook his head again.

"I can't stop thinking about Nat. How intense she was, so real and vibrant. There was nothing phony about that girl. And here I am—the polar opposite. If I died tomorrow, it would be like I was never here at all."

"What? Ben, you're real as all hell. You're like the high-definition version of everything."

"No, I'm not. I'm a fucking illusionist, and I'm tired. I'm so tired of role-playing every single second. Amy, I . . ." He took a breath and faced me, eyes blinking back a wash of tears. "You and me, we've always been alike. Always had plenty in common—right down to our looks, our messed-up heads, our family shit. Everything. Right down to the one person neither of us can live without."

A wave of realization rolled over me, throwing his words into sharp, clear relief. Magnifying all the confusion of last summer and sorting it into individual sketches—his persistent attempts to discourage my feelings; his cryptic comments and weird, unblinking gaze; his refusal to consider leaving River Run; the two of them arguing in hushed voices, unspoken cracks already showing along the seams; the explosion of rage when he'd caught us kissing, a reaction far removed from reason or sense.

Panic skittered across Ben's face, displacing misery as he watched the truth sink into my brain.

"You—oh my God, Ben. What he said—that you—"

"That I was obsessed? That I'm a pathetic, lying mess who wasted years pining for the guy in love with my cousin? Let's just say Teddy's always known me better than anyone else on earth." Ben sighed, dropping his face into his hand. "Just do me a favor and don't tell anyone, okay? And maybe hear me out before you stop speaking to me."

"Why would I—wait, do you seriously think I would? All the shit you've done, and you think *this* is my final straw?" I almost laughed it was so absurd. Instead I reached out, rested my hand gently on his hunched shoulder. "The people I know back home—it's barely worth mentioning, it's so common. Like, I don't even care, Ben. I mean, of course I care about *you*, but it doesn't *bother* me if you're gay."

"God, don't just *say* it like that. You've met our family—I don't know what the hell I'll tell them, or *if* I'll tell them, or anyone else, ever. I can't even believe I'm telling you *now*. Fuck. This was a mistake. Forget I said anything."

"Might as well clue us both in while you're at it," said a voice at my back. "Officially, anyway."

We turned as one toward Teddy. He stood behind us, awkward and sleep-rumpled, eyes fixed on the far wall. Ben's face went absolutely gray.

"Oh God. Oh shit. You've been—no. Nooo. Oh *God*." He covered his eyes with both hands and banged his forehead to the table, letting loose a long, wordless wail. "Go away, man. Please, just go away."

"Nope. This conversation should have happened months ago." Teddy shifted uneasily, rubbed a hand over his face. "And not to eavesdrop, but dude, you should know these walls are basically made of cardboard."

"So you heard everything." Ben spoke directly to his own feet, arms bracketing his head on the tabletop. "My life. Fuck my entire life."

"Ben, it's okay," I said. "There's no shame in this. None."

"That's easy for you to say—you're in art school, in a Blue state, where it's more or less part of normal life. But Mom let me know years ago exactly how fast I'd be out on my ass if I ever 'chose that lifestyle,' as she put it. Can't have that in the family, not in River Run."

"Are you serious?"

"Oh, definitely. No inheritance, no college, no place with them ever. Full disownment guaranteed, and all that after what I can only assume would be the beating of a lifetime. Plus, you know—the god-damn Hansen name. I have a duty to the legacy, don't you know?"

"God. I really hate them sometimes."

"Me too, Ames." He was quiet for a moment, then lifted his head, scrubbing a hand across his nose. "You and Teddy—you two have always been crazy about each other; that wasn't news. But last summer . . . I could tell it was different from the very first day. I knew what was coming—so I lied. I told him you were out of his league, and your mom wouldn't allow it. And I told you he had commitment issues. That he'd get what he wanted and pull his typical slow fade. I thought you'd stay away from him to save your friendship. But he'd be staring at you, and I'd just sit there and wish—ah, God. Forget it; I changed my mind. I don't want to talk about any of this ever."

"What did you wish?" I reached out, rubbed my hand over his back. "Talk to me. Talk to *me,* no one else. You can tell me anything, just like you always could."

"Yeah." He sat back and sniffled hard, jamming his fists into his eyes. "I'd wish I was imagining it. I'd get all up in my own head, try to trick myself into seeing what wasn't there. I knew I'd never be with him. I knew that; I'm not delusional. But I thought I could handle it—it would be okay as long as I didn't have to see him with you."

"You thought it would be *okay*?" Teddy's outburst startled us both. "What do you think my commitment issues were about, Ben? I tried for years to get over Amy, and you *know* it never worked. It was always going to be her."

"I know," he wailed, twisting in his chair to face us. "I know, I do. It's fucked up, but you don't get it. You can have anyone you want—you always could, and if Amy never looks at you again after today, at least right now you know she loves you back. I can't even admit who I *am*. Not if I want to set foot in my own home ever again."

"Goddamn it, Benny—"

Ben shot out of the chair all at once, strode across the room until he and Teddy were nose to nose. Anger rose off them both like smoke, ringed us all in its heavy funk. When Ben spoke, his voice was low and clear, absent of any trace of sorrow. Furious.

"No. You will *never* know what it's like to be alone this way. You'll never have *any* idea. And by the way, fuck you, Teddy. Fuck you for using it against me. You knew all along, didn't you?"

"Of course I knew, you dumb shit. You've been giving me that look since middle school."

"I can't believe you. That's so fucked up. It's—"

"Oh, it's what? Not sure why 'it's' a thing in the first place. I mean, why would Benjamin Hansen get his hands dirty with some-one like me? I'm beneath you, remember?"

"I didn't mean—"

"You know what? You did. Whatever you say now, at least some part of you meant it then. So fuck you too."

I could see it unfolding once again, and once again I was help-less, relegated to an observer as they spat poison in each other's eyes. Everything we'd rebuilt was crashing right back down, and I couldn't take it. I couldn't let us break again.

"Well, *I* never knew," I burst out. They both shut up and stared at me, as if surprised to see me still in the room. "How is *that* possible?"

"I'm actually not sure, Amy," Ben said. "You were there for the argument, right? You heard what he said."

"How was I supposed to know what he meant? You were both yelling at each other, and you called me a piece of ass—and thanks for *that,* by the way—then started in on me and my parents. You know how that ended up. And anyway, why would I even guess that option? You date girls, Ben. You *sleep* with girls."

"Well, obviously. Like I can just blow them off when they're all up on my junk like it's their job? Turning them down would be like, the fastest way to out myself."

"That's ridiculous."

"That's actually true," Teddy interjected, "and it's not really an option. I know how it sounds, but you don't get it—you're only here for the summers. But when we're in school—Christ, you wouldn't believe it. You've never seen anything like the way people love Ben Hansen."

"It's not my fault they can't get enough." Ben sulked. "Not that I can blame them, but my God."

"My point is, River Run's messed up in all kinds of ways, with almost zero diversity, or like, progressive views. If someone like Ben doesn't feel safe coming out in this town, who would? He's in that boat with the rest of us, for once in his life. And if you're a guy our age and you don't try to score, that's the biggest red flag around."

"And you threw it in his face." I glared at Teddy's sheepish side-eye, scowled at the nod that followed. "That was a real dick move, Teddy."

"Yeah, I know it was. I'm not proud." He looked away from me, caught Ben's eyes. His own were sad and regretful, dark with shame. "For what it's worth, Benny, I know I fucked up. You pissed me off, but it never should have gone that far. It's the worst thing I could have done, and I'm sorry. Truly."

"So, this won't—I mean, you've still got my back, right? Even though I'm—"

"Look, man, I'm not shit as far this town's concerned. I'm broke as hell, and no one cares what I think unless they're trying to hang out or get laid. My mom—she's got her problems, that's no secret. But I saw what it did to her, losing Nat." He turned away and dropped into the recliner, leaning forward to rest his elbows on his knees. "She'd have died in a second to bring that kid back, and she'd do the same for me. There's never been a day in my life I doubted that. So if your parents throw you away over something like this—if they lose you *by choice* when they're supposed to love you—well, fuck them. Fuck all their bullshit, and fuck River Run too. You're damn right I have your back. Always."

"Thanks. Really." Ben's mouth trembled and slackened, went soft with a gladness that lived beyond a smile. He rubbed his face and cleared his throat, lifted his chin to its usual haughty tilt. "In any case, you guys can feel free to do your thing. I could've lived without walking in on you just now, but I'm basically over it, so cheers to your future and all that shit."

"Wow. Back up." I stood, pressing my hands to my face. Pacing the tiny room, trying like hell to sort my thoughts. "You're over it? All of a sudden, after all this time?"

"Not all of a sudden. It took months, actually—teen heartbreak, the stages of grief, etcetera. But it's done. I've been over it since before you came back and will proceed as per usual as soon as we're finished here."

"I can't believe I fucking *missed* this," I said, still nonplused. "How did you hide it from me all this time?"

"It's easy enough when you don't live here, Ames. For all you're an artist, you can be unobservant as fuck, even when something's right in your face." He shrugged, mouth quirking at my glare. "I counted on you assuming the default, and that's exactly what happened. Plus, you know. The ladies can't resist me and all."

"Oh, whatever. What happens now? I mean, what will you do?"

"What *is* there to do? I'll just . . . continue. You know me— nothing in my life a pill can't fix, right? Block out my parents, keep me acting right. Keep that smile on like I'm supposed to. And everyone loves me. So it must be working."

"God. Benjamin—"

"I know. One thing at a time, huh? Let me at least get it all out."

"I wish you'd done that years ago. I've been hurting you, and I never knew, and if you'd only told me—"

"Not your fault, Amy. It's no one's fault the way this went in the end. And everything else aside, I can't think of a better match for either of you." Ben dropped back into his chair and raised his eyes to mine as I returned to my seat beside him. "So take care of him for me, okay? He loves you like you wouldn't believe."

"Oh, Ben. I'm sorry. I—"

"Don't. I'm the one who's sorry. And I can say it over and over, all day long, but I can't take back what I did to us. Guys, I'd give anything I have if it meant I could take it all back."

I reached out and held on to him, resting my cheek against his trembling back. My cousin. My family.

"I love you," I whispered. "I love you both so much."

"I love you too, Ames." Teddy rose and crossed the room to us, smoothed a gentle hand over my hair. "Both of you. Hear that, Benny? I love you guys no matter what."

"Fuck, Teddy. I'm so sorry. I'm so, so—" He dropped his head again as Teddy knelt beside him and squeezed his shoulder, giving him a rough, affectionate shake.

"It's okay, man—*we're* okay. I'm sorry too."

We left Teddy that evening in high spirits—we three were together again, done with secrets, solid and unbreakable like we'd been before we'd begun to grow up. Before we'd begun to shed our innocence and weave a knotted mess around one another's hearts.

Ben drove with one hand on the wheel, grinned at me as we turned onto the main drive.

"Can you come over? Help me get my case notes and stuff together? I think I need to finally let this go."

"Of course. What happened with Darrow after I left? Did he book you for running your mouth, or what?"

"Nah, he was cool about all that. We actually sat down and went over every detail, and it really does look like they're right—it was an accident. You know how strong the current gets. They think she took a wrong step, maybe slipped and hit her head, got sucked under. Which is exactly what happened years ago, only we weren't there this time to pull her out. And I feel like such an asshole, wasting the summer trying to prove otherwise."

"You're not an asshole. You might have gone a little overboard, but your intentions were pure. You were trying to make sense of a tragedy and seek justice for someone you love. There's something beautiful in that."

"I guess. I mean, you're wrong—I *am* an asshole. Maybe not about this, but still."

Our laughter rang out the open windows. The night seemed brighter as we drove up the hill, both of us calm and happy—truly hopeful for the first time all summer. The tree-lined lane enveloped us, familiar and safe and speckled with fireflies. A peaceful tunnel that ended as the Hansen ranch burst into view.

The house hulked dark and silent on the hilltop, barely a shadow against the purple sky. The door was a stifled yawn; the windows sightless eyes. Even the porch light was off.

"Guess we're on our own for supper," Ben groaned as we pulled up to the house. "They must be at some bullshit society thing. Want to order pizza? I could totally destroy some deep dish right about now."

We made it to the porch with the help of Ben's phone flashlight. I aimed it at the doorknob while he fumbled his key chain, got the key halfway into the lock. Pushed the door open with hardly a nudge, as one does when a door is unlocked and unengaged. Open already, though barely a crack.

"What the hell?" Ben's fingers jerked away, as if the knob had gone hot. His key followed the rest of the key chain as it fell to the threshold. We stared at the shadows behind the frosted glass, senses straining for an explanation—a door slam, footsteps, the reassuring countdown of the alarm system. Nothing.

"Ben," I said, "let's go. We can call the cops from Grandma's."

"Let me at least get the lights on, see if we've been robbed before crawling back up Darrow's ass for the second time today."

"Are you insane? I'm not going in there."

"There's no one here, Ames. Maybe there was, but they're not lying in wait for us in the fucking dark. They're probably halfway to Lexington with all our shit."

He reached through the doorway, thumbed the chandelier switch. The mirrors and framed art still hung on the walls; the accent tables and their knickknacks were undisturbed.

"Well, if we did get robbed it was by a bunch of fucking amateurs." Ben strolled down the hall, swept his hand around the kitchen doorjamb in search of the light. "These paintings alone are worth half the value of the house itself. If my Xbox is gone, though, I'll find those fuckers and salt the earth with their blood. That would be some typical River Run bullshit, taking my console and leaving the—OH MY CHRIST. DAD, WHAT THE HELL?!"

The track lighting burst to life, washed the kitchen in a dismal glow. Uncle Peter sat at the breakfast table, straight-backed and still, head bowed over his clasped hands.

"Holy God, I just aged a decade. What are you doing in here?" Ben's face worked itself into a frown around the answering silence. "Dad?"

Uncle Peter started slightly and raised his head, taking us in slowly. Building a complete picture, piece by tiny piece. A strange ringing began in my ears, tingled through my fingers and toes.

"Oh. Hey there, Benny. Amy. Is it very late?"

"It's past eight," I said when Ben didn't move. My eyes found a scrap of paper; a trail of scraps, heavy with purple *X* marks. It ended at Ben's suspect list, the word *MOTIVE* ripped through its line of question marks. The name *PETER HANSEN*, stark and unblemished in the middle of the page—the only name we hadn't crossed out. Our maps and notes littered the tabletop. "Ben. Look."

"Shit." We stood there, a pair of panicked, cornered rabbits catching an unknown scent on the breeze. "Um, I can explain all that, Dad. We were sort of drunk this one time, and I—"

"No need to explain, son—I'm proud of you for this. You're a good boy, looking out for Natasha and Teddy. Like a brother. Like Sam and I used to be. Did I ever tell you that, how close we were? Me and Sam and Junie. Always and forever."

"Yeah, Dad, you did." Ben's smile was a stretched parody, terrible and terrified. His eye twitch surfaced, a few tics at a time. "Is everything okay?"

"You tell me, son. They said it was an accident—said she drowned. But you three—you never believed that?"

"Not at first, but we were wrong. It turns out—"

"I know I'm not a perfect man, but I try to be a good father. A father should care for his children, sacrifice his own happiness for the sake of theirs. Accept them at all costs. I accept you, don't I? I mean, deep in my heart, I don't care that you're a homosexual. Is that the word you prefer I use? Homosexual?"

Ben's face went utterly green, broke out in a visible sweat. His mouth stuttered open and closed, spitting out a broken answer.

"Oh. Well, I don't—that's fine, I guess. How, um, how did you—"

"You're my boy, Benny. You could have told me at any time." His voice darkened, rising with each word. "Do you think I'd judge you? Worry about the gossips in this town—as if they matter more to me than my own son? I love you no matter what, and if I ever catch wind of you suffering any mistreatment, those responsible will suffer tenfold. Understand?"

"Yes, sir. But Mom—she said—"

"What your mother says is incidental. I didn't get. To where I am today. By worrying what people THINK." His hands turned to fists, crashed down on the table.

The gasp was mine; an instinctive, terrified flinch that snapped his eyes my way. He blinked at me, confused then sad, understanding creeping across his face.

"Sit on down, kiddo. Amy. I won't hurt you. I could never hurt my family. Sit on down, both of you. Let's talk this out."

"Dad, what did you do? Where's Mom?"

Uncle Peter started, stared, ran a hand through his thick, pale hair. Ben stayed on his feet, moved to my side as I slid into a chair. Anchored me to the room with a hand on my shoulder.

"It's been a long game with us, your mother and me. Lots of talking, lots of deals, lots of compromises. Many cards on the table. She loves you, Benny, I'll give her that. But she never loved me. Didn't even bother pretending once you were born. Knew I wouldn't leave you, no matter what hell she put me through."

"Of course you wouldn't. Why would you even say that?"

"You won't need either of us soon enough. My time was almost up—she had to know we couldn't live like this forever. I was finally going to do something for *me*." He leaned forward, stared straight into my eyes. "Don't I deserve happiness, Amy? Don't you think everyone deserves to get what they want every now and then?"

The few syllables I stuttered lost their way in the air between us. Ben's hand was a solid, grounding pressure, clenching in my shirt as Uncle Peter continued.

"We tried to make it work. Find the good in a bad situation. But then, Natasha—" He broke in front of me; just folded up on the tabletop, arms cradling his bowed head. "They said it was an accident. And you two—you *three* think I *killed* her."

"Dad, we don't. We had to consider every possibility, but—"

"What must you think of me, son, to add me to that list? I've done terrible things, but I would never—she was so beautiful. She never hurt a soul, and someone *did* that to her."

"Jesus, would you listen to me? We made a mistake. The police said—"

"Hellooo?"

Her voice was an easy lilt, cleaving off the end of Ben's reply. I heard the front door close, heard the efficient beeps of the alarm as Aunt Mattie entered the code and armed the system. Her heels tapped a chipper trail toward us then, swept her into the room on a waft of Chanel.

"Oh, there you are. Why is everything so dark? Amy, I didn't expect you over this late."

I smiled at her with all my teeth, secretly glad for an excuse to flee the house, and the weird shadows that teemed beneath its shine.

"I'm sorry, ma'am. I should get back, anyway."

"Bless your heart, honey, you're welcome to stay. Have you all eaten?"

"No, Madeleine, we haven't eaten." Uncle Peter was the flat, hard slap of rock on water, staring up from a festering abyss. "Natasha was murdered."

"Dad, for the final goddamn time, it wasn't a murder. Would you maybe listen to a single fucking word that leaves my mouth?"

"Language, Benjamin." Aunt Mattie set her Birkin on the table, right on top of the property map. "Peter, what in the world are you talking about?"

"Look." He shoved a crunch of papers at her, clutched at his hair while she studied them. "The kids have spent their summer all but proving it. We need to take this down to June, call the police over to her place. We need to—"

"We will do no such thing." A list of clues disappeared in the ball of her fist. "You will not drag the family down this rabbit hole. The case is settled. June's trying to move on. Think of what it would do to her, to rip the whole thing open. Think of what people will say about you—about me and Benny—if you drag this out again."

Uncle Peter huffed a sharp laugh and stood, stalking around the table until they were toe to toe.

"This is bigger than our family, Mattie. This more than eclipses our standing in this town, so why should it matter what I do? You just don't care about anything, do you? All that matters to you is the Hansen name."

Ben's eyes slid closed at his words, ones he'd weathered a million times before. Aunt Mattie tossed the wadded list back on the table, wiped her fingertips on her skirt.

"Well, what else have you ever had to offer? This land is *my* inheritance. I have my own money. I have my own life. Ben is the only good thing to come from this marriage, and you never thought twice of siphoning off his future to feed your mistakes."

Something darker than rage engulfed his face, chased my mild, kind uncle into the creases of his clenched fists.

"Don't you call her that. I've made plenty of mistakes, but not once have I counted her among them."

"Of course you don't. Meanwhile, your *son*—your *rightful* heir—is the one who suffers. What chance does he have with a role model like you? A pathetic, slavering fool who can't find his own two feet, let alone stand on them at any given moment?"

"Mom," Ben groaned. "Could you please just not, for once? Could you guys just *listen*? Dad, please?"

"Me?" Uncle Peter snapped, ignoring Ben. "You think *I'm* the problem when it comes to Ben? He can't get through the day without his pill bottle, Mattie, and that's on you. You won't let him be who he is, or live life on his own terms, and you do the same to me. You couldn't just let me love my child."

"Your child is right in front of you, Peter. If you'd prioritized him—if you'd prioritized *us*, none of this would have happened. You never put anyone before your own whims."

"That's all I *ever* did." His voice shattered somewhere between a wail and a sob. "You and Benny. Sam. Everyone. And now June can't even look me in the face."

"Oh, shed a single tear for that whore, I dare you—I'll cut the eyes from your head myself."

The words twisted in my gut, tore the perfectly blended mask from my aunt's familiar face. What lay beneath was dark and ugly, hideous as an unearthed corpse. Seething with blight and worms and putrid decay.

"You two can rot in misery for all I care," Aunt Mattie continued, "but did you really think you'd get your happy ending at the expense of my son? Did you really think I'd stand aside and let you claim that girl as one of us?"

"What the fuck?" Ben's voice was a bewildered muddle of realization and creeping, thorn-studded dread. "Mom, what are you—"

"You chose trash over me years ago, Peter, but you won't leave Ben high and dry. I'll put you in the ground next to her before I live to see that happen."

I'd seen Aunt Mattie crack before. Seen the shift of her features, the slow crumble of her perfect facade. My uncle had seen it too, no doubt, over decades of regret; it was likely as familiar as the cadence of her breath. It flaked away as he stared at her, a horrible understanding flowing across his face—first a trickle, then a swell, then a strong, dark rush, silent and bleak as the river itself.

Beautiful and lethal. There all along.

"Mattie. *You*—"

"*You* killed her, Peter, as much as anyone—you put *her* first, from the moment she was born. You *destroyed* my family." Her voice dropped low, slid out sweet and dark and deadly sharp. "How does it feel?"

"No." The word fell from Ben's lips, shattered on the tiles at his feet. "Mom, no."

Aunt Mattie turned to him, her smile twisting into madness. Her eyes met his, then widened, hollowed out into wells of panic as the color drained from her face.

"Oh, Benny. I'm so sorry. It was an accident. I mean—I never *planned* to—she was just there all at once, right in front of the car. Jumped out from behind those mailboxes like it was a game—like she was trying to scare me, and I hit the brakes, but it was too late." Her breath doubled, voice dropping to a thin, barely coherent hiss. "She was always just *there*, no matter what I did."

"Christ. Jesus *Christ*. You—"

"It was *too late*, and I *couldn't* tell—what would that have meant for you, my sweet boy, if it all came out? I had to hide it for *your* sake—all I've done with this *life* has been for you, don't you see?" Her face caved, eyes overflowing as he flinched away from her outstretched hand. "Everything."

Uncle Peter's knuckles broke open against her teeth.

They went to the floor together, a flurry of claws and incoherency, every cry washed in years of agony. She fought like a hellcat—like a Langston girl, fierce and unhinged, her pearl-pink nails clawing at his neck and face. More like family than I'd ever seen before. His fingers closed around her throat, cutting off her screech. Cutting off her air. Her face went from red to purple, snapping Ben and me out of our shocked paralysis.

"DAD. STOP."

I was a breeze against Uncle Peter's back, no match for massive arms and quarry-born shoulders. My head hit the china hutch, knocked the stars from orbit, knocked me to the floor, where I cowered just shy of my uncle's wild swings. Ben slammed into him, shoved him halfway off Aunt Mattie, then took an elbow to the jaw when Uncle Peter lunged for her throat once more, his growl ripped to a high, animal keen as her thumb disappeared into his eye.

My cousin ended up on the floor next to the fireplace, grabbed the wrought iron hearth shovel and brandished it like a bat. Brought it down hard on the back of his father's head.

Uncle Peter rolled to the wall, braced himself against it as he struggled to sit up. His face was a horror of bloody scratches, his eye a mangled, rotten plum. Ben sank to the floor beside him, breath heaving out in high, hysterical yelps.

"I'm sorry, Benny," he moaned, reaching for us both. Sagging into tired sobs when Ben shoved his hand away.

"Don't touch me. My mother—LOOK AT HER. LOOK WHAT YOU DID TO MY MOM."

"I had to. She drowned her." He slumped back to the floor, a scarlet smear mapping the journey of his head. "She drowned my little girl."

His words slammed through me like a bullet train and the world cracked open, scattered in shards, realigned into stark, horrible truth. A laughing, bright-haired truth who'd flitted in our footsteps for ten long years, crashed through life in a flash of innocent beauty. Who'd washed up, cold and still, on a distant riverbank.

My mother's sister shifted and sighed, coughed up a thick, pink glut of foam. Ben scrabbled across the floor on hands and knees, his frantic sobs escalating to wails at the sight of her shattered face.

"Mama."

Her head turned toward his voice; her swollen eyes took in the void of her son. She lifted a hand that didn't quite make it to his cheek.

Ben's cry cut through my fog, a horrid wind whipping at my heels as I crawled away from it, fought through a sunburst flare of pain to pull myself to standing, and then I ran. I slammed into the door at the end of that long hallway, yanked it open, and staggered through it into the muggy air, the house alarm beeping in protest, then starting its countdown. Eight. Seven. Six.

I collapsed against the porch rail, turned my gaze to the river view beyond the cliffs. The countdown ended and Ben's voice was drowned out as the siren blew the doors off the night.

Help roared toward me on a silent wave, sirens swallowed by the house alarm. I watched through sheets of fun-house glass—struggled to focus on the night-black road, the swirls of blue and red lights pouring from the dark cup of the tree line.

The lawn filled up with squad cars, and Darrow was there, yanking me off the porch, yelling at me to tell him what under God's blue canopy was happening inside that shrieking house. I blinked up at his narrow, horrified face and it all came out: Uncle Peter's raving. The truth about him and June and Nat. Aunt Mattie's slow descent into madness, sparking to life in a child's too-familiar face, ending at the bloody hands of her own husband.

It took four cops to pry Ben away from his mother.

"It's for his own safety, honey," Darrow said as they guided him past us—the wreck of my cousin, quivering and handcuffed. "I'll get those bracelets off him as soon as he's calm."

He didn't bother extending that promise with regards to Ben's parents.

The ambulance arrived next, followed by my grandmother. More wailing, more explaining, all through the barrier anchored around my mind. Aunt Mattie rolled by, strapped to a stretcher, semiconscious and struggling to speak. Expending what remained of but he's not more than a few hours behind me. We've both been so worried—what in the world is going on here? Natasha—did Madeleine really—" She broke off as I nodded, pressed her fingers to her mouth, then took my tired hand in both of hers. "God. This is so horrible, I just can't—how are you, really? Please talk to me, Amy. Please tell me what you need."

She was referring to my mental state, I could tell—she wanted information, maybe absolution; my side of whatever story Grandma and the doctors had told. That old news was the least of my worries, though. There would be plenty of time to discuss the complexities of both our psyches and our relationship, haggle over my future and my love life and whatever other bullshit we usually dredged up. My mother was right in front me, practically begging me to communicate. I wasn't about to waste the chance.

"Why were you sneaking around River Run with your boyfriend the day Nat died?"

It wasn't what I'd *planned* to say. It wasn't even on my conscious agenda. But when you've spent your life braced for a moment of reckoning, what do you do when that moment finally arrives? How do you navigate it in any sense when it's right there in front of you and looks nothing like you'd thought it would?

If you're me, you apparently rip off the filters and sweep aside the expectations. You open your mouth and just let loose with whatever comes to mind.

My mother blinked at me, eyes wide, mouth a question mark of confusion.

"I'm sorry—what did you say? My *boyfriend*? Amy, what on earth are you—"

her strength in a vain attempt to shake off the policeman's grip as he cuffed her wrist to the gurney frame. The ambulance doors slammed on her wail. My uncle, at least, went quietly.

Still more vehicles rolled up the driveway, bearing plainclothes detectives and white-coated, stone-faced technicians. Then, the hospital. The submission to bright lights and blood pressure cuffs, one image after another, blipping in disconnected, clinical flashbulbs.

"You've got a nasty bump, some bruising and laceration, but no concussion. Nothing too serious." The voice was a soft, sweet drawl. Its owner loomed into view, a bright-eyed nurse wrapped in cheerful scrubs. "We'll give you something for the pain, get you on your feet in no time. What did you have for supper tonight, honey?"

"I didn't." I hadn't even gotten around to eating the sandwich at Ben's earlier that day; what with the events of the afternoon, I'd been running on little more than adrenaline, force of will, and endorphins. All of which were slowly, finally, ebbing.

"What about dinner? Breakfast? When was the last time you ate something? Honey?" The smile faded from her face as she checked my color, shone a light in my unfocused eyes. Dropped off altogether at my muttered reply.

Shit got real after that. The oxygen and IV needles, the cold compress shock to the back of my neck. Discussion of acute stress reaction, of possible dissociation, depersonalization, the risk of PTSD. The blink in and out of consciousness when they finally let me rest. My grandmother's quiet tears.

"I didn't know about any of this. Lord, if I'd known, I'd—dear, tell me the truth. Did you know how bad this was?"

"No, ma'am." Teddy's broken voice pierced through my slow-drip haze. "Ben said she had trouble with her mother, but I didn't know details before today. She never told me. I'm so sorry."

"This is not your fault, young man. As for Eleanor . . ." Grandma's voice seethed over the name. "She will reap what she's sown. Pass me my handbag, please—I need to use the FaceTime."

I drifted out again, woke to Darrow, a flurry of fury, of gestures and whispered profanity as he paced the room with his ever-buzzing phone.

"A misdirection, sir. She all but confessed to her family—the son's and husband's stories match up. Waiting on the third witness to wake up, but she's—yes, sir. Said a bit during transport last night— enough to piece together a probable—yes, I'll get her official state- ment as soon as I can. We think Mrs. Hansen struck the victim with her vehicle unintentionally, then took her on up the driveway and dumped her off the edge out there. No, the cliffs—the ones at the top of the property. Coroner's report notes pre- and postmortem injuries consistent with sudden impact, which we'd previously assumed was sustained on rocks or boulders. Very likely that *was* the intention, yes. Carried her things down to the woods afterward. Yes, sir—a hair clip of some kind, beneath the driver's seat. Yes, trace amounts. A few strands, but—I'm on it. I'll get that to the lab today if I have to drive it over myself."

I shut down at that, closed my eyes and slid back into painless slumber before he noticed I'd stirred. Woke later to Teddy asleep in the bedside chair, his face marred by tearstains and fatigue. Woke again to Grandma's vicious snarls, jerked fully awake all at once at my mother's hysterical protests, closer than any FaceTime call. Their voices drifted in from the hallway, through the partially open door. She was here.

"—and what you've done, Eleanor, will not be swept asi Grandma said. "You *will* ease up on that child."

"What *I've* done? What have I ever done besides push her tow the best possible future? I was setting her up for a *life*. Independer Self-sufficiency. So she'd never have to rely on anyone who'd fail the way you failed me."

Silence. I quietly scooted sideways on the narrow mattre leaned over the railing as if closing such a miniscule gap would ma a difference.

"I knew nothing of that before this evening," Grandma fina said. "If you'd told me then—"

"I couldn't tell you because I couldn't trust you'd take me ser ously. You barely believe me now—if I'd come to you when I w sixteen? Not a chance. So what does that tell you about yoursel Mother, when you really get down into the—"

The call button slid off the bed as I shifted my weight, hit the floc with a clatter that cut their argument short. Grandma appeared in th doorway for a split second before she was displaced by my mothe who flew toward me as if she'd been launched from a cannon. He clothes were rumpled; her hair was held back from her flushed, bar face by a plum silk scarf. She smelled like coffee and hand sanitizer, n trace of her usual heady perfume. I must have been out longer than I' realized if she'd had time to make it all the way back home.

"Amy. My God, are you okay? Your head—"

"I'll be fine." I slid a hand through my hair experimentally, cringec when my fingertips brushed the swollen, tender bump. She settled or the mattress beside me, hovered over me like a worried hawk. "Is Dad—"

"He's on his way. We couldn't get seats on the same flight

her strength in a vain attempt to shake off the policeman's grip as he cuffed her wrist to the gurney frame. The ambulance doors slammed on her wail. My uncle, at least, went quietly.

Still more vehicles rolled up the driveway, bearing plainclothes detectives and white-coated, stone-faced technicians. Then, the hospital. The submission to bright lights and blood pressure cuffs, one image after another, blipping in disconnected, clinical flashbulbs.

"You've got a nasty bump, some bruising and laceration, but no concussion. Nothing too serious." The voice was a soft, sweet drawl. Its owner loomed into view, a bright-eyed nurse wrapped in cheerful scrubs. "We'll give you something for the pain, get you on your feet in no time. What did you have for supper tonight, honey?"

"I didn't." I hadn't even gotten around to eating the sandwich at Ben's earlier that day; what with the events of the afternoon, I'd been running on little more than adrenaline, force of will, and endorphins. All of which were slowly, finally, ebbing.

"What about dinner? Breakfast? When was the last time you ate something? Honey?" The smile faded from her face as she checked my color, shone a light in my unfocused eyes. Dropped off altogether at my muttered reply.

Shit got real after that. The oxygen and IV needles, the cold compress shock to the back of my neck. Discussion of acute stress reaction, of possible dissociation, depersonalization, the risk of PTSD. The blink in and out of consciousness when they finally let me rest. My grandmother's quiet tears.

"I didn't know about any of this. Lord, if I'd known, I'd—dear, tell me the truth. Did you know how bad this was?"

"No, ma'am." Teddy's broken voice pierced through my slow-drip haze. "Ben said she had trouble with her mother, but I didn't know details before today. She never told me. I'm so sorry."

"This is not your fault, young man. As for Eleanor . . ." Grandma's voice seethed over the name. "She will reap what she's sown. Pass me my handbag, please—I need to use the FaceTime."

I drifted out again, woke to Darrow, a flurry of fury, of gestures and whispered profanity as he paced the room with his ever-buzzing phone.

"A misdirection, sir. She all but confessed to her family—the son's and husband's stories match up. Waiting on the third witness to wake up, but she's—yes, sir. Said a bit during transport last night— enough to piece together a probable—yes, I'll get her official statement as soon as I can. We think Mrs. Hansen struck the victim with her vehicle unintentionally, then took her on up the driveway and dumped her off the edge out there. No, the cliffs—the ones at the top of the property. Coroner's report notes pre- and postmortem injuries consistent with sudden impact, which we'd previously assumed was sustained on rocks or boulders. Very likely that *was* the intention, yes. Carried her things down to the woods afterward. Yes, sir—a hair clip of some kind, beneath the driver's seat. Yes, trace amounts. A few strands, but—I'm on it. I'll get that to the lab today if I have to drive it over myself."

I shut down at that, closed my eyes and slid back into painless slumber before he noticed I'd stirred. Woke later to Teddy asleep in the bedside chair, his face marred by tearstains and fatigue. Woke again to Grandma's vicious snarls, jerked fully awake all at once at my mother's hysterical protests, closer than any FaceTime call. Their voices drifted in from the hallway, through the partially open door. She was here.

"—and what you've done, Eleanor, will not be swept aside," Grandma said. "You *will* ease up on that child."

"What *I've* done? What have I ever done besides push her toward the best possible future? I was setting her up for a *life*. Independence. Self-sufficiency. So she'd never have to rely on anyone who'd fail her the way you failed me."

Silence. I quietly scooted sideways on the narrow mattress, leaned over the railing as if closing such a miniscule gap would make a difference.

"I knew nothing of that before this evening," Grandma finally said. "If you'd told me then—"

"I couldn't tell you because I couldn't trust you'd take me seriously. You barely believe me now—if I'd come to you when I was sixteen? Not a chance. So what does that tell you about yourself, Mother, when you really get down into the—"

The call button slid off the bed as I shifted my weight, hit the floor with a clatter that cut their argument short. Grandma appeared in the doorway for a split second before she was displaced by my mother, who flew toward me as if she'd been launched from a cannon. Her clothes were rumpled; her hair was held back from her flushed, bare face by a plum silk scarf. She smelled like coffee and hand sanitizer, no trace of her usual heady perfume. I must have been out longer than I'd realized if she'd had time to make it all the way back home.

"Amy. My God, are you okay? Your head—"

"I'll be fine." I slid a hand through my hair experimentally, cringed when my fingertips brushed the swollen, tender bump. She settled on the mattress beside me, hovered over me like a worried hawk. "Is Dad—"

"He's on his way. We couldn't get seats on the same flight,

but he's not more than a few hours behind me. We've both been so worried—what in the world is going on here? Natasha—did Madeleine really—" She broke off as I nodded, pressed her fingers to her mouth, then took my tired hand in both of hers. "God. This is so horrible, I just can't—how are you, really? Please talk to me, Amy. Please tell me what you need."

She was referring to my mental state, I could tell—she wanted information, maybe absolution; my side of whatever story Grandma and the doctors had told. That old news was the least of my worries, though. There would be plenty of time to discuss the complexities of both our psyches and our relationship, haggle over my future and my love life and whatever other bullshit we usually dredged up. My mother was right in front me, practically begging me to communicate. I wasn't about to waste the chance.

"Why were you sneaking around River Run with your boyfriend the day Nat died?"

It wasn't what I'd *planned* to say. It wasn't even on my conscious agenda. But when you've spent your life braced for a moment of reckoning, what do you do when that moment finally arrives? How do you navigate it in any sense when it's right there in front of you and looks nothing like you'd thought it would?

If you're me, you apparently rip off the filters and sweep aside the expectations. You open your mouth and just let loose with whatever comes to mind.

My mother blinked at me, eyes wide, mouth a question mark of confusion.

"I'm sorry—what did you say? My *boyfriend*? Amy, what on earth are you—"

"His alibi." I held her gaze, watched her eyes widen, swap confusion for comprehension, then settle into bewilderment as I ran through a heavily edited summary of our investigation. "Noah Franklin's alibi, Mom. The police told us he was with you when Nat disappeared," I concluded. "But why? And how? Is that why Dad's gone? Are you having—"

The word stuck in my mouth. If I got even a waft of River Run off the bomb that blew apart my family, I was done with her forever, no matter what she said.

My mother waited, brow arched, for me to finish the question. When that didn't happen, she filled in the blanks, voice calm and self-assured.

"Am I having what—an affair? With Noah *Franklin*? I hadn't heard a thing from him in almost thirty years. We bumped into each other in the pharmacy completely by chance—I wasn't 'sneaking around' anywhere, young lady, and I'm not having an affair of any sort. Neither is your father." She fixed me with a careful glare, indignation tempered by an almost frantic cloak of fear. "Now, let me get this straight: your cousin thought Noah was a serial killer, and his first impulse was to launch an *investigation* into him? Are you kids out of your minds? Do you know how dangerous it is, the three of you playing detective in a case like—"

"Dangerous? Really?" That was a pretty big way to miss the point when there'd been a murderer right up the hill, smiling at us through her sister's teeth. "It was for Nat, Mom. That's all that mattered. Anyway, *you* try talking Ben down when he latches on to something like this."

"I'm sure I can imagine," she said, the corner of her mouth

forming a half smile. "And I understand. I didn't know Natasha well, but I do know how much she meant to you. That poor, sweet girl."

"But you *were* with Noah Franklin when she went missing," I pressed. "Your River Run boy. I found pictures of you and some kid down in the cove. It was him, right? The pictures in your desk?"

"I know exactly which pictures you mean. The day I took them was almost perfect in every way. It's one of my last truly good memories, both of Noah and of River Run. I couldn't just toss them out, even after—but I suppose I eventually forgot where I'd left them. Now that I think about it, I'm surprised you didn't find them ages ago."

"Mom. What *happened*?"

It was a simple question only on the surface. The answer, I knew, would go one way or the other—a dreamy reflection in a calm, glassy river, or every dark and deadly ghost beneath. There had never been a middle ground in my family.

Still, I wasn't sure which path my mother's words would take, until she met my eyes. Hers were lifeless, drained of even the usual bite of sarcasm. My mother, blank as a paint-stripped canvas. Retreating, in the same way I so often did from whatever she was poised to say. Was that how I looked when I shut down? Would that be my face thirty years on if nothing ever changed?

"I don't know where to start. You know the Franklins were our closest neighbors. Noah and I were in the same class, went to the same church. Our mothers were friends. She was a good, Christian lady—organized the charity collections and food drives, always ran the church fundraisers. Collected winter coats for impoverished kids, that sort of thing. A genuinely kind and caring person. She got cancer when we were small, and after she passed, Noah started coming by the house now and then, when he needed a button sewn on, or his pant legs let down. Some little thing that a widower couldn't be bothered with. After a while, we started meeting up in the woods to play. Swam in the river, climbed up to that tree house, just like you and the boys always did. I expect you can guess how things evolved from there."

"I expect I can," I muttered, rolling my eyes. After the metric shit ton of grief I'd caught from her over the years regarding my own evolving feelings, I wasn't about to let her little River Run romance slide without comment.

"Noah was *so* sweet," she continued, ignoring my attitude. "To everyone, not just me. But he was terrified of his father. I never understood it; Gerald seemed perfectly normal. He worked out at the quarry, went to church, hunted on the weekends like every other man around. He was a bit quick to discipline sometimes, but not to an extreme—no worse than most parents were back then. And then, one day . . . I caught him."

"You—*what*?" I sat up too quickly, winced at the ache in my head and the tug of my IV needle. "Mom—"

"We were supposed to meet at the cove after supper. Noah and me, I mean—we were 'sneaking out.'" Her laugh was an empty ache. "It was so forbidden, so exciting. But when I arrived—*he* was there. Noah's father, coming off the path that led from his house. Carrying a little girl toward the water."

My heart went into free fall, dropped from my body and kept on sinking. Her eyes were wasteland blank, free of deception or exaggeration. Marked by nothing but the hollow where her light had been.

"I was so stupid. I didn't understand what was happening at first, and I ran toward him, thinking he needed help—by the time I *saw* her, and it registered that she was . . . very clearly dead, it was too late. I knew that man my whole life, and he'd never so much as frowned at me, but he dropped that child and ran at me like a bull. Chased me all the way up the trail. I could see our kitchen door through the trees when he caught me by the hair. Put a knife to my throat before I could call for help."

I felt her skin change in my grip, felt her palm go clammy as she relived the moment. Her mouth tightened; her jaw flexed. Then, as I watched, the tension melted from her face and shoulders. Her back straightened and her chin lifted, as her expression reset into one of quiet neutrality, the way mine so often did. I watched her disconnect.

It took every shred of my resolve not to do the same.

She spoke her next words carefully, as if she could shape them into something less horrendous before setting them free.

"He dragged me back to that cove and made me sit there while he cut off a piece of that girl's hair and dumped her in the water. Once she was out of sight, he cut a piece of *my* hair and stuck it in his pocket. Said if he got so much as a bad feeling that I'd said a word, he'd come in the night and finish the job—slit my throat and burn our house to the ground, with my family inside. Then he'd do the same to Noah." Her eyes slid closed over the memory. "I truly thought he'd kill me right there in that cove. But he let me go."

"And you cut your hair short," I interrupted, the pieces of her story whirling through my head, finding one another like magnets and clicking into place. "So—the braid. Was that yours?"

"Braid? I don't—how did you know I cut my hair?"

"Grandma told me. The braid was in the wall. The box. I mean—" I took a deep breath that did precisely nothing, not to clear my head nor to make sense of the words tripping around in my mouth. "We found a box in the attic of his old house. It was full of trophies—trinkets, jewelry. Locks of hair. Do you think Mr. Franklin might have kept the piece he took from you?"

"I don't have any idea, Amy. It's possible. But this is the first I've heard of any . . . box of *hair*." She rubbed her temples. "*God*. I need to go to the police. There's just so *much*. They'll want to know why I didn't come in thirty years ago."

"It's a pretty fair question, Mother," I said. "What if he'd changed his mind and come after you anyway? What about the other kids he took? Did you ever think of them?"

"Did I? It consumed my life—to this day I see that girl's face. But Noah made me swear to keep quiet, said it was the only way to—"

"Wait. He knew the whole time?" For all I'd dismissed Ben's teen killer theories, had he actually stumbled onto some twisted version of the right track? "Mom, was Noah—involved with what happened to those kids?"

"Absolutely not." The vehemence snapped back into her voice, startling us both. She reined it in to just above a murmur. "Amy, he would never. He was the most sensitive, gentle boy I'd ever met. But—yes. He knew what his father was."

"And he never said a word? *How?* Mom, how could he sit there and let those kids die and just do—*nothing?* How could *you?*"

"It was her or me," she said simply, terribly, "and she was already gone. Gerald said he'd kill us all, and I believed him—to this day I don't know why he let me go. Maybe I was too close to home, or maybe he couldn't go through with it—but I expect it was the best way he had to keep Noah cowed. And I didn't *know* there were others, not until much later. Even the one, though—" Her voice caught on the words. "I *should* have said something then. I knew better. But Noah told me he'd take care of me . . . and he was my everything. I had to trust him."

I couldn't help the pang it sent through my body—the thought of her so freely in love, unencumbered by rules or expectations or pain-in-the-ass cousins. How perfect that love must have been, that she'd put her faith, without hesitation, in the boy whose father had been seconds from ending her life.

"He never told me any of it until afterward, when it was too late," she continued. "I wanted to tell someone—our pastor, my parents—anyone who could help us. Noah said he'd been gathering evidence, planning to go to the police, but he wouldn't do it until I was out of reach. I can only assume his father caught on to his plans—or maybe he just got scared, I don't know. He was supposed to wait until it all blew over, and then come find me so we could be together. But that was the last time we spoke. By the time it really clicked—that maybe that girl wasn't the only one—Gerald was dead, and Noah was God knows where. He'd joined the army as soon as I left, all but fell off the face of the earth, and I had no proof of any of it. So when I met your dad at Georgetown, I made the choice. I buried my head in the sand and tried to forget."

"Does he know? Dad, I mean. About—"

"No. Oh no, are you kidding me? Even once I was safe at college, your grandparents, your aunt—they were still here. Mattie and

Peter were on the verge of their engagement, building their house right up the hill. The Franklins were one of the first River Run families, a huge name in the community, and I was just a girl. What if I came forward and no one believed me—I couldn't risk it. None of it holds up in hindsight, but at the time I was absolutely paralyzed by fear, and Jake would've chased that story to the ends of the earth. Blown the whole town apart in the name of justice—like you eventually did, I suppose. So much of your fire comes from him." A soft smile quavered at the edges of her lips, disappeared too quickly into a quiet sigh. "It used to be good with us, Amy. Your parents *were* happy together—none of that is here nor there now, but you should know we had something real, however long ago."

That idea was a fresh and different take on "real," to say the least. *She* was the blaze in our household butting up against his frostbite sting. But was my father really carved from ice, or was he the blue core of a flame, burning with such intensity you could hardly feel its heat? I watched her warily, waiting for her next words. Wondering how much of me was *me*, not some strange mosaic of their flaws and virtues. When she didn't speak, I pressed on, determined to tug at every loose end until my life was recognizable.

"Why did you stay that extra day?" I asked. "When Nat disappeared—you're usually gone the same afternoon. And why would you bring me back here at all after what happened to you?"

"Why did I—Amy, I wanted to help. Your grandpa had an appointment—you know it's hard for him to get around, and Mom's gotten too frail to manage him on her own. Mattie usually handles it, but she had that event, so I changed my flight. Once Natasha disappeared, I pushed everything out again to the last possible second. I wanted to be there for June and your grandparents while I could. And Pete." She shook her head. "He's always been useless when it comes to his women, but he loved that little girl. I can't fault him for that. And I needed to make sure you were okay. I need you to *be* okay."

"I was. I am." It wasn't the truth, not technically; more a prophecy in progress, stumbling its way toward accurate. I *would* be okay again, someday. The idea that she could truly be a part of that—it was a wish too fierce and deep to voice, its origin in roots far stronger than resentment. "It makes more sense now, at least. How much you hate this place. Why you never want me staying longer than a summer."

"I never set foot in this town again while that man lived. When I heard he was gone, I thought I could finally go home. Your father was open to it for a time, before our careers took off. We even talked about moving back, building our own place on my land. But it wasn't what I expected. Living away from here opened my eyes to a lot of things I never realized growing up. The politics, the toxic viewpoints and behavior—all the old family grudges. All the dark, ugly secrets. You know how isolated it is; very little has changed since then. I wanted you to know your family, but I couldn't let you get pulled into River Run. I had to make sure the things about this place that hurt me never had a chance to reach you."

"And Noah Franklin . . ."

"Was my best friend, and my first love, and inextricably tied to the person who destroyed everything I was. He was always so set on getting out—he hated this town *so much*, and I never understood why. These were our roots. Good family names, built-in social circles, money, land—why would we leave when we had everything we'd need?"

Ben's words from my mother's mouth. Entitlement passed down through my family like heirloom jewels, throwing their sparkle across River Run like sun on water. Gleaming so brightly on the surface you'd never think to check for sinkholes beneath.

"I can't fathom his childhood in that house," she whispered. "He must have known about the others—seen unthinkable things living with that monster. But he loved me. He loved me, and his father used that love to keep him quiet. Made him submit to save my life." Her face folded; the facade cracked and collapsed as she pressed her palms to her eyes, too late to catch her tears. "Which is why it scares me so much to see how you are with Teddy. It's utterly illogical, but it brings back what I had with Noah, and triggers fear beyond my control."

"He's not Noah, Mom. And I'm *not* you."

"I realize that. I do. My issues . . . they're *mine*. It's not fair to project them onto him—or onto you. I'm so sorry for so many, many things." She rubbed her face and raised her head, tucked a strand of hair behind my ear, made sure I met her sorrowful gaze before continuing. "I want you to be happy, Amy, no matter what it does to me. I owe you years of penance—and I know we can't go back. I know that. But I *will* do the work to move forward. All I can hope is that you'll give me a chance to try."

I could see it on her as she sat beside me—the way that childhood sticks. How the things that happen when we're small cling to everything else, each memory burst of pain traveling like an electric current, hopping from point to point. Engulfing every fragile thing we touch.

"Okay," I whispered, finally curling my fingers around hers. "I think I can work with that."

My mother had left it all behind. She'd given up her hopes, cut herself out of her own family to protect me, and still it hadn't been enough. Nothing that happened back then had been her fault—she'd been a girl, coping in the only way she could. But she'd fled her home with demons scuttling beneath her skin, let the fear that drove her away cling and shift and grow within until it wore a normal face. Until it infected everything she did.

And Noah Franklin had gone his own way, ceased to exist beyond those photographs—a dark-haired memory with gentle, timid eyes. The polar opposite of the man my mother ultimately chose to be her partner. She might as well have built him from scratch, my father—customized his features and temperament and personality, forged and shaped them into the perfect antithesis of her childhood love. As if she'd never stopped trying to outrun that boy, long after he'd faded into the past.

It wasn't perfect. It never would be perfect, not by my family's standards, or by the world's. Still, I let her pull me into a hug, let my eyes dampen the collar of her silk blouse as my heart overflowed. Her arms circled me gently, as if unsure which of us might shatter. Cradled me closer as I squeezed her tight, for once not waiting for her to let me go.

CHAPTER 41

SUMMER 2019—THE LAST DAY

The river ran past us, silent and deep, moonlight cast in sheets across its dark and constant pull. We built our fire as we always did: my rocks, Teddy's fuel, Ben's flame. The Zippo worked on the first try for once, sparks catching on the kindling, throwing light and shadows through the close-ringed trees of our cove.

Three weeks. That's how long it took for us to find our way there, past the screams and the blood, past the howling, broken disaster of our families.

Ben had emerged with a bruise on his jaw and a blade through his life. He hadn't been back to the house since, tucked himself instead into a spare bedroom at our grandparents' place a few doors down from my own. He took the time to ascertain only that his mother was alive and had been transferred from the hospital to a psychiatric facility to await her trial, then set about dismantling their relationship, brick by brick. He hung up on her collect calls, blocked her e-mail, burned her snail mail letters. Spent hours crafting replies, only to destroy the finished pages in various impulsive, violent ways.

"They're not *for* her," he'd informed me, the one time I'd worked up the nerve to ask why he bothered. "Nat was my sister. I had a *sister*—we could have grown up together, had this awesome life, and my mother stole that from me. She took us from each other way before this summer, just like she took everything else that meant anything. The things I have to say—she'd kill herself for real if I let loose."

"Sounds like an easy fix to me," I muttered, earning an appreciative chuckle that closer resembled a gasp.

"Jesus, Ames. I thought I was the vindictive one." He shook his head. "But nah. I don't literally want her dead—I don't want her blood on my hands. I want to make her live with what she did, knowing she's dead to *me*. Forever."

If she ended up in the water, it's because someone put her there. Ben's words, spoken in what seemed like another life, had been the answer all along. The car accident had been just that—a distracted driver and a carefree, mischievous child. A tragedy so commonplace it wouldn't have garnered more than a mention from any but the most local news outlets. But Nat *had* drowned, in the end—sank into the river with life in her veins and air in her lungs. Left both beneath the surface long before she washed ashore. My aunt had erased her from the world with the same cold-blooded precision with which she'd years ago erased her from the family, robbing both my boys of a bond both precious and irreplaceable. Robbing us all of past and future both.

Forgiveness is finite in even the best of times. Absolution, for this, was nonexistent.

So Ben—mama's boy Ben, who'd spent years clawing after love and brushing off his own abuse—did what he always did at the point of no return: scorched every square inch of visible earth. Instead of a long, rambling missive of accusations and pleas for explanations, he'd sent Aunt Mattie a short, brutal note. It hadn't stopped the onslaught of letters, but he no longer bothered doing more than dropping them straight into the trash, unopened.

He'd seen his father once, though—at the police station, the day after the world imploded. Uncle Peter was a broken, one-eyed mess, wracked with guilt, brimming with excuses and justifications. His marriage had been in name only for more than fifteen years. With Ben on the way out, his gaze had naturally returned, as it always did, to June—his childhood love, sweet and vulnerable and needy and *there*, forever hovering a shade past his fingertips. His second chance to grasp the happiness he'd long ago relinquished for the sake of his lifelong friendship with Sam Fox—trusting, oblivious, faithful Sam, who'd loved her just as much. His second chance to have a family.

June and Pete. A match so untenable yet so instinctively obvious we'd made it a joke. Twisted an unspoken inkling into a decoy and set it in a full-blast spotlight so we wouldn't have to see its face.

And Aunt Mattie, who apparently cared more than she let on, was having none of it. The sight of her own husband's eyes peering from a childlike copy of June's face had mocked her for years, chipping away until she turned her wrath on Uncle Peter. She'd hurled accusations he didn't bother denying, dared him to break up his real family, leave his son and lawful wife for the sake of his bastard daughter—the daughter who'd be left with even less than the little she had once the lawyers cleaned him out. And when he appeared more than willing to call her bluff—and fate had unexpectedly put Nat's life into her hands—Aunt Mattie had made a split-second choice, tearing the roots out of every possible compromise.

Ben had listened in silence, stood up from his chair, and walked away. Turned his back on his father like only a Hansen could.

Uncle Peter had been released soon after, ordered to remain in town pending various possible charges. He knew better than to come to the house. We hadn't seen him since.

Three weeks later and the fervor had faded, the phones had stopped ringing, and it all came down to us, gathered once more in the place that had borne quiet witness to our history—to the beginning and the end of everything. The night belonged to the flames and the trees and the call of the rapids. To Nat's memory, woven through it all. To the three of us, huddled together beneath a dark, indifferent sky.

"So this is it," Ben said, breaking a long stretch of silence. "The last bonfire—probably forever. If I'd known things would shake out the way they did, I never would have fucked up last year's."

"It's okay," I told him, sending over a soft smile. "It's sort of pointless to hold that against you now."

"Yeah, man, no worries," Teddy added. "We know you can't help being a fuckup."

"It is one of my more endearing qualities." The shadows hid the corner of his smile. "Tonight just feels too final. Who knows where we'll all be next summer."

"No real mystery here," Teddy said. "If you need me, just wave from the top of the quarry. Toss me down a beer every now and then."

"Goddamn it, Teddy, if I see even a trace of your ass in that pit, I'll fire you on the spot. You're not breaking rocks on my watch, man."

"Rent's not paying itself, Benny. Staying with Mom even a day longer than I have to is just not doable."

Since Nat's death, June had clung to sanity with ever-weakening fingers; Aunt Mattie's arrest pushed her over the edge. During the mess that followed, she'd admitted her primary source of income since Sam's death had been Hansen guilt money—an arrangement she'd neglected to mention to Teddy. He'd handed over his paychecks for household expenses, and she'd dumped them straight into the offering plate at her weird church. Things had been less than stable between them once that little detail slipped into the light.

"I get it," Ben said. "I won't live in *my* old house ever again, that's for sure, and fuck the old Franklin place too. I'm eighteen in two months. I guess I'll stay with Grandma and Grandpa until I graduate, officially inherit my trust, all that. They still have to work out the legalities with the money and the business once Mom is sentenced, but who knows how long that'll take to iron out."

"Wait—are you broke? Dude. *Dude.*"

"It's temporary," Ben huffed, tossing his head, cheeks pinkening at Teddy's laughter. "But yes—my money is technically theirs until I'm no longer a minor, which means right now I have access to exactly jack shit. But Dad said everything that's left of Mom's will eventually belong to me, including her share of Hansen, Inc. He wants me taken care of, I guess. Not that I'm talking to *him* ever again, business partner or not."

"Oh good, I was worried there for a second. So I'm hired, right?"

"Not in the pit. What do you know about quarterly reports?"

"Literally nothing."

"Yeah, me neither. Seriously, name the job and it's yours. I'll have the lawyers appoint someone to run things in my place for the next few years, sort shit out, get everything set up for my takeover.

Until then, who knows? Maybe I'll get out there, see the world. Don't want to deprive the world of Ben Hansen, after all."

"The real Ben Hansen?" I asked, giving him a careful look. In the weeks since he'd come out to us, Ben had resumed the status quo as promised, upped his douche factor threefold to cover his tracks.

"For someone who spent all summer perfecting the art of the secret hand job," Ben drawled, "you're way into up-front honesty all of a sudden, Ames."

"I was *not* giving secret—" I huffed the end off my denial as both boys cackled. "Our entire family tree is rooted in fiction. Every horrible thing that happened this summer can be traced back to people's secrets and their lies and hiding the things that made them suffer. Things that ruined our lives before we were even born. If we don't do better than *that*, what was the point in any of this?"

"I get what you're saying. And I *will* do better—eventually. But it has to be on my time. Let me get through the school year first. Get on my own two feet so I don't end up on the way to conversion camp or some shit."

"I just can't see our family doing that to you," I persisted, voice catching at the horrible but very real possibility that Ben's fears weren't unfounded. "I know you're scared, but I'll be there the whole time. We can tell them together. And if they have a problem—"

"Then *what*, Amy? It's fine for you to say that like I have a choice—you could come out at breakfast and, assuming they bothered to give a fuck either way, your parents would have a Pride flag on the porch by sundown. The grandparents? Maybe not so much."

"Maybe not, but you don't know for sure. You could be completely wrong."

"Or I could be right. Look, I get it—we both want to think the best of the few people we have left. But that's not my reality. They're all I care about apart from you guys, and until I know where they stand, I'm keeping it to myself. I have to." Ben sighed, turned his face toward the water. "Because if *you're* wrong, and they can't handle it? I have nowhere else to go."

"The air mattress offer is always on the table, dude," Teddy said, the gentle pressure of his fingers around mine quelling my protest. "I'm in your corner either way, but do what you need to do. This town's not changing any time soon."

"I don't care about *this town*," Ben scoffed. "Let them try to fuck with me when I'm months away from owning most of their jobs. If they want to play hardball, they should take a hot second to remember who runs the playing field."

"You're not worried?"

"Sure I am. This is borrowed time, my dude—maybe not out in the open, but behind the scenes, at school and stuff? Regular ass-kickings are basically guaranteed. Most likely delivered by the same guys who've been sucking up to me since grade school."

"Nope. Fuck that." I felt the shudder run through Teddy's frame as he spoke, and tightened my grip on his hand. He slid an arm around my waist, pulling me close. "They come for you, they better hope they catch me on an off day. All I ask is that you spot me bail money if it gets too wild."

"Anytime."

We fell silent, sobered by the horrible road we'd walked to arrive at that moment. Ben stared into the fire, but Teddy looked to the river, his face a collection of shadows and ghosts. I leaned into his heartbeat, let my eyes fall shut at the brush of his lips against my hair as he turned back toward us.

"Hey," he said, pressing something small and flat into my hand. "I have something for you."

"What's that?" I squinted, then did a double take. "Whoa, seriously? Where did you get this?"

"Nat's room. Looks like she found it in the cove, after you left last year." His chuckle drew an answering smile from my lips. "Check out the back."

I flipped through my lost sketchbook, joy and nostalgia warring with the sorrowful squeeze of my heart. My drawings were untouched, but the last page in the book was filled top to bottom with Nat's handwriting.

> Hi Amy,
> Don't worry, I didn't take your book. It was in the old tree house down in the woods. I didn't show it to Bear because I didn't think you'd like that. I think he would, though. I think it would make him happy to see how you see him. You should show him your pictures, and you should tell him you love him, because I think he'd like to say it back. FINALLY.
> Your friend,
> Nat

The words went soft through a well of tears that promised full-on waterworks had they not been interrupted by Ben's howl of laughter. He'd butted his head in between ours to read over Teddy's shoulder. Of course he had.

"That kid," he cackled. "I swear to Christ, you guys, no one had your number like Nat had your goddamn number, am I right? You should be ashamed of yourselves."

"I'm not worried," Teddy said, palming Ben's face and pushing him playfully away. "If I had to get a message from beyond the grave or whatever, this is the best one I can think of."

"I'm fine with it too," I said. "At least we know she'd approve, wherever she is."

"And she was right." His finger appeared on the page, brushed gently over the last word of the note: *finally*. "All the time we spent in denial—with each other, ourselves, our parents—it was nothing but a waste. We're here now—that's what matters—but I feel like it would've been nice to skip over all that shit. Get here on *our* terms, you know?"

It wasn't unfamiliar, the weight of that specific, useless regret—the months, maybe even years, swallowed up by what we couldn't face. Lies of a different, silent sort, no less damaging for all that had gone unsaid. Everything we'd missed; no one to blame but ourselves.

It ate away at me in random intervals. It likely always would.

I closed the book and set it aside, rested my head against Teddy's chest. Felt the rhythm of his breathing: slow, then faster, stuttering to nerves. I looked up, saw the words hanging just behind his lips.

"You okay?" I asked. He nodded, frowning, then raised his eyes to Ben's.

"I asked Mom, you know—if Dad knew about Nat. She said he

never had a doubt from the moment she was born. Even though she looked like Mom, same face and hair and coloring and all that, he knew a Hansen kid when he saw one."

"We are all kind of the same," Ben said. "All pale and beautiful and fucked up. Devoid of shame and boundaries. Still, he stuck around."

"Only just barely. Mom said he went nuts. She went around behind his back with your dad for years, and everyone knew—your mom, Amy's mom, even your grandparents. Pete was always in love with her, all the way since high school. Never denied it, and never did get over it, even after Nat died."

"Damn." Ben shook his head. "Sorry about all those 'your mom' jokes, I guess."

"Dude, you and me both. But Dad lost his shit in a big way. Almost took me and left for good, but couldn't go through with it. He loved Nat anyway—blood or no blood, he was her dad. All the way to the end."

I thought of Sam, of the countless times I'd seen him with Nat. Her riding his shoulders every Fourth of July, a pair of spitting sparklers clutched in each fist. Him teaching her to currycomb a horse, his work-worn hand huge over her tiny, spidery fingers. Her proudly clutching a handful of brightly painted river rocks, "paperweights" she'd made for Father's Day, and his sheer delight at receiving them. Him broken and weeping the day she'd almost drowned, slumped on the trailer steps, clenched fists pressed to his eyes. A better dad to that girl on any given day than my own had been to me at the best of times.

"This might sound weird," Ben said, "but I think old Sam got the better end of the deal, even if he was being royally screwed over.

Hey, Teddy, I know I can be a dick, but at least you never have to worry about me knocking up your girlfriend and leaving you to raise the kid."

"Dude." Teddy put up a valiant struggle, but his poker face caved to laughter in under a minute. "That's disgusting. On many, many levels."

"It's a silver lining." He stared into the fire, a spasm of sorrow breaking his impish grin. "Gotta break that cycle somehow."

"This is what I'm hoping." I sighed, still feeling a twinge of dread at the thought of returning home, reconciliation notwithstanding. "I think things can be better with Mom now—I want them to be. But what if nothing changes? I can't go back to how it was."

"You won't," Teddy said, lifting my chin to look in my eyes. "You're strong, Amy, and you're not alone. No matter what happens, I'm in your corner."

"We both are." Ben reached across to nudge my knee. "Anything you need. And when we're together again and can legally take you across state lines without risking prison time, we can really start some shit."

"Countdown begins now. In the meantime, I think she's genuinely sorry. Plus, Grandma ripped her a new one, so there's that."

"If you're really worried, you can always stay. I know the town's a steaming turd, but you can draw from anywhere. I'll introduce you to my therapist and everything."

"It's only a couple years. I need to give her a chance to be better. My dad—I thought that ship capsized on the high seas sometime back in middle school, but he seemed genuine enough a couple weeks ago. And if Mom really wants to try, I do too."

"And if she backslides?"

"I guess I'll deal with it. Long enough to get my tuition paid, anyway. I've made it this far. I can do what I have to, and then she'll never hear from me again."

"Nope, not good enough. If she fucks it up you'll come back here and she'll shell out no matter where you live, because it's that or I'll put all her shit on blast, on every platform I can think of. She may have defected from River Run, but she's still a Langston—you can't tell me money matters more to her than reputation."

"So you'll blackmail her. Even knowing what we know now—even if she genuinely does try with the whole grow-and-change thing?"

"With a smile on my face. It's called atonement, Ames—the bare minimum start for the shit she's pulled. I'll burn her world to the ground before she even smells the smoke. It'll be awesome—we'll do our whole European dream tour on her dime. I'll even drop you off in Paris myself on the way back from the fjords. Make her fork out for your boy's ticket, just to twist the knife. We should all go anyway, even if everything works out—yep, it's happening, I just decided. Next summer, you guys. The perfect end to senior year."

"You'll have to get Teddy on a plane first, Ben. Get him a passport, trick him into your suitcase. Poke holes in the sides so he doesn't suffocate."

"I'll go."

My breath caught at Teddy's words—at the determination in his voice, the hesitance and hope in his eyes. At the sorrowful lines of his mouth, which smoothed into a reflection of my halting smile.

"You will?"

"Always wanted out of this place. Can't think of a better way to make it happen."

"Jesus God, dude." Ben lit a cigarette in the fire, shaking his head as Teddy fell into him under the momentum of my kiss. "Get a room."

"Deal with it, Benny. There's more where this came from if she sticks around."

"*If,*" I scoffed. "Like I went through this whole dumpster fire of a summer for nothing."

"So that's a yes?"

"That's a hell yes." I reached past him to squeeze my cousin's hand. "If you're in, I'm in."

"World without end, Ames."

The firelight played tag across my boys, bouncing beams off Ben's gleaming hair, teasing shadows from the angles of Teddy's face. We three, bound by choice. In the same way Sam Fox had bound himself to a daughter—gave her his name and his life, loved her despite her twisted origins.

We'd been raised to conform. To let their rot creep through our veins and past our fingertips; to chain ourselves to time and blood and obligation. All of us, butterflies beneath the lid, racing in the same predestined circles.

Together we were stronger than what they'd made. We were more than their children—more than limbs and joints and dangling strings. So much of what we'd almost lost still shone through, bright and vital as any sun. We were our own family, stretching upward through the pull of the unchanging current, past the surface and the sky.

My boys and me, reaching endlessly for that burning, distant light.

RESOURCES

Resources for families of missing persons under the age of eighteen, including abducted children and endangered runaways:
https://www.missingkids.com/MissingChild
National Center for Missing and Exploited Children (NCMEC):
1-800-THE-LOST (843-5678)

Resources for young people in abusive households, relationships, or situations:
https://www.nrcdv.org/rhydvtoolkit/teens/
National Domestic Violence Hotline: 1-800-799-7233

24/7 Crisis intervention and suicide prevention for LGBTQ+ people under age twenty-five:
https://www.thetrevorproject.org/resources/
TrevorLifeline: 1-866-488-7386 or text START to 678-678

Mental health support for teens and young adults:
https://www.nami.org/Your-Journey/Teens-Young-Adults
NAMI Helpline: 1-800-950-NAMI (6264) or text NAMI to 741-741

Grief and bereavement support for all ages, including kids, teens, and young adults:
https://www.dougy.org/grief-resources/

ACKNOWLEDGMENTS

The first flashes of this story came to me at a seemingly mundane moment, during a very scary and uncertain time in my young family's life. To see it realized more than ten years (and even more drafts) later is like finally arriving at a destination I thought I'd never reach. I have so many people to thank for helping me along the way.

Liesa Abrams, thank you for taking on this book and helping me transform it into more than I ever imagined it could be. The care you take with every scene, your kindness and sensitivity, your patience and humor, and your rare ability to empathize and understand the core of what I'm trying to say even when I say it badly make you the best kind of person to have in my corner, both as an editor and a friend. I hope we never tire of telling stories together.

Mara Anastas, Rebecca Vitkus, and the rest of the Simon & Schuster team, thank you—for being the perfect landing place for my stories and my voice, and for bringing this book to life. Your guidance and support has been invaluable; I'll always be proud of the Simon Pulse logo on my books.

Christa Heschke, I will always remember the day you took a chance on an unknown writer with an awkward query letter, a dismal social media presence, and a manuscript crowded with angst, metaphors, and semicolons, and gave her the opportunity to become a real live author. Thank you so much for believing in my work and in me, and for supporting all my twisted, barely realized inklings, from the moment they spark to life until I manage, somehow, to pummel them into books. I couldn't ask for a better—or more patient—agent or advocate. I'm so grateful to be on #TeamMandO.

ACKNOWLEDGMENTS

Shannon Powers, few appreciate my gritty dark side quite like you. Thank you for all you did to bring this book to this point, and for helping me navigate "being an author" in the early days.

Daniele Hunter, thank you for your unending support. You're the awesome fangirl every writer hopes to have, and I'm so lucky to work with you, now and in the future.

Julie Hutchings, your enthusiasm for this book gave me the push I needed to reach for more than I thought I deserved. I can't imagine where I'd be without your help—the world would be a markedly drearier place without your lovely words, keen eye, and generous heart. Thank you.

Much appreciation to Katie Rogers at Pages and Pugs for hosting the cover reveal, for your kindness in promoting my work, and for all your (and Cubert's!) help and support. Thank you so much, for everything.

Everlasting gratitude to Jennifer Moffett, Alex Richards, Shannon Takaoka, Shana Youngdahl, Liz Lawson, Rachel Lynn Solomon, and every other author whose words inspired me and whose support and friendship helped so very much during the infamous 2020 debut year. And to everyone who read my words and loved them, thank you— for the beautiful aesthetics and heartfelt reviews; for navigating my cynical, possum-choked Twitter feed and the tangle of yarn, flowers, baked goods, and reposts of other people's art and aesthetics that is my Instagram presence; for reaching out to me, even in the smallest ways. You are seen and appreciated, always.

Jill Corddry and Ron Walters, each of you hold a permanent place in these pages. Without you, Ron, there would be no Nat, and this book would be a very different thing. Thank you for reminding me that I actually do control the outcome of my own stories, at least to a certain extent. Jill, without your encouragement, friendship, and willingness to extract me from my own head and talk sense into the space left behind, who even knows what I'd be doing? The EWC is invaluable to me, not only for the infinite patience you both have for what must, by this point, be a higher total word count than any of us care to admit, but for your honesty, humor, commiseration, and constant, steady support over the many years and many, many, many (many) drafts. I can never thank either of you enough.

This book, above all else, is about family, so it *almost* goes without saying that it would've been pretty tough for me to write it without the eternal tempest of love and chaos that comprises my own family—nuclear and extended, blood and chosen—and the absolute avalanche of friends and relatives who came out of the woodwork to cheer me on: Mom and Dad, Pat, Justin, Erika, David, Johnny, Brad, Susan, Maggie, Ed (and Odin!), Liss, Tara, Bridget, Jenn, Renard, Joe, Allison, Heidi, Sarah, Kim, Nicole, Kat, Holly, Tisheena, and far too many more to name in this small space. Your outpour of love, acceptance, and encouragement has overwhelmed me in the very best way. Cynthia Thornton, thank you for the early read, conversation, feedback, and sangria, and for always being awesome. Betsy Davis, for your extreme generosity in the coordination and execution of the sneakiest of redhead-devised plots, I am so very grateful. You're an amazing friend (as is the aforementioned redhead). Thanks to Alexa King, whose land was the literal and figurative jumping-off point. And special thanks to Emily, for loving this story even in its ghastly early days, and for being my cocreator in my earliest Charlene-and-Minnie-based storytelling adventures. So much love to all of you.

ACKNOWLEDGMENTS

Henry and Cora, thank you for your patience with my "work time," for making me laugh and think and keep on keeping on. You are the heart and soul of everything I do. That you're "proud of Mama" means the world—I can't wait until you're old enough to read the rest of these pages.

Brandon, this book would not exist without our journey—the literal one and the metaphorical one. We've come a long way from our starting point; I couldn't be prouder of the family we've built, nor could I be happier that we've stayed the course. Thank you for continuing forward with me, every day.

And, once again, for Gini—the very first of my found family. Miss you forever.